—— PRAISE FOR ——

Hollow City

THE SECOND NOVEL OF
MISS PEREGRINE'S PECULIAR CHILDREN

A *New York Times* Best Seller
A *USA Today* Best Seller
An IndieBound Best Seller

"A stunning achievement. . . . This sophomore novel, which is even richer than Riggs's imaginative debut, will not disappoint. The cinematic qualities of the writing are high-definition bold, the love story more dramatic, and . . . the characters are given greater depth." —*Boston Globe*

"I was blown away. . . . *Hollow City* is fantastic." —*USA Today*

"This harrowing tale picks up right where *Miss Peregrine's Home for Peculiar Children* left off. . . . Quirky and creepy snapshots perfectly illustrate the characters and settings, reinforcing the dark atmosphere of the narrative. Fans of the first title will find this book a treasure." —*School Library Journal*

"Like the first volume, this novel is generously illustrated with peculiar period photographs that capture and enhance the eerie mood and mode. Fans will be pleased with this second volume and downright delighted to know that a third in the series is in the offing." —*Booklist*

"A perfect blend of creepiness and thoughtfulness." —Popmatters.com

"What makes the series soar . . . is not the world-building, as intriguing as it is, but the heartfelt intensity of the emotions." —*Virginian-Pilot*

"A tasty adventure for any reader with an appetite for the peculiar." —*Kirkus Reviews*

"As hauntingly sinister as the first book and unequivocally worth the wait . . . . A rare sequel that improves on the series' beginning. . . . A must-read!" —RT Book Reviews

"Riggs deftly moves between fantasy and reality, prose and photography to create an enchanting and at times positively terrifying story."

—Associated Press

"It's an enjoyable, eccentric read, distinguished by well-developed characters, a believable Welsh setting, and some very creepy monsters."

—*Publishers Weekly*

"An original work that defies categorization, this first novel should appeal to readers who like quirky fantasies. Riggs includes many vintage photographs that add a critical touch of the peculiar to his unusual tale."

—*Library Journal*

"Somewhat reminiscent of Jack Finney's *Time and Again*, Riggs's first novel is enchanting. . . . Highly recommended."

—*Ellery Queen Mystery Magazine*

"In a time when so much summer entertainment seems to be more of the same, *Miss Peregrine's Home for Peculiar Children* is a pleasant surprise—a story that is fresh and new, engrosses and grips, and provides enough clues so that the ending makes sense and seems thoughtful."

—Popmatters.com

"Brace yourself for the last 70 pages of relentless, squirm-in-your-chair action. I loved every minute of it."

—*Cleveland Plain Dealer*

"An unforgettable novel that mixes fiction and photography in a thrilling reading experience." —*Savannah Morning News*

"This is a Book of the Year candidate and right now I'm calling it the front runner. Absolutely magical in every sense of the word, *Miss Peregrine* has a peerless combination of witty, intelligent dialogue and prose, combined with an absolutely beautiful design. . . . *Miss Peregrine's Home for Peculiar Children* is the sharpest thing you'll read all year." —*Shelf Unbound*

HOLLOW

CITY

HOLLOW CITY

═══ THE SECOND NOVEL OF ═══

MISS PEREGRINE'S

⬥ PECULIAR CHILDREN ⬥

BY RANSOM RIGGS

QUIRK BOOKS
PHILADELPHIA

First paperback edition, Quirk Books, 2015.
Originally published by Quirk Books in 2014.

Library of Congress Cataloging in Publication Number: 2013914959
(hardcover edition)

ISBN: 978-1-59474-735-9

Printed in the United States of America
Typeset in Sabon, Belwe, and Dear Sarah

Designed by Doogie Horner
Cover photograph courtesy of John Van Noate, Rex USA, and the Everett Collection
Production management by John J. McGurk

Quirk Books
215 Church St.
Philadelphia, PA 19106
quirkbooks.com

10 9 8 7

FOR TAHEREH

And lo! towards us coming in a boat
    An old man, grizzled with the hair of eld,
    Moaning: "Woe unto you, debased souls!

Hope nevermore to look upon the heavens.
    I come to lead you to the other shore;
    Into eternal darkness; into fire and frost.

And thou, that yonder standest, living soul,
    Withdraw from these people, who are dead!"
    But he saw that I did not withdraw . . .

—Dante's *Inferno*, Canto III

JACOB PORTMAN

Our hero, who can see and
sense hollowgast

EMMA BLOOM

A girl who can make fire with
her hands, formerly involved
with Jacob's grandfather

ABRAHAM PORTMAN
(DECEASED)

Jacob's grandfather, killed
by a hollowgast

BRONWYN BRUNTLEY

An unusually strong girl

PECULIAR PERSONAE

MILLARD NULLINGS

An invisible boy, scholar of all things peculiar

OLIVE ABROHOLOS ELEPHANTA

A girl who is lighter than air

HORACE SOMNUSSON

A boy who suffers from premonitory visions and dreams

ENOCH O'CONNOR

A boy who can animate the dead for brief periods of time

◆ PECULIAR PERSONAE ◆

HUGH APISTON

A boy who commands and
protects the many bees that
live in his stomach

CLAIRE DENSMORE

A girl with an extra mouth
in the back of her head; the
youngest of Miss Peregrine's
peculiar children

FIONA FRAUENFELD

A silent girl with a peculiar
talent for making plants grow

ALMA LEFAY PEREGRINE

Ymbryne, shape-shifter,
manipulator of time;
headmistress of Cairnholm's
loop; arrested in bird form

PECULIAR PERSONAE

ESMERELDA AVOCET

An ymbryne whose loop was raided by the corrupted; kidnapped by wights

NONPECULIAR PERSONAE

FRANKLIN PORTMAN

Jacob's father; bird hobbyist, wannabe writer

MARYANN PORTMAN

Jacob's mother; heiress to Florida's second-largest drugstore chain

RICKY PICKERING

Jacob's only normal friend

DOCTOR GOLAN (DECEASED)

A wight who posed as a psychiatrist to deceive Jacob and his family; later killed by Jacob

RALPH WALDO EMERSON (DECEASED)

Essayist, lecturer, poet

PART

ONE

CHAPTER ONE

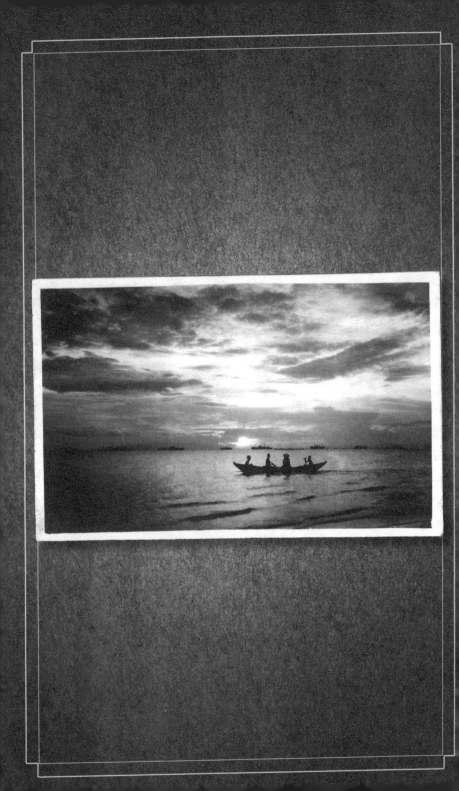

We rowed out through the harbor, past bobbing boats weeping rust from their seams, past juries of silent seabirds roosting atop the barnacled remains of sunken docks, past fishermen who lowered their nets to stare frozenly as we slipped by, uncertain whether we were real or imagined; a procession of waterborne ghosts, or ghosts soon to be. We were ten children and one bird in three small and unsteady boats, rowing with quiet intensity straight out to sea, the only safe harbor for miles receding quickly behind us, craggy and magical in the blue-gold light of dawn. Our goal, the rutted coast of mainland Wales, was somewhere before us but only dimly visible, an inky smudge squatting along the far horizon.

We rowed past the old lighthouse, tranquil in the distance, which only last night had been the scene of so many traumas. It was there that, with bombs exploding around us, we had nearly drowned, nearly been torn apart by bullets; that I had taken a gun and pulled its trigger and killed a man, an act still incomprehensible to me; that we had lost Miss Peregrine and got her back again—snatched from the steel jaws of a submarine—though the Miss Peregrine who was returned to us was damaged, in need of help we didn't know how to give. She perched now on the stern of our boat, watching the sanctuary she'd created slip away, more lost with every oar stroke.

Finally we rowed past the breakwater and into the great blank open, and the glassy surface of the harbor gave way to little waves that chopped at the sides of our boats. I heard a plane threading the clouds high above us and let my oars drag, neck craning up, arrested by a vision of our little armada from such a height: this world I had chosen, and everything I had in it, and all our precious, peculiar lives, contained in three splinters of wood adrift upon the vast, unblinking eye of the sea.

Mercy.

* * *

Our boats slid easily through the waves, three abreast, a friendly current bearing us coastward. We rowed in shifts, taking turns at the oars to stave off exhaustion, though I felt so strong that for nearly an hour I refused to give them up. I lost myself in the rhythm of the strokes, my arms tracing long ellipses in the air as if pulling something toward me that refused to come. Hugh manned the oars opposite me, and behind him, at the bow, sat Emma, her eyes hidden beneath the brim of a sun hat, head bent toward a map spread across her knees. Every so often she'd look up from her map to consult the horizon, and just the sight of her face in the sun gave me energy I didn't know I had.

I felt like I could row forever—until Horace shouted from one of the other boats to ask how much ocean was left between us and the mainland, and Emma squinted back toward the island and then down at her map, measuring with spread fingers, and said, somewhat doubtfully, "Four miles?" But then Millard, who was also in our boat, muttered something in her ear and she frowned and turned the map sideways, and frowned again, then said, "I mean, five." As the words left her mouth, I felt myself—and saw everyone else—wilt a little.

Five miles: a journey that would've taken an hour in the stomach-churning ferry that had brought me to Cairnholm weeks ago. A distance easily covered by an engine-powered boat of any size. Roughly one mile less than my out-of-shape uncles ran on odd weekends for charity, and only a bit more than my mother boasted she could manage during rowing-machine classes at her fancy gym. But the ferry between the island and the mainland wouldn't start running for another thirty years, and rowing machines weren't loaded down with passengers and luggage, nor did they require constant course corrections just to stay pointed in the right direction. Worse still, the ditch of water we were crossing was treacherous, a notorious ship-swallower: five miles of moody, changeable sea, its floor fanned with greening wrecks and sailors' bones and, lurking somewhere in the fathoms-deep darkness, our enemies.

Those of us who worried about such things assumed the wights were nearby, somewhere below us in that German submarine, waiting. If they didn't already know we'd fled the island, they'd find out soon enough. They hadn't gone to such lengths to kidnap Miss Peregrine only to give up after one failed attempt. The warships that inched along like centipedes in the distance and the British planes that kept watch overhead made it too dangerous for the submarine to surface in broad daylight, but come nightfall, we'd be easy prey. They would come for us, and take Miss Peregrine, and sink the rest. So we rowed, our only hope that we could reach the mainland before nightfall reached us.

*   *   *

We rowed until our arms ached and our shoulders knotted. We rowed until the morning breeze stilled and the sun blazed down as through a magnifying glass and sweat pooled around our collars, and I realized no one had thought to bring fresh water, and that sunblock in 1940 meant standing in the shade. We rowed until the skin wore away from the ridges of our palms and we were certain we absolutely couldn't row another stroke, but then did, and then another, and another.

"You're sweating buckets," Emma said. "Let me have a go at the oars before you melt away."

Her voice startled me out of a daze. I nodded gratefully and let her switch into the oar seat, but twenty minutes later I asked for it back again. I didn't like the thoughts that crept into my head while my body was at rest: imagined scenes of my father waking to find me gone from our rooms on Cairnholm, Emma's baffling letter in my place; the panic that would ensue. Memory-flashes of terrible things I'd witnessed recently: a monster pulling me into its jaws; my former psychiatrist falling to his death; a man buried in a coffin of ice, torn momentarily from the next world to croak into my ear with half a throat. So I rowed despite my exhaustion and a spine that felt like it might never bend straight again and hands rubbed raw from friction, and tried to think of exactly nothing, those leaden oars both a life sentence and a life raft.

Bronwyn, seemingly inexhaustible, rowed one of the boats all by herself. Olive sat opposite but was no help; the tiny girl couldn't pull the oars without pushing herself up into the air, where a stray gust of wind might send her flying away like a kite. So Olive shouted encouragement while Bronwyn did the work of two—or three or four, if you took into account all the suitcases and boxes weighing down their boat, stuffed with clothes and food and maps and books and a lot of less practical things, too, like several jars of pickled reptile hearts sloshing in Enoch's duffel bag; or the blown-off front doorknob to Miss Peregrine's house, a memento Hugh had found in the grass on our way to the boats and decided he couldn't live without; or the bulky pillow Horace had rescued from the house's flaming shell—it was his lucky pillow, he said, and the only thing that kept his paralyzing nightmares at bay.

Other items were so precious that the children clung to them even as they rowed. Fiona kept a pot of wormy garden dirt pressed between her knees. Millard had striped his face with a handful of bomb-pulverized brick dust, an odd gesture that seemed part mourning ritual. If what they kept and clung to seemed strange, part of me sympathized: it was all they had left of their home. Just because they knew it was lost didn't mean they knew how to let it go.

After three hours of rowing like galley slaves, distance had shrunk the island to the size of an open hand. It looked nothing like the foreboding, cliff-ringed fortress I had first laid eyes upon a few weeks ago; now it seemed fragile, a shard of rock in danger of being washed away by the waves.

"Look!" Enoch shouted, standing up in the boat next to ours. "It's disappearing!" A spectral fog enshrouded the island, blanking it from view, and we broke from rowing to watch it fade.

"Say goodbye to our island," Emma said, standing and removing her big hat. "We may never see it again."

"Farewell, island," said Hugh. "You were so good to us."

Horace set his oar down and waved. "Goodbye, house. I shall miss all your rooms and gardens, but most of all I shall miss my bed."

"So long, loop," Olive sniffled. "Thank you for keeping us safe all these years."

"Good years," said Bronwyn. "The best I've known."

I, too, said a silent goodbye, to a place that had changed me forever—and the place that, more than any graveyard, would forever contain the memory, and the mystery, of my grandfather. They were linked inextricably, he and that island, and I wondered, now that both were gone, if I would ever really understand what had happened to me: what I had become; was becoming. I had come to the island to solve my grandfather's mystery, and in doing so I had discovered my own. Watching Cairnholm disappear felt like watching the only remaining key to that mystery sink beneath the dark waves.

And then the island was simply gone, swallowed up by a mountain of fog.

As if it had never existed.

*　　*　　*

Before long the fog caught up to us. By increments we were blinded, the mainland dimming and the sun fading to a pale white bloom, and we turned circles in the eddying tide until we'd lost all sense of direction. Finally we stopped and put our oars down and waited in the doldrummy quiet, hoping it would pass; there was no use going any farther until it did.

"I don't like this," Bronwyn said. "If we wait too long it'll be night, and we'll have worse things to reckon with than bad weather."

Then, as if the weather had heard Bronwyn and decided to put us in our place, it turned *really* bad. A strong wind blew up, and within moments our world was transformed. The sea around us whipped into white-capped waves that slapped at our hulls and broke into our boats, sloshing cold water around our feet. Next came rain, hard as little bullets on our skin. Soon we were being tossed around like rubber toys in a bathtub.

"Turn into the waves!" Bronwyn shouted, slicing at the water with her oars. "If they broadside us we'll flip for sure!" But most of us were too spent to row in calm water, let alone a boiling sea, and the rest were too scared even to reach for the oars, so instead we grabbed for the gunwales and held on for dear life.

A wall of water plowed straight toward us. We climbed the massive wave, our boats turning nearly vertical beneath us. Emma clung to me and I clung to the oarlock; behind us Hugh held on to the seat with his arms. We crested the wave like a roller coaster, my stomach dropping into my legs, and as we raced down the far side, everything in our boat that wasn't nailed down—Emma's map, Hugh's bag, the red roller suitcase I'd lugged with me since Florida— went flying out over our heads and into the water.

There was no time to worry about what had been lost, because initially we couldn't even see the other boats. When we'd resumed an even keel, we squinted into the maelstrom and screamed our friends' names. There was a terrible moment of silence before we heard voices call back to us, and Enoch's boat appeared out of the mist, all four passengers aboard, waving their arms at us.

"Are you all right?" I shouted.

"Over there!" they called back. "Look over there!"

I saw that they weren't waving hello, but directing our attention to something in the water, some thirty yards away—the hull of an overturned boat.

"That's Bronwyn and Olive's boat!" Emma said.

It was upside down, its rusty bottom to the sky. There was no sign of either girl around it.

"We have to get closer!" Hugh shouted, and forgetting our exhaustion we grabbed the oars and paddled toward it, calling their names into the wind.

We rowed through a tide of clothes ejected from split-open suitcases, every swirling dress we passed resembling a drowning girl. My heart hammered in my chest, and though I was soaked and shivering I hardly felt the cold. We met Enoch's boat at the overturned hull of Bronwyn's and searched the water together.

"Where are they?" Horace moaned. "Oh, if we've lost them . . ."

"Underneath!" Emma said, pointing at the hull. "Maybe they're trapped underneath it!"

I pulled one of my oars from its lock and banged it against the overturned hull. "If you're in there, swim out!" I shouted. "We'll rescue you!"

For a terrible moment there was no response, and I could feel any hope of recovering them slipping away. But then, from the underside of the overturned boat, there was a knock in reply—and then a fist smashed through the hull, wood chips flying, and we all jumped in surprise.

"It's Bronwyn!" Emma cried. "They're alive!"

With a few more strikes Bronwyn was able to knock a person-sized hole in the hull. I extended my oar to her and she grabbed it, and with Hugh and Emma and me all pulling, we managed to drag her through the churning water and into our boat just as hers sank, vanishing beneath the waves. She was panicked, hysterical, shouting with breath she didn't have to spare. Shouting for Olive, who hadn't been under the hull with her. She was still missing.

"Olive—got to get Olive," Bronwyn sputtered once she'd tumbled into the boat. She was shivering, coughing up seawater. She stood up in the pitching boat and pointed into the storm. "There!" she cried. "See it?"

I shielded my eyes from the stinging rain and looked, but all I could see were waves and fog. "I don't see anything!"

"She's there!" Bronwyn insisted. "The rope!"

Then I saw what she was pointing at: not a flailing girl in the water but a fat thread of woven hemp trailing up from it, barely visible in all the chaos. A strand of taut brown rope extended up from the water and disappeared into the fog. Olive must've been attached to the other end, unseen.

We paddled to the rope and Bronwyn reeled it down, and after a minute Olive appeared from the fog above our heads, one end of the rope knotted around her waist. Her shoes had fallen off when her boat flipped, but Bronwyn had already tied Olive to the anchor line, the other end of which was resting on the seafloor. If not for that, she surely would've been lost in the clouds by now.

Olive threw her arms around Bronwyn's neck and crowed, "You saved me, you saved me!"

They embraced. The sight of them put a lump in my throat.

"We ain't out of danger yet," said Bronwyn. "We still got to reach shore before nightfall, or our troubles have only just begun."

*   *   *

The storm had weakened some and the sea's violent chop died down, but the idea of rowing another stroke, even in a perfectly calm sea, was unimaginable now. We hadn't made it even halfway to the mainland and already I was hopelessly exhausted. My hands throbbed. My arms felt heavy as tree trunks. Not only that, but the endless diagonal rocking of the boat was having an undeniable effect on my stomach—and judging from the greenish color of the faces around me, I wasn't alone.

"We'll rest awhile," Emma said, trying to sound encouraging.

"We'll rest and bail out the boats until the fog clears . . ."

"Fog like this has a mind of its own," said Enoch. "It can go days without breaking. It'll be dark in a few hours, and then we'll have to hope we can last until morning without the wights finding us. We'll be utterly defenseless."

"And without water," said Hugh.

"Or food," added Millard.

Olive raised both hands in the air and said, "*I* know where it is!"

"Where what is?" said Emma.

"Land. I saw it when I was up at the end of that rope." Olive had risen above the fog, she explained, and briefly caught a clear view of the mainland.

"Fat lot of good that does," grumbled Enoch. "We've circled back on ourselves a half-dozen times since you were dangling up there."

"Then let me up again."

"Are you certain?" Emma asked her. "It's dangerous. What if a wind catches you, or the rope snaps?"

Olive's face went steely. "Reel me up," she repeated.

"When she gets like this, there's no arguing," said Emma. "Fetch the rope, Bronwyn."

"You're the bravest little girl I ever knew," Bronwyn said, then set to working. She pulled the anchor out of the water and up into our boat, and with the extra length of rope it gave us we lashed together our two remaining boats so they couldn't be separated again, then reeled Olive back up through the fog and into the sky.

There was an odd quiet moment when we were all staring at a rope in the clouds, heads thrown back—waiting for a sign from heaven.

Enoch broke the silence. "Well?" he called, impatient.

"I can see it!" came the reply, Olive's voice barely a squeak over the white noise of waves. "Straight ahead!"

"Good enough for me!" Bronwyn said, and while the rest of us clutched our stomachs and slumped uselessly in our seats, she clambered into the lead boat and took the oars and began to row, guided only by Olive's tiny voice, an unseen angel in the sky.

"Left . . . more left . . . not that much!"

And like that we slowly made our way toward land, the fog pursuing us always, its long, gray tendrils like the ghostly fingers of some phantom hand, ever trying to draw us back.

As if the island couldn't quite let us go, either.

CHAPTER TWO

*O*ur twin hulls ground to a halt in the rocky shallows. We hove up onto shore just as the sun was dimming behind acres of gray clouds, perhaps an hour left until full dark. The beach was a stony spit clogged with low-tide sea wrack, but it was beautiful to me, more beautiful than any champagne-white tourist beach back home. It meant we had made it. What it meant to the others I could hardly imagine; most of them hadn't been off Cairnholm in a lifetime, and now they gazed around in wonder, bewildered to still be alive and wondering what on earth to do about it.

We staggered from our boats with legs made of rubber. Fiona scooped a handful of slimy pebbles into her mouth and rolled them over her tongue, as if she needed all five senses to convince herself she wasn't dreaming—which was just how I'd felt about being in Miss Peregrine's loop, at first. I had never, in all my life, so distrusted my own eyes. Bronwyn groaned and sank to the ground, exhausted beyond words. She was surrounded and fussed over and showered with thanks for all she'd done, but it was awkward; our debt was too great and the words *thank you* too small, and she tried to wave us away but was so tired she could barely raise her hand. Meanwhile, Emma and the boys reeled Olive down from the clouds.

"You're positively *blue*!" Emma exclaimed when Olive appeared through the fog, and she leapt up to pull the little girl into her arms. Olive was soaked and frozen, her teeth chattering. There were no blankets, nor even a stitch of dry clothing to give her, so Emma ran her ever-hot hands around Olive's body until the worst of her shudders subsided, then sent Fiona and Horace away to gather driftwood for a fire. While waiting for their return, we gathered round the boats to take stock of all we'd lost at sea. It was a grim tally. Nearly everything we'd brought now littered the seafloor.

What we had left were the clothes on our backs, a small amount of food in rusty tins, and Bronwyn's tank-sized steamer trunk, indestructible and apparently unsinkable—and so absurdly heavy that only Bronwyn herself could ever hope to carry it. We tore open its metal latches, eager to find something useful, or better yet, edible, but all it held was a three-volume collection of stories called *Tales of the Peculiar*, the pages spongy with seawater, and a fancy bath mat embroidered with the letters *ALP*, Miss Peregrine's initials.

"Oh, thank heavens! Someone remembered the bath mat," Enoch deadpanned. "We are saved."

Everything else was gone, including both our maps—the small one Emma had used to navigate us across the channel and the massive leather-bound loop atlas that had been Millard's prized possession, the Map of Days. When Millard realized it was gone he began to hyperventilate. "That was one of only five extant copies!" he moaned. "It was of incalculable value! Not to mention it contained years of my personal notes and annotations!"

"At least we still have the *Tales of the Peculiar*," said Claire, wringing seawater from her blonde curls. "I can't get to sleep at night without hearing one."

"What good are fairy tales if we can't even find our way?" Millard asked.

I wondered: *Find our way to where?* It occurred to me that, in our rush to escape the island, I had only ever heard the children talk about reaching the mainland, but we'd never discussed what to do once we got there—as if the idea of actually surviving the journey in those tiny boats was so far-fetched, so comically optimistic, that planning for it was a waste of time. I looked to Emma for reassurance, as I often did. She gazed darkly down the beach. The stony sand backed up to low dunes swaying with saw grass. Beyond was forest: an impenetrable-looking barrier of green that continued in both directions as far as I could see. Emma with her now-lost map had been aiming for a certain port town, but after the storm hit, just making it to dry land had become our goal. There was no telling how far we'd strayed off course. There were no roads I could see, or signposts, or even footpaths. Only wilderness.

Of course, we didn't really need a map, or a signpost, or anything else. We needed Miss Peregrine—a whole, healed one—the Miss Peregrine who would know just where to go and how to get us there safely. The one perched before us now, fanning her feathers dry on a boulder, was as broken as her maimed wing, which hooked downward in an alarming V. I could tell it pained the children to see her like this. She was supposed to be their mother, their protector. She'd been queen of their little island world, but now she couldn't speak, couldn't loop time, couldn't even fly. They saw her and winced and looked away.

Miss Peregrine kept her eyes trained on the slate-gray sea. They were hard and black and contained unutterable sorrow.

They seemed to say: *I failed you.*

*   *   *

Horace and Fiona arced toward us through the rocky sand, the wind poofing Fiona's wild hair like a storm cloud, Horace bouncing with his hands pressed against the sides of his top hat to keep it secure on his head. Somehow he had kept hold of it throughout our near disaster at sea, but now it was stove in on one side like a bent muffler pipe. Still, he refused to let it go; it was the only thing, he said, that matched his muddy, sopping, finely tailored suit.

Their arms were empty. "There's no wood anywhere!" Horace said as they reached us.

"Did you look in the *woods*?" said Emma, pointing at the dark line of trees behind the dunes.

"Too scary," Horace replied. "We heard an owl."

"Since when are you afraid of birds?"

Horace shrugged and looked at the sand. Then Fiona elbowed him, and he seemed to remember himself, and said: "We found something else, though."

"Shelter?" asked Emma.

"A road?" asked Millard.

"A goose to cook for supper?" asked Claire.

"No," Horace replied. "Balloons."

There was a brief, puzzled silence.

"What do you mean, balloons?" said Emma.

"Big ones in the sky, with men inside."

Emma's face darkened. "Show us."

We followed them back the way they'd come, curving around a bend in the beach and climbing a small embankment. I wondered how we could have possibly missed something as obvious as hot air balloons, until we crested a hill and I saw them—not the big, colorful teardrop-shaped things you see in wall calendars and motivational posters (*"The sky's the limit!"*), but a pair of miniature zeppelins: black egg-shaped sacs of gas with skeletal cages hung below them, each containing a single pilot. The craft were small and flew low, banking back and forth in lazy zigzags, and the noise of the surf had covered the subtle whine of their propellers. Emma herded us into the tall saw grass and we dropped down out of sight.

"They're submarine hunters," Enoch said, answering the question before anyone had asked it. Millard might've been the authority when it came to maps and books, but Enoch was an expert in all things military. "The best way to spot enemy subs is from the sky," he explained.

"Then why are they flying so close to the ground?" I asked. "And why aren't they farther out to sea?"

"That I don't know."

"Do you think they could be looking for . . . us?" Horace

ventured.

"If you mean could they be wights," said Hugh, "don't be daft. The wights are with the Germans. They're on that German sub."

"The wights are allied with whomever it suits their interests to be allied with," Millard said. "There's no reason to think they haven't infiltrated organizations on both sides of the war."

I couldn't take my eyes off the strange contraptions in the sky. They looked unnatural, like mechanical insects bloated with tumorous eggs.

"I don't like the way they're flying," Enoch said, calculating behind his sharp eyes. "They're searching the coastline, not the sea."

"Searching for what?" asked Bronwyn, but the answer was obvious and frightening and no one wanted to say it aloud.

They were searching for us.

We were all squeezed together in the grass, and I felt Emma's body tense next to mine. "Run when I say run," she hissed. "We'll hide the boats, then ourselves."

We waited for the balloons to zag away, then tumbled out of the grass, praying we were too far away to be spotted. As we ran I found myself wishing that the fog which had plagued us at sea would return again to hide us. It occurred to me that it had very likely saved us once already; without the fog those balloons would've spotted us hours ago, in our boats, when we'd had nowhere to run. And in that way, it was one last thing that the island had done to save its peculiar children.

We dragged our boats across the beach toward a sea cave, its entrance a black fissure in a hill of rocks. Bronwyn had spent her strength completely and could hardly manage to carry herself, much less the boats, so the rest of us struggled to pick up the slack, groaning and straining against hulls that kept trying to bury their noses in the wet sand. Halfway across the beach, Miss Peregrine let out a warning cry, and the two zeppelins bobbed up over the dunes and into our line of sight. We broke into an adrenaline-fueled sprint, flying those boats into the cave like they were on rails, while Miss Peregrine hopped lamely alongside us, her broken wing dragging in the sand.

When we were finally out of sight we dropped the boats and flopped onto their overturned keels, our wheezing breaths echoing in the damp and dripping dark. "Please, please let them not have seen us," Emma prayed aloud.

"Ah, birds! Our tracks!" Millard yelped, and then he stripped off the overcoat he'd been wearing and scrambled back outside to cover the drag marks our boats had made; from the sky they'd look like arrows pointing right to our hiding place. We could only watch his footsteps trail away. If anyone but Millard had ventured out, they'd have been seen for sure.

A minute later he came back, shivering, caked in sand, a red stain outlining his chest. "They're getting close now," he panted. "I did the best I could."

"You're bleeding again!" Bronwyn fretted. Millard had been grazed by a bullet during our melee at the lighthouse the previous night, and though his recovery so far was remarkable, it was far from complete. "What have you done with your wound dressing?"

"I threw it away. It was tied in such a complicated manner that I couldn't remove it quickly. An invisible must always be able to disrobe in an instant, or his power is useless!"

"He's even more useless dead, you stubborn mule," said Emma. "Now hold still and don't bite your tongue. This is going to hurt." She squeezed two fingers in the palm of her opposite hand, concentrated for a moment, and when she took them out again they glowed, red hot.

Millard balked. "Now then, Emma, I'd rather you didn't—"

Emma pressed her fingers to his wounded shoulder. Millard gasped. There was the sound of singeing meat, and a curl of smoke rose up from his skin. In a moment the bleeding stopped.

"I'll have a scar!" Millard whined.

"Yes? And who'll see it?"

He sulked and said nothing.

The balloons' engines grew louder, then louder still, amplified by the cave's stone walls. I pictured them hovering above the cave, studying our footprints, preparing their assault. Emma leaned her shoulder into mine. The little ones ran to Bronwyn and buried their faces in her lap, and she hugged them. Despite our peculiar powers, we felt utterly powerless: it was all we could do to sit hunched and blinking at one another in the pale half-light, noses running from the cold, hoping our enemies would pass us by.

Finally the engines' whine began to dwindle, and when we could hear our own voices again, Claire mumbled into Bronwyn's lap, "Tell us a story, Wyn. I'm scared and I don't like this at all and I think I'd like to hear a story instead."

"Yes, would you tell one?" Olive pleaded. "A story from the *Tales*, please. They're my favorite."

The most maternal of the peculiars, Bronwyn was more like a mother to the young ones than even Miss Peregrine. It was Bronwyn who tucked them into bed at night, Bronwyn who read them stories and kissed their foreheads. Her strong arms seemed made to gather them in warm embraces, her broad shoulders to carry them. But this was no time for stories—and she said as much.

"Why, certainly it is!" Enoch said with singsongy sarcasm. "But skip the *Tales* for once and tell us the story of how Miss Peregrine's wards found their way to safety without a map or any food and weren't eaten by hollowgast along the way! I'm ever so keen to hear how *that* story ends."

"If only Miss Peregrine could tell us," Claire sniffled. She disentangled herself from Bronwyn and went to the bird, who'd been watching us from her perch on one of the boats' overturned keels. "What are we to do, headmistress?" said Claire. "Please turn human again. Please wake up!"

Miss Peregrine cooed and stroked Claire's hair with her wing. Then Olive joined in, her face streaking with tears: "We need you, Miss Peregrine! We're lost and in danger and increasingly peckish and we've got no home anymore nor any friends but one another and we *need* you!"

Miss Peregrine's black eyes shimmered. She turned away, unreachable.

Bronwyn knelt down beside the girls. "She can't turn back right now, sweetheart. But we'll get her fixed up, I promise."

"But *how*?" Olive demanded. Her question reflected off the stone walls, each echo asking it again.

Emma stood up. "*I'll* tell you how," she said, and all eyes went to her. "We'll *walk*." She said it with such conviction that I got a chill. "We'll walk and walk until we come to a town."

"What if there's no town for fifty miles?" said Enoch.

"Then we'll walk for fifty-one miles. But I know we weren't blown *that* far off course."

"And if the wights should spot us from the air?" said Hugh.

"They won't. We'll be careful."

"And if they're waiting for us in the town?" said Horace.

"We'll pretend to be normal. We'll pass."

"I was never much good at that," Millard said with a laugh.

"You won't be seen at all, Mill. You'll be our advance scout, and our secret procurer of necessary items."

"I *am* quite a talented thief," he said with a touch of pride. "A veritable master of the five-fingered arts."

"And then?" Enoch muttered sourly. "Maybe we'll have food in our bellies and a warm place to sleep, but we'll still be out in the open, exposed, vulnerable, loopless . . . and Miss Peregrine is . . . is still . . ."

"We'll find a loop somehow," said Emma. "There are landmarks and signposts for those who know what to look for. And if there aren't, we'll find someone like us, a fellow peculiar who can show us where the nearest loop is. And in that loop there will be an ymbryne, and that ymbryne will be able to give Miss Peregrine the help she needs."

I'd never met anyone with Emma's brash confidence. Everything about her exuded it: the way she carried herself, with shoulders thrown back; the hard set of her teeth when she made up her mind about something; the way she ended every sentence with a declarative period, never a question mark. It was infectious and I loved it, and I had to fight a sudden urge to kiss her, right there in front of everyone.

Hugh coughed, and bees tumbled out of his mouth to form a question mark that shivered in the air. "How can you be so bloody *sure*?" he asked.

"Because I am, that's all." And she brushed her hands as if that were that.

"You make a nice rousing speech," said Millard, "and I hate to spoil it, but for all we know, Miss Peregrine is the only ymbryne left uncaptured. Recall what Miss Avocet told us: the wights have been raiding loops and abducting ymbrynes for *weeks* now. Which means that even if we *could* find a loop, there'd be no way of knowing whether it still had its ymbryne—or was occupied instead by our enemies. We can't simply go knocking on loop doors and hoping they aren't full of wights."

"Or surrounded by half-starved hollows," Enoch said.

"We won't *have* to hope," Emma said, then smiled in my direction. "Jacob will tell us."

My entire body went cold. "*Me?*"

"You can sense hollows from a distance, can't you?" said Emma. "In addition to seeing them?"

"When they're close, it kind of feels like I'm going to puke," I admitted.

"How close do they have to be?" asked Millard. "If it's only a few meters, that still puts us within devouring range. We'd need you to sense them from much farther away."

"I haven't exactly tested it," I said. "This is all so new to me."

I'd only ever been exposed to Dr. Golan's hollow, Malthus—the creature who'd killed my grandfather, then nearly drowned me in Cairnholm's bog. How far away had he been when I'd first felt him stalking me, lurking outside my house in Englewood? It was impossible to know.

"Regardless, your talent can be developed," said Millard. "Peculiarities are a bit like muscles—the more you exercise them, the bigger they grow."

"This is madness!" Enoch said. "Are you all really so desperate that you'd stake everything on *him*? Why, he's just a boy—a soft-bellied normal who knows next to nothing of our world!"

"He isn't *normal*," Emma said, grimacing as if this were the direst insult. "He's one of us!"

"Stuff and rubbish!" yelled Enoch. "Just because there's a dash of peculiar blood in his veins doesn't make him my brother. And it certainly doesn't make him my protector! We don't know what he's capable of—he probably wouldn't know the difference between a hollow at fifty meters and gas pains!"

"He *killed* one of them, didn't he?" said Bronwyn. "Stabbed it through the eyes with a pair of sheep shears! When's the last time you heard of a peculiar so young doing anything like that?"

"Not since Abe," Hugh said, and at the mention of his name a reverent hush fell over the children.

"I heard he once killed one with his bare hands," said Bronwyn.

"*I* heard he killed one with a knitting needle and a length of twine," said Horace. "In fact, I dreamed it, so I'm certain he did."

"Half of those stories are just tall tales, and they get taller with every year that passes," said Enoch. "The Abraham Portman I knew never did a single thing to help us."

"He was a great peculiar!" said Bronwyn. "He fought bravely and killed scores of hollows for our cause!"

"And then he ran off and left us to hide in that house like refugees while he galavanted around America, playing hero!"

"You don't know what you're talking about," Emma said, flushing with anger. "There was a lot more to it than that."

Enoch shrugged. "Anyway, that's all beside the point," he said. "Whatever you thought of Abe, this boy isn't him."

In that moment I hated Enoch, and yet I couldn't blame him for his doubts about me. How could the others, so sure and seasoned in their abilities, put so much faith in mine—in something I was only beginning to understand and had known I was capable of for only a few days? Whose grandson I was seemed irrelevant. I simply didn't know what I was doing.

"You're right, I'm not my grandfather," I said. "I'm just a kid from Florida. I probably got lucky when I killed that hollow."

"Nonsense," said Emma. "You'll be every bit the hollow-slayer Abe was, one day."

"One day soon, let's hope," said Hugh.

"It's your destiny," said Horace, and the way he said it made me think he knew something I didn't.

"And even if it ain't," said Hugh, clapping his hand on my back, "you're all we've got, mate."

"If that's true, bird help us all," said Enoch.

My head was spinning. The weight of their expectations threatened to crush me. I stood, unsteady, and moved toward the cave exit. "I need some air," I said, pushing past Enoch.

"Jacob, wait!" cried Emma. "The balloons!"

But they were long gone.

"Let him go," Enoch grumbled. "If we're lucky, he'll swim back to America."

Walking down to the water's edge, I tried to picture myself the way my new friends saw me, or wanted to: not as Jacob, the kid who once broke his ankle running after an ice cream truck, or who reluctantly and at the behest of his dad tried and failed three times to get onto his school's noncompetitive track team, but as Jacob, inspector of shadows, miraculous interpreter of squirmy gut feelings, seer and slayer of real and actual monsters—and all that might stand between life and death for our merry band of peculiars.

How could I ever live up to my grandfather's legacy?

I climbed a stack of rocks at the water's edge and stood there, hoping the steady breeze would dry my damp clothes, and in the dying light I watched the sea, a canvas of shifting grays, melded and darkening. In the distance a light glinted every so often. It was Cairnholm's lighthouse, flashing its hello and last goodbye.

My mind drifted. I lapsed into a waking dream.

I see a man. He is of middle age, cloaked in excremental mud, crabbing slowly along the knife tip of a cliff, his thin hair uncombed and hanging wet across his face. Wind whips his thin jacket like a sail. He stops, drops to his elbows. Slips them into divots he'd made weeks before, when he was scouting these coves for mating terns and shearwaters' nests. He raises a pair of binoculars to his eyes but aims them low, below the nests, at a thin crescent of beach where the swelling tide collects things and heaves them up: driftwood and seaweed, shards of smashed boats—and sometimes, the locals say, bodies.

The man is my father. He is looking for something that he desperately does not want to find.

He is looking for the body of his son.

I felt a touch on my shoe and opened my eyes, startled out of my half-dream. It was nearly dark, and I was sitting on the rocks with my knees drawn into my chest, and suddenly there was Emma, breeze tossing her hair, standing on the sand below me.

"How are you?" she asked.

It was a question that would've required some college-level math and about an hour of discussion to answer. I felt a hundred conflicting things, the great bulk of which canceled out to equal cold and tired and not particularly interested in talking. So I said, "I'm fine, just trying to dry off," and flapped the front of my soggy sweater to demonstrate.

"I can help you with that." She clambered up the stack of rocks and sat next to me. "Gimme an arm."

I offered one up and Emma laid it across her knees. Cupping her hands over her mouth, she bent her head toward my wrist. Then, taking a deep breath, she exhaled slowly through her palms and an incredible, soothing heat bloomed along my forearm, just on the edge of painful.

"Is it too much?" she said.

I tensed, a shudder going through me, and shook my head.

"Good." She moved farther up my arm to exhale again. Another pulse of sweet warmth. Between breaths, she said, "I hope you're not letting what Enoch said bother you. The rest of us believe in you, Jacob. Enoch can be a wrinkle-hearted old titmouse, especially when he's feeling jealous."

"I think he's right," I said.

"You don't really. Do you?"

It all came pouring out. "I have no idea what I'm doing," I said. "How can any of you depend on me? If I'm really peculiar then it's just a little bit, I think. Like I'm a quarter peculiar and the rest of you guys are full-blooded."

"It doesn't work that way," she said, laughing.

"But my grandfather was more peculiar than me. He had to be. He was so strong . . ."

"No, Jacob," she said, narrowing her eyes at me. "It's astounding. In so many ways, you're just like him. You're different, too, of course—you're gentler and sweeter—but everything you're saying . . . you sound like Abe, when he first came to stay with us."

"I do?"

"Yes. He was confused, too. He'd never met another peculiar. He didn't understand his power or how it worked or what he was capable of. Neither did we, to tell the truth. It's very rare, what you can do. Very rare. But your grandfather learned."

"How?" I asked. "Where?"

"In the war. He was part of a secret all-peculiar cell of the British army. Fought hollowgast and Germans at the same time. The sorts of things they did you don't win medals for—but they were heroes to us, and none more than your grandfather. The sacrifices they made set the corrupted back decades and saved the lives of countless peculiars."

And yet, I thought, *he couldn't save his own parents. How strangely tragic.*

"And I can tell you this," Emma went on. "You're every bit as peculiar as he was—and as brave, too."

"Ha. Now you're just trying to make me feel better."

"No," she said, looking me in the eye. "I'm not. You'll learn, Jacob. One day you'll be an even greater hollow-slayer than he was."

"Yeah, that's what everyone keeps saying. How can you be so sure?"

"It's something I feel very deeply," she said. "You're *supposed to*, I think. Just like you were supposed to come to Cairnholm."

"I don't believe in stuff like that. Fate. The stars. Destiny."

"I didn't say destiny."

"*Supposed to* is the same thing," I said. "Destiny is for people in books about magical swords. It's a lot of crap. I'm here because my grandfather mumbled something about your island in the ten seconds before he died—and that's it. It was an accident. I'm glad he did, but he was delirious. He could just as easily have rattled off a grocery list."

"But he *didn't*," she said.

I sighed, exasperated. "And if we go off in search of loops, and you depend on me to save you from monsters and instead I get you all killed, is that destiny, too?"

She frowned, put my arm back in my lap. "I didn't say *destiny*," she said again. "What I believe is that when it comes to big things in life, there are no accidents. Everything happens for a reason. *You're* here for a reason—and it's not to fail and die."

I didn't have the heart to keep arguing. "Okay," I said. "I don't think you're right—but I do *hope* you are." I felt bad for snapping at her before, but I'd been cold and scared and feeling defensive. I had good moments and bad, terrified thoughts and confident ones—though my terror-to-confidence ratio was pretty dismal at present, like three-to-one, and in the terrified moments it felt like I was being pushed into a role I hadn't asked for; volunteered for front-line duty in a war, the full scope of which none of us yet knew. "Destiny" sounded like an obligation, and if I was to be thrust into battle against a legion of nightmare creatures, that had to be my choice.

Though in a sense the choice had been made already, when I agreed to sail into the unknown with these peculiar children. And it wasn't true, if I really searched the dusty corners of myself, that I hadn't asked for this. Really, I'd been dreaming of such adventures since I was small. Back then I'd believed in destiny, and believed in it absolutely, with every strand and fiber of my little kid heart. I'd felt it like an itch in my chest while listening to my grandfather's extraordinary stories. *One day that will be me.* What felt like obligation now had been a promise back then—that one day I would escape my little town and live an extraordinary life, as he had done; and that one day, like Grandpa Portman, I would do something that mattered. He used to say to me: "You're going to be a great man, Yakob. A very great man."

"Like you?" I would ask him.

"Better," he'd reply.

I'd believed him then, and I still wanted to. But the more I learned about him, the longer his shadow became, and the more impossible it seemed that I could ever matter the way he had. That maybe it would be suicidal even to try. And when I imagined myself trying, thoughts of my father crept in—my poor about-to-be-devastated father—and before I could push them out of my mind, I wondered how a great man could do something so terrible to someone who loved him.

I began to shiver. "You're cold," Emma said. "Let me finish what I started." She picked up my other arm and kissed with her breath the whole length of it. It was almost more than I could handle. When she reached my shoulder, instead of placing the arm in my lap, she hung it around her neck. I lifted my other arm to join it, and she put her arms around me, too, and our foreheads nodded together.

Speaking very quietly, Emma said, "I hope you don't regret the choice you made. I'm so glad you're here with us. I don't know what I'd do if you left. I fear I wouldn't be all right at all."

I thought about going back. For a moment I really tried to play it out in my head, how it would be if I could somehow row one of our boats back to the island again, and go back home.

But I couldn't do it. I couldn't imagine.

I whispered: "How could I?"

"When Miss Peregrine turns human again, she'll be able to send you back. If you want to go."

My question hadn't been about logistics. I had meant, simply: *How could I leave you?* But those words were unsayable, couldn't find their way past my lips. So I held them inside, and instead I kissed her.

This time it was Emma whose breath caught short. Her hands rose to my cheeks but stopped just shy of making contact. Heat radiated from them in waves.

"Touch me," I said.

"I don't want to burn you," she said, but a sudden shower of sparks inside my chest said *I don't care*, so I took her fingers and raked them along my cheek, and both of us gasped. It was hot but I didn't pull away. Dared not, for fear she'd stop touching me. And then our lips met again and we were kissing again, and her extraordinary warmth surged through me.

My eyes fell closed. The world faded away.

If my body was cold in the night mist, I didn't feel it. If the sea roared in my ears, I didn't hear it. If the rock I sat on was sharp and jagged, I hardly noticed. Everything outside the two of us was a distraction.

And then a great crash echoed in the dark, but I thought nothing of it—could not take myself away from Emma—until the sound doubled and was joined by an awful shriek of metal, and a blinding light swept over us, and finally I couldn't shut it out anymore.

The lighthouse, I thought. *The lighthouse is falling into the sea.* But the lighthouse was a pinpoint in the distance, not a sun-bright flash, and its light only traveled in one direction, not back and forth, searching.

It wasn't a lighthouse at all. It was a searchlight—and it was coming from the water close to shore.

It was the searchlight of a submarine.

*   *   *

Brief second of terror in which brain and legs were disconnected. My eyes and ears registered the submarine not far from shore: metal beast rising from the sea, water rushing from its sides, men bursting onto its deck from open hatches, shouting, training cannons of light at us. And then the stimulus reached my legs and we slid, fell, and pitched ourselves down from the rocks and ran like hell.

The spotlight threw our pistoning shadows across the beach,

ten feet tall and freakish. Bullets pocked the sand and buzzed the air.

A voice boomed from a loudspeaker. "STOP! DO NOT RUN!"

We burst into the cave—*They're coming, they're here, get up, get up*—but the children had heard the commotion and were already on their feet—all but Bronwyn, who had so exhausted herself at sea that she had fallen asleep against the cave wall and couldn't be roused. We shook her and shouted in her face, but she only moaned and brushed us away with a sweep of her arm. Finally we had to hoist her up by the waist, which was like lifting a tower of bricks, but once her feet touched the ground, her red-rimmed eyelids split open and she took her own weight.

We grabbed up our things, thankful now that they were so small and so few. Emma scooped Miss Peregrine into her arms. We tore outside. As we ran into the dunes, I saw behind us a gang of silhouetted men splashing the last few feet to shore. In their hands, held above their heads to keep them dry, were guns.

We sprinted through a stand of windblown trees and into the trackless forest. Darkness enveloped us. What moon wasn't already hidden behind clouds was blotted out now by trees, branches filtering its pale light to nil. There was no time for our eyes to adjust or to feel our way carefully or to do anything other than run in a gasping, stumbling herd with arms outstretched, dodging trunks that seemed to coalesce suddenly in the air just inches from us.

After a few minutes we stopped, chests heaving, to listen. The voices were still behind us, only now they were joined by another sound: dogs barking.

We ran on.

CHAPTER THREE

We tumbled through the black woods for what seemed like hours, no moon or movement of stars by which to judge the passing time. The sound of men shouting and dogs barking wheeled around us as we ran, menacing us from everywhere and nowhere. To throw the dogs off our scent, we waded into an icy stream and followed it until our feet went numb, and when we crossed out of it again, it felt like I was stumbling along on prickling stumps.

After a time we began to fail. Someone moaned in the dark. Olive and Claire started to fall behind, so Bronwyn hefted them into her arms, but then she couldn't keep up, either. Finally, when Horace tripped over a root and fell to the ground and then lay there begging for a rest, we all stopped. "Up, you lazy sod!" Enoch hissed at him, but he was wheezing, too, and then he leaned against a tree to catch his breath and the fight seemed to go out of him.

We were reaching the limit of our endurance. We had to stop.

"It's no use running circles in the dark like this, anyway," said Emma. "We could just as easily end up right back where we started."

"We'll be able to make better sense of this forest in the light of day," said Millard.

"Provided we live that long," said Enoch.

A light rain hissed down. Fiona made a shelter for us by coaxing a ring of trees to bend their lower branches together, petting their bark and whispering to their trunks until the branches meshed to form a watertight roof of leaves just high enough for us to sit beneath. We crawled in and lay listening to the rain and the distant barking of dogs. Somewhere in the forest, men with guns were still hunting us. Alone with our thoughts, I'm sure each of us was wondering the same thing—what might happen to us if we were caught.

Claire began to cry, softly at first but then louder and louder, until both of her mouths were bawling and she could hardly catch a breath between sobs.

"Get ahold of yourself!" Enoch said. "They'll hear you—and then we'll all have something to cry about!"

"They're going to feed us to their dogs!" she said. "They're going to shoot holes in us and take Miss Peregrine away!"

Bronwyn scooted next to her and wrapped the little girl in a bear hug. "Please, Claire! You've got to think about something else!"

"I'm truh-trying!" she wailed.

"Try *harder*!"

Claire squeezed her eyes shut, drew in a deep breath, and held it until she looked like a balloon about to pop—then burst into a fit of gasping cough-sobs that were louder than ever.

Enoch clapped his hands over her mouths. "*Shhhhhhh!*"

"I'm suh-suh-sorry!" she blubbered. "Muh-maybe if I could hear a story . . . one of the tuh-*Tales* . . ."

"Not this again," said Millard. "I'm beginning to wish we'd lost those damned books at sea with the rest of our things!"

Miss Peregrine spoke up—inasmuch as she was able to—hopping atop Bronwyn's trunk and tapping it with her beak. Inside, along with the rest of our meager possessions, were the *Tales*.

"I'm with Miss P," said Enoch. "It's worth a try—anything to stop her bawling!"

"All right then, little one," Bronwyn said, "but just one tale, and you've got to promise to stop crying!"

"I pruh-promise," Claire sniffled.

Bronwyn opened the trunk and pulled out a waterlogged volume of *Tales of the Peculiar*. Emma scooted close and lit the tiniest wisp of flame on her fingertip to read by. Then Miss Peregrine, apparently impatient to pacify Claire, took one edge of the book's cover in her beak and opened it to a seemingly random chapter. In a hushed voice, Bronwyn began to read.

"Once upon a peculiar time, in a forest deep and ancient, there roamed a great many animals. There were rabbits and deer and foxes, just as there are in every forest, but there were animals of a less common sort, too, like stilt-legged grimbears and two-headed lynxes and talking emu-raffes. These peculiar animals were a favorite target of hunters, who loved to shoot them and mount them on walls and show them off to their hunter friends, but loved even more to sell them to zookeepers, who would lock them in cages and charge money to view them. Now, you might think it would be far better to be locked in a cage than to be shot and mounted upon a wall, but peculiar creatures must roam free to be happy, and after a while the spirits of caged ones wither, and they begin to envy their wall-mounted friends."

"This is a sad story," Claire groused. "Tell a different one."

"I like it," said Enoch. "Tell more about the shooting and mounting."

Bronwyn ignored them both. "Now this was an age when giants still roamed the Earth," she went on, "as they did in the long-ago *Aldinn* times, though they were few in number and diminishing. And it just so happened that one of these giants lived near the forest, and he was very kind and spoke very softly and ate only plants and his name was Cuthbert. One day Cuthbert came into the forest to gather berries, and there saw a hunter hunting an emu-raffe. Being the kindly giant that he was, Cuthbert picked up the little 'raffe by the scruff of its long neck, and by standing up to his full height, on tiptoe, which he rarely did because it made all his old bones crackle, Cuthbert was able to reach up very high and deposit the emu-raffe on a mountaintop, well out of danger. Then, just for good measure, he squashed the hunter to jelly between his toes.

"Word of Cuthbert's kindness spread throughout the forest,

and soon peculiar animals were coming to him every day, asking to be lifted up to the mountaintop and out of danger. And Cuthbert said, 'I'll protect you, little brothers and sisters. All I ask in return is that you talk to me and keep me company. There aren't many giants left in the world, and I get lonely from time to time.'

"And they said, 'Of course, Cuthbert, we will.'

"So every day Cuthbert saved more peculiar animals from the hunters, lifting them up to the mountain by the scruffs of their necks, until there was a whole peculiar menagerie up there. And the animals were happy there because they could finally live in peace, and Cuthbert was happy, too, because if he stood on his tiptoes and rested his chin on the top of the mountain he could talk to his new friends all he liked. Then one morning a witch came to see Cuthbert. He was bathing in a little lake in the shadow of the mountain when she said to him, 'I'm terribly sorry, but I've got to turn you into stone now.'

"'Why would you do something like that?' asked the giant. 'I'm very kindly. A helping sort of giant.'

"And she said, 'I was hired by the family of the hunter you squashed.'

"'Ah,' he replied. 'Forgot about him.'

"'I'm terribly sorry,' the witch said again, and then she waved a birch branch at him and poor Cuthbert turned to stone.

"All of the sudden Cuthbert became very heavy—so heavy that he began to sink into the lake. He sank and sank and didn't stop sinking until he was covered in water all the way up to his neck. His animal friends saw what was happening, and though they felt terrible about it, they decided they could do nothing to help him.

"'I know you can't save me,' Cuthbert shouted up to his friends, 'but at least come and talk to me! I'm stuck down here, and so very lonely!'

"'But if we come down there the hunters will shoot us!' they called back.

"Cuthbert knew they were right, but still he pleaded with them.

"'Talk to me!' he cried. 'Please come and talk to me!'

"The animals tried singing and shouting to poor Cuthbert from the safety of their mountaintop, but they were too distant and their voices too small, so that even to Cuthbert and his giant ears they sounded quieter than the whisper of leaves in the wind.

"'Talk to me!' he begged. 'Come and talk to me!'

"But they never did. And he was still crying when his throat turned to stone like the rest of him. The end."

Bronwyn closed the book.

Claire looked appalled. "That's *it*?"

Enoch began to laugh.

"That's it," Bronwyn said.

"That's a *terrible* story," said Claire. "Tell another one!"

"A story's a story," said Emma, "and now it's time for bed."

Claire pouted, but she had stopped crying, so the tale had served its purpose.

"Tomorrow's not likely to be any easier than today was," said Millard. "We'll need what rest we can get."

We gathered cuts of springy moss to use as pillows, Emma drying the rain from them with her hands before we tucked them under our heads. Lacking blankets, we nestled together for warmth: Bronwyn cuddling the small ones; Fiona entangled with Hugh, whose bees came and went from his open mouth as he snored, keeping watch over their sleeping master; Horace and Enoch shivering with their backs to one another, too proud to snuggle; myself with Emma. I lay on my back and she in the crook of my arm, head on my chest, her face so invitingly close to mine that I could kiss her forehead anytime I liked—and I wouldn't have stopped except that I was as tired as a dead man and she was as warm as an electric blanket and pretty soon I was asleep and dreaming pleasant, forgettable nothings.

I never remember nice dreams; only the bad ones stick.

It was a miracle that I could sleep at all, given the circumstances. Even here—running for our lives, sleeping exposed, facing death—even here, in her arms, I was able to find some measure of peace.

Watching over us all, her black eyes shining in the dark, was Miss Peregrine. Though damaged and diminished, she was still our protector.

The night turned raw, and Claire began to shake and cough. Bronwyn nudged Emma awake and said, "Miss Bloom, the little one needs you; I'm afraid she's taking ill," and with a whispered apology Emma slipped out of my arms to go and attend to Claire. I felt a twinge of jealousy, then guilt for being jealous of a sick friend. So I lay alone feeling irrationally forsaken and stared into the dark, more exhausted than I had ever been and yet unable now to sleep, listening to the others shift and moan in the grip of nightmares that could not have equalled the one we would likely wake to. And eventually the dark peeled back layer by layer, and with imperceptible gradations the sky feathered to a delicate pale blue.

*　　*　　*

At dawn we crawled from our shelter. I picked moss out of my hair and tried in vain to brush the mud from my pants, but succeeded only in smearing it, making me look like some bog creature vomited from the earth. I was hungry in a way I'd never experienced, my belly gnawing at itself from the inside, and I ached just about everywhere it was possible to ache, from rowing and running and sleeping on the ground. Still, a few mercies prevailed: overnight the rain had let up, the day was warming by degrees, and we seemed to have evaded the wights and their dogs, at least for the time being; either they'd stopped barking or were too far away to be heard.

In doing so we'd gotten ourselves hopelessly lost. The forest was no easier to navigate by day than it had been in the dark. Green-boughed firs stretched away in endless, disordered rows, each direction a mirror of the others. The ground here was a carpet of fallen leaves that hid any tracks we might've made the night before. We'd woken in the heart of a green labyrinth without a map or compass, and Miss Peregrine's broken wing meant she couldn't fly above the treeline to guide us. Enoch suggested we raise Olive above the trees, like we had in the fog, but we didn't have any rope to hold her, and if she slipped and fell into the sky, we'd never get her back again.

Claire was sick and getting sicker, and lay curled in Bronwyn's lap, sweat beading her forehead despite a chill in the air. She was so skinny I could count her ribs through her dress.

"Will she be all right?" I asked.

"She's feverish," Bronwyn said, pressing a hand to the girl's cheek. "She needs medicine."

"First we'll have to find our way out of this accursed forest," said Millard.

"First we should eat," said Enoch. "Let's eat and discuss our options."

"What options?" said Emma. "Pick a direction and we'll walk in it. Any one's as good as another."

In sullen silence we sat and ate. I've never tasted dog food but I'm sure this was worse—brownish squares of congealed meat fat from rusted tins, which, lacking utensils, we dug out with our fingers.

"I packed five salted game hens and three tins of foie gras with cornichons," Horace said bitterly, "and *this* is what survives our shipwreck." He held his nose and dropped a gelatinous nugget down his throat without chewing. "I think we're being punished."

"For what?" said Emma. "We've been perfect angels. Well, most of us."

"The sins of past lives, maybe. I don't know."

"Peculiars don't have past lives," said Millard. "We live them all at once."

We finished quickly, buried our empty tins, and prepared to go. Just as we were about to, Hugh burst through a thicket of bushes into our makeshift camp, bees circling his head in an agitated cloud. He was out of breath with excitement.

"Where have *you* been?" Enoch demanded.

"I needed some privacy to attend to my morning never-you-minds," Hugh said, "and I found—"

"Who gave you permission to be out of visual range?" Enoch said. "We nearly left without you!"

"Who says I need permission? Anyway, I saw—"

"You can't just wander away like that! What if you'd gotten lost?"

"We're *already* lost."

"You ignoramus! What if you couldn't find your way back?"

"I left a trail of bees, like I always do—"

"Would you kindly *let him finish*!" Emma shouted.

"Thank you," said Hugh, and then he turned and pointed back the way he'd come. "I saw water. Quite a lot of it, through the trees there."

Emma's face clouded. She said, "We're trying to get *away* from the sea, not back to it. We must've doubled back on ourselves in the night."

We followed Hugh back the way he'd come, Bronwyn carrying Miss Peregrine on her shoulder and poor sick Claire in her arms. After a hundred yards, a glisten of gray ripples appeared beyond the trees: some wide body of water.

"Oh, this is just *awful*," said Horace. "They've chased us right back into their arms!"

"I don't *hear* any soldiers," said Emma. "In fact, I don't hear anything at all. Not even the ocean."

Enoch said, "That's because it's *not* the ocean, you dolt," and he stood up and ran toward the water. When we caught up with him he was standing with his feet planted in wet sand, looking back at us with a self-satisfied *I-told-you-so* grin. He'd been right: this wasn't the sea. It was a misty, gray lake, wide and ringed with firs, its calm surface smooth as slate. But its most distinguishing feature was something I didn't notice right away; not until Claire pointed out a large rock formation jutting from the shallows nearby. My eyes skimmed it at first but then went back for a second glance. There was something eerie about it—and decidedly familiar.

"It's the giant from the story!" said Claire, pointing from her place in Bronwyn's arms. "It's Cuthbert!"

Bronwyn stroked her head. "Shh, honey, you've got fever."

"Don't be ridiculous," said Enoch. "It's just a rock."

But it wasn't. Though wind and rain had worn its features some, it looked just like a giant who'd sunk up to its neck in the lake. You could see clearly that it had a head and a neck and a nose and even an Adam's apple, and some scrubby trees were growing atop it like a crown of wild hair. But what was really uncanny was the position of its head—thrown back with its mouth open, as if, like the giant in the story we'd heard just last night, it had turned to stone while crying out to its friends on the mountaintop.

"And look!" said Olive, pointing at a rocky bluff rising in the distance. "That must be Cuthbert's mountain!"

"Giants are real," Claire murmured, her voice weak but full of wonder. "And so are the *Tales*!"

"Let's not jump to absurd conclusions," said Enoch. "What's more likely? That the writer of the tale we read last night was inspired by a rock that just happened to be shaped like a giant head, or that this head-shaped rock was really a giant?"

"You take the fun out of everything," said Olive. "*I* believe in giants, even if you don't!"

"The *Tales* are just tales and nothing more," Enoch grumbled.

"Funny," I said, "that's exactly what I thought all of *you* were, before I met you."

Olive laughed. "Jacob, you're silly. You really thought we were made up?"

"Of course. And even after I met you I still did, for a while. Like maybe I was losing my mind."

"Real or not, it's an incredible coincidence," said Millard. "To have been reading that story just last night, and then happen upon the very bit of geography that inspired it the next morning? What are the chances?"

"I don't think it's a coincidence," Emma said. "Miss Peregrine opened the book herself, remember? She must've chosen that story on purpose."

Bronwyn turned to look at the bird on her shoulder and said, "Is that right, Miss P? Why?"

"Because it means something," said Emma.

"Absolutely," said Enoch. "It means we should go and climb that bluff. Then maybe we'll see a way out of this forest!"

"I mean the *tale* means something," said Emma. "In the story, what was it the giant wanted? That he asked for over and over again?"

"Someone to talk to!" Olive answered like an eager student.

"Exactly," said Emma. "So if he wants to talk, let's hear what he has to say." And with that, she waded into the lake.

We watched her go, slightly perplexed.

"Where's she heading?" said Millard. He seemed to be asking me. I shook my head.

"We've got wights chasing us!" Enoch shouted after her. "We're desperately lost! What on bird's green earth are you thinking?"

"I'm thinking peculiarly!" Emma shouted back. She sloshed through the shallows to the base of the rock, then climbed up to its jaw and peered into its open mouth.

"Well?" I called. "What do you see?"

"Don't know!" she replied. "Looks like it goes down a long way, though. I'd better get a closer look!"

Emma hoisted herself into the giant's stone mouth.

"You'd better come down from there before you get hurt!" shouted Horace. "You're making everyone anxious!"

"Everything makes *you* anxious," Hugh said.

Emma tossed a rock down the giant's throat, listening for whatever sound came back. She started to say "I think it might be a . . ." but then slipped on loose gravel, and her last word was lost as she scrambled and caught herself before she could fall.

"Be careful!" I shouted, my heart racing. "Wait, I'm coming, too!"

I splashed into the lake after her.

"It might be a what?" called Enoch.

"Only one way to find out!" Emma said excitedly, and climbed farther into the giant's mouth.

"Oh, Lord," said Horace. "There she goes . . ."

"Wait!" I shouted again—but she was gone already, disappeared down the giant's throat.

*   *   *

The giant appeared even larger up close than it had from the shore, and peering down into its dark throat, I swore I could almost hear old Cuthbert breathing. I cupped my hands and called Emma's name. My own voice came echoing back. The others were wading into the lake now, too, but I couldn't wait for them—what if she was in trouble down there?—so I gritted my teeth, lowered my legs into the dark, and let go.

I fell for a long time. A full second. Then *splash*—a plunge into water so cold it made me gasp, all my muscles constricting at once. I had to remind myself to tread water or sink. I was in a dim, narrow chamber filled with water, with no way back up the giant's long, smooth throat; no rope, no ladder, no footholds. I shouted for Emma, but she was nowhere around.

Oh God, I thought. *She's drowned!*

But then something tickled my arms, and bubbles began breaking all around me, and a moment later Emma broke the surface, gasping for breath.

She looked okay by the pale light. "What are you waiting for?" she said slapping the water with her hand like she wanted me to dive down with her. "Come on!"

"Are you insane?" I said. "We're trapped in here!"

"Of course we're not!" she said.

Bronwyn's voice called from above. "Hellooooo, I hear you down there! What have you found?"

"I think it's a loop entrance!" Emma called back. "Tell everyone to jump in and don't be afraid—Jacob and I will meet you on the other side!"

And then she took my hand, and though I didn't quite understand what was going on, I drew a deep breath and let her pull me underwater. We flipped and scissor-kicked downward toward a person-sized hole in the rock through which a gleam of daylight was visible. She pushed me inside and then came after, and we swam through a shaft about ten feet long and then out into the lake. Above us I could see its rippling surface, and above that the blue, refracted sky, and as we rose toward it the water warmed dramatically. Then we broke into the air and gasped for breath, and instantly I could feel that the weather had changed: it was hot and muggy now, and the light had changed to that of a golden afternoon. The depth of the lake had changed, too—now it came all the way to the giant's chin.

"See?" Emma said, grinning. "We're somewhen else!"

And just like that, we'd entered a loop—abandoned a mild morning in 1940 for a hot afternoon in some other, older year, though it was difficult to tell just how much older, here in the forest, away from the easily datable cues of civilization.

One by one, the other children surfaced around us, and seeing how much things had changed, had their own realizations.

"Do you realize what this *means*?" Millard squealed. He was splashing around, turning in circles, out of breath with excitement. "It means there's secret knowledge embedded in the *Tales*!"

"Not so useless now, are they?" said Olive.

"Oh, I can't *wait* to analyze and annotate them," said Millard, rubbing his hands together.

"Don't you dare write in my book, Millard Nullings!" said Bronwyn.

"But what *is* this loop?" asked Hugh. "Who do you think lives here?"

Olive said, "Cuthbert's animal friends, of course!"

Enoch rolled his eyes but stopped short of saying what he was probably thinking—*It's just a story!*—maybe because his mind was starting to change, too.

"Every loop has an ymbryne," said Emma, "even mystery loops from storybook tales. So let's go and find her."

"All right," said Millard. "Where?"

"The only place the story made mention of aside from this lake was that mountain," Emma said, indicating the bluff beyond the trees. "Who's ready to do some climbing?"

We were tired and hungry, every one of us, but finding the loop had given us a burst of new energy. We left the stone giant behind and set off through the woods toward the foot of the bluff, our clothes drip-drying quickly in the heat. As we neared the bluff, the ground began to slope upward, and then a well-worn path appeared and we followed it up and up through clusters of brushy firs and winding rocky passages, until the path became so vertical in places that we had to go on all fours, clawing at the angled ground to pull ourselves forward.

"There'd better be something wonderful at the end of this trail," said Horace, dabbing sweat from his forehead. "A gentleman doesn't perspire!"

The path narrowed to a ribbon, the ground rising sharply on our right side and dropping away on the left, a carpet of green tree-tops spreading beyond it. "Hug the wall!" Emma warned. "It's a long way down."

Just glancing at the drop-off made me dizzy. Suddenly, it seemed, I had developed a new and stomach-clenching fear of heights, and it took all my concentration simply to put one foot in front of the other.

Emma touched my arm. "Are you all right?" she whispered. "You look pale."

I lied and said I was, and succeeded in faking allrightness for exactly three more twists in the path, at which point my heart was racing and my legs shaking so badly that I had to sit down, right there in the middle of the narrow path, blocking everyone behind me.

"Oh, dear," Hugh muttered. "Jacob's cracking up."

"I don't know what's wrong with me," I muttered. I'd never been afraid of heights before, but now I couldn't so much as look off the edge of the path without my stomach doing flips.

Then something terrible occurred to me: what if this wasn't a fear of heights I was feeling—but of hollows?

It couldn't be, though: we were inside a loop, where hollows couldn't go. And yet the more I studied the feeling churning in my gut, the more convinced I became that it wasn't the drop itself that bothered me, but something *beyond* it.

I had to see for myself.

Everyone chattered anxiously in my ear, asking what was the matter, was I okay. I shut out their voices, tipped forward onto my hands, and crawled toward the edge of path. The closer I got, the worse my stomach felt, like it was being clawed to shreds from the inside. Inches away, I pressed my chest flat to the ground and reached out to hook my fingers over the ledge, then dragged myself forward until I could peek over it.

It took my eyes a moment to spot the hollow. At first it was just a shimmer against the craggy mountainside; a quivering spot in the air like heat waves rising from a hot car. An error, barely detectable.

This was how they looked to normals, and to other peculiars— to anyone who could not do what I did.

Then I actually experienced my peculiar ability coming to life. Very quickly, the churning in my belly contracted and focused into a single point of pain; and then, in a way I can't fully explain, it became *directional*, lengthening from a point into a line, from one dimension to two. The line, like a compass needle, pointed diagonally at that faltering spot a hundred yards below and to the left on the mountainside, the waves and shimmers of which began to gather and coalesce into solid black mass, a humanoid thing made from tentacles and shadow, clinging to the rocks.

And then it saw me see it and its whole awful body drew taut. Hunkering close against the rocks, it unhinged its saw-toothed mouth and let loose an ear-splitting shriek.

My friends didn't need me to describe what I was seeing. The sound alone was enough.

"*Hollow!*" someone shouted.

"*Run!*" shouted another, belaboring the obvious.

I scrambled back from the ledge and was pulled to my feet, and then we were all running in a pack, not down the mountain but up it, farther into the unknown rather than back toward the flat ground and loop exit that lay behind us. But it was too late to turn back; I could feel the hollow leaping from boulder to crag up the cliffside—but away from us, down the path, to cut us off in case we tried to run past it down the mountain. It was trapping us.

This was new. I'd never been able to track a hollow with anything other than my eyes before, but now I felt that little compass needle inside me pointing behind us, and I could almost picture the creature scrambling toward flat ground. It was as if, upon seeing the hollow, I'd planted a sort of homing beacon in it with my eyes.

We raced around a corner—my fleeting fear of heights now apparently gone—and were confronted by a smooth wall of rock, fifty feet high at least. The path ended here; all around us the ground fell away at crazy angles. The wall had no ladders, no handholds. We searched frantically for some other way—a secret passage in the rock, a door, a tunnel—but there was none, and no way forward but up; and no way up, apparently, other than via hot air balloon or the helping hand of a probably mythical giant.

Panic took hold. Miss Peregrine began to screech and Claire to cry as Horace stood and wailed, "This is the end, we're all going to die!" The rest looked for last-ditch ways to save ourselves. Fiona dragged her hands along the wall, searching for crevices that might contain soil from which she could grow a vine or something else we could climb. Hugh ran to the edge of the path and peered over the drop-off. "We could jump, if only we had a parachute!"

"I can be a parachute!" said Olive. "Take hold of my legs!"

But it was a long way down, and at the bottom was dark and dangerous forest. It was better, Bronwyn decided, to send Olive up the rock face than down the mountain, and with limp, feverish Claire in one arm, Bronwyn led Olive by the hand to the wall. "Give me your shoes!" she said to Olive. "Take Claire and Miss P and get to the top as quick as you can!"

Olive looked terrified. "I don't know if I'm strong enough!" she cried.

"You've got to try, little magpie! You're the only one who can keep them safe!" And she knelt and set Claire down on her feet, and the sick girl tottered into Olive's arms. Olive squeezed her tight, slipped off her leaden shoes, and then, just as they began to rise, Bronwyn transferred Miss Peregrine from her shoulder to the top of Olive's head. Weighed down, Olive rose very slowly—it was only when Miss Peregrine began to flap her good wing and pull Olive up by the hair, Olive yelping and kicking her feet, that the three of them really took off.

The hollow had nearly reached level ground. I knew it as surely as if I could see it with my eyes. Meanwhile, we scoured the ground for anything that might be used as a weapon—but all we could find were pebbles. "*I* can be a weapon," said Emma, and she clapped her hands and drew them apart again, an impressive fireball roaring to life between them.

"And don't forget about my bees!" said Hugh, opening his mouth to let them out. "They can be fierce when provoked!"

Enoch, who always found a way to laugh at the most inappropriate times, let out a big guffaw. "What're you going to do," he said, "pollinate it to death?"

Hugh ignored him, turning to me instead. "You'll be our eyes, Jacob. Just tell us where the beast is and we'll sting his brains out!"

My compass needle of pain told me it was on the path now, and the way its venom was expanding to fill me meant it was closing in fast. "Any minute now," I said, pointing to the bend in the path we'd come around. "Get ready." If not for the adrenaline flooding my system, the pain would've been totally debilitating.

We assumed fight-or-flight positions, some of us crouching with fists raised like boxers, others like sprinters before the starting gun, though no one knew which way to run.

"What a depressing and inauspicious end to our adventures,"

said Horace. "Devoured by a hollow in some Welsh backwater!"

"I thought they couldn't enter loops," said Enoch. "How the hell did it get in here?"

"It would seem they have evolved," said Millard.

"Who gives a chuck how it happened!" Emma snapped. "It's here and it's hungry!"

Then from above us a small voice cried, "Look out below!" and I craned my neck to see Olive's face pull back and disappear over the top of the rock wall. A moment later something like a long rope came sailing over the ledge. It unreeled and snapped taut, and then a net unfurled at the end of it and smacked against the ground. "Hurry!" came Olive's voice again. "There's a lever up here—everyone grab hold of the net and I'll pull it!"

We ran to the net, but it was tiny, hardly large enough for two. Pinned to the rope at eye level was a photograph of a man inside the net—this very net—with his legs folded in front of him and hanging just above the ground before a sheer rock face—this very rock face. On the back of the photo a message was printed:

ONLY ACCESS TO MENAGERIE: CLIMB INSIDE!

WEIGHT LIMIT: ONE RIDER

STRICTLY ENFORCED

This contraption was some sort of primitive elevator—meant for one rider at a time, not eight. But there was no time to use it as intended, so we all dog-piled onto it, sticking our arms and legs through its holes, clinging to the rope above it, attaching ourselves any way we could.

"Take us up!" I shouted. The hollow very close now; the pain extraordinary.

For a few endless seconds, nothing happened. The hollow bolted around the bend, using its muscular tongues like legs, its atrophied human limbs hanging useless. Then a metallic squeal rang out, the rope pulled taut, and we lurched into the air.

The hollow had nearly closed the distance between us. It galloped with jaws wide open, as if to collect us between its teeth the way a whale feeds on plankton. We weren't quite halfway up the wall when it reached the ground below us, looked up, and squatted like a spring about to uncoil.

"It's going to jump!" I shouted. "Pull your legs into the net!"

The hollow drove its tongues into the ground and sprang upward. We were rising fast and it seemed like the hollow would miss us, but just as it reached the apex of its jump, one of its tongues shot out and lassoed Emma around the ankle.

Emma screamed and kicked at it with her other foot as the net came to a jolting stop, the pulley above too weak to raise all of us and the hollow, too.

"Get it off me!" Emma shouted. "Get it off get it off get it off!"

I tried kicking at it, too, but the hollow's tongue was as strong as woven steel and the tip was covered in hundreds of wriggling sucker-cups, so that anyone who tried to pry the tongue off would only get stuck to it themselves. And then the hollow was reeling itself up, its jaws inching closer until we could smell its stinking grave-breath.

Emma shouted for someone to hold her and with one hand I grabbed the back of her dress. Bronwyn let go of the net entirely, clinging to it with just her legs, then threw her arms around Emma's waist. Then Emma let go, too—Bronwyn and I being all that kept her from falling—and with her hands now free she reached down and clapped them around the tongue.

The hollow shrieked. The sucker-cups along its tongue, withered and reeking black smoke, hissed from its flesh. Emma squeezed harder and closed her eyes and howled, not a cry of pain, I thought, but a kind of war cry, until the hollow was forced to release, its injured tentacle unslithering from around her ankle. There was a surreal moment where it was no longer the hollow who was holding Emma but Emma who was holding the hollow, the thing writhing and shrieking below us, the acrid smoke of its burned flesh filling our noses, until finally we had to shout at her to *let go*, and Emma's eyes flew open again and she seemed to remember where she was and pulled her hands apart.

The hollow tumbled away from us, grasping at empty space as it fell. We rocketed up and away in the net, the tension that had been holding us down suddenly released, and soaring over the lip of the wall, we collapsed in a heap on top of it. Olive, Claire, and Miss Peregrine were waiting there for us, and as we extricated ourselves from the net and stumbled away from the cliff's edge, Olive cheered, Miss Peregrine screeched and beat her good wing, and Claire raised her head from where she'd been lying on the ground and gave a weak smile.

We were giddy—and for the second time in as many days, stunned to be alive. "That's twice you've saved our necks, little magpie," Bronwyn said to Olive. "And Miss Emma, I already knew you were brave, but that was beyond anything!"

Emma shrugged it off. "It was him or me," she said.

"I can't believe you *touched* it," said Horace.

Emma wiped her hands on her dress, held them to her nose, and made a face. "I just hope this smell comes off soon," she said. "That beast stank like a landfill!"

"How's your ankle?" I asked her. "Does it hurt?"

She knelt and pushed down her sock to reveal a fat, red welt ringing it. "Not too bad," she said, touching the ankle gingerly. But when she stood up again and put weight on it, I caught her wincing.

"A lot of help *you* were," Enoch growled at me. "'Run away!'

says the hollow-slayer's grandson!"

"If my grandfather had run from the hollow that killed him, he might still be alive," I said. "It's good advice."

I heard a thud from beyond the wall we'd just scaled, and the Feeling churned up inside me again. I went to the ledge and looked over. The hollow was alive and well at the base of the wall, and busy punching holes in the rock with its tongues.

"Bad news," I said. "The fall didn't kill it."

In a moment Emma was at my side. "What's it doing?"

I watched it twist one of its tongues into a hole it had made, then hoist itself up and begin making a second. It was creating footholds—or tongue-holds, rather.

"It's trying to climb the wall," I said. "Good God, it's like the freaking Terminator."

"The what?" said Emma.

I almost started to explain, then shook my head. It was a stupid comparison, anyway—hollowgast were scarier, and probably deadlier, than any movie monster.

"We have to stop it!" said Olive.

"Or better yet, run!" said Horace.

"No more running!" said Enoch. "Can we please just kill the damn thing?"

"Sure," Emma said. "But how?"

"Anyone got a vat of boiling oil?" said Enoch.

"Will this do instead?" I heard Bronwyn say, and turned to see her lifting a boulder above her head.

"It might," I said. "How's your aim? Can you drop it where I tell you?"

"I'll certainly try," Bronwyn said, tottering toward the ledge with the rock balanced precariously on her hands.

We stood looking over the ledge. "Farther this way," I said, urging her a few steps to the left. Just as I was about to give the signal for her to drop the boulder, though, the hollow leapt from one hold to the next, and now she was standing in the wrong place.

The hollow was getting faster at making the holds; now it was a moving target. To make matters worse, Bronwyn's boulder was the only one in sight. If she missed, we wouldn't get a second shot.

I forced myself to stare at the hollow despite a nearly unbearable urge to look away. For a few strange, head-swimmy seconds, the voices of my friends faded away and I could hear my own blood pumping in my ears and my heart thumping in the cavity of my chest, and my thoughts drifted to the creature that killed my grandfather; that stood over his torn and dying body before fleeing, cowardly, into the woods.

My vision rippled and my hands shook. I tried to steady myself.

You were born for this, I thought to myself. *You were built to kill monsters like this.* I repeated it under my breath like a mantra.

"Hurry up, please, Jacob," Bronwyn said.

The creature faked left, then jumped right. I didn't want to guess, and throw away our best chance at killing it. I wanted to *know*. And somehow, for some reason, I felt that I could.

I knelt, so close to the cliff's edge now that Emma hooked two fingers through the back of my belt to keep me from falling. Focusing on the hollow, I repeated the mantra to myself—*built to kill you, built to kill*—and though the hollow was for the moment stationary, hacking away at one spot on the wall, I felt the compass needle in my gut prick ever so slightly to the right of it.

It was like a premonition.

Bronwyn was beginning to tremble under the boulder's weight. "I can't hold this much longer!" she said.

I decided to trust my instinct. Even though the spot my compass pointed to was empty, I shouted for Bronwyn to drop the boulder there. She angled toward it and, with a groan of relief, let go of the rock.

The moment after she let go, the hollow leapt to the right— into the very place my compass had pointed. The hollow looked up to see the rock sailing toward it and poised to jump again—but there wasn't time. The boulder slammed into the creature's head and swept its body off the wall. With a thunderous crash, hollow and boulder hit the ground together. Tentacle tongues shot out from beneath the rock, shivered, went limp. Black blood followed, fanning around the boulder in a great, viscous puddle.

"Direct hit!" I yelled.

The kids began to jump and cheer. "It's dead, it's dead," Olive cried, "the horrible hollow is dead!"

Bronwyn threw her arms around me. Emma kissed the top of my head. Horace shook my hand and Hugh slapped me on the back. Even Enoch congratulated me. "Good work," he said a bit reluctantly. "Now don't go getting a big head over it."

I should've been overjoyed, but I hardly felt anything, just a spreading numbness as the trembling pain of the Feeling receded. Emma could see I was drained. Very sweetly, and in a way no one else could quite detect, she took my arm and half supported me as we walked away from the ledge. "That wasn't luck," she whispered in my ear. "I was right about you, Jacob Portman."

*   *   *

The path that had dead-ended at the bottom of the wall began again here at the top, following the spine of a ridge up and over a hill.

"The sign on the rope said *Access to Menagerie*," said Horace. "Do you suppose that's what's ahead?"

"You're the one who dreams about the future," said Enoch. "Suppose you tell *us*."

"What's a menagerie?" asked Olive.

"A collection of animals," Emma explained. "Like a zoo, sort of."

Olive squeaked and clapped her hands. "It's Cuthbert's friends!

From the story! Oh, I can't wait to meet them. Do you suppose that's where the ymbryne lives, too?"

"At this juncture," Millard said, "it's best not to suppose anything."

We started walking. I was still reeling from my encounter with the hollow. My ability did seem to be developing, as Millard said it would, growing like a muscle the more I worked it. Once I'd seen a hollow I could track it, and if I focused on it in just the right way, I could anticipate its next move, in some felt-more-than-known, gut-instinctual way. I felt a certain satisfaction at having learned something new about my peculiarity, and with nothing to teach me but experience. But this wasn't a safe, controlled environment I was learning in. There were no bumper lanes to keep my ball out of the gutter. Any mistake I made would have immediate and deadly consequences, for both myself and those around me. I worried the others would start believing the hype about me—or worse yet, *I* would. And I knew that the minute I got cocky—the minute I stopped being pants-wettingly terrified of hollowgast—something terrible would happen.

Maybe it was lucky, then, that my terror-to-confidence ratio was at an all-time low. Ten-to-one, easy. I stuck my hands in my pockets as we walked, afraid the others would see them shaking.

"Look!" said Bronwyn, stopping in the middle of the path. "A house in the clouds!"

We were halfway up the ridge. Up ahead of us, high in the distance, was a house that almost seemed to be balanced on a cloudbank. As we walked farther and crested the hill, the clouds parted and the house came into full view. It was very small, and perched not atop a cloud but on a very large tower constructed entirely from stacked-up railroad ties, the whole thing set smack in the middle of a grassy plateau. It was one of the strangest man-made structures I'd ever seen. Around it on the plateau were scattered a few shacks, and at the far end was a small patch of woods, but we paid no attention—our eyes were on the tower.

"What *is* it?" I whispered.

"A lookout tower?" guessed Emma.

"A place to launch airplanes from?" said Hugh.

But there were no airplanes anywhere, nor any evidence of a landing strip.

"Perhaps it's a place to launch zeppelins from," said Millard.

I remembered old footage of the ill-fated Hindenburg docking to the top of what looked like a radio tower—a structure not so different from this—and felt a cold wave of dread pass through me. What if the balloons that hunted us on the beach were based here, and we'd unwittingly stumbled into a nest of wights?

"Or maybe it's the ymbryne's house," said Olive. "Why does everyone always leap to the awfullest conclusions right away?"

"I'm sure Olive's right," said Hugh. "There's nothing to be afraid of here."

He was answered right away by a loud, inhuman growl, which seemed to come from the shadows beneath the tower.

"What was *that*?" said Emma. "Another hollow?"

"I don't think so," I said; the Feeling still fading in me.

"I don't know and I don't want to know," said Horace, backing away.

But we didn't have a choice; it wanted to meet us. The growl came again, prickling the hairs on my arms, and a moment later a furry face appeared between two of the lower railroad ties. It snarled at us like a rabid dog, reels of saliva dripping from its fang-toothed mouth.

"What in the name of the Elderfolk is *that*?" muttered Emma.

"Capital idea, coming into this loop," said Enoch. "Really working out well for us so far."

The whatever-it-was crawled out from between the ties and into the sun, where it crouched on its haunches and leered at us with an unbalanced smile, as if imagining how our brains might taste. I couldn't tell if it was human or animal; dressed in rags, it had the body of a man but carried itself like an ape, its hunched form like some long-lost ancestor of ours whose evolution had been arrested millions of years ago. Its eyes and teeth were a dull yellow, its skin pale and blotched with dark spots, its hair a long, matted nest.

"Someone make it die!" Horace said. "Or at least make it quit looking at me!"

Bronwyn set Claire down and assumed a fighting stance, while Emma held out her hands to make a flame—but she was too stunned, apparently, to summon more than a sputter of smoke. The man-thing tensed, snarled, and then took off like an Olympic sprinter—not toward us but *around* us, diving behind a pile of rocks and popping up again with a fang-bearing grin. It was toying with us, like a cat toys with its prey just before the kill.

It seemed about to make another run—*at us* this time—when a voice from behind commanded it to "Sit down and behave!" And the thing did, relaxing onto its hindquarters, tongue lolling from its mouth in a dopey grin.

We turned to see a dog trotting calmly in our direction. I looked past it to see who had spoken, but there was no one—and then the dog itself opened its mouth and said, "Don't mind Grunt, he's got no manners at all! That's just his way of saying thank you. That hollowgast was *most* bothersome."

The dog seemed to be talking to me, but I was too surprised to respond. Not only was it speaking in an almost-human voice—and a refined British one at that—but it held in its jowly mouth a pipe and on its face wore a pair of round, green-tinted glasses. "Oh dear, I hope you're not *too* offended," the dog continued, misinterpreting my silence. "Grunt means well, but you'll have to excuse him. He was, quite literally, raised in a barn. I, on the other hand, was educated on a grand estate, the seventh pup of the seventh pup in an illustrious line of hunting dogs." He bowed as well as a dog could, dipping his nose to the ground. "Addison MacHenry, at your humble service."

"That's a fancy name for a dog," said Enoch, apparently unimpressed to meet a talking animal.

Addison peered over his glasses at Enoch and said, "And by what appellation, dare I ask, are *you* denominated?"

"Enoch O'Connor," Enoch said proudly, sticking his chest out a little.

"That's a fancy name for a grimy, pudge-faced boy," Addison said, and then he stood up on his hind legs, rising nearly to Enoch's height. "I am a dog, yes, but a peculiar one. Why, then, should I be saddled with a common dog's name? My former master called me 'Boxie' and I despised it—an assault on my dignity!—so I bit him on the face and took his name. Addison: much more befitting an animal of my intellectual prowess, I think. That was just before Miss Wren discovered me and brought me here."

Faces brightened at the mention of an ymbryne's name, a pulse of hope firing through us.

"Miss Wren brought you?" said Olive. "But what about Cuthbert the giant?"

"Who?" Addison said, and then he shook his head. "Ah, right, the story. It's just that, I'm afraid—a *story*, inspired long ago by that curious rock down below and Miss Wren's peculiar menagerie."

"Told you," muttered Enoch.

"Where's Miss Wren now?" Emma said. "We've got to speak to her!"

Addison looked up at the house atop the tower and said, "That's her residence, but she isn't home at the moment. She winged off some days ago to help her ymbryne sisters in London. There's a war on, you see . . . I assume you've heard all about it? Which explains why you're traveling in the degraded style of refugees?"

"Our loop was raided," said Emma. "And then we lost our things at sea."

"And nearly ourselves," Millard added.

At the sound of Millard's voice, the dog startled. "An invisible! What a rare surprise. And an American, too," he said, nodding at me. "What a peculiar lot you are, even for peculiars." He fell back onto all fours and turned toward the tower. "Come, I'll introduce you to the others. They'll be absolutely fascinated to meet you. And you must be famished from your journey, poor creatures. Nutrifying provender shall be forthcoming!"

"We need medicine, too," said Bronwyn, kneeling to pick up Claire. "This little one is very ill!"

"We'll do all we can for her," the dog said. "We owe you that and more for solving our little hollowgast problem. *Most* bothersome, as I was saying."

"Nutrifying *what* did he say?" said Olive.

"Sustenance, comestibles, rations!" the dog replied. "You'll eat like royalty here."

"But I don't like dog food," said Olive.

Addison laughed, the timbre surprisingly human. "Neither do I, miss."

CHAPTER FOUR

ddison walked on all fours with his snub nose in the air while the man-thing called Grunt scampered around us like a psychotic puppy. From behind tufts of grass and the shacks scattered here and there, I could see faces peeking out at us—furry, most of them, and of all different shapes and sizes. When we came to the middle of the plateau, Addison reared up on his hind legs and called out, "Don't be afraid, fellows! Come and meet the children who dispatched our unwelcome visitor!"

One by one, a parade of bizarre animals ventured out into the open. Addison introduced them as they came. The first creature looked like the top half of a miniature giraffe sutured onto the bottom half of a donkey. It walked awkwardly on two hind legs—its only limbs. "This is Deirdre," said Addison. "She's an emu-raffe, which is a bit like a donkey and a giraffe put together, only with fewer legs and a peevish temper. She's a terrible sore loser at cards," he added in a whisper. "*Never* play an emu-raffe at cards. Say hello, Deirdre!"

"Goodbye!" Deirdre said, her big horse lips pulling back into a bucktoothed grin. "Terrible day! Very displeased to meet you!" Then she laughed—a braying, high-pitched whinny—and said, "Only teasing!"

"Deirdre thinks she's quite funny," Addison explained.

"If you're like a donkey and a giraffe," said Olive, "then why aren't you called a donkey-raffe?"

Deirdre frowned and answered, "Because what kind of an aw-

ful name is that? Emu-raffe rolls off the tongue, don't you think?"
And then she stuck out her tongue—fat, pink, and three feet long—
and pushed Olive's tiara back on her head with its tip. Olive squealed
and ran behind Bronwyn, giggling.

"Do all the animals here talk?" I asked.

"Just Deirdre and I," Addison said, "and a good thing, too.
The chickens won't shut up as it is, and they can't say a word!"
Right on cue, a flock of clucking chickens bobbled toward us from
a burned and blackened coop. "Ah!" said Addison. "Here come the
girls now."

"What happened to their coop?" Emma asked.

"Every time we repair it, they burn it down again," he said.
"Such a bother." Addison turned and nodded in the other direction.
"You might want to back away a bit. When they get excited . . ."

BANG!—a sound like a quarter-stick of dynamite going off
made us all jump, and the coop's last few undamaged boards splintered and flew into the air.

". . . their eggs go off," he finished.

When the smoke cleared, we saw the chickens still coming
toward us, unhurt and seemingly unsurprised by the blast, a little
cloud of feathers wafting around them like fat snowflakes.

Enoch's jaw fell open. "Are you telling me these chickens lay
exploding eggs?!" he said.

"Only when they get excited," said Addison. "Most of their
eggs are quite safe—and delicious! But it was the exploding ones
that earned them their rather unkind name: Armageddon chickens."

"Keep away from us!" Emma shouted as the chickens closed
in. "You'll blow us all up!"

Addison laughed. "They're sweet and harmless, I assure you,
and they don't lay anywhere but inside their coop." The chickens
clucked happily around our feet. "You see?" the dog said. "They
like you!"

"This is a madhouse!" said Horace.

Deirdre laughed. "No, doveling. It's a menagerie."

Then Addison introduced us to a few animals whose peculiarities were subtler, including an owl who watched us from a branch, silent and intense, and a cadre of mice who seemed to fade subtly in and out of view, as if they spent half their time on some other plane of reality. There was a goat, too, with very long horns and deep black eyes; an orphan from a herd of peculiar goats who once roamed the forest below.

When all the animals were assembled, Addison cried, "Three cheers for the hollow-killers!" Deirdre brayed and the goat stamped the ground and the owl hooted and the chickens clucked and Grunt grunted his appreciation. And while all this was going on, Bronwyn and Emma kept trading looks—Bronwyn glancing down at her coat, where Miss Peregrine was hiding, and then raising her eyebrows at Emma to ask, *Now?* and Emma shaking her head in reply: *Not quite yet.*

Bronwyn laid Claire in a patch of grass beneath a shade tree. She was sweating and shivering, fading in and out of consciousness.

"There's a special elixir I've seen Miss Wren prepare for treating fever," Addison said. "Foul-tasting but effective."

"My mom used to make me chicken soup," I offered.

The chickens squawked with alarm, and Addison shot me a nasty look. "He was joking!" he said. "Only joking, such an absurd joke, ha-ha! There's no such thing as chicken soup!"

With the help of Grunt and his opposable thumbs, Addison and the emu-raffe went to prepare the elixir. In a little while they returned with a bowl of what looked like dirty dishwater. Once Claire had drunk every drop and fallen back asleep, the animals laid out a modest feast for us: baskets of fresh bread and stewed apples and hard-boiled eggs—of the nonexploding variety—all served straight into our hands, as they had no plates or silverware. I didn't realize how hungry I'd been until I wolfed down three eggs and a loaf of bread in under five minutes.

When I was done I belched and wiped my mouth and looked up to see all the animals looking back, watching us eagerly, their faces so alive with intelligence that I went a little numb and had to fight an overwhelming sensation that I was dreaming.

Millard was eating next to me, and I turned to him and asked, "Before this, had you ever heard of peculiar animals?"

"Only in children's stories," he said through a mouthful of bread. "How strange, then, that it was one such story that led us to them."

Only Olive seemed unfazed by it all, perhaps because she was still so young—or part of her was, anyway—and the distance between stories and real life did not yet seem so great. "Where are the other animals?" she asked Addison. "In Cuthbert's tale there were stilt-legged grimbears and two-headed lynxes."

And just like that, the animals' jubilant mood wilted. Grunt hid his face in his big hands and Deirdre let out a neighing groan. "Don't ask, don't ask," she said, hanging her long head. But it was too late.

"These children helped us," Addison said. "They deserve to hear our sad story, if they wish."

"If you don't mind telling us," said Emma.

"I love sad stories," said Enoch. "Especially ones where princesses get eaten by dragons and everyone dies in the end."

Addison cleared his throat. "In our case, it's more that the dragon got eaten by the princess," he said. "It's been a rough few years for the likes of us, and it was a rough few centuries prior to that." The dog paced back and forth, his voice taking on a preacherly kind of grandness. "Once upon a time, this world was full of peculiar animals. In the *Aldinn* days, there were more peculiar animals on Earth than there were peculiar folk. We came in every shape and size you could imagine: whales that could fly like birds, worms as big as houses, dogs twice as intelligent as I am, if you can believe it. Some had kingdoms all their own, ruled over by animal leaders." A spark moved behind the dog's eyes, barely detectable—as if he were old enough to remember the world in such a state—and then he sighed deeply, the spark snuffed, and continued. "But our numbers are not a fraction of what they were. We have fallen into near extinction. Do any of you know what became of the peculiar animals that once roamed the world?"

We chewed silently, ashamed that we didn't.

"Right, then," he said. "Come with me and I'll show you." And he trotted out into the sun and looked back, waiting for us to follow.

"Please, Addie," said the emu-raffe. "Not now—our guests are eating!"

"They asked, and now I'm telling them," said Addison. "Their bread will still be here in a few minutes!"

Reluctantly, we put down our food and followed the dog. Fiona stayed behind to watch Claire, who was still sleeping, and with Grunt and the emu-raffe loping after us, we crossed the plateau to the little patch of woods that grew at the far edge. A gravel path wound through the trees, and we crunched along it toward a clearing. Just before we reached it, Addison said, "May I introduce you to the finest peculiar animals who ever lived!" and the trees parted to reveal a small graveyard filled with neat rows of white headstones.

"Oh, *no*," I heard Bronwyn say.

"There are probably more peculiar animals buried here than are currently alive in all of Europe," Addison said, moving through the graves to reach one in particular, which he leaned on with his forepaws. "This one's name was Pompey. She was a fine dog, and could heal wounds with a few licks of her tongue. A wonder to behold! And yet *this* is how she was treated." Addison clicked his tongue and Grunt scurried forward with a little book in his hands, which he thrust into mine. It was a photo album, opened to a picture of a dog that had been harnessed, like a mule or a horse, to a little wagon. "She was enslaved by carnival folk," Addison said, "forced to pull fat, spoiled children like some common beast of burden— whipped, even, with riding crops!" His eyes burned with anger. "By the time Miss Wren rescued her, Pompey was so depressed she was nearly dead from it. She lingered on for only a few weeks after she arrived, then was interred here."

I passed the book around. Everyone who saw the photo sighed or shook their head or muttered bitterly to themselves.

Addison crossed to another grave. "Grander still was Ca'ab Magda," he said, "an eighteen-tusked wildebeest who roamed the loops of Outer Mongolia. She was terrifying! The ground thundered under her hooves when she ran! They say she even marched over the Alps with Hannibal's army in 218 BC. Then, some years ago, a hunter shot her."

Grunt showed us a picture of an older woman who looked like she'd just gotten back from an African safari, seated in a bizarre chair made of horns.

"I don't understand," said Emma, peering at the photo. "Where's Ca'ab Magda?"

"Being sat upon," said Addison. "The hunter fashioned her horns into a chair."

Emma nearly dropped the album. "That's disgusting!"

"If that's her," said Enoch, tapping the photo, "then what's buried here?"

"The chair," said Addison. "What a pitiful waste of a peculiar life."

"This burying ground is filled with stories like Magda's," Addison said. "Miss Wren meant this menagerie to be an ark, but gradually it's become a tomb."

"Like all our loops," said Enoch. "Like peculiardom itself. A failed experiment."

"'This place is dying,' Miss Wren often said." Addison's voice rose in imitation of her. "'And I am nothing but the overseer of its long funeral!'"

Addison's eyes glistened, remembering her, but just as quickly went hard again. "She was very theatrical."

"Please don't refer to our ymbryne in the past tense," Deirdre said.

"Is," he said. "Sorry. *Is.*"

"They hunted you," said Emma, her voice wavering with emotion. "Stuffed you and put you in zoos."

"Just like the hunters did in Cuthbert's story," said Olive.

"Yes," said Addison. "Some truths are expressed best in the form of myth."

"But there was no Cuthbert," said Olive, beginning to understand. "No giant. Just a bird."

"A very *special* bird," said Deirdre.

"You're worried about her," I said.

"Of course we are," said Addison. "To my knowledge, Miss Wren is the only remaining uncaptured ymbryne. When she heard that her kidnapped sisters had been spirited away to London, she flew off to render assistance without a moment's thought for her own safety."

"Nor ours," Deirdre muttered.

"London?" said Emma. "Are you sure that's where the kidnapped ymbrynes were taken?"

"Absolutely certain," the dog replied. "Miss Wren has spies in the city—a certain flock of peculiar pigeons who watch everything and report back to her. Recently, several came to us in a state of terrible distress. They had it on good information that the ymbrynes were—and still are—being held in the punishment loops."

Several of the children gasped, but I had no idea what the dog meant. "What's a punishment loop?" I asked.

"They were designed to hold captured wights, hardened criminals, and the dangerously insane," Millard explained. "They're nothing like the loops we know. Nasty, nasty places."

"And now it is the wights, and undoubtedly their hollows, who are guarding them," said Addison.

"Good God!" exclaimed Horace. "Then it's worse than we feared!"

"Are you joking?" said Enoch. "This is *precisely* the sort of thing I feared!"

"Whatever nefarious end the wights are seeking," Addison said, "it's clear that they need all the ymbrynes to accomplish it. Now only Miss Wren is left . . . brave, foolhardy Miss Wren . . . and who knows for how long!" Then he whimpered the way some dogs do during thunderstorms, tucking his ears back and lowering his head.

*   *   *

We went back to the shade tree and finished our meals, and when we were stuffed and couldn't eat another bite, Bronwyn turned to Addison and said, "You know, Mister Dog, everything's not quite as dire as you say." Then she looked at Emma and raised her eyebrows, and this time Emma nodded.

"Is that so," Addison replied.

"Yes, it is. In fact, I have something right here that may just cheer you up."

"I rather doubt that," the dog muttered, but he lifted his head from his paws to see what it was anyway.

Bronwyn opened her coat and said, "I'd like you to meet the

second-to-last uncaptured ymbryne, Miss Alma Peregrine." The bird poked her head out into the sunlight and blinked.

Now it was the animals' turn to be amazed. Deirdre gasped and Grunt squealed and clapped his hands and the chickens flapped their useless wings.

"But we heard your loop was raided!" Addison said. "Your ymbryne stolen!"

"She was," Emma said proudly, "but we stole her back!"

"In that case," said Addison, bowing to Miss Peregrine, "it is a most extraordinary pleasure, madam. I am your servant. Should you require a place to change, I'll happily show you to Miss Wren's private quarters."

"She *can't* change," said Bronwyn.

"What's that?" said Addison. "Is she shy?"

"No," said Bronwyn. "She's stuck."

The pipe dropped from Addison's mouth. "Oh, no," he said quietly. "Are you quite certain?"

"She's been like this for two days now," said Emma. "I think if she could change back, she would've done it by now."

Addison shook the glasses from his face and peered at the bird, his eyes wide with concern. "May I examine her?" he asked.

"He's a regular Doctor Dolittle," said the emu-raffe. "Addie treats us all when we're sick."

Bronwyn lifted Miss Peregrine out of her coat and set the bird on the ground. "Just be careful of her hurt wing," she said.

"Of course," said Addison. He began by making a slow circle around the bird, studying her from every angle. Then he sniffed her head and wings with his big, wet nose. "Tell me what happened to her," he said finally, "and when, and how. Tell me all of it."

Emma recounted the whole story: how Miss Peregrine was kidnapped by Golan, how she nearly drowned in her cage in the ocean, how we'd rescued her from a submarine piloted by wights. The animals listened, rapt. When we'd finished, the dog took a moment to gather his thoughts, then delivered his diagnosis: "She's been poisoned. I'm certain of it. Dosed with something that's keeping her in bird form artificially."

"Really?" said Emma. "How do you know?"

"To kidnap and transport ymbrynes is a dangerous business when they're in human form and can perform their time-stopping tricks. As birds, however, their powers are very limited. This way, your mistress is compact, easily hidden . . . much less of a threat." He looked at Miss Peregrine. "Did the wight who took you spray you with anything?" he asked her. "A liquid or a gas?"

Miss Peregrine bobbed her head in the air—what seemed to be a nod.

Bronwyn gasped. "Oh, miss, I'm so awfully sorry. We had no idea."

I felt a stab of guilt. *I* had led the wights to the island. *I* was the reason this had happened to Miss Peregrine. *I* had caused the peculiar children to lose their home, at least partly. The shame of it lodged like a stone in my throat.

I said, "She'll get better though, won't she? She'll turn back?"

"Her wing will mend," Addison replied, "but without help she won't turn human again."

"What sort of help does she need?" Emma asked. "Can you give it to her?"

"Only another ymbryne can assist her. And she's running very short on time."

I tensed. This was something new.

"What do you mean?" Emma said.

"I hate to be the bearer of bad news," said Addison, "but two days is a very long time for an ymbryne to be arrested like this. The more time she spends as a bird, the more her human self will be lost. Her memory, her words—everything that made her who she was— until, eventually, she won't be an ymbryne at all anymore. She'll just be a bird, for good and ever."

An image came to me of Miss Peregrine splayed on an emergency room table, buzzed around by doctors, her breathing stopped—every second that ticked by doing her brain some new and irreparable harm.

"How long?" asked Millard. "How much longer does she have?"

Addison squinted, shook his head. "Two days, if she's strong."

Whispers and gasps. We collectively went pale.

"Are you sure?" said Emma. "Are you absolutely, positively certain?"

"I've seen it happen before." Addison padded over to the little owl, who was perched on a branch nearby. "Olivia here was a young ymbryne who had a bad accident during her training. They brought her to us five days later. Miss Wren and I did everything we could to try to change her back, but she was beyond help. That was ten years ago; she's been this way ever since."

The owl stared mutely. There was no life in her anymore beyond that of an animal; you could see it in the dullness of her eyes.

Emma stood. She seemed about to say something—to rally us, I hoped, kick us into action with some inspiring speech—but she couldn't seem to get the words out. Choking back a sob, she stumbled away from us.

I called after her, but she didn't stop. The others just watched her go, stunned by the terrible news; stunned, too, by any sign of weakness or indecision from Emma. She had maintained her strength in the face of all this for so long that we had come to take it for granted, but she wasn't bulletproof. She might've been peculiar, but she was also human.

"You'd better fetch her, Mister Jacob," Bronwyn said to me. "We mustn't linger here too long."

*   *   *

When I caught up to Emma she was standing near the plateau's edge, gazing out at the countryside below, sloping green hills falling away to a distant plain. She heard me coming but didn't turn to look.

I shuffled up next to her and tried to think of something comforting to say. "I know you're scared, and—and three days doesn't seem like a long time, but—"

"*Two* days," she said. "Two days *maybe*." Her lip trembled. "And that's not even the worst of it."

I balked. "How could things possibly be worse?"

She'd been waging a battle against tears, but now, in a sudden break, she lost it. She sank to the ground and sobbed, a storm overtaking her. I knelt and wrapped my arms around her and hung on. "I'm so sorry," she said, repeating it three times, her voice raw, a fraying rope. "You never should've stayed. I shouldn't have let you. But I was selfish . . . so terribly selfish!"

"Don't say that," I said. "I'm here—I'm here, and I'm not going anywhere."

That only seemed to make her cry harder. I pressed my lips to her forehead and kissed it until the storm began to pass out of her, the sobs fading to whimpers. "Please talk to me," I said. "Tell me what's wrong."

After a minute she sat up, wiped her eyes, and tried to compose herself. "I had hoped I'd never have to say this," she said. "That it wouldn't matter. Do you remember when I told you, the night you decided to come with us, that you might never be able to go home again?"

"Of course I do."

"I didn't know until just now how true that really was. I'm afraid I've doomed you, Jacob, my sweet friend, to a short life trapped in a dying world." She drew a quivering breath, then continued. "You came to us through Miss Peregrine's loop, and that means only Miss Peregrine or her loop can send you back. But her loop is gone now—or if it isn't yet, it will be soon—which leaves

Miss Peregrine herself as your only way home. But if she never turns human again . . ."

I swallowed hard, my throat dry. "Then I'm stuck in the past."

"Yes. And the only way to return to the time you knew as your own would be to wait for it—day by day, year by year."

Seventy years. By then my parents, and everyone I ever knew or cared about, would be dead, and I'd be long dead to all of them. Of course, provided we survived whatever tribulations we were about to face, I could always go and find my parents in a few decades, once they were born—but what would be the point? They'd be children, and strangers to me.

I wondered when my present-day back-home parents would give up on finding me alive. What story they'd tell themselves to make sense of my disappearance. Had I run away? Gone insane? Thrown myself off a sea cliff?

Would they have a funeral for me? Buy me a coffin? Write my name on a gravestone?

I'd become a mystery they would never solve. A wound that would never heal.

"I'm so sorry," Emma said again. "If I'd known Miss Peregrine's condition was so dire, I swear to you, I never would've asked you to stay. The present means nothing to the rest of us. It'll kill us if we stay there too long! But you—you still have family, a life . . ."

"No!" I said, shouting, slapping the ground with my hand—chasing away the self-pitying thoughts that had started to cloud my head. "That's all gone now. I chose *this*."

Emma laid her hand atop mine and said gently: "If what the animals say is true, and all our ymbrynes have been kidnapped, soon even *this* won't be here." She gathered some dirt in her hand and scattered it in the breeze. "Without ymbrynes to maintain them, our loops will collapse. The wights will use the ymbrynes to re-create their damned experiment and it'll be 1908 all over again—and either they'll fail and turn all creation into a smoking crater, or they'll succeed and make themselves immortal, and we'll be ruled by those monsters. Either way, before long we'll be more extinct than the peculiar animals! And now I've dragged *you* into this hopeless mess—and for what?"

"Everything happens for a reason," I said.

I couldn't believe those words had come out of my mouth, but as soon as they were spoken I felt the truth of them, resonating in me loud as a bell.

I was here for a reason. There was something I was meant not simply to *be*, but to *do*—and it wasn't to run or hide or give up the minute things seemed terrifying and impossible.

"I thought you didn't believe in destiny," said Emma, assessing me skeptically.

I didn't—not exactly—but I wasn't quite sure how to explain what I *did* believe, either. I thought back to the stories my grandfather used to tell me. They were filled with wonder and adventure, but something deeper ran through them, as well—a sense of abiding gratitude. As a kid I'd focused on Grandpa Portman's descriptions of a magical-sounding island and peculiar children with fantastic powers, but at heart his stories were about Miss Peregrine, and how, in a time of great need, she had helped him. When he arrived in Wales, my grandfather had been a young, frightened boy who didn't speak the language, a boy hunted by two kinds of monsters: one that would eventually kill most of his family, and the other, cartoonishly grotesque and invisible to all but him, which must've seemed lifted directly from his nightmares. In the face of all this, Miss Peregrine had hidden him, given him a home, and helped him discover who he really was—she had saved his life, and in doing so had enabled my father's life, and by extension, my own. My parents had birthed and raised and loved me, and for that I owed them a debt. But I would never have been born in the first place if not for the great and selfless kindness Miss Peregrine had shown my grandfather. I was coming to believe I had been sent here to repay that debt—my own, my father's, and my grandfather's, too.

I tried my best to explain. "It's not about destiny," I said, "but I do think there's balance in the world, and sometimes forces we don't understand intervene to tip the scales the right way. Miss Peregrine saved my grandfather—and now I'm here to help save *her*."

Emma narrowed her eyes and nodded slowly. I couldn't tell if she was agreeing with me or thinking of a polite way to tell me I'd lost my mind.

Then she hugged me.

I didn't need to explain any further. She understood.

She owed Miss Peregrine her life, too.

"We've got three days," I said. "We'll go to London, free one of the ymbrynes, and fix Miss Peregrine. It's not hopeless. We'll save her, Emma—or we'll die trying." The words sounded so brave and resolute that for a moment I wondered if it was really me who'd said them.

Emma surprised me by laughing, as if this struck her as funny somehow, and then she looked away for a moment. When she looked back again her jaw was set and her eyes shone; her old confidence was returning. "Sometimes I can't decide whether you're completely mad or some sort of miracle," she said. "Though I'm starting to think it's the latter."

She put her arms around me again and we held each other for a long moment, her head on my shoulder, breath warm on my neck, and suddenly I wanted nothing more than to close all the little gaps that existed between our bodies, to collapse into one being. But then she pulled away and kissed my forehead and started back toward the others. I was too dazed to follow right away, because there was something new happening, a wheel inside my heart I'd never noticed before, and it was spinning so fast it made me dizzy. And the farther away she got, the faster it spun, like there was an invisible cord unreeling from it that stretched between us, and if she went too far it would snap—and kill me.

I wondered if this strange, sweet pain was love.

*   *   *

The others were clustered together beneath the shade tree, children and animals together. Emma and I strode toward them. I had an impulse to link arms with her, and nearly did before something caught me and I thought better of it. I was suddenly aware—as Enoch turned to look at us with that certain suspicion he always reserved for me and now, increasingly, for both of us—that Emma and I were becoming a unit apart from the others, a private alliance with its own secrets and promises.

Bronwyn stood as we approached. "Are you all right, Miss Emma?"

"Yes, yes," Emma said quickly, "had something caught in my eye, was all. Now, everyone gather your things. We must go to London at once, and see about making Miss Peregrine whole again!"

"We're thrilled you agree," Enoch said with an eye roll. "We came to the same conclusion several minutes ago, while you two were over there whispering."

Emma flushed, but she declined to take Enoch's bait. There were more important things to attend to now than petty conflicts—namely, the many exotic dangers of the journey we were about to undertake. "As I'm sure you're all aware," Emma said, "this is by most standards a very poor plan with little hope of success." She laid out some of the reasons why. London was far away—not by the standards of the present-day world, maybe, when we might've GPSed our way to the nearest train station and caught an express that would've whisked us to the city center in a few hours. In 1940, though, in a Britain convulsed by war, London was a world away: the roads and rails might be clogged by refugees, or ruined by bombs, or monopolized by military convoys, any of which would cost us time Miss Peregrine didn't have to spare. Worse, we would be hunted—

and even more intensely than we had already been, now that nearly all the other ymbrynes had been captured.

"Forget the journey!" said Addison. "That's the least of your worries! Perhaps I was not sufficiently dissuasive when we discussed this earlier. Perhaps you do not fully understand the circumstances of the ymbrynes' incarceration." He enunciated each syllable as if we were hard of hearing. "Haven't any of you read about the punishment loops in your peculiar history books?"

"Of course we have," said Emma.

"Then you'll know that attempting to breach them is tantamount to suicide. They're death traps, every one of them, containing the very bloodiest episodes from London's history—the Great Fire of 1666; the exceedingly lethal Viking Siege of 842; the pestilent height of the terrible Plague! They don't publish temporal maps of these places, for obvious reasons. So unless one of you has a working knowledge of the secretest parts of peculiardom . . ."

"I am a student of obscure and unpleasant loops," Millard spoke up. "Been a pet hobby for many years."

"Bully for you!" said Addison. "Then I suppose you have a way to get past the horde of hollows who'll be guarding their entrances as well!"

Suddenly it felt like everyone's eyes were on me. I swallowed hard, kept my chin high, and said, "Yeah, in fact, we do."

"We'd better," grumbled Enoch.

Then Bronwyn said, "I believe in you, Jacob. I haven't known you too long, but I feel I know your heart, and it's a strong, true thing—a peculiar heart—and I trust you." She leaned against me and hugged my shoulder with one arm, and I felt my throat tighten.

"Thank you," I said, feeling lame and small in the face of her big emotion.

The dog clucked his tongue. "Madness. You children have no self-preservation instincts at all. It's a wonder any of you are still breathing."

Emma stepped in front of Addison and tried to shut him down. "Yes, wonderful," she said, "thank you for illuminating us with your opinion. Now, doomsaying aside, I have to ask the rest of you: Are there any objections to what we're proposing? I don't want anyone volunteering because they feel pressured."

Slowly, timidly, Horace raised his hand. "If London is where all the wights are, won't going there be walking right into their hands? Is that a good idea?"

"It's a *genius* idea," Enoch said irritably. "The wights are convinced we peculiar children are docile and weak. Us coming after *them* is the last thing they'd expect."

"And if we fail?" said Horace. "We'll have hand-delivered Miss Peregrine right to their doorstep!"

"We don't *know* that," said Hugh. "That London is their doorstep."

Enoch snorted. "Don't sugarcoat things. If they've broken open the prison loops and they're using them to keep our ymbrynes, then you can bet your soft parts they've overrun the rest of the city, too! It'll be absolutely *crawling* with them, mark my words. If it weren't, the wights would never have bothered coming after us in little old Cairnholm. It's basic military strategy. In battle you don't aim for the enemy's pinky toe first—you stab him right through the heart!"

"Please," Horace moaned, "enough talk of smashing loops and stabbing hearts. You'll frighten the little ones!"

"I ain't scared!" said Olive.

Horace shrank into himself. Someone muttered the word *coward*.

"None of that!" Emma said sharply. "There's nothing wrong with being frightened. It means you're taking this very serious thing we're proposing very seriously. Because, yes, it *will* be dangerous. Yes, the chances of success are abysmal. And should we even make it to London, there's no guarantee we'll be able to *find* the ymbrynes, much less rescue one. It's entirely likely that we'll end our days wasting away in some wightish prison cell or dissolved in the belly of a hollowgast. Everyone got that?"

Grim nods of understanding.

"Am I sugarcoating anything, Enoch?"

Enoch shook his head.

"If we try this," Emma went on, "we may well lose Miss Peregrine. That much is uncontroversial. But if we *don't* try, if we *don't* go, then there's no *question* we'll lose her—and the wights will likely catch us anyway! That said, anyone who doesn't feel up to it can stay behind." She meant Horace and we all knew it. Horace stared at a spot on the ground. "You can stay here where it's safe, and we'll come collect you later, when the trouble's through. There's no shame in it."

"My left ventricle!" said Horace. "If I sat this out, I'd never live it down."

Even Claire refused to be left behind. "I've just had eighty years of pleasantly boring days," she said, raising up on one elbow from the shady spot where she'd been sleeping. "Stay here while the rest of you go adventuring? Not a chance!" But when she tried to stand, she found she couldn't, and lay back again, coughing and dizzy. Though the dishwatery liquid she'd drunk had cooled her fever some, there was no way she'd be able to make the journey to London—not today, not tomorrow, and certainly not in time to help Miss Peregrine. Someone would have to stay behind with Claire while she recuperated.

Emma asked for volunteers. Olive raised her hand, but Bronwyn told her to forget it—she was too young. Bronwyn started to raise her own hand, then thought better of it. She was torn, she said, between wanting to protect Claire and her sense of duty to Miss Peregrine.

Enoch elbowed Horace. "What's the matter with you?" Enoch taunted. "Here's your big chance to stay behind!"

"I *want* to go adventuring, I really and truly do," Horace insisted. "But I should also like to see my 105th birthday, if at all possible. Promise we won't try to save the whole blasted world?"

"We just want to save Miss P," said Emma, "but I make no guarantees about anyone's birthday."

Horace seemed satisfied with this, and his hands stayed planted at his sides.

"Anyone else?" said Emma, looking around.

"It's all right," Claire said. "I can manage on my own."

"Out of the question," said Emma. "We peculiars stick together."

Fiona's hand drifted up. She'd been so quiet, I'd nearly forgotten she was sitting with us.

"Fee, you can't!" said Hugh. He looked hurt, as if by volunteering to stay behind she was rejecting him. She looked at him with big, sad eyes, but her hand stayed in the air.

"Thank you, Fiona," said Emma. "With any luck, we'll see you both again in just a few days."

"Bird willing," said Bronwyn.

"Bird willing," echoed the others.

*   *   *

Afternoon was slipping toward evening. In an hour the animals' loop would be dark, and finding our way down the mountain would be much more dangerous. As we made preparations to leave, the animals kindly outfitted us with stores of fresh food and sweaters spun from the wool of peculiar sheep, which Deirdre swore had some peculiar property, though what exactly it was she couldn't quite remember. "Impervious to fire, I think—or perhaps water. Yes, they never sink in water, like fluffy little lifejackets. Or maybe—oh, I don't know, they're warm in any case!"

We thanked her and folded them into Bronwyn's trunk. Then Grunt came loping forward holding a package wrapped up with paper and twine. "A gift from the chickens," Deirdre explained, winking as Grunt pressed it into my hands. "Don't drop it."

A smarter person than I might've thought twice about bringing explosives along on our trip, but we were feeling vulnerable, and both the dog and emu-raffe swore that if we were gentle with the eggs they wouldn't go off, so we nestled them carefully between the sweaters in Bronwyn's trunk. Now at least we wouldn't have to face men with guns without weapons of our own.

Then we were nearly ready, except for one thing: when we left the animals' loop, we'd be just as lost as when we'd come in. We needed directions.

"I can show you the way out of the forest," said Addison. "Meet me at the top of Miss Wren's tower."

The space up top was so small that only two of us could fit at a time, so Emma and I went, climbing its railroad ties like the rungs of a giant ladder. Grunt monkeyed his way up in half the time, delivering Addison to the top under one arm.

The view from the top was amazing. To the east, forested slopes stretched away to a vast, barren plain. To the west, you could see all the way to the ocean, where an old-looking ship rigged with giant, complicated sails glided down the coast. I'd never asked what year it was here—1492? 1750?—though to the animals I guess it hardly mattered. This was a safe place apart from the world of people, and only in the world of people did the year make any difference.

"You'll head north," Addison said, jabbing his pipe in the direction of a road, just visible, tracing through the trees below like a faint, pencil-drawn line. "Down that road is a town, and in that town—in your time, anyway—is a train station. Your medium of inter-loop travel is when—1940?"

"That's right," Emma replied.

Though I only vaguely understood what they were talking about, I'd never been afraid to ask dumb questions. "Why can't we just go out into this world?" I asked. "Travel to London through whatever year it is here?"

"The only way is by horse and carriage," said Addison, "which takes several days . . . and causes considerable chafing, in my experience. I'm afraid you don't have that much time to spare." He turned and nosed open the door to the tower's little shack. "Please," he said, "there's one more thing I'd like to show you."

We followed him inside. The shack was modest and tiny, a far cry from Miss Peregrine's queenly setup. The entirety of its furniture was a small bed, a wardrobe, and a rolltop desk. A telescope sat mounted on a tripod, aimed out the window: Miss Wren's lookout station, where she watched for trouble, and the comings and goings of her spy pigeons.

Addison went to the desk. "Should you have any difficulty locating the road," he said, "there's a map of the forest in here."

Emma opened the desk and found the map, an old, yellowed roll of paper. Underneath it was a creased snapshot. It showed a woman in a black sequined shawl with gray-streaked hair worn in a dramatic upsweep. She was standing next to a chicken. At first glance the photo looked like a discard, taken during an off moment when the woman was looking away with her eyes closed, and yet there was something just right about it, too—how the woman's hair and clothes matched the black-and-white speckle of the chicken's feathers; how she and the chicken were facing opposite directions, implying some odd connection between them, as if they were speaking without words; dreaming at one another.

This, clearly, was Miss Wren.

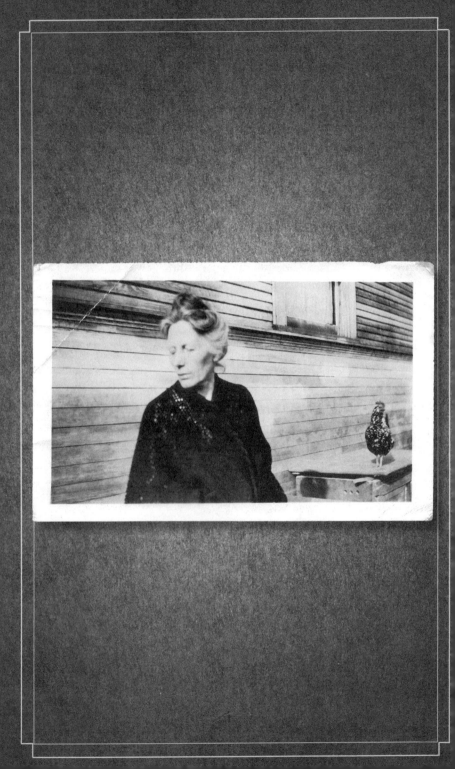

Addison saw the photo and seemed to wince. I could tell he was worried for her, much more than he wanted to admit. "Please don't take this as an endorsement of your suicidal plans," he said, "but if you should succeed in your mad quest . . . and should happen to encounter Miss Wren along the way . . . you might consider . . . I mean, *might* you consider . . ."

"We'll send her home," Emma said, and then scratched him on the head. It was a perfectly normal thing to do to a dog, but seemed a strange thing to do to a talking one.

"Dog bless you," Addison replied.

Then I tried petting him, but he reared up on his hind legs and said, "Do you mind? Keep your hands at bay, sir!"

"Sorry," I mumbled, and in the awkward moment that followed it became obvious that it was time to go.

We climbed down the tower to join our friends, where we exchanged tearful goodbyes with Claire and Fiona under the big shade tree. By now Claire had been given a cushion and blanket to lie on, and like a princess she received us one by one at her makeshift bedside on the ground, extracting promises as we knelt down beside her.

"Promise you'll come back," she said to me when it was my turn, "and promise you'll save Miss Peregrine."

"I'll try my best," I said.

"That isn't good enough!" she said sternly.

"I'll come back," I said. "I promise."

"And save Miss Peregrine!"

"And save Miss Peregrine," I repeated, though the words felt empty; the more confident I tried to sound, the less confident I actually felt.

"Good," she said with a nod. "It's been awfully nice knowing you, Jacob, and I'm glad you came to stay."

"Me, too," I said, and then I got up quickly because her bright, blonde-framed face was so earnest it killed me. She believed, unequivocally, everything we told her: that she and Fiona would be all right here, among these strange animals, in a loop abandoned by its ymbryne. That we'd return for them. I hoped with all my heart that it was more than just theater, staged to make this hard thing we had to do seem possible.

Hugh and Fiona stood off to one side, their hands linked and foreheads touching, saying goodbye in their own quiet way. Finally, we'd all finished with Claire and were ready to go, but no one wanted to disturb them, so we stood watching as Fiona pulled away from Hugh, shook a few seeds from her nest of wild hair, and grew a rose bush heavy with red flowers right where they stood. Hugh's bees rushed to pollinate it, and while they were occupied—as if she'd done it just so they could have a moment to themselves—Fiona embraced him and whispered something in his ear, and Hugh nodded and whispered something back. When they finally turned and saw all of us looking, Fiona blushed, and Hugh came toward us with his hands jammed in his pockets, his bees trailing behind him, and growled, "Let's go, show's over."

We began our trek down the mountain just as dusk was falling. The animals accompanied us as far as the sheer rock wall.

Olive said to them, "Won't you all come with us?"

The emu-raffe snorted. "We wouldn't last five minutes out there! *You* can at least hope to pass for normal. But one look at *me* . . ." She wiggled her forearm-less body. "I'd be shot, stuffed, and mounted in no time."

Then the dog approached Emma and said, "If I could ask one last thing of you . . ."

"You've been so kind," she replied. "Anything."

"Would you mind terribly lighting my pipe? We have no matches here; I haven't had a real smoke in years."

Emma obliged him, touching a lit finger to the bowl of his pipe. The dog took a long, satisfied puff and said, "Best of luck to you, peculiar children."

CHAPTER FIVE

*W*e clung to the swinging net like a tribe of monkeys, bumping clumsily down the rock face while the pulley squealed and the rope creaked. Coming to earth in a knotted pile, we extricated ourselves from its tangles in what could've been a lost Three Stooges bit; several times I thought I was free, only to try standing and fall flat on my face again with a cartoonish *whump!* The dead hollow lay just feet away, its tentacles splayed like starfish arms from beneath the boulder that had crushed it. I almost felt embarrassed for it: that such a fearsome creature had let itself be laid low by the likes of us. Next time—if there was a next time—I didn't think we'd be so lucky.

We tiptoed around the hollow's reeking carcass. Charged down the mountain as fast as we could, given the limits of the treacherous path and Bronwyn's volatile cargo. Once we'd reached flat land we were able to follow our own tracks back through the squishy moss of the forest floor. We found the lake again just as the sun was setting and bats were screeching out of their hidden roosts. They seemed to bear some unintelligible warning from the world of night, crying and circling overhead as we splashed through the shallows toward the stone giant. We climbed up to his mouth and pitched ourselves down his throat, then swam out the back of him into the instantly cooler water and brighter light of midday, September 1940.

The others surfaced around me, squealing and holding their ears, everyone feeling the pressure that accompanied quick temporal shifts.

"It's like an airplane taking off," I said, working my jaw to release the air.

"Never flown in an airplane," said Horace, brushing water from the brim of his hat.

"Or when you're on the highway and someone rolls down a window," I said.

"What's a highway?" asked Olive.

"Forget it."

Emma shushed us. "Listen!"

In the distance I could hear dogs barking. They seemed far away, but sound traveled strangely in deep woods, and distances could be deceiving. "We'll have to move quickly," Emma said. "Until I say different, no one make a sound—and that includes you, headmistress!"

"I'll throw an exploding egg at the first dog that gets near us," said Hugh. "That'll teach them to chase peculiars."

"Don't you dare," said Bronwyn. "Mishandle one egg and you're liable to set them all off!"

We waded out of the lake and started back through the forest, Millard navigating with Miss Wren's creased map. After half an hour we came to the dirt road Addison had pointed to from the top of the tower. We stood in the ruts of an old wagon track while Millard studied the map, turning it sideways, squinting at its microscopic markings. I reached into the pocket of my jeans for my phone, thinking I'd call up a map of my own—an old habit—then found myself tapping on a blank rectangle of glass that refused to light up. It was dead, of course: wet, chargeless, and fifty years from the nearest cell tower. My phone was the only thing I owned that had survived our disaster at sea, but it was useless here, an alien object. I tossed it into the woods. Thirty seconds later I felt a pang of regret and ran to retrieve it. For reasons that weren't entirely clear to me, I wasn't quite ready to let it go.

Millard folded his map and announced that the town was to our left—a five- or six-hour walk, at least. "If we want to arrive before dark, we'd better move quickly."

We hadn't been walking long when Bronwyn noticed a cloud of dust rising on the road behind us, way in the distance. "Someone's coming," she said. "What should we do?"

Millard removed his greatcoat and threw it into the weeds by the side of the road, making himself invisible. "I recommend you make yourselves disappear," he said, "in whatever limited way you are able."

We got off the road and crouched behind a screen of brush. The dust cloud expanded, and with it came a clatter of wooden wheels and the clip-clop of horses' hooves. It was a caravan of wagons. When they emerged clanking and rumbling from the dust and began to pass us, I saw Horace gasp and Olive break into a smile. These were not the gray, utilitarian wagons I'd gotten used to seeing on Cairnholm, but like something from a circus, painted every color of the rainbow, sporting ornately carved roofs and doors, pulled by long-maned horses, and driven by men and women whose bodies fluttered with beaded necklaces and bright scarves. Remembering Emma's stories of performing in traveling sideshows with Miss Peregrine and the others, I turned to her and asked, "Are they peculiar?"

"They're Gypsies," she replied.

"Is that good news or bad?"

She narrowed her eyes. "Dunno yet."

I could see her weighing a decision, and I was pretty sure I knew what it was. The town we were heading for was far away, and these wagons were moving a lot faster than we could ever travel on foot. With wights and dogs hunting us, the extra speed might mean the difference between getting caught and getting away. But we didn't know who these Gypsies were, or whether we could trust them.

Emma looked at me. "What do you think, should we hitch a ride?"

I looked at the wagons. Looked back at Emma. Thought about

how my feet would feel after a six-hour walk in still-wet shoes. "Absolutely," I said.

Signaling to the others, Emma pointed at the last wagon and mimed running after it. It was shaped like a miniature house, with a little window on each side and a platform that jutted from the back like a porch, probably just wide and deep enough to hold all of us if we squeezed tight together. The wagon was moving fast but not faster than we could sprint, so when it had passed us and we were out of the last driver's sight, we leapt out of the brush and scurried after it. Emma climbed on first, then held out a hand for the next person. One by one we pulled ourselves up and settled into cramped positions along the wagon's rear porch, careful to do so quietly lest the driver hear us.

We rode like that for a long time, until our ears rang with the clatter of wagon wheels and our clothes were caked with dust, until the midday sun had wheeled across the sky and dipped behind the trees, which rose up like the walls of a great green canyon on either side of us. I scanned the forest constantly, afraid that at any moment the wights and their dogs would burst out and attack us. But for hours we didn't see anyone—not a wight, not even another traveler. It was as if we'd arrived in an abandoned country.

Now and then the caravan would stop and we'd all hold our breath, ready to flee or fight, sure we were about to be discovered. We'd send Millard out to investigate, and he would creep down from the wagon only to find that the Gypsies were just stretching their legs or reshoeing a horse, and then we'd start moving again. Eventually I stopped worrying about what would happen if we were discovered. The Gypsies seemed road-weary and harmless. We'd pass as normal and appeal to their pity. *We're just orphans with no home*, we'd say. *Please, could you spare a morsel of bread?* With any luck, they'd give us dinner and escort us to the train station.

It wasn't long before my theory was put to the test. The wagons pulled abruptly off the road and shuddered to a stop in a small clearing. The dust had hardly settled when a large man came striding around back of our wagon. He wore a flat cap on his head, a caterpillar mustache below his nose, and a grim expression that pulled down the corners of his mouth.

Bronwyn hid Miss Peregrine inside her coat while Emma leapt off the wagon and did her best impression of a pathetic orphan. "Sir, we throw ourselves at your mercy! Our house was hit by a bomb, you see, and our parents are dead, and we're terribly lost . . ."

"Shut your gob!" the man boomed. "Get down from there, all of you!" It was a command, not a request, emphasized by the decorative-but-deadly-looking knife balanced in his hand.

We looked at one another, unsure what to do. Should we fight him and run, and probably give away our secret in the process—or play normal for a while longer and wait to see what he does? Then dozens more of them appeared, piling out of their wagons to range around us in a wide circle, many holding knives of their own. We were surrounded, our options dramatically narrowed.

The men were grizzled and sharp-eyed, dressed in dark, heavy-knit clothes built to hide layers of road dust. The women wore bright, flowing dresses, their long hair held back by scarves. Children gathered behind and between them. I tried to square what little I knew about Gypsies with the faces before me. Were they about to massacre us—or were they just naturally grumpy?

I looked to Emma for a cue. She stood with her hands pressed to her chest, not held out like she was about to make flame. If she wasn't going to fight them, I decided, then neither was I.

I got down from the wagon like the man had asked, hands above my head. Horace and Hugh did the same, and then the others—all but Millard, who had slipped away, unseen, presumably to lurk nearby, waiting and watching.

The man with the cap, whom I'd pegged as their leader, began to fire questions at us. "Who are you? Where do you come from? Where are your elders?"

"We come from the west," Emma said calmly. "An island off the coast. We're orphans, as I already explained. Our houses were smashed by bombs in an air raid, and we were forced to flee. We rowed all the way to the mainland and nearly drowned." She attempted to manufacture some tears. "We have nothing," she sniffled. "We've been lost in the woods for days with no food to eat and no clothes but the ones we have on. We saw your wagons passing but were too frightened to show ourselves. We only wanted to ride as far as the town . . ."

The man studied her, his frown deepening. "Why were you forced to flee your island after your house was bombed? And why did you run into the woods instead of following the coast?"

Enoch spoke up. "No choice. We were being chased."

Emma gave him a sharp look that said: *Let me do this.*

"Chased by who?" asked the leader.

"Bad men," Emma said.

"Men with guns," added Horace. "Dressed like soldiers, although they aren't, really."

A woman in a bright yellow scarf stepped forward. "If soldiers are after them, they're trouble we don't need. Send them away, Bekhir."

"Or tie them to trees and leave them!" said a rangy-looking man.

"No!" cried Olive. "We have to get to London before it's too late!"

The leader cocked an eyebrow. "Too late for what?" We hadn't aroused his pity—only his curiosity. "We'll do nothing until we find out who you are," he said, "and what you're worth."

*   *   *

Ten men holding long-bladed knives marched us toward a flatbed wagon with a big cage mounted on top of it. Even from a distance I could see that it was something meant for animals, twenty feet by ten, made of thick iron bars.

"You're not going to lock us in there, are you?" Olive said.

"Just until we sort out what to do with you," said the leader.

"No, you can't!" cried Olive. "We have to get to London, and quick!"

"And why's that?"

"One of us is ill," said Emma, shooting Hugh a meaningful look. "We need to get him a doctor!"

"You don't need to go all the way to London for no doctor," said one of the Gypsy men. "Jebbiah's a doctor. Ain't you, Jebbiah?"

A man with scabrous lesions spanning his cheeks stepped forward. "Which one of ye's ill?"

"Hugh needs a *specialist*," said Emma. "He's got a rare condition. Stinging cough."

Hugh put a hand to his throat as if it hurt him and coughed, and a bee shot out of his mouth. Some of the Gypsies gasped, and a little girl hid her face in her mother's skirt.

"It's some sort of trick!" said the so-called doctor.

"Enough," said their leader. "Get in the cage, all of you."

They shoved us toward a ramp that led to it. We clustered together at the bottom. No one wanted to go first.

"We can't let them do this!" whispered Hugh.

"What are you waiting for?" Enoch hissed at Emma. "Burn them!"

Emma shook her head and whispered, "There are too many." She led the way up the ramp and into the cage. Its barred ceiling was low, its floor piled deep with rank-smelling hay. When we were all inside, the leader slammed the door and locked it behind us, slipping the key into his pocket. "No one goes near them!" he shouted to anyone within earshot. "They could be witches, or worse."

"Yes, that's what we are!" Enoch said through the bars. "Now let us go, or we'll turn your children into warthogs!"

The leader laughed as he walked away down the ramp. Meanwhile, the other Gypsies retreated to a safe distance and began to set up camp, pitching tents and starting cookfires. We sank down into the hay, feeling defeated and depressed.

"Look out," Horace warned. "There are animal droppings everywhere!"

"Oh, what does it matter, Horace?" Emma said. "No one gives a chuck if your clothes are dirty!"

"*I* do," Horace replied.

Emma covered her face with her hands. I sat down next to her and tried to think of something encouraging to say, but came up blank.

Bronwyn opened her coat to give Miss Peregrine some fresh air, and Enoch knelt beside her and cocked his ear, as if listening for something. "Hear that?" he said.

"What?" Bronwyn replied.

"The sound of Miss Peregrine's life slipping away! Emma, you should've burned those Gypsies' faces off while you had the chance!"

"We were surrounded!" Emma said. "Some of us would've gotten hurt in a big fight. Maybe killed. I couldn't risk that."

"So you risked Miss Peregrine instead!" said Enoch.

"Enoch, leave her be," said Bronwyn. "It ain't easy, deciding for everyone. We can't take a vote every time there's a choice to be made."

"Then maybe you should let *me* decide for everyone," Enoch replied.

Hugh snorted. "We would've been killed ages ago if *you* were in charge."

"Look, it doesn't matter now," I said. "We have to get out of this cage and make it to that town. We're a lot closer now than if we hadn't hitched a ride in the first place, so there's no need to cry over milk that hasn't even spilled yet. We just need to think of a way to escape."

So we thought, and came up with lots of ideas, but none that seemed workable.

"Maybe Emma can burn through this floor," Bronwyn suggested. "It's made of wood."

Emma swept a clear patch in the hay and knocked on the floor. "It's too thick," she said miserably.

"Wyn, can you bend these bars apart?" I asked.

"Maybe," she replied, "but not with those Gypsies so close by. They'll see and come running with their knives again."

"We need to *sneak* out, not *break* out," said Emma.

Then we heard a whisper from outside the bars. "Did you forget about me?"

"Millard!" Olive exclaimed, nearly floating out of her shoes with excitement. "Where have you been?"

"Getting the lay of the land, as it were. And waiting for things to calm down."

"Think you can steal the key for us?" said Emma, rattling the cage's locked door. "I saw the head man put it in his pocket."

"Prowling and purloinment are my specialty," he assured us, and with that he slipped away.

*　　*　　*

The minutes crawled by. Then a half hour. Then an hour. Hugh paced the length of the cage, an agitated bee circling his head. "What's taking him so long?" he grumbled.

"If he doesn't come back soon, I'm going to start tossing eggs," said Enoch.

"Do that and you'll get us all killed," said Emma. "We're sitting ducks in here. Once the smoke clears, they'll flay us alive."

So we sat and waited more, watching the Gypsies, the Gypsies watching back. Every minute that ticked by felt like another nail in Miss Peregrine's coffin. I found myself staring at her, as if by looking closely enough I might be able to detect the changes happening to her—to see the still-human spark within her slowly winking out. But she looked the same as she always had, only calmer somehow, asleep in the hay next to Bronwyn, her small, feathered chest rising and falling softly. She seemed to have no awareness of the trouble we were in, or of the countdown that was hanging over her head. Maybe the fact that she could sleep at a time like this was evidence enough that she was changing. The old Miss Peregrine would've been having nervous fits.

Then my thoughts strayed to my parents, as they always did when I didn't keep a tight rein on them. I tried to picture their faces as I'd last seen them. Bits and pieces coalesced in my mind: the thin rim of stubble my dad had developed after a few days on the island; the way my mom, without realizing it, would fiddle with her wedding ring when my dad talked too long about something that disinterested her; my dad's darting eyes, always checking the horizon on his never-ending search for birds.

Now they'd be searching for me.

As evening settled in, the camp came alive around us. The Gypsies talked and laughed, and when a band of children with battered horns and fiddles struck up a song, they danced. Between songs one of the boys from the band snuck around back of our cage with a bottle in his hands. "It's for the sick one," he said, checking behind him nervously.

"Who?" I said, and then he nodded at Hugh, who wilted to the floor in spasms of coughing, right on cue.

The boy slipped the bottle through the bars. I twisted off the cap, gave it a sniff, and nearly fell over. It smelled like turpentine mixed with compost. "What *is* it?" I said.

"Works, that's all I know." He looked behind him again. "All right, I done something for you. Now you owes. So tell me—what crime did you do? You're thieves, aincha?" Then he lowered his voice and said, "Or didja *kill* someone?"

"What's he talking about?" said Bronwyn.

We didn't kill anyone, I came close to saying, but then an image of Golan's body tumbling through the air toward a battery of rocks flashed in my mind, and I kept quiet.

Emma said it for me instead. "We didn't kill anyone!"

"Well, you musta done *something*," the boy said. "Why else would they have a reward out for you?"

"There's a reward?" said Enoch.

"Sure as rain. They're offering a whole pile of money."

"*Who* is?"

The boy shrugged.

"Are you going to turn us in?" Olive asked.

The boy twisted his lip. "Dunno if we will or we won't. The big shots are chewing it over. Though I'll say they don't much trust the sort of people who's offerin' the reward. Then again, money's money, and they don't much like it that you won't answer their questions."

"Where we come from," Emma said haughtily, "you don't question people who come to you asking for help."

"And you don't put 'em in cages, either!" said Olive.

Just then a tremendous bang went off in the middle of the camp. The Gypsy boy lost his balance and fell off the ramp into the grass, and the rest of us ducked as pots and pans went flying through the air away from a cookfire. The Gypsy woman who'd been tending it sped off screaming bloody murder, her dress on fire, and she might've run all the way to the ocean if someone hadn't picked up a horse's drinking bucket and doused her with it.

A moment later we heard the footsteps of an invisible boy pounding up the ramp outside our cage. "That's what happens when you try and make an omelet from a peculiar chicken egg!" said Millard, out of breath and laughing.

"*You* did that?" said Horace.

"Everything was too orderly and quiet . . . bad weather for

pickpocketing! So I slipped one of our eggs in with theirs, *et voilà*!"
Millard made a key appear out of thin air. "People are much less
likely to notice my hand in their pockets when dinner's just exploded
in their faces."

"Took you long enough," said Enoch. "Now let us out of
here!"

But before Millard could get the key in the door, the Gypsy boy
stood up and shouted, "Help! They're trying to get away!"

The boy had heard everything—but in the confusion following
the blast, hardly anyone noticed his shouts.

Millard twisted the key in the lock. The door wouldn't open.
"Oh, drat," he said. "Perhaps I stole the wrong key?"

"*Ahhhh!*" the boy screamed, pointing at the space Millard's
voice emanated from. "*A ghost!*"

"Will someone *please* shut him up!" said Enoch.

Bronwyn obliged, reaching through the cage to grab the boy's
arms, then pulling him off his feet and up against the bars.

"*Haaaaalp!*" he screamed. "They've got *mmmfff*—"

She slapped a hand over his mouth, but she'd silenced him too
late. "Galbi!" a woman shouted. "Let him go, you savages!"

And suddenly, without really meaning to, we'd taken a hostage. Gypsy men rushed at us, knives flashing in the failing light.

"What are you doing?" cried Millard. "Let that boy go before
they murder us!"

"No, don't!" Emma said, and then she screamed, "Free us or
the boy dies!"

The Gypsies surrounded us, shouting threats. "If you harm him
in any way," the leader yelled, "I'll kill every last one of you with
my bare hands!"

"Stay back!" Emma said. "Just let us go and we won't hurt
anyone."

One of the men made a run at the cage, and instinctively, Emma
flicked out her hands and sparked a roaring fireball between them.

The crowd gasped and the man skidded to a stop.

"Now you've done it!" hissed Enoch. "They'll hang us for being witches!"

"I'll burn the first one that tries!" Emma shouted, widening the space between her palms to make the fireball even larger. "Come on, let's show them who they're messing with!"

It was time to put on a show. Bronwyn went first: with one hand she raised the boy even higher, his feet kicking in the air, and with the other she grabbed one of the roof bars and began to bend it. Hugh stuck his face between the bars and shot a line of bees from his open mouth, and then Millard, who'd sprinted away from the cage the moment the boy had noticed him, shouted from somewhere behind the crowd, "And if you think you can contend with them, you haven't met me!" and launched an egg into the air. It arced above their heads and landed in a nearby clearing with a huge bang, scattering dirt as high as the treetops.

As the smoke cleared, there was a breathless moment in which no one moved or spoke. I thought at first that our display had paralyzed the Gypsies with awe—but then, when the ringing in my ears had faded, I realized they were listening for something. Then I was, too.

From the darkening road came the sound of an engine. A pair of headlights flickered into view beyond the trees, along the road. Everyone, Gypsy and peculiar, watched as the lights passed the turnoff to our clearing—then slowed, then came back. A canvas-topped military vehicle rumbled toward us. From inside it, the sounds of angry voices shouting and dogs, their throats hoarse from barking but unable to stop now that they'd caught our scent again.

It was the wights who'd been hunting us—and here we were inside a cage, unable even to run.

Emma extinguished her flame with a clap of her hands. Bronwyn dropped the boy and he stumbled away. The Gypsies fled back to their wagons or into the woods. In moments we were left alone, seemingly forgotten.

Their leader strode toward us.

"Open the cage!" Emma begged him.

She was ignored. "Hide yourselves under the hay and don't make a sound!" the man said. "And no magic tricks—unless you'd rather go with them."

There was no time for more questions. The last thing we saw before everything went black were two Gypsy men running at us with a tarp in their hands. They flipped it over the top of our cage.

Instant night.

*   *   *

Boots tromped by outside the cage, heavy and thudding, as if the wights sought to punish the very ground they walked upon. We did as instructed and dug ourselves into the stinking hay.

Nearby, I heard a wight talking to the Gypsy leader. "A group of children were seen along the road this morning," the wight said, his voice clipped, accent obscure—not quite English, not quite German. "There's a reward for their capture."

"We haven't run across anyone all day, sir," the leader said.

"Don't let their innocent faces fool you. They're traitors to the war effort. Spies for Germany. The penalty for hiding them . . ."

"We aren't hiding anything," the leader said gruffly. "See for yourself."

"I'll do that," said the wight. "And if we find them here, I'll cut your tongue out and feed it to my dog."

The wight stomped away.

"*Don't. Even. Breathe,*" the leader hissed at us, and then his footsteps trailed away, too.

I wondered why he would lie for us, given the harm these wights could cause his people. Maybe it was out of pride, or some deep-rooted disdain for authority—or, I thought with a cringe, maybe the

Gypsies just wanted the satisfaction of killing us themselves.

All around us we could hear the wights spreading throughout the camp, kicking things over, throwing open caravan doors, shoving people. A child screamed and a man reacted angrily, but was cut short with the sound of wood meeting flesh. It was excruciating to lie there and listen to people suffer—even if those same people had been ready to tear us limb from limb just minutes ago.

From the corner of my eye I saw Hugh rise from the hay and crawl to Bronwyn's trunk. He slipped his fingers over the latch and began to open the lid, but Bronwyn stopped him. "What are you doing?" she mouthed.

"We've got to get them before they get us!"

Emma lifted herself out of the hay on her elbows and rolled toward them, and I got closer too, to listen.

"Don't be insane," said Emma. "If we throw the eggs now, they'll shoot us to ribbons."

"So what, then?" said Hugh. "We should just lie here until they find us?"

We clustered around the trunk, speaking in whispers.

"Wait until they unlock the door," said Enoch. "Then I'll throw an egg through the bars behind us. That'll distract the wights long enough for Bronwyn to crack the skull of whichever one comes into the cage first, which should give the rest of us time to run. Scatter to the outer edges of camp, then turn and throw your eggs back at the middle-most campfire. Everyone in a thirty-meter radius will be a memory."

"I'll be damned," said Hugh. "That just might work."

"But there are children in the camp!" said Bronwyn.

Enoch rolled his eyes. "Or we can worry about collateral damage, run into the woods, and leave the wights and their dogs to hunt us down one by one. But if we plan on reaching London—or living beyond tonight—I don't recommend it."

Hugh patted Bronwyn's hand, which was covering the trunk

latch. "Open it," he said. "Give them out."

Bronwyn hesitated. "I can't. I can't kill children who've done nothing to harm us."

"But we don't have a choice!" whispered Hugh.

"You always have a choice," said Bronwyn.

Then we heard a dog snarl very near the bottom rim of the cage, and went silent. A moment later a flashlight shone against the outside of the tarp. "Tear this sheet down!" someone said—the dog's handler, I assumed.

The dog barked, its nose snuffling to get beneath the tarp and up through the cage bars. "Over here!" shouted the handler. "We've got something!"

We all looked to Bronwyn. "Please," Hugh said. "At least let us defend ourselves."

"It's the only way," said Enoch.

Bronwyn sighed and took her hand away from the latch. Hugh nodded gratefully and opened the trunk lid. We all reached in and took an egg from between the layered sweaters—everyone but Bronwyn. Then we stood and faced the cage door, eggs in hand, and prepared for the inevitable.

More boots marched toward us. I tried to prepare myself for what was coming. *Run,* I told myself. *Run and don't look back and then throw it.*

But knowing that innocent people would die, could I really do it? Even to save my own life? What if I just dropped the egg in some grass and ran into the woods?

A hand grabbed one edge of the tarp and pulled. The tarp began to slide away.

Then, just shy of exposing us, it stopped.

"What's the matter with you?" I heard the dog's handler say.

"I'd steer well away from that cage if I was you," said another voice—a Gypsy's.

I could see half the sky above us, stars twinkling down through the branches of oaks.

"Yeah? And why is that?" said the handler.

"Old Bloodcoat ain't been fed in a few days," the Gypsy said. "He don't usually care for the taste of humans, but when he's this hungry he ain't so discriminating!"

Then came a sound that stole the breath right out of me—the roar of a giant bear. Impossibly, it seemed to be coming from among us, inside our cage. I heard the dog's handler shout in surprise and then scramble down the ramp, pulling his yelping dog along with him.

I couldn't fathom how a bear had gotten into the cage, only that I needed to get away from it, so I pressed myself hard against the bars. Next to me I saw Olive stick her little fist in her mouth to keep from crying out.

Outside, other soldiers were laughing at the handler. "Idiot!" he said, embarrassed. "Only Gypsies would keep an animal like that in the middle of their camp!"

I finally worked up the courage to turn around and look behind me. There was no bear in our cage. What had made that awful roar?

The soldiers kept searching the camp, but now they left our cage alone. After a few minutes we heard them pile back into their truck and restart the engine, and then, at last, they were gone.

The tarp slid away from our cage. The Gypsies were all gathered around us. I held my egg in one trembling hand, wondering if I'd have to use it.

The leader stood before us. "Are you all right?" he said. "I'm sorry if that frightened you."

"We're alive," Emma replied, looking around warily. "But where's this bear of yours?"

"You aren't the only ones with unusual talents," said a young man at the edge of the crowd, and then in quick succession he growled like a bear and yowled like a cat, throwing his voice from one place to another with slight turns of his head so that it sounded like we were being stalked from all directions. When we'd gotten over our shock, we broke into applause.

"I thought you said they weren't peculiar," I whispered to Emma.

"Anyone can do parlor tricks like that," she said.

"Apologies if I failed to properly introduce myself," said the Gypsy leader. "My name is Bekhir Bekhmanatov. And you are our honored guests." He bowed deeply. "Why didn't you tell us you were *syndrigasti*?"

We gaped at him. He had used the ancient name for peculiars, the one Miss Peregrine had taught us.

"Do we know you from somewhere?" Bronwyn asked.

"Where did you hear that word?" said Emma.

Bekhir smiled. "If you'll accept our hospitality, I promise to explain everything." Then he bowed again and strode forward to unlock our cage.

*   *   *

We sat with the Gypsies on fine, handwoven carpets, talking and eating stew by the shimmering light of twin campfires. I dropped the spoon I'd been given and slurped straight from a wooden bowl, my table manners a distant memory as greasy, delicious broth dribbled down my chin. Bekhir walked among us, making sure each peculiar child was comfortable, asking if we had enough to eat and drink, and apologizing repeatedly for the state of our clothes, now covered in filthy bits of hay from the cage. Since witnessing our peculiar display he'd changed his attitude toward us completely; in the span of a few minutes we'd graduated from being prisoners to guests of honor.

"I'm very sorry for the way you were treated," he said, lowering himself onto a cushion between the fires. "When it comes to the safety of my people, I must take every precaution. There are many strangers wandering the roads these days—people who aren't what they appear to be. If you'd only told me you were *syndrigasti* . . ."

"We were taught never, ever to tell anyone," said Emma.

"*Ever*," Olive added.

"Whoever taught you that is very wise," Bekhir said.

"How do you know about us?" Emma asked. "You speak the old tongue."

"Only a few words," Bekhir said. He gazed into the flames, a spit of darkening meat roasting there. "We have an old understanding, your people and mine. We aren't so different. Outcasts and wanderers all—souls clinging to the margins of the world." He pinched a hunk of meat from the spit and chewed it thoughtfully. "We are allies of a sort. Over the years, we Gypsies have even taken in and raised some of your children."

"And we're grateful for it," said Emma, "and for your hospitality as well. But at the risk of seeming rude, we can't possibly stay with you any longer. It's very important that we reach London quickly. We have a train to catch."

"For your sick friend?" Bekhir asked, raising an eyebrow at Hugh, who had long ago dropped his act and was now gulping down stew with abandon, bees buzzing happily around his head.

"Something like that," said Emma.

Bekhir knew we were hiding something, but he was kind enough to let us have our secrets. "There won't be any more trains tonight," he said, "but we'll rise at dawn and deliver you to the station before the first one leaves in the morning. Good enough?"

"It'll have to be," Emma said, her brow pinched with worry. Even though we'd saved time by hitching a ride instead of walking, Miss Peregrine had still lost an entire day. Now she had only two left, at most. But that was in the future; right now we were warm, well fed, and out of immediate danger. It was hard not to enjoy ourselves, if only for the moment.

We made fast friends with the Gypsies. Everyone was eager

to forget what had happened between us earlier. Bronwyn tried to apologize to the boy she'd taken hostage, but he brushed it off like it had been nothing. The Gypsies fed us relentlessly, refilling my bowl again and again—overfilling it when I tried to refuse more. When Miss Peregrine hopped out of Bronwyn's coat and announced her appetite with a screech, the Gypsies fed her, too, tossing hunks of raw meat in the air and cheering when she leapt up to snatch them. "She's hungry!" Olive laughed, clapping as the bird shredded a pig knuckle with her talons.

"Now aren't you glad we didn't blow them up?" Bronwyn whispered to Enoch.

"Oh, I *suppose*," he replied.

The Gypsy band struck up another song. We ate and danced. I convinced Emma to take a turn around the fire with me, and though I was usually shy about dancing in public, this time I let myself go. Our feet flew and our hands clapped in time to the music, and for a few shining minutes we lost ourselves in it. I was able to forget how much danger we were in, and how that very day we had nearly been captured by wights and devoured by a hollow, our meat-stripped bones spat off a mountainside. In that moment I was deeply grateful to the Gypsies, and for the simplemindedness of the animal part of my brain; that a hot meal and a song and a smile from someone I cared about could be enough to distract me from all that darkness, if only for a little while. Then the song ended and we stumbled back to our seats, and in the lull that followed I felt the mood change. Emma looked at Bekhir and said, "May I ask you something?"

"Of course," he said.

"Why did you risk your lives for us?"

He waved his hand. "You would've done the same."

"I'm not sure we would've," said Emma. "I just want to understand. Was it because we're peculiar?"

"Yes," he said simply. A moment passed. He looked away at the trees that edged our clearing, their firelit trunks and the blackness beyond. Then he said, "Would you like to meet my son?"

"Of course," Emma said.

She stood, and so did I and several others.

Bekhir raised a hand. "He's shy, I'm afraid. Just you," he said, pointing to Emma, "and you"—he pointed at me—"and the one who can be heard but not seen."

"Impressive," said Millard. "And I was trying so hard to be subtle!"

Enoch sat down again. "Why am I always being left out of things? Do I smell?"

A Gypsy woman in a flowing robe swept into the campfire circle. "While they're gone, I'll read your palms and tell your fortunes," she said. She turned to Horace. "Maybe you'll climb Kilimanjaro one day!" Then to Bronwyn—"Or marry a rich, handsome man!"

Bronwyn snorted. "My fondest dream."

"The future is *my* specialty, madam," said Horace. "Let me show you how it's done!"

Emma, Millard, and I left them and started across the camp with Bekhir. We came to a plain-looking caravan wagon, and he climbed its short ladder and knocked on the door.

"Radi?" he called gently. "Come out, please. There are people here to see you."

The door opened a crack and a woman peeked out. "He's scared. Won't leave his chair." She looked us over carefully, then opened the door wide and beckoned us in. We mounted the steps and ducked into a cramped but cozy space that appeared to be a living room, bedroom, and kitchen all in one. There was a bed under a narrow window, a table and chair, and a little stove that vented out a chimney in the roof; everything you'd need to be self-sufficient on the road for weeks or months at a time.

In the room's lone chair sat a boy. He held a trumpet in his lap. I'd seen him play earlier, I realized, as part of the Gypsy children's band. This was Bekhir's son, and the woman, I assumed, was

Bekhir's wife.

"Take off your shoes, Radi," the woman said.

The boy kept his gaze trained on the floor. "Do I have to?" he asked.

"Yes," Bekhir said.

The boy tugged off one of his boots, then the other. For a second I wasn't sure what I was seeing: there was nothing inside his shoes. He appeared to have no feet. And yet he'd had to work to get his boots off, so they had to have been attached to *something*. Then Bekhir asked him to stand, and reluctantly the boy slid forward in the chair and rose out of it. He seemed to be levitating, the cuffs of his pants hanging empty a few inches above the floor.

"He began disappearing a few months ago," the woman explained. "First just his toes. Then his heels. Finally the rest, both feet. Nothing I've given him—no tincture, no tonic—has had the slightest effect in curing him."

So he had feet, after all—invisible ones.

"We don't know what to do," said Bekhir. "But I thought, perhaps there's a healer among you . . ."

"There's no healing what he's got," said Millard, and at the sound of his voice in the empty air the boy's head jerked up. "We're alike, he and I. It was just the same for me when I was young. I wasn't born invisible; it happened a little at a time."

"Who's speaking?" the boy said.

Millard picked up a scarf that lay on the edge of the bed and wrapped it around his face, revealing the shape of his nose, his forehead, his mouth. "Here I am," he said, moving across the floor toward the boy. "Don't be frightened."

As the rest of us watched, the boy reached up his hand and touched Millard's cheek, then his forehead, then his hair—the color and style of which it had never occurred to me to imagine—and even pulled a little hank of it, gently, as if testing its realness.

"You're *there*," the boy said, his eyes sparkling with wonder.

"You're really there!"

"And you'll be, too, even after the rest of you goes," said Millard. "You'll see. It doesn't hurt."

The boy smiled, and when he did, the woman's knees wobbled and she had to steady herself against Bekhir. "Bless you," she said to Millard, near tears. "Bless you."

Millard sat down at Radi's disappeared feet. "There's nothing to be afraid of, my boy. In fact, once you adjust to invisibility, I think you'll find it has many advantages . . ."

And as he began to list them, Bekhir went to the door and nodded at Emma and me. "Let's let them be," he said. "I'm sure they have a lot to talk about."

We left Millard alone with the boy and his mother. Returning to the campfire, we found nearly everyone, peculiar and Gypsy alike, gathered around Horace. He was standing on a tree stump before the astounded fortune teller, his eyes closed and one hand atop her head, and seemed to be narrating a dream as it came to him: ". . . and your grandson's grandson will pilot a giant ship that shuttles between the Earth and the moon like an omnibus, and on the moon he'll have a very small house, and he'll fall behind on the mortgage and have to take in lodgers, and one of those lodgers will be a beautiful woman with whom he'll fall very deeply in moon-love, which isn't quite the same as Earth-love because of the difference in gravity there . . ."

We watched from the edge of the crowd. "Is he for real?" I asked Emma.

"Might be," she replied. "Or he might just be having a bit of fun with her."

"Why can't he tell *our* futures like that?"

Emma shrugged. "Horace's ability can be maddeningly useless. He'll reel off lifetimes of predictions for strangers, but with us he's almost totally blocked. It's as if the more he cares about someone, the less he can see. Emotion clouds his vision."

"Doesn't it all of us," came a voice from behind us, and we turned to see Enoch standing there. "And on that tip, I hope you aren't distracting the American too much, Emma dear. It's hard to keep a lookout for hollowgast when there's a young lady's tongue in your ear."

"Don't be disgusting!" Emma said.

"I couldn't ignore the Feeling if I wanted to," I said, though I did wish I could ignore the icky feeling that Enoch was jealous of me.

"So, tell me about your secret meeting," Enoch said. "Did the Gypsies really protect us because of some dusty old alliance none of us have heard of?"

"The leader and his wife have a peculiar son," said Emma. "They hoped we could help him."

"That's madness," said Enoch. "They nearly let themselves be filleted alive by those soldiers for the sake of one boy? Talk about emotion clouding vision! I figured they wanted to enslave us for our abilities, or at the very least sell us at auction—but then I'm always overestimating people."

"Oh, go find a dead animal to play with," said Emma.

"I'll never understand ninety-nine percent of humanity," said Enoch, and he went away shaking his head.

"Sometimes I think that boy is part machine," Emma said. "Flesh on the outside, metal on the inside."

I laughed, but secretly I wondered if Enoch was right. *Was it crazy*, what Bekhir had risked for his son? Because if Bekhir was crazy, then certainly I was. How much had I given up for the sake of just one girl? Despite my curiosity, despite my grandfather, despite the debts we owed Miss Peregrine, ultimately I was here—now—for one reason alone: because from the day I met Emma I'd known I wanted to be part of any world she belonged to. Did that make me crazy? Or was my heart too easily conquered?

Maybe I could use a little metal on the inside, I thought. If I'd kept my heart better armored, where would I be now?

Easy—I'd be at home, medicating myself into a monotone. Drowning my sorrows in video games. Working shifts at Smart Aid. Dying inside, day by day, from regret.

You coward. You weak, pathetic child. You threw your chance away.

But I hadn't. In reaching toward Emma, I'd risked everything— was risking it again, every day—but in doing so I had grasped and pulled myself into a world once unimaginable to me, where I lived among people who were more alive than anyone I'd known, did things I'd never dreamed I could do, survived things I'd never dreamed I could survive. All because I'd let myself feel something for one peculiar girl.

Despite all the trouble and danger we found ourselves in, and despite the fact that this strange new world had started to crumble the moment I'd discovered it, I was profoundly glad I was here. Despite everything, this peculiar life was what I'd always wanted. Strange, I thought, how you can be living your dreams and your nightmares at the very same time.

"What is it?" Emma said. "You're staring at me."

"I wanted to thank you," I said.

She wrinkled her nose and squinted like I'd said something funny. "Thank me for what?" she said.

"You give me strength I didn't know I had," I said. "You make me better."

She blushed. "I don't know what to say."

Emma, bright soul. I need your fire—the one inside you.

"You don't have to say anything," I said. And then I was seized with the sudden urge to kiss her, and I did.

*　　*　　*

Though we were dead tired, the Gypsies were in a buoyant mood and seemed determined to keep the party going, and after a few cups of hot, sweet, highly caffeinated something and a few more songs, they'd won us over. They were natural storytellers and beautiful singers; innately charming people who treated us like long-lost cousins. We stayed up half the night trading stories. The young guy who'd thrown his voice like a bear did a ventriloquist act that was so good I almost believed his dummies had come alive. He seemed to have a little crush on Emma and delivered the whole routine to her, smiling encouragingly, but she pretended not to notice and made a point of holding my hand.

Later they told us the story of how, during the First World War, the British army had taken all their horses, and for a while they'd had none to pull their wagons. They had been left stranded in the forest—this very forest—when one day a herd of long-horned goats wandered into their camp. They looked wild but were tame enough to eat out of your hand, so someone got the idea to hitch one to a wagon, and these goats turned out to be nearly as strong as the horses they'd lost. So the Gypsies got unstuck, and until the end of the war their wagons were pulled by these peculiarly strong goats, which is how they became known throughout Wales as Goat People. As proof they passed around a photo of Bekhir's uncle riding a goat-pulled wagon. We knew without anyone having to say it that this was the lost herd of peculiar goats Addison had talked about. After the war, the army gave back the Gypsies' horses, and the goats, no longer needed, disappeared again into the forest.

Finally, campfires dwindling, they laid out sleeping rolls for us and sang a lullaby in a lilting foreign language, and I felt pleasantly like a child. The ventriloquist came to say good night to Emma. She shooed him away, but not before he left a calling card. On the back was an address in Cardiff where he picked up mail every few months, whenever the Gypsies stopped through. On the front was his photo, with dummies, and a little note written to Emma. She showed it to me and snickered, but I felt bad for the guy. He was guilty only of liking her, same as me.

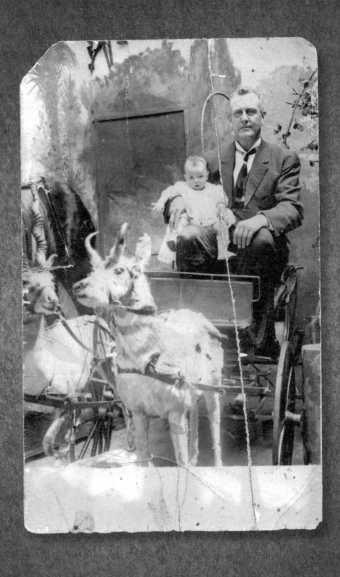

To Emma,

Yours for a smile

G. M. S. etc.

I curled up with Emma in a sleeping roll at the forest's edge. Just as we were drifting off, I heard footsteps in the grass nearby, and opened my eyes to see no one at all. It was Millard, back again after having spent the evening talking with the Gypsy boy.

"He wants to come with us," said Millard.

"Who?" Emma mumbled groggily. "Where?"

"The boy. With us."

"And what did you say?"

"I told him it was a bad idea. But I didn't say no, precisely."

"You know we can't take on anyone else," Emma said. "He'll slow us down."

"I know, I know," said Millard. "But he's disappearing very rapidly, and he's frightened. Soon he'll be entirely invisible, and he's afraid he'll fall behind their group one day and the Gypsies won't notice and he'll be lost forever in the woods among the wolves and spiders."

Emma groaned and rolled over to face Millard. He wasn't going to let us sleep until this was decided. "I know he'll be disappointed," she said. "But it's really impossible. I'm sorry, Mill."

"Fair enough," Millard said heavily. "I'll give him the news."

He rose and slipped away.

Emma sighed, and for a while she tossed and turned, restless.

"You did the right thing," I whispered. "It isn't easy being the one everybody looks to."

She said nothing, but snuggled into the hollow of my chest. Gradually we drifted off, the whispers of breeze-blown branches and the breathing of horses gentling us to sleep.

*　　*　　*

It was a night of thin sleep and bad dreams, spent much as I'd spent the previous day: being chased by packs of nightmare dogs. By morning I was worn out. My limbs felt heavy as wood, my head cottony. I might've felt better if I hadn't slept at all.

Bekhir woke us at dawn. "Rise and shine, *syndrigasti*!" he shouted, tossing out hunks of brick-hard bread. "There'll be time for sleeping when you're dead!"

Enoch knocked his bread against a rock and it clacked like wood. "We'll be dead soon enough, with breakfast like this!"

Bekhir roughed Enoch's hair, grinning. "Ahh, come on. Where's your peculiar spirit this morning?"

"In the wash," said Enoch, covering his head with the sleeping roll.

Bekhir gave us ten minutes to prepare for the ride to town. He was making good on his promise and would have us there before the morning's first train. I got up, stumbled to a bucket of water, splashed some on my face, brushed my teeth with my finger. Oh, how I missed my toothbrush. How I longed for my minty floss, my ocean-breeze-scented deodorant stick. What I wouldn't have given, just then, to find a Smart Aid store.

My kingdom for a pack of fresh underwear!

As I raked bits of hay from my hair with my fingers and bit into a loaf of inedible bread, the Gypsies and their children watched us with mournful faces. It was as if they knew, somehow, that the previous night's fun had been a last hurrah, and now we were being led off to the gallows. I tried to cheer one of them up. "It's okay," I said to a towheaded little boy who seemed on the verge of tears. "We're going to be fine."

He looked at me as if I were a talking ghost, his eyes wide and uncertain.

Eight horses were rounded up, and eight Gypsy riders—one for each of us. Horses would get us to town much faster than a caravan of wagons could. They were also terrifying to me.

I'd never ridden a horse. I was probably the only marginally rich kid in America who hadn't. It wasn't because I didn't think horses were beautiful, majestic creatures, the pinnacle of animal creation, etc., etc.—it's just that I didn't believe any animal had the slightest interest in being mounted or ridden by a human being. Besides, horses were very large, with rippling muscles and big, grinding teeth, and they looked at me as if they knew I was afraid and were hoping for an opportunity to kick my head in. Not to mention the lack of a seatbelt on a horse—no secondary restraint systems of any kind—and yet horses could go nearly as fast as cars but were much bouncier. So the whole endeavor just seemed inadvisable.

I said none of this, of course. I shut up and set my jaw and hoped I'd live at least long enough to die in a more interesting way than by falling off a horse.

From the first *giddyap!* we were at full gallop. I abandoned my dignity right away and bear-hugged the Gypsy man on the saddle in front of me who held the reins—so quickly that I didn't have a chance to wave goodbye to the Gypsies who had gathered to see us off. Which was just as well: goodbyes had never been my strong suit anyway, and lately my life had felt like an unbroken series of them. Goodbye, goodbye, goodbye.

We rode. My thighs went numb from squeezing the horse. Bekhir led the pack, his peculiar boy riding with him in the saddle. The boy rode with his back straight and arms at his sides, confident and unafraid, such a contrast from last night. He was in his element here, among the Gypsies. He didn't need us. *These* were his people.

Eventually we slowed to a trot and I found the courage to unbury my face from the rider's jacket and take in the changing landscape. The forest had flattened into fields. We were descending into a valley, in the middle of which was a town that, from here, looked no bigger than a postage stamp, overwhelmed by green on all sides. Tracing toward it from the north was a long ellipsis of puffy white dots: the smoky breath of a train.

Bekhir stopped the horses just shy of the town gates. "This is as far as we go," he said. "We're not much welcome in towns. You don't want the sort of attention we'd draw."

It was hard to imagine anyone objecting to these kindly people. Then again, similar prejudices were among the reasons peculiars had withdrawn from society. Such was the way the sad world turned.

The children and I dismounted. I stood behind the others, hoping no one would notice my trembling legs. Just as we were about to go, Bekhir's boy sprang down from his father's horse and cried, "Wait! Take me with you!"

"I thought you were going to talk to him," Emma said to Millard.

"I *did*," Millard replied.

The boy pulled a knapsack from the saddlebag and slung it over his shoulder. He was packed and ready to go. "I can cook," he said, "and chop wood, and ride a horse, and tie all sorts of knots!"

"Someone give him a merit badge," said Enoch.

"I'm afraid it's impossible," Emma said to him gently.

"But I'm like you—and becoming more so all the time!" The boy began to unbuckle his pants. "Look what's happening to me!"

Before anyone could stop him, he'd sent his pants to his ankles. The girls gasped and looked away. Hugh shouted, "Keep your trousers on, you depraved lunatic!"

But there was nothing to see—he was invisible from the midsection down. Morbid curiosity compelled me to peek at the underside of his visible half, which earned me a crystal-clear view of the inner workings of his bowels.

"Look how much I've disappeared since yesterday," Radi said, his voice panicky. "Soon I'll be gone altogether!"

The Gypsy men gawked and murmured. Even their horses

seemed disturbed, shying away from what seemed to be a disembodied child.

"I'll be winged!" said Enoch. "He's only half there."

"Oh, you poor thing," said Bronwyn. "Can't we keep him?"

"We aren't some traveling circus you can join whenever the notion takes you," said Enoch. "We're on a dangerous mission to save our ymbryne, and in no position to play babysitter to a clueless new peculiar!"

The boy's eyes grew wide and began to water, and he let his knapsack slide off his shoulder and fall to the road.

Emma took Enoch aside. "That was too harsh," she said. "Now tell him you're sorry."

"I won't. This is a ridiculous waste of our precious and dwindling time."

"These people saved our lives!"

"Our lives wouldn't have *needed* saving if they hadn't stuck us in that blessed cage!"

Emma gave up on Enoch and turned to the boy. "If circumstances were different, we'd welcome you with open arms. But as it stands, our entire civilization and way of life are in danger of being snuffed out. So it's rather bad timing, you see."

"It isn't fair," the boy moped. "Why couldn't I have started disappearing ages ago? Why did it have to happen *now*?"

"Every peculiar's ability manifests in its own time," said Millard. "Some in infancy; others not until they're quite old. I once heard of a man who didn't realize he could levitate objects with his mind until he was ninety-two years of age."

"I was lighter than air from the minute I was born," Olive said proudly. "I popped out of me mum and floated straight up to the hospital ceiling! Only thing that stopped me from rolling out the window and into the clouds was the umbilical cord. They say the doctor fainted from the shock!"

"You're *still* quite shocking, love," Bronwyn said, giving her a reassuring pat on the back.

Millard, visible thanks to the coat and boots he wore, went to the boy. "What does your father think about all of this?" he said.

"Naturally, we don't want him to go," Bekhir said, "but how can we properly care for our son if we can't even *see* him? He wants to leave—and I wonder if perhaps he'd be better off among his own kind."

"Do you love him?" Millard asked bluntly. "Does he love you?"

Bekhir's brow furrowed. He was a man of traditional sensibilities, and the question made him uncomfortable. But after some hemming and hawing, he growled, "Of course. He's my child."

"Then *you* are his kind," said Millard. "The boy belongs with you, not us."

Bekhir was loath to show emotion in front of his men, but at this I saw his eyes flicker and his jaw tighten. He nodded, looked down at his son, and said, "Come on, then. Pick up your bag and let's go. Your mother'll have tea waiting."

"All right, Papa," the boy said, seeming at once disappointed and relieved.

"You'll be fine," Millard assured the boy. "Better than fine. And when this is all over, I'll look for you. There are more like us out there, and we'll find them one day, together."

"Promise?" the boy said, his eyes full of hope.

"I do," said Millard.

And with that the boy climbed back onto his father's horse, and we turned and walked through the gates into town.

CHAPTER SIX

*T*he town was named Coal. Not Coaltown or Coalville. Just Coal. The stuff was everywhere, piled in gritty drifts by the side doors of houses, wafting up from the chimneys as oily smoke, smeared on the overalls of men walking to work. We hurried past them toward the depot in a tight pack.

"Quickly now," Emma said. "No talking. Eyes down."

It was a well-established rule that we were to avoid unnecessary eye contact with normals, because looks could lead to conversations, and conversations to questions, and peculiar children found questions posed by normal adults difficult to answer in a way that didn't invite still more questions. Of course, if anything was going to invite questions, it was a group of bedraggled-looking children traveling alone during wartime—especially with a big, sharp-taloned bird of prey perched on one of the girls' shoulders—but the townspeople hardly seemed to notice us. They haunted the laundry lines and pub doorways of Coal's twisting lanes, drooping like wilted flowers, eyes flicking toward us and away again. They had other worries.

The train depot was so small I wondered if trains ever bothered stopping there. The only covered portion was the ticket counter, a little hut in the middle of an open-air platform. Inside the hut was a man asleep in a chair, bottle-thick bifocals slipping down his nose.

Emma rapped sharply on the window, startling the clerk awake. "Eight tickets to London!" she said. "We must be there this very afternoon."

The clerk peered at us through the glass. Took off his bifocals and wiped them clean and put them on again, just to make sure he was seeing properly. I'm sure we were a shocking sight: our clothes were mud-splotched, our hair greasy and sticking up at odd angles. We probably stank, too.

"So sorry," the clerk said. "The train is full."

I looked around. Aside from a few people dozing on benches, the depot was empty.

"That's absurd!" said Emma. "Sell us the tickets at once or I shall report you to the rail authority for child discrimination!"

I might've handled the clerk with a softer touch, but Emma had no patience for the self-important authority of petty bureaucrats.

"If there were any such statute," the clerk replied, his nose rising disdainfully, "it would certainly not apply to *you*. There's a war on, you know, and more important things to be hauled about her majesty's countryside than children and animals!" He gave Miss Peregrine a hard look. "Which aren't allowed in any case!"

A train hissed into the station and squealed to a stop. The conductor stuck his head out of one of its windows and shouted, "Eight-thirty to London! All aboard!" The bench-sleepers in the depot roused themselves and began to shuffle across the platform.

A man in a gray suit shoved past us to the window. He pushed money at the clerk, received a ticket in exchange, and hurried off toward the train.

"You said it was full!" Emma said, rapping hard on the glass. "You can't *do* that!"

"That gentleman bought a *first-class* ticket," the clerk said. "Now be gone with you, pestilent little beggars! Go find pockets to pick somewhere else!"

Horace stepped to the ticket window and said, "Beggars, by definition, do not carry large sums of money," and then he reached into his coat pocket and slapped a fat wad of bills down on the counter. "If it's first-class tickets you're selling, then that's what we'll have!"

The clerk sat up straight, gaping at the pile of money. The rest of us gaped too, baffled as to where Horace had gotten it. Riffling through the bills, the clerk said, "Why, this is enough to buy seats to an entire first-class car!"

"Then give us an entire car!" said Horace. "That way you can be sure we'll pick no one's pocket."

The clerk turned red and stammered, "Y-yes sir—sorry, sir— and I hope you won't take my previous comments as anything other than jest . . ."

"Just give us the blasted tickets so we can get on the train!"

"Right away, sir!"

The clerk slid a stack of first-class tickets toward us. "Enjoy your trip!" he said. "And please don't tell anyone I said so, sirs and madams, but if I were you, I'd hide that bird out of sight. The conductors won't like it, first-class tickets or not."

As we strode away from the counter with tickets in hand, Horace's chest puffed out like a peacock's.

"Where on earth did you get all that money?" said Emma.

"I rescued it from Miss Peregrine's dresser drawer before the house burned," Horace replied. "Tailored a special pocket in my coat to keep it safe."

"Horace, you're a genius!" said Bronwyn.

"Would a real genius have given away every cent of our money like that?" said Enoch. "Did we really need an *entire* first-class car?"

"No," said Horace, "but making that man look stupid felt good, didn't it?"

"I suppose it did," Enoch said.

"That's because the true purpose of money is to manipulate others and make them feel lesser than you."

"I'm not entirely sure about that," Emma said.

"Only kidding!" said Horace. "It's to buy clothes, of course."

We were about to board the train when the conductor stopped us. "Let's see your tickets!" he said, and he was reaching for the stack in Horace's hand when he noticed Bronwyn stuffing something into her coat. "What's that you've got there?" the conductor said, rounding on her suspiciously.

"What's what I've got where?" Bronwyn replied, trying to seem casual while holding her coat closed over a wriggling lump.

"In your coat there!" the conductor said. "Don't toy with me, girl."

"It's, ahhh . . ." Bronwyn tried to think fast and failed. "A bird?"

Emma's head fell. Enoch put a hand over his eyes and groaned.

"No pets on the train!" the conductor barked.

"But you don't understand," said Bronwyn. "I've had her ever since I was a child . . . and we *must* get on this train . . . and we paid *so much* for our tickets!"

"Rules are rules!" the conductor said, his patience fraying. "Do *not* toy with me!"

Emma's head bopped up, her face brightening. "A toy!" she said.

"Excuse me?" said the conductor.

"It isn't a *real* bird, conductor sir. We'd never dream of breaking the rules like that. It's my sister's favorite toy, you see, and she thinks you mean to take it away from her." She clasped her hands pitifully, imploring. "You wouldn't take away a child's favorite toy, would you?"

The conductor studied Bronwyn doubtfully. "She looks too old for toys, wouldn't you say?"

Emma leaned in and whispered, "She's a bit *delayed*, you see . . ."

Bronwyn frowned at this but had no choice but to play along. The conductor stepped toward her. "Let's see this toy, then."

Moment of truth. We held our breath as Bronwyn opened her coat, reached inside, and slowly withdrew Miss Peregrine. When I saw the bird, I thought for one terrible moment that she had died. Miss Peregrine had gone completely stiff, and lay in Bronwyn's hand with her eyes closed and legs sticking out rigidly. Then I realized she was just playing along.

"See?" Bronwyn said. "Birdy ain't real. She's stuffed."

"I saw it moving earlier!" the conductor said.

"It's a—ehm—a wind-up model," said Bronwyn. "Watch."

Bronwyn knelt down and set Miss Peregrine on the ground on her side, then reached under her wing and pretended to wind something. A moment later Miss Peregrine's eyes flew open and she began to toddle around, her head swiveling mechanically and legs kicking out as if spring-loaded. Finally she jerked to a stop and toppled over, stiff as a board. Truly an Oscar-worthy performance.

The conductor seemed almost—but not quite—convinced. "Well," he hemmed, "if it's a toy, you won't mind putting it away in your toy chest." He nodded at the trunk, which Bronwyn had set down on the platform.

Bronwyn hesitated. "It isn't a—"

"Yes, fine, that's no bother," said Emma, flipping open the trunk's latches. "Put it away now, sister!"

"But what if there's no *air* in there?" Bronwyn hissed at Emma.

"Then we'll poke some blessed *holes* in the side of it!" Emma hissed back.

Bronwyn picked up Miss Peregrine and set her gently inside the trunk. "Ever so sorry, ma'am," she whispered, lowering and then latching the lid.

The conductor finally took our tickets. "First class!" he said, surprised. "Your car's all the way down front." He pointed to the far end of the platform. "You'd best hurry!"

"*Now* he tells us!" said Emma, and we took off down the platform at a jog.

With a chug of steam and a metallic groan, the train began to move beside us. For now it was just inching along, but with each turn of its wheels it sped up a little more.

We came even with the first-class car. Bronwyn was first to

jump through the open door. She set her trunk down in the aisle and reached out a hand to help Olive on board.

Then, from behind us, a voice shouted, "Stop! Get away from there!"

It wasn't the conductor's voice. This one was deeper, more authoritative.

"I swear," Enoch said, "if *one more person* tries to stop us getting on this train . . ."

A gunshot rang out, and the sudden shock of it made my feet tangle. I stumbled out the doorway and back onto the platform.

"I said *stop!*" the voice bellowed again, and looking over my shoulder I saw a uniformed soldier standing on the platform, his knees bent in firing stance, rifle aimed at us. With a pair of loud cracks he volleyed two more bullets over our heads, just to drive his point home. "Off the train and on your knees!" he said, striding toward us.

I thought of making a run for it, but then I caught a glimpse of the soldier's eyes, and their bulging, pupil-less whites convinced me not to. He was a wight, and I knew he wouldn't think twice about shooting any one of us. Better not to give him an excuse.

Bronwyn and Olive must've been thinking along the same lines, because they got off the train and dropped to their knees alongside the rest of us.

So close, I thought. *We were* so *close.*

The train pulled out of the station without us, our best hope for saving Miss Peregrine steaming away into the distance.

And Miss Peregrine with it, I realized with a queasy jolt. Bronwyn had left her trunk on board the train! Something automatic took hold of me and I leapt up to chase down the train—but then the barrel of a rifle appeared just inches from my face, and I felt all the power drain from my muscles in an instant.

"Not. Another. *Step*," the soldier said.

I sank back to the ground.

We were on our knees, hands up, hearts hammering. The soldier circled us, tense, his rifle aimed and his finger on its trigger. It was the closest, longest look I'd gotten at a wight since Dr. Golan. He had on a standard-issue British army uniform—khaki shirt tucked into wool pants, black boots, helmet—but he wore them awkwardly, the pants crooked and the helmet seated too far back on his head, like a costume he wasn't used to wearing yet. He seemed nervous, too, his head cocking this way and that as he sized us up. He was outnumbered, and though we were just a bunch of unarmed children, we'd been responsible for the death of one wight and two hollowgast in the last three days. He was scared of us, and that, more than anything else, made me scared of him. His fear made him unpredictable.

He pulled a radio from his belt and chattered into it. There was a burst of static, and then a moment later an answer came back. It was all in code; I couldn't understand a word.

He ordered us to our feet. We stood.

"Where are we going?" Olive asked timidly.

"For a walk," he said. "A nice, orderly walk." He had a clipped, vowel-flattened way of speaking that told me he was from somewhere else but faking a British accent, though not particularly well. Wights were supposed to be masters of disguise, but this one was clearly not a star pupil.

"You will not fall out of line," he said, staring down each of us in turn. "You will not run. I have fifteen rounds in my clip—enough to put two holes in each of you. And don't think I don't see your jacket, invisible boy. Make me chase you and I'll slice off your invisible thumbs for souvenirs."

"Yes, sir," said Millard.

"No talking!" the soldier boomed. "Now *march*!"

We marched past the ticket booth, the clerk now gone, then down off the platform, out of the depot, and into the streets. Though the denizens of Coal hadn't given us a second glance when we'd come through town earlier, now their heads swiveled like owls as we trudged by in single file, at gunpoint. The soldier kept us in tight formation, barking at us when anyone strayed too far. I was at the rear, him behind me, and I could hear his ammunition belt clinking as we walked. We were heading back the way we'd come, straight out of town.

I dreamed up a dozen escape plans. We'd scatter. No—he'd shoot at least a few of us. Maybe someone could pretend to faint in the road, then the person behind would trip, and in the confusion—no, he was too disciplined to fall for anything like that. One of us would have to get close enough to take his gun away.

Me. I was closest. Maybe if I walked a little slower, let him catch up, then ran at him . . . but who was I kidding? I was no action hero. I was so scared I could hardly breathe. Anyway, he was ten whole yards behind me, and had his gun aimed right at my back. He'd shoot me the second I turned around, and I'd bleed out in the middle of the road. That was my idea of stupidity, not heroism.

A jeep zoomed up from behind and pulled alongside us, slowing to match our pace. There were two more soldiers in it, and though both wore mirrored sunglasses, I knew what was behind them. The wight in the passenger seat nodded to the one who'd captured us and gave a little salute—*Nice going!*—then turned to us and stared. From that moment he never took his eyes off us or his hands off his rifle.

Now we had escorts, and one rifle-wielding wight had become three. Any hope of escape I'd had was dashed.

We walked and walked, our shoes crunching on the gravel road, the jeep's engine grumbling beside us like a cheap lawnmower. The town receded and a farm sprang up on either side of the tree-lined road, its fields fallow and bare. The soldiers never exchanged a word. There was something robotic about them, as if their brains had been scooped out and replaced with wires. Wights were supposed to be brilliant, but these guys seemed like drones to me. Then I heard a drone in my ear, and looked up to see a bee circle my head and fly away.

Hugh, I thought. *What's he up to?* I looked for him in line, worried he might be planning something that would get us all shot—but I didn't see him.

I did a quick head count. *One-two-three-four-five-six*. In front of me was Emma, then Enoch, Horace, Olive, Millard, and Bronwyn.

Where was Hugh?

I nearly leapt into the air. Hugh wasn't here! That meant he hadn't been rounded up with the rest of us. He was still free! Maybe in the chaos at the depot he'd slipped down into the gap between the train and the platform, or hopped onto the train without the soldier noticing. I wondered if he was following us—wished I could look back at the road behind without giving him away.

I hoped he wasn't, because that might mean he was with Miss Peregrine. Otherwise, how would we ever find her again? And what if she ran out of air, locked in that trunk? And what did they do with suspiciously abandoned baggage in 1940, anyway?

My face flushed hot and my throat tightened. There were too many things to be terrified of, a hundred horror scenarios all vying for attention in my brain.

"Back in line!" the soldier behind me shouted, and I realized that it was me he was talking to—that in my fevered state I'd strayed too far from the center of the road. I hurried back to my place behind Emma, who gave me a pleading look over her shoulder—*Don't make him angry!*—and I promised myself I'd keep it together.

We walked on in edgy silence, tension humming through us like an electric current. I could see it in Emma as she clenched and unclenched her fists; in Enoch as he shook his head and muttered to himself; in Olive's uneven steps. It seemed like just a matter of time before one of us did something desperate and bullets started flying.

Then I heard Bronwyn gasp and I looked up, a horror scenario I hadn't yet imagined taking shape before my eyes. Three massive forms lay ahead of us, one in the road and two more in the field adjacent, just the other side of a shallow ditch. Heaps of black earth, I thought at first, refusing to see.

Then we got closer, and I couldn't pretend they were anything other than what they were: three horses dead in the road.

Olive screamed. Bronwyn instinctively went to comfort her—"Don't look, little magpie!"—and the soldier riding shotgun fired into the air. We dove to the ground and covered our heads.

"Do that again and you'll be lying in the ditch beside them!" he shouted.

As we returned to our feet, Emma angled toward me and breathed the word *Gypsies*, then nodded at the closest horse. I took her meaning: these were their horses. I even recognized the markings on one—white spots on its hind legs—and realized it was the very horse I'd been clinging to just an hour ago.

I felt like I was about to be sick.

It all came together, playing out like a movie in my head. The wights had done this—the same ones who'd raided our camp the night before. The Gypsies had met them along the road after leaving us at the edge of town. There'd been a skirmish, then a chase. The wights had shot the Gypsies' horses right out from under them.

I knew the wights had killed people—killed peculiar children, Miss Avocet had said—but the brutality of shooting these animals seemed to exceed even that evil. An hour ago they'd been some of the most fully alive creatures I'd ever seen—eyes gleaming with intelligence, bodies rippling with muscle, radiating heat—and now, thanks to the intervention of a few pieces of metal, they were nothing but heaps of cold meat. These proud, strong animals, shot down and left in the road like garbage.

I shook with fear, seethed with anger. I was sorry, too, that I'd been so unappreciative of them. What a spoiled, ungrateful ass I was.

Pull it together, I told myself. *Pull yourself together.*

Where were Bekhir and his men now? Where was his son? All I knew was that the wights were going to shoot us. I was sure of it now. These impostors in soldiers' costumes were nothing but animals themselves; more monstrous even than the hollowgast they controlled. The wights, at least, had minds that could reason—but they used that creative faculty to dismantle the world. To make living things into dead things. And for what? So that *they* might live a little longer. So that they might have a little more power over the world around them, and the creatures in it, for whom they cared so little.

Waste. Such a stupid waste.

And now they were going to waste us. Lead us to some killing field where we'd be interrogated and dumped. And if Hugh had been dumb enough to follow us—if the bee flying up and down our line meant he was nearby—then they'd kill him, too.

God help us all.

The fallen horses were well behind us when the soldiers ordered us to turn off the main road and down a narrow farm lane. It was hardly more than a footpath, just a few feet wide, so the soldiers who'd been riding alongside us had to park their jeep and walk, one in front and two behind. On either side of us the fields grew wild, bursting with flowering weeds and humming with late-summer insects.

A beautiful place to die.

After a while, a thatch-roofed shack came into sight at the edge of the fields. *That's where they'll do it*, I thought. *That's where they'll kill us.*

As we got closer, a door opened and a soldier stepped out of the shack. He was dressed differently than the ones around us: instead of a helmet he wore a black-brimmed officer's hat, and instead of a rifle he carried a holstered revolver.

This one was in charge.

He stood in the lane as we approached, rocking on his heels and flashing a pearly grin. "We meet at last!" he called out. "You've given us quite the go-round, but I knew we'd catch you in the end. Only a matter of time!" He had pudgy, boyish features, thin hair that was so blond it was almost white, and he was full of weird, chipper energy, like an overcaffeinated Cub Scout leader. But all I could think when I looked at him was: *Animal. Monster. Murderer.*

"Come in, come in," the officer said, pulling open the shack's door. "Friends of yours are waiting inside."

As his soldiers shoved us past him, I caught a glimpse of the name stitched on his shirt: WHITE. Like the color.

Mister White. A joke, maybe? Nothing about him seemed genuine; that least of all.

We were pushed inside, shouted into a corner. The shack's one room was bare of furniture and crowded with people. Bekhir and his men sat on the floor with their backs to the walls. They'd been treated badly; they were bruised, bleeding, and slouched in attitudes of defeat. A few were missing, including Bekhir's boy. Standing guard were two more soldiers—that made six altogether, including Mr. White and our escorts.

Bekhir caught my eye and nodded gravely. His cheeks were purpled with bruises. *I'm sorry*, he mouthed to me.

Mr. White saw our exchange and skipped over to Bekhir. "Aha! You recognize these children?"

"No," Bekhir said, looking down.

"No?" Mr. White feigned shock. "But you apologized to that one. You must know him, unless you make a habit of apologizing to strangers?"

"They aren't the ones you're looking for," Bekhir said.

"I think they are," said Mr. White. "I think these are the *very* children we've been looking for. And furthermore, I think they spent last night in your camp."

"I told you, I've never seen them before."

Mr. White clucked his tongue like a disapproving schoolmarm. "Gypsy, do you remember what I promised to do if I found out you were lying to me?" He unsheathed a knife from his belt and held it against Bekhir's cheek. "That's right. I promised to cut your lying tongue out and feed it to my dog. And I always keep my promises."

Bekhir met Mr. White's blank stare and stared back, unflinching. The seconds spun out in unbearable silence. My eyes were fixed on the knife. Finally, Mr. White cracked a smile and stood smartly upright again, breaking the spell. "But," he said cheerily, "first things first!" He turned to face the soldiers who had escorted us. "Which of you has their bird?"

The soldiers looked at one another. One shook his head, then another.

"We didn't see it," said the one who'd taken us prisoner at the depot.

Mr. White's smile faltered. He knelt down next to Bekhir. "You told me they had the bird with them," he said.

Bekhir shrugged. "Birds have wings. They come and go."

Mr. White stabbed Bekhir in the thigh. Just like that: quick and emotionless, the blade going in and out. Bekhir howled in surprise and pain and rolled onto his side, gripping his leg as blood began to flow.

Horace fainted and slid to the floor. Olive gasped and covered her eyes.

"That's twice you've lied to me," Mr. White said, wiping the blade clean on a handkerchief.

The rest of us clenched our teeth and held our tongues, but I could see Emma plotting revenge already, clasping her hands together behind her back, getting them nice and warm.

Mr. White dropped the bloody handkerchief on the floor, slid the knife back into its sheath, and stood up to face us. He was almost but not quite smiling, his eyes wide, unibrow raised in a capital M. "Where is your bird?" he asked calmly. The nicer he pretended to be, the more it scared the hell out of me.

"She flew away," Emma said bitterly. "Just like that man told you."

I wished she hadn't said anything; now I was afraid he'd single her out for torment.

Mr. White stepped toward Emma and said, "Her wing was injured. You were seen with her just yesterday. She couldn't be far from here." He cleared his throat. "I'll ask you again."

"She died," I said. "We threw her in a river."

Maybe if I were a bigger pain in his butt than Emma, he'd forget she'd ever spoken.

Mr. White sighed. His right hand glided across his holstered gun, lingered over the handle of his knife, then came to rest on his belt's brass buckle. He lowered his voice, as if what he was about to say were meant for my ears only.

"I see what the trouble is. You believe there's nothing to be gained by being honest with me. That we will kill you regardless of what you do or say. I need you to know this is not the case. However, in the spirit of total honesty, I will say this: you shouldn't have made us chase you. That was a mistake. This could've been so much easier, but now everyone's *angry*, you see, because you've wasted so much of our time."

He flicked a finger toward his soldiers. "These men? They'd like very much to hurt you. I, on the other hand, am able to consider things from your point of view. We *do* seem frightening, I understand that. Our first meeting, on board my submarine, was regrettably uncivil. What's more, your ymbrynes have been poisoning you with misinformation about us for generations. So it's only natural that you'd run. In light of all that, I'm willing to make you what I believe to be a reasonable offer. Show us to the bird right now, and rather than hurting you, we'll send you off to a nice facility where you'll be well looked after. Fed every day, each with your own bed . . . a place no more restrictive than that ridiculous loop you've been hiding in all these years."

Mr. White looked at his men and laughed. "Can you believe they spent the last—what is it, seventy years?—on a tiny island, living the same day over and over? Worse than any prison camp I can think of. It would've been so much easier to cooperate!" He shrugged, looked back at us. "But pride, venal pride, got the better of you. And to think, all this time we could've been working together toward a common good!"

"Working together?" said Emma. "You hunted us! Sent monsters to kill us!"

Damn it, I thought. *Keep quiet.*

Mr. White made a sad puppy-dog face. "Monsters?" he said. "That hurts. That's *me* you're talking about, you know! Me and all my men here, before we evolved. I'll try not to take your slight personally, though. The adolescent phase is rarely attractive, whatever the species." He clapped his hands sharply, which made me jump. "Now then, down to business!"

He raked us with a slow, icy stare, as if scanning our ranks for weakness. Which of us would crack first? Which would actually tell him the truth about where Miss Peregrine was?

Mr. White zeroed in on Horace. He'd recovered from his faint but was still on the floor, crouched and shaking. Mr. White took a decisive step toward him. Horace flinched at the click of his boots.

"Stand up, boy."

Horace didn't move.

"Someone get him up."

A soldier yanked Horace up roughly by his arm. Horace cowered before Mr. White, his eyes on the floor.

"What's your name, boy?"

"Huh-huh-Horace . . ."

"Well, Huh-Horace, you seem like someone with abundant common sense. So I'll let *you* choose."

Horace raised his head slightly. "Choose . . . ?"

Mr. White unsheathed the knife from his belt and pointed it at the Gypsies. "Which of these men to kill first. Unless, of course, you'd like to tell me where your ymbryne is. Then no one has to die."

Horace squeezed his eyes shut, as if he could simply wish himself away from here.

"Or," Mr. White said, "if you'd rather not choose one of them, I'd be happy to choose one of *you*. Would you rather do that?"

"No!"

"Then *tell me*!" Mr. White thundered, his lips snarling back to reveal gleaming teeth.

"Don't tell them anything, *syndrigasti*!" shouted Bekhir—and then one of the soldiers kicked him in the stomach, and he groaned and fell quiet.

Mr. White reached out and grabbed Horace by the chin, trying to force him to look right into his horrible blank eyes. "You'll tell me, won't you? You'll tell me, and I won't hurt you."

"Yes," Horace said, still squeezing his eyes shut—still wishing himself gone, yet still here.

"Yes, *what*?"

Horace drew a shaking breath. "Yes, I'll tell you."

"Don't!" shouted Emma.

Oh God, I thought. *He's going to give her up. He's too weak.*

We should've left him at the menagerie . . .

"Shh," Mr. White hissed in his ear. "Don't listen to them. Now, go ahead, son. Tell me where that bird is."

"She's in the drawer," said Horace.

Mr. White's unibrow knit together. "The drawer. What drawer?"

"Same one she's always been in," said Horace.

He shook Horace by the jaw and shouted, "*What drawer?!*"

Horace started to say something, then closed his mouth. Swallowed hard. Stiffened his back. Then his eyes came open and he looked hard into Mr. White's and said, "Your mother's knickers drawer," and he spat right in Mr. White's face.

Mr. White slammed Horace in the side of the head with the handle of his knife. Olive screamed and several of us flinched in vicarious pain as Horace dropped to the floor like a sack of potatoes, loose change and train tickets spilling out of his pockets.

"What's this?" said Mr. White, bending down to look.

"I caught them trying to catch a train," said the soldier who'd caught us.

"Why are you just telling me this *now*?"

The soldier faltered. "I thought—"

"Never mind," Mr. White said. "Go intercept it. Now."

"Sir?"

Mr. White glanced at the ticket, then at his watch. "The eight-thirty to London makes a long stop at Porthmadog. If you're quick, it'll be waiting for you there. Search it from front to back—starting with first class."

The soldier saluted him and ran outside.

Mr. White turned to the other soldiers. "Search the rest of them," he said. "Let's see if they're carrying anything else of interest. If they resist, shoot them."

While two soldiers with rifles covered us, a third went from peculiar to peculiar, rooting through our pockets. Most of us had nothing but crumbs and lint, but the soldier found an ivory comb on Bronwyn—"Please, it belonged to my mother!" she begged, but he only laughed and said, "She might've taught you how to use it, mannish girl!"

Enoch was carrying a small bag of worm-packed grave dirt, which the soldier opened, sniffed, and dropped in disgust. In my pocket he found my dead cell phone. Emma saw it clatter to the floor and looked at me strangely, wondering why I still had it. Horace lay unmoving on the floor, either knocked out or playing possum. Then it was Emma's turn, but she wasn't having it. When the soldier came toward her, she snarled, "Lay a hand on me and I'll burn it off!"

"Please, hold your fire!" he said, and broke out laughing. "Sorry, couldn't resist."

"I'm not joking," Emma said, and she took her hands out from behind her back. They were glowing red, and even from three feet away I could feel the heat they gave off.

The soldier jumped out of her reach. "Hot touch and a temper to match!" he said. "I like that in a woman. But burn me and Clark there'll spackle the wall with your brainy bits."

The soldier he'd indicated pressed the barrel of his rifle to Emma's head. Emma squeezed her eyes shut, her chest rising and falling fast. Then she lowered her hands and folded them behind her back. She was positively vibrating with anger.

So was I.

"Careful, now," the soldier warned her. "No sudden moves."

My fists clenched as I watched him slide his hands up and down her legs, then run his fingers under the neckline of her dress, all with unnecessary slowness and a leering grin. I'd never felt so powerless in all my life, not even when we were trapped in that animal cage.

"She doesn't have anything!" I shouted. "Leave her alone!"

I was ignored.

"I like this one," the soldier said to Mr. White. "I think we should keep her awhile. For . . . science."

Mr. White grimaced. "You are a disgusting specimen, corporal.

But I agree with you—she is fascinating. I've heard about you, you know," he said to Emma. "I'd give anything to do what you can do. If only we could bottle those hands of yours . . ."

Mr. White smiled weirdly before turning back to the soldier. "Finish up," he snapped, "we don't have all day."

"With pleasure," the soldier replied, and then he stood, dragging his hands up Emma's torso as he rose.

What happened next seemed to unfold in slow motion. I could see that this disgusting letch was about to lean in and give Emma a kiss. I could also see that, behind her back, Emma's hands were now lined with flame. I knew where this was going: the second his lips got near her, she was going to reach around and melt his face—even if it meant taking a bullet. She'd reached a breaking point.

So had I.

I tensed, ready to fight. These, I was convinced, were our last moments. But we'd live them on our own terms—and if we were going to die, by God, we'd take a few wights with us along the way.

The soldier slid his hands around Emma's waist. The barrel of another's rifle dug into her forehead. She seemed to be pushing back against it, daring it to fire. Behind her back I saw her hands begin to spread, white-hot flame tracing along each of her fingers.

Here we go—

Then *CRACK!*—the report of a gun, stunning and sharp.

I shut down, blacked out for a second.

When my sight came back, Emma was still standing. Her head still intact. The rifle that had been pressed against it was pointed down now, and the soldier who'd been about to kiss her had pulled away and spun around to face the window.

The gunshot had come from outside.

Every nerve in my body had gone numb, tingling with adrenaline.

"What was that?" said Mr. White, rushing to the window.

I could see through the glass over his shoulder. The soldier who'd gone to intercept the train was standing outside, waist-deep in wildflowers. His back was to us, his rifle aimed at the field.

Mr. White reached through the bars that covered the window and pushed it open. "What the hell are you shooting at?" he shouted. "Why are you still here?"

The soldier didn't move, didn't speak. The field was alive with the whine of insects, and briefly, that's all we could hear.

"Corporal Brown!" bellowed Mr. White.

The man turned slowly, unsteady on his feet. The rifle slipped from his hands and fell into the tall grass. He took a few doddering steps forward.

Mr. White took the revolver from his holster and pointed it out the window at Brown. "Say something, damn you!"

Brown opened his mouth and tried to speak—but where his voice should've been, an eerie droning noise came echoing up from his guts, mimicking the sound that was everywhere in the fields around him.

It was the sound of bees. Hundreds, thousands of them. Next came the bees themselves: just a few at first, drifting through his parted lips. Then some power beyond his own seemed to take hold of him: his shoulders pulled back and his chest pressed forward and his jaws ratcheted wide open, and from his gaping mouth there poured forth such a dense stream of bees that they were like one solid object; a long, fat hose of insects unspooling endlessly from his throat.

Mr. White stumbled back from the window, horrified and baffled.

Out in the field, Brown collapsed in a cloud of stinging insects. As his body fell, another was revealed behind him.

It was a boy.

Hugh.

He stood defiantly, staring through the window. The insects swung around him in a great, whirling sphere. The fields were packed with them—honeybees and hornets, wasps and yellow jackets, stinging things I couldn't know or name —and every last one of them seemed to be at his command.

Mr. White raised his gun and fired. Emptied his clip.

Hugh went down, disappearing in the grass. I didn't know whether he had fallen to the ground or dived to it. Then three other soldiers ran to the window, and while Bronwyn cried "Please, don't kill him!" they raked the field with bullets, filling our ears with the thunder of their guns.

Then there were bees in the room. A dozen, maybe, furious and flinging themselves at the soldiers.

"Shut the window!" Mr. White screamed, swatting the air around him.

A soldier slammed the window closed. They all went to work smacking the bees that had gotten in. While they were busy with that, more and more collected outside—a giant, seething blanket of them pulsing against the other side of the glass—so many that by the time Mr. White and his men had finished killing the bees *inside* the room, the ones outside had nearly shut out the sun.

The soldiers clustered in the middle of the floor, backs together, rifles bristling out like porcupine quills. It was dark and hot, and the alien whine of a million manic bees reverberated through the room like something out of a nightmare.

"Make them leave us alone!" Mr. White shouted, his voice cracking, desperate.

As if anyone but Hugh could do that—if he was still alive.

"I'll make you another offer," said Bekhir, pulling himself to his feet using the window bars, his hobbled silhouette outlined against the dark glass. "Put down your guns or I open this window."

Mr. White spun to face him. "Even a Gypsy wouldn't be stupid enough to do that."

"You think too highly of us," Bekhir said, sliding his fingers toward the handle.

The soldiers raised their rifles.

"Go ahead," said Bekhir. "Shoot."

"Don't, you'll break the glass!" Mr. White shouted. "Grab him!"

Two soldiers threw down their rifles and lunged at Bekhir, but not before he punched his fist through the glass.

The entire window shattered. Bees flushed into the room. Chaos erupted—screams, gunfire, shoving—though I could hardly hear it over the roar of the insects, which seemed to fill not just my ears but every pore of my body.

People were climbing over one another to get out. To my right I saw Bronwyn push Olive to the floor and cover her with her body. Emma shouted "Get down!" and we ducked for cover as bees tumbled over our skin, our hair. I waited to die, for the bees to cover every exposed inch of me in stings that would shut down my nervous system.

Someone kicked open the door. Light blasted in. A dozen boots thundered across the floorboards.

It got quiet. I slowly uncovered my head.

The bees were gone. So were the soldiers.

Then, from outside, a chorus of panicked screams. I jumped up and rushed to the shattered window, where a knot of Gypsies and peculiars were already gathered, peering out.

At first I didn't see the soldiers at all—just a giant, swirling mass of insects, so dense it was opaque, about fifty feet down the footpath.

The screams were coming from inside it.

Then, one by one, the screamers fell silent. When it was all over, the cloud of bees began to spread and scatter, unveiling the bodies of Mr. White and his men. They lay clustered in the low grass, dead or nearly so.

Twenty seconds later, their killers were gone, their monstrous hum fading as they settled back into the fields. In their wake fell a strange and bucolic calm, as if it were just another summer day, and nothing out of the ordinary had happened.

Emma counted the soldiers' bodies on her fingers. "Six. That's all of them," she said. "It's over."

I put my arms around her, shaking with gratitude and disbelief.

"Which of you are hurt?" said Bronwyn, looking around frantically. Those last moments had been crazy—countless bees, gunfire in the dark. We checked ourselves for holes. Horace was dazed but conscious, a trickle of blood running from his temple. Bekhir's stab wound was deep but would heal. The rest of us were shaken but unhurt—and miraculously, not a single one of us was bee-stung.

"When you broke the window," I said to Bekhir, "how did you know the bees wouldn't attack us?"

"I didn't," he said. "Luckily, your friend's power is strong."

Our friend . . .

Emma pulled away from me suddenly. "Oh my God!" she gasped. "Hugh!"

In all the chaos, we'd forgotten about him. He was probably bleeding to death right now, somewhere in the tall grass. But just as we were about to tear outside and look for him, he appeared in the doorway—bedraggled and grass-stained, but smiling.

"Hugh!" Olive cried, rushing to him. "You're alive!"

"I am!" he said heartily. "Are all of you?"

"Thanks to you we are!" Bronwyn said. "Three cheers for Hugh!"

"You're our man in a pinch, Hugh!" cried Horace.

"Nowhere am I deadlier than in a field of wildflowers," Hugh said, enjoying the attention.

"Sorry about all the times I made fun of your peculiarity," said Enoch. "I suppose it's not so useless."

"Additionally," said Millard, "I'd like to compliment Hugh on his impeccable timing. Really, if you'd arrived just a few seconds later . . ."

Hugh explained how he'd evaded capture at the depot by slipping down between the train and the platform—just like I'd thought.

He'd sent one of his bees trailing after us, which allowed him to follow from a careful distance. "Then it was just a matter of finding the perfect time to strike," he said proudly, as if victory had been assured from the moment he decided to save us.

"And if you hadn't accidentally stumbled across a field packed with bees?" Enoch said.

Hugh dug something from his pocket and held it up: a peculiar chicken egg. "Plan B," he said.

Bekhir hobbled to Hugh and shook his hand. "Young man," he said, "we owe you our lives."

"What about your peculiar boy?" Millard asked Bekhir.

"He managed to escape with two of my men, thank God. We lost three fine animals today, but no people." Bekhir bowed to Hugh, and I thought for a moment he might even take Hugh's hand and kiss it. "You must allow us to repay you!"

Hugh blushed. "There's no need, I assure you—"

"And no time, either," said Emma, pushing Hugh out the door. "We have a train to catch!"

Those of us who hadn't yet realized Miss Peregrine was gone went pale.

"We'll take their jeep," said Millard. "If we're lucky—and if that wight was correct—we might just be able to catch the train during its stopover in Porthmadog."

"I know a shortcut," Bekhir said, and he drew a simple map in the dirt with his shoe.

We thanked the Gyspies. I told Bekhir we were sorry we'd caused them so much trouble, and he unleashed a big, booming laugh and waved us on down the path. "We'll meet again, *syndrigasti*," he said. "I'm certain of it!"

*   *   *

We squeezed into the wights' jeep, eight kids packed like sardines into a vehicle built for three. Because I was the only one who'd driven a car before, I took the wheel. I spent way too long figuring out how to start the damn thing—not with a key, it turned out, but by pushing a button on the floor—and then there was the matter of shifting gears; I'd only driven a manual transmission a few times, and always with my dad coaching me from the passenger seat. Despite all that, after a minute or two we were—bumpily, jerkily, somewhat hesitatingly—on our way.

I stomped the accelerator and drove as fast as the overloaded jeep would take us, while Millard shouted directions and everyone else held on for dear life. We reached the town of Porthmadog twenty minutes later, the train's whistle blowing as we sped down the main street toward the station. We came to a skidding stop by the depot and tumbled out. I didn't even bother to kill the engine. Racing through the station like cheetahs after a gazelle, we leapt on board the last car of the train just as it was pulling out of the station.

We stood doubled over and panting in the aisle while astonished passengers pretended not to stare. Sweating, dirty, and disheveled—we must've been a sight.

"We made it," Emma gasped. "I can't believe we made it."

"I can't believe I drove stick," I said.

The conductor appeared. "You're back," he said with a beleaguered sigh. "I trust you still have your tickets?"

Horace fished them from his pocket in a wad.

"This way to your cabin," said the conductor.

"Our trunk!" Bronwyn said, clutching at the conductor's elbow. "Is it still there?"

The conductor pried his arm away. "I tried taking it to lost and found. Couldn't move the blessed thing an inch."

We ran from car to car until we reached the first-class cabin, where we found Bronwyn's trunk sitting just where she'd left it. She rushed to it and threw open the latches, then the lid.

Miss Peregrine wasn't inside.

I had a mini heart attack.

"My bird!" Bronwyn cried. "Where's my bird?!"

"Calm down, it's right here," said the conductor, and he pointed above our heads. Miss Peregrine was perched on a luggage rack, fast asleep.

Bronwyn stumbled back against the wall, so relieved she nearly fainted. "How did she get up *there*?"

The conductor raised an eyebrow. "It's a *very* lifelike toy." He turned and went to the door, then stopped and said, "By the way, where can I get one? My daughter would just love it."

"I'm afraid she's one of a kind," Bronwyn said, and she took Miss Peregrine down and hugged her to her chest.

* * *

After all we'd been through over the past few days—not to mention the past few hours—the luxury of the first-class cabin came as a shock. Our car had plush leather couches, a dining table, and wide picture windows. It looked like a rich man's living room, and we had it all to ourselves.

We took turns washing up in the wood-paneled bathroom, then availed ourselves of the dining menu. "Order anything you like," Enoch said, picking up a telephone that was attached to the arm of a reclining chair. "Hello, do you have goose liver pâté? I should like all of it. Yes, all that you have. And toast triangles."

No one said anything about what had happened. It was too much, too awful, and for now we just wanted to recover and forget. There was so much else to be done, so many more dangers left to reckon with.

We settled in for the journey. Outside, Porthmadog's squat houses shrank away and Miss Wren's mountain came into view, rising grayly above the hills. While the others drifted into conversations, my nose stayed glued to the window, and the endless unfolding *thereness* of 1940 beyond it—1940 being a place that had until recently been merely pocket-sized in my experience, no wider than a tiny island, and a place I could leave any time I wished by passing through the dark belly of Cairnholm's cairn. Since leaving the island, though, it had become a world, a whole world of marshy forests and smoke-wreathed towns and valleys crisscrossed with shining rivers; and of people and things that looked old but weren't yet, like props and ex-tras in some elaborately staged but plotless period movie—all of it flashing by and by and by out my window like a dream without end.

I fell asleep and woke, fell asleep and woke, the train's rhythm hypnotizing me into a hazy state in which it was easy to forget that I was more than just a passive viewer, my window more than just a movie screen; that *out there* was every bit as real as in here. Then, slowly, I remembered how I'd come to be part of this: my grandfa-ther; the island; the children. The pretty, flint-eyed girl next to me, her hand resting atop mine.

"Am I really here?" I asked her.

"Go back to sleep," she said.

"Do you think we'll be all right?"

She kissed me on the tip of my nose.

"Go back to sleep."

CHAPTER SEVEN

*M*ore terrible dreams, all mixed up, fading in and out of one another. Snippets of horrors from recent days: the steel eye of a gun barrel staring me down from close range; a road strewn with fallen horses; a hollowgast's tongues straining toward me across a chasm; that awful, grinning wight and his empty eyes.

Then this: I'm back home again, but I'm a ghost. I drift down my street, through my front door, into my house. I find my father asleep at the kitchen table, a cordless phone clutched to his chest.

I'm not dead, I say, but my words don't make sound.

I find my mother sitting on the edge of her bed, still in night-clothes, staring out the window at a pale afternoon. She's gaunt, wrung out from crying. I reach out to touch her shoulder, but my hand passes right through it.

Then I'm at my own funeral, looking up from my grave at a rectangle of gray sky.

My three uncles peer down, their fat necks bulging from starched white collars.

Uncle Les: *What a pity. Right?*

Uncle Jack: *You really gotta feel for Frank and Maryann right now.*

Uncle Les: *Yeah. What're people gonna think?*

Uncle Bobby: *They'll think the kid had a screw loose. Which he did.*

Uncle Jack: *I knew it, though. That he'd pull something like this one day. He had that look, you know? Just a little . . .*

Uncle Bobby: *Screwy.*

Uncle Les: *That comes from his dad's side of the family, not ours.*

Uncle Jack: *Still. Terrible.*

Uncle Bobby: *Yeah.*

Uncle Jack: . . .

Uncle Les: . . .

Uncle Bobby: *Buffet?*

My uncles shuffle away. Ricky comes along, his green hair extra spiked for the occasion.

Bro. Now that you're dead, can I have your bike?

I try to shout: *I'm not dead!*

I am just far away

I'm sorry

But the words echo back at me, trapped inside my head.

The minister peers down. It's Golan, holding a Bible, dressed in robes. He grins.

We're waiting for you, Jacob.

A shovelful of dirt rains down on me.

We're waiting.

*   *   *

I bolted upright, suddenly awake, my mouth dry as paper. Emma was next to me, hands on my shoulders. "Jacob! Thank God—you gave us a scare!"

"I did?"

"You were having a nightmare," said Millard. He was seated across from us, looking like an empty suit of clothes starched into position. "Talking in your sleep, too."

"I was?"

Emma dabbed sweat from my forehead with one of the first-class napkins. (Real cloth!) "You were," she said. "But it sounded like gobbledygook. I couldn't understand a word."

I looked around self-consciously, but no else seemed to have noticed. The other children were spread throughout the car, catnapping, daydreaming out the window, or playing cards.

I sincerely hoped I was not starting to lose it.

"Do you often have nightmares?" asked Millard. "You should describe them to Horace. He's good at sussing hidden meanings from dreams."

Emma rubbed my arm. "You sure you're all right?"

"I'm fine," I said, and because I don't like being fussed over, I changed the subject. Seeing that Millard had the *Tales of the Peculiar* open in his lap, I said, "Doing some light reading?"

"Studying," he replied. "And to think I once dismissed these as just stories for children. They are, in fact, extraordinarily complex—cunning, even—in the way they conceal secret information about peculiardom. It would take me years, probably, to decode them all."

"But what good is that to us now?" Emma said. "What good are loops if they can be breached by hollowgast? Even the secret ones in that book will be found out eventually."

"Maybe it was just the one loop that was breached," I said hopefully. "Maybe the hollow in Miss Wren's loop was a freak, somehow."

"A peculiar hollow!" said Millard. "That's amusing—but no. He was no accident. I'm certain these 'enhanced' hollows were an integral part of the assault on our loops."

"But how?" said Emma. "What's changed about hollows that they can get into loops now?"

"That's something I've been thinking about a great deal," said Millard. "We don't know a lot about hollows, having never had the chance to examine one in a controlled setting. But it's thought that, like normals, they lack something which you and I and everyone in this train car possesses—some essential peculiarness—which is what allows us to interact with loops; to bind with and be absorbed into them."

"Like a key," I said.

"Something like that," said Millard. "Some believe that, like blood or spinal fluid, our peculiarness has physical substance. Others think it's inside us but insubstantial. A second soul."

"Huh," I said. I liked this idea: that peculiarness wasn't a deficiency, but an abundance; that it wasn't we who lacked something normals had, but they who lacked peculiarness. That we were more, not less.

"I hate all that crackpot stuff," said Emma. "The idea that you could capture the second soul in a jar? Gives me the quivers."

"And yet, over the years, some attempts have been made to do just this," said Millard. "What did that wight soldier say to you, Emma? 'I wish I could bottle what you have,' or something to that effect?"

Emma shuddered. "Don't remind me."

"The theory goes that if somehow our peculiar essence could be distilled and captured—in a bottle, as he said, or more likely a petri dish—then perhaps that essence could also be transferred from one being to another. If this were possible, imagine the black market in peculiar souls that might spring up among the wealthy and unscrupulous. Peculiarities like your spark or Bronwyn's great strength sold to the highest bidder!"

"That's disgusting," I said.

"Most peculiars agree with you," said Millard, "which is why such research was outlawed many years ago."

"As if the wights cared about our laws," said Emma.

"But the whole idea seems crazy," I said. "It couldn't really work, could it?"

"I didn't think so," said Millard. "At least, not until yesterday. Now I'm not so sure."

"Because of the hollow in the menagerie loop?"

"Right. Before yesterday I wasn't even certain I believed in a 'second soul.' To my mind, there was only one compelling argument for its existence: that when a hollowgast consumes enough of us, it transforms into a different sort of creature—one that can travel through time loops."

"It becomes a wight," I said.

"Yes," he said. "But only if it consumes *peculiars*. It can eat as many normals as it likes and it will never turn into a wight. Therefore, we must have something normals lack."

"But that hollow at the menagerie didn't become a wight," said Emma. "It became a hollow that could enter loops."

"Which makes me wonder if the wights have been tinkering with nature," said Millard, "vis-à-vis the transference of peculiar souls."

"I don't even want to think about it," said Emma. "Can we please, *please* talk about something else?"

"But where would they even *get* the souls?" I asked. "And how?"

"That's it, I'm sitting somewhere else," Emma said, and she got up to find another seat.

Millard and I rode in silence for a while. I couldn't stop imagining being strapped to a table while a cabal of evil doctors removed my soul. How would they do it? With a needle? A knife?

To derail this morbid train of thought, I tried changing the subject again. "How did we all get to be peculiar in the first place?" I asked.

"No one's certain," Millard answered. "There are legends, though."

"Like what?"

"Some people believe we're descended from a handful of peculiars who lived a long, long time ago," he said. "They were very powerful—and enormous, like the stone giant we found."

I said, "Why are we so small, then, if we used to be giants?"

"The story goes that over the years, as we multiplied, our power diluted. As we became less powerful, we got smaller, too."

"That's all pretty hard to swallow," I said. "I feel about as powerful as an ant."

"Ants are quite powerful, actually, relative to their size."

"You know what I mean," I said. "The thing I really don't get is, why *me*? I never asked to be this way. Who decided?"

It was a rhetorical question; I wasn't really expecting an answer, but Millard gave me one anyway. "To quote a famous peculiar: 'At the heart of nature's mystery lies another mystery.'"

"Who said that?"

"We know him as Perplexus Anomalous. An invented name, probably, for a great thinker and philosopher. Perplexus was a cartographer, too. He drew the very first edition of the Map of Days, a thousand-something years ago."

I chuckled. "You talk like a teacher sometimes. Has anyone ever told you that?"

"All the time," Millard said. "I would've liked to try my hand at teaching. If I hadn't been born like this."

"You would've been great at it."

"Thank you," he said. Then he went quiet, and in the silence I could feel him dreaming it: scenes from a life that might've been. After a while he said, "I don't want you to think that I don't like being invisible. I do. I love being peculiar, Jacob—it's the very core of who I am. But there are days I wish I could turn it off."

"I know what you mean," I said. But of course I didn't. My peculiarity had its challenges, but at least I could participate in society.

The door to our compartment slid open. Millard quickly flipped up the hood of his jacket to hide his face—or rather, his apparent lack of one.

A young woman stood in the door. She wore a uniform and held a box of goods for sale. "Cigarettes?" she asked. "Chocolate?"

"No, thanks," I said.

She looked at me. "You're an American."

"Afraid so."

She gave me a pitying smile. "Hope you're having a nice trip. You picked an awkward time to visit Britain."

I laughed. "So I've been told."

She went out. Millard shifted his body to watch her go. "Pretty," he said distantly.

It occurred to me that it had probably been a lot of years since he'd seen a girl outside of those few who lived on Cairnholm. But what chance would someone like him have with a normal girl, anyway?

"Don't look at me like that," he said.

It hadn't occurred to me that I'd been looking at him any particular way. "Like what?"

"Like you feel bad for me."

"I don't," I said.

But I did.

Then Millard stood up from his seat, took off his coat, and disappeared. I didn't see him again for a while.

*   *   *

The hours rolled on, and the children passed them by telling stories. They told stories about famous peculiars and about Miss Peregrine in the strange, exciting, early days of her loop, and eventually they came around to telling their own stories. Some I had heard before—like how Enoch had raised the dead in his father's funeral parlor, or the way Bronwyn, at the tender age of ten, had snapped her abusive stepfather's neck without quite meaning to—but others were new to me. For as old as they were, the kids didn't often lapse into bouts of nostalgia.

Horace's dreams had started when he was just six, but he didn't realize they were predictive of anything until two years later, when one night he dreamed about the sinking of the *Lusitania* and the next day heard about it on the radio. Hugh, from a young age, had loved honey more than any other food, and at five he'd started eating honeycomb along with it—so ravenously that the first time he accidentally swallowed a bee, he didn't notice until he felt it buzzing around in his stomach. "The bee didn't seem to mind a bit," Hugh said, "so I shrugged and went on eating. Pretty soon I had a whole hive down there." When the bees needed to pollinate, he'd gone to find a field of blooming flowers, and that's where he met Fiona, who was sleeping among them.

Hugh told her story, too. Fiona was a refugee from Ireland, he said, where she'd been growing food for the people in her village during the famine of the 1840s—until she was accused of being a witch and chased out. This is something Hugh had gleaned only after years of subtle, nonverbal communication with Fiona, who didn't speak not because she couldn't, Hugh said, but "because the things she'd witnessed in the famine were so horrific they stole her voice away."

Then it was Emma's turn, but she had no interest in telling her story.

"Why not?" whined Olive. "Come on, tell about when you found out you were peculiar!"

"It's ancient history," Emma muttered, "relevant to nothing. And hadn't we better be thinking about the future instead of the past?"

"Someone's being a grumplepuss," said Olive.

Emma got up and left, heading to the back of the car where no one would bother her. I let a minute or two pass so that she wouldn't feel hounded, then went and sat next to her. She saw me coming and hid behind a newspaper, pretending to read.

"Because I don't care to discuss it," she said from behind the paper. "That's why!"

"I didn't say anything."

"Yes, but you were going to ask, so I saved you the trouble."

"Just to make it fair," I said, "I'll tell you something about me first."

She peeked over the top of the paper, slightly intrigued. "But don't I know everything about you already?"

"Ha," I said. "Not hardly."

"All right, then tell me three things about you I don't know. Dark secrets only, please. Quickly, now!"

I racked my brain for interesting factoids about myself, but I could only think of embarrassing ones. "Okay, one. When I was little, I was really sensitive to seeing violence on TV. I didn't understand that it wasn't real. Even if it was just a cartoon mouse punching a cartoon cat, I would freak out and start crying."

Her newspaper came down some. "Bless your tender soul!" she said. "And now look at you—impaling monstrous creatures right through their leaky eyeballs."

"Two," I said. "I was born on Halloween, and until I was eight years old my parents had me convinced that the candy people gave out when I knocked on their doors was birthday presents."

"Hmm," she said, lowering the paper a little more. "That one was only middlingly dark. You may continue nevertheless."

"Three. When we first met, I was convinced you were about to cut my throat. But scared as I was, there was this tiny voice in my head saying: *If this is the last face you ever see, at least it's a beautiful one.*"

The paper fell to her lap. "Jacob, that's . . ." She looked at the floor, then out the window, then back at me. "What a sweet thing to say."

"It's true," I said, and slid my hand across the seat to hers. "Okay, your turn."

"I'm not trying to hide anything, you know. It's just that those musty stories make me feel ten years old again, and unwanted. That never goes away, no matter how many magical summer days have come between."

That hurt was still with her, raw even all these years later.

"I want to know you," I said. "Who you are, where you come

from. That's all."

She shifted uncomfortably. "I never told you about my parents?"

"All I know I heard from Golan, that night in the icehouse. He said they gave you away to a traveling circus?"

"No, not quite." She slid down in her seat, her voice falling to a whisper. "I suppose it's better for you to know the truth than rumors and speculation. So, here goes.

"I started manifesting when I was just ten. Kept setting my bed on fire in my sleep, until my parents took away all my sheets and made me lie on a bare metal cot in a bare room with nothing flammable at all in it. They thought I was a pyromaniac and a liar, and the fact that I myself never seemed to get burned was as good as proof. But I *couldn't* be burned, something even I didn't know at first. I was ten: I didn't know fig about anything! It's a very scary thing, manifesting without understanding what's happening to you, though it's a fright nearly all peculiar children experience because so few of us are born to peculiar parents."

"I can imagine," I said.

"One day, as far as anyone knew, I was as common as rice pudding, and the next I felt a curious itch in the palms of my hands. They grew red and swollen, then hot—so hot that I ran to the grocer's and buried them in a case of frozen cod! When the fish began to thaw and stink, the grocer chased me home again, where he demanded that my mother pay for all I'd ruined. My hands were burning up by this time; the ice had only made it worse! Finally, they caught fire, and I was sure I'd gone stark raving mad."

"What did your parents think?" I asked.

"My mother, who was a deeply superstitious person, ran out of the house and never came back. She thought I was a demon, arrived straight from Hell via her womb. The old man took a different approach. He beat me and locked me in my room, and when I tried to burn through the door he tied me down with asbestos sheets. Kept me like that for days, feeding me once in a while by hand, since he didn't trust me enough to untie me. Which was a good thing for him, 'cause the minute he did I would've burned him black."

"I wish you had," I said.

"That's sweet of you. But it wouldn't have done any good. My parents were horrible people—but if they hadn't been, and if I'd stayed with them much longer, there's no question the hollows would've found me. I owe my life to two people: my younger sister, Julia, who freed me late one night so that I could finally run away; and Miss Peregrine, who discovered me a month later, working as a fire-eater at a traveling circus." Emma smiled wistfully. "The day I met her, that's what I call my birthday. The day I met my true mum."

My heart melted a little. "Thank you for telling me," I said. Hearing Emma's story made me feel closer to her, and less alone in my own confusion. Every peculiar had struggled through a period of painful uncertainty. Every peculiar had been tried. The glaring difference between us was that my parents still loved me—and despite the problems I'd had with them, I loved them, too, in my own quiet way. The thought that I was hurting them now was a constant ache.

What did I owe them? How could it be reckoned against the debt I owed Miss Peregrine, or my obligation to my grandfather—or the sweet, heavy thing I felt for Emma, which seemed to grow stronger every time I looked at her?

The scales tipped always toward the latter. But eventually, if I lived through this, I would have to face up to the decision I had made and the pain I had caused.

If.

If always propelled my thoughts back to the present, because *if* depended so much on keeping my wits about me. I couldn't properly sense things if I was distracted. *If* demanded my full presence and participation in *now*.

If, as much as it scared me, also kept me sane.

London approached, villages giving way to towns giving way

to unbroken tracts of suburbia. I wondered what was waiting for us there; what new horrors lay ahead.

I glanced at a headline in the newspaper still open in Emma's lap: AIR RAIDS RATTLE CAPITAL. SCORES DEAD.

I closed my eyes and tried to think of nothing at all.

PART

TWO

I anyone had been watching as the eight-thirty train hissed into the station and ground to a steaming halt, they wouldn't have noticed anything out of the ordinary about it: not about the conductors and porters who wrestled open its latches and threw back its doors; not about the mass of men and women, some in military dress, who streamed out and disappeared into the swarming crowd; not even about the eight weary children who filed heavily from one of its first-class cars and stood blinking in the hazy light of the platform, their backs pressed together in a protective circle, dazed by the cathedral of noise and smoke in which they found themselves.

On an ordinary day, any group of children as lost and forlorn-looking as these would've been approached by some kindly adult and asked what the matter was, or whether they needed help, or where their parents were. But today the platform teemed with hundreds of children, all of whom looked lost and forlorn. So no one paid much attention to the little girl with tumbling brown hair and button shoes, or the fact that her shoes did not quite touch the floor. No one noticed the moon-faced boy in the flat cap, or the honeybee that drifted from his mouth, tested the sooty air, then dove back from whence it came.

No one's gaze lingered on the boy with dark-ringed eyes, or saw the clay man who peeked from his shirt pocket only to be pushed down again by the boy's finger. Likewise the boy who was dressed to the nines in a muddy but finely tailored suit and stove-in top hat, his face drawn and haggard from lack of sleep, for he hadn't allowed *himself any in days, so afraid was he of his dreams.*

No one more than glanced at the big girl in the coat and simple dress, who was built like a stack of bricks and had lashed to her back a steamer trunk nearly as large as herself. None who saw her could have guessed how stupendously heavy the trunk was, or what it held, or why a screen of tiny holes had been punched into one side. Overlooked completely was the young man next to her, so wrapped in scarves and a hooded coat that not an inch of his bare skin could be seen, though it was early September and the weather still warm.

Then there was the American boy, so ordinary-looking he hardly merited notice; so apparently normal that people's eyes skipped over him—even as he studied them, on tiptoe, neck swiveling, his gaze sweeping across the platform like a sentry's. The girl by his side stood with her hands clasped together, concealing a tendril of flame that curled stubbornly around the nail of her pinky, which happened sometimes when she was upset. She tried shaking her finger as one might to extinguish a match, then blowing on it. When that didn't work, she slipped it into her mouth and let a puff of smoke coil from her nose. No one saw that, either.

In fact, no one looked closely enough at the children from the first-class car of the eight-thirty train to notice anything peculiar about them at all. Which was just as well.

CHAPTER EIGHT

*E*mma nudged me.

"So?"

"I need another minute," I said.

Bronwyn had set down her trunk and I was standing on it now, head above the crowd, casting my eyes over a shifting sea of faces. The long platform teemed with children. They squirmed like amoebas under a microscope, row upon row receding into a haze of smoke. Hissing black trains loomed up on either side, anxious to swallow them.

I could feel my friends' eyes on my back, watching me as I scanned the crowd. I was supposed to know whether, somewhere in that great, seething mass, there were monsters who meant to kill us—and I was supposed to know it simply by looking; by assessing some vague feeling in my gut. Usually it was painful and obvious when a hollow was nearby, but in a giant space like this—among hundreds of people—my warning might only be a whisper, the faintest twinge, easy to miss.

"Do the wights know we're coming?" Bronwyn asked, talking low for fear she'd be overheard by a normal—or worse yet, a wight. They had ears everywhere in the city, or so we'd been led to believe.

"We killed every one of them that might've known where we were going," Hugh said proudly. "Or rather, *I* did."

"Which means they'll be looking for us even harder," Millard said. "And they'll want more than the bird now—they'll want revenge."

"Which is why we can't stand here much longer," Emma said,

tapping me on the leg. "Are you almost finished?"

My focus slipped. I lost my place in the crowd. Began again. "One more minute," I said.

Personally, it wasn't wights that concerned me most, but hollows. I'd killed two of them now, and each encounter had nearly been the end of me. My luck, if that's what had been keeping me alive thus far, had to be running out. That's why I was determined never to be surprised by another hollow. I would do everything in my power to sense them from a distance and avoid contact altogether. There was less glory in running away from a fight, sure, but I didn't care about glory. I just wanted to survive.

The real danger, then, wasn't the figures on the platform, but the shadows that lay between and beyond them; the darkness at the margins. That's where I focused my attention. It gave me an out-of-body sort of feeling, to cast my sense out into a crowd this way, prodding distant corners for traces of danger. It wasn't something I could've done a few days ago. My ability to direct it like a spotlight—this was new.

What else, I wondered, was left to discover about myself?

"We're okay," I said, stepping down from the trunk. "No hollows."

"*I* could've told you that," grumbled Enoch. "If there had been, they'd have eaten us by now!"

Emma took me aside. "If we're to have a fighting chance here, you've got to be faster."

It was like asking someone who'd just learned to swim to compete in the Olympics. "I'm doing my best," I said.

Emma nodded. "I know you are." She turned to the others and snapped her fingers for attention. "Let's head for that phone box," she said, pointing to a tall, red phone booth across the platform, just visible through the surging crowd.

"Who are we calling?" Hugh asked.

"The peculiar dog said that all of London's loops had been

raided and their ymbrynes kidnapped," Emma said, "but we can't simply take his word for it, can we?"

"You can *call* a time loop?" I said, flabbergasted. "On the *phone*?"

. Millard explained that the Council of Ymbrynes maintained a phone exchange, though it could be used only within the boundaries of the city. "Quite ingenious how it works, given all the time differences," he said. "Just because we live in time loops doesn't mean we're stuck in the Stone Age!"

Emma took my hand and told the others to join hands, too. "It's crucial we stay together," she said. "London is vast, and there's no lost and found here for peculiar children."

We waded into the crowd, hands linked, our snaking line slightly parabolic in the middle where Olive buoyed up like an astronaut walking on the moon.

"You losing weight?" Bronwyn asked her. "You need heavier shoes, little magpie."

"I get feathery when I ain't had proper meals," Olive said.

"Proper meals? We just ate like kings!"

"Not me," said Olive. "They didn't have any meat pies."

"You're awfully picky for a refugee," said Enoch. "Anyway, since Horace wasted all our money, the only way we're getting more food is if we steal it, or find a not-kidnapped ymbryne who'll cook us some."

"We still have money," Horace said defensively, jingling the coins in his pocket. "Though not enough for meat pies. We could perhaps afford a jacket potato."

"If I have another jacket potato, I'll turn *into* a jacket potato," Olive whined.

"That's impossible, dear," said Bronwyn.

"Why? Miss Peregrine can turn into a bird!"

A boy we were passing turned to stare. Bronwyn shushed Olive angrily. Telling our secrets in front of normals was strictly forbidden, even if they were so fantastic-sounding no one would believe them.

We shouldered through one last knot of children to arrive at the phone booth. It was only large enough to hold three, so Emma, Millard, and Horace squeezed inside while the rest of us crowded around the door. Emma worked the phone, Horace fished our last few coins from his pocket, and Millard paged through a chunky phone book that dangled from a cord.

"Are you kidding?" I said, leaning into the booth. "There are ymbrynes in the phone book?"

"The addresses listed are fakes," said Millard, "and the calls won't connect unless you whistle the right passcode." He tore out a listing and handed it to Emma. "Give this one a go. Millicent Thrush."

Horace fed a coin into the slot and Emma dialed the number. Then Millard took the phone, whistled a bird call into the receiver, and handed it back to Emma. She listened for a moment, then frowned. "It just rings," she said. "No one's picking up."

"No bother!" Millard said. "That was just one of many. Let me find another . . ."

Outside the booth, the crowd that had been flowing around us slowed to a stop, bottlenecking somewhere out of sight. The train platform was reaching capacity. There were normal children on every side of us, chattering to one another, shouting, shoving—and one, who stood right next to Olive, was crying bitterly. She had pigtails and puffy red eyes, and she carried a blanket in one hand and a raggedy cardboard suitcase in the other. Pinned to her blouse was a tag with words and numbers stenciled in large print:

115-201
London → Sheffield

Olive watched the girl cry until her own eyes began to shimmer with tears. Finally, she couldn't take it anymore and asked what the matter was. The girl looked away, pretending not to have heard.

Olive didn't take the hint. "What's the matter?" she asked again. "Are you crying because you've been sold?" She pointed to the tag on the girl's blouse. "Was that your price?"

The girl tried to scoot away but was blocked by a wall of people.

"I would buy you and set you free," Olive went on, "but I fear we've spent all our money on train tickets and haven't enough even for meat pies, much less a slave. I'm awfully sorry."

The girl spun to face Olive. "I'm not for sale!" she said, stamping her foot.

"Are you certain?"

"Yes!" the girl shouted, and in a fit of frustration she ripped the tag off her blouse and threw it away. "I just don't want to go and live in the stupid country, that's all."

"I didn't want to leave my home, either, but we had to," Olive said. "It got smashed by a bomb."

The girl's face softened. "Mine did, too." She put down her suitcase and held out her hand. "Sorry I got cross. My name is Jessica."

"I'm Olive."

The two little girls shook hands like gentlemen.

"I like your blouse," Olive said.

"Thanks," said Jessica. "And I like your—the—the whatsit on your head."

"My tiara!" Olive reached up to touch it. "It isn't real silver, though."

"That's okay. It's pretty."

Olive smiled as wide as I'd ever seen her smile, and then a loud whistle blew and a booming voice crackled over a loudspeaker. "All children onto the trains!" it said. "Nice and orderly now!"

The crowd began to flow around us again. Here and there, adults herded the children along, and I heard one say, "Don't worry, you'll see your mummies and daddies again soon!"

That's when I realized why there were so many children here. They were being evacuated. Of all the many hundreds of kids in the train station this morning, my friends and I were the only ones arriving. The rest were leaving, being shuttled out of the city for their own safety—and from the look of the winter coats and overstuffed cases some of them carried, maybe for a long time.

"I have to go," Jessica said, and Olive had hardly begun to say goodbye when her new friend was borne away by the crowd toward a waiting train. Just that quickly, Olive made and lost the only normal friend she'd ever had.

Jessica looked back as she was boarding. Her grim expression seemed to say: *What will become of me?*

We watched her go and wondered the same about ourselves.

Inside the phone box, Emma scowled at the receiver. "No one's answering," she said. "All the numbers just ring and ring."

"Last one," said Millard, handing her another ripped-out page. "Cross your fingers."

I was focused on Emma as she dialed, but then a commotion broke out behind me and I turned to see a crimson-faced man waving an umbrella at us. "What are you dallying about for?" he said. "Vacate that phone box and board your train at once!"

"We just got off one," said Hugh. "We ain't about to get on another!"

"And what have you done with your tag numbers?" the man shouted, flecks of spittle flying from his lips. "Produce them at once or by God I'll have you shipped somewhere a great deal less pleasant than Wales!"

"Piss off this instant," said Enoch, "or we'll have *you* shipped straight to Hell!"

The man's face went so purple I thought he'd burst a blood vessel in his neck. Clearly, he wasn't used to being spoken to this way by children.

"I said *get out of that phone box!*" he roared, and raising the umbrella over his head like an executioner's ax, he brought it down on the cable that stretched between the top of the booth and the wall, snapping it in half with a loud *thwack!*

The phone went dead. Emma looked up from the receiver, boiling with quiet rage. "If he wants to use the phone so badly," she said, "then let's give it to him."

As she, Millard, and Horace squeezed out of the booth, Bronwyn grabbed the man's hands and pinned them behind his back. "Stop!" he screamed. "Unhand me!"

"Oh, I'll unhand you," said Bronwyn, and then she picked

him up, stuffed him headfirst into the booth, and barred the door shut with his umbrella. The man screamed and banged on the glass, jumping up and down like a fat fly trapped in a bottle. Although it would've been fun to stick around and laugh at him, the man had drawn too much attention, and now adults were converging on us from all across the station. It was time to go.

We linked hands and raced off toward the turnstiles, leaving behind us a wake of tripped and flailing normals. A train whistle screeched and was echoed inside Bronwyn's trunk, where Miss Peregrine was being tossed around like laundry in the wash. Too light on her feet to run, Olive clung to Bronwyn's neck, trailing behind her like a half-deflated balloon on a string.

Some of the adults were closer to the exit than we were, and rather than running around them, we tried to barrel straight through.

This didn't work.

The first to intercept us was a big woman who smacked Enoch upside the head with her purse, then tackled him. When Emma tried to pull her off, two men grabbed her by the arms and wrestled her to the floor. I was about to jump in and help her when a third man grabbed *my* arms.

"Someone *do* something!" Brownyn cried. We all knew what she meant, but it wasn't clear which of us was free to act. Then a bee whizzed past Enoch's nose and buried its stinger in the haunches of the woman sitting astride him, and she squealed and leapt up.

"Yes!" Enoch shouted. "More bees!"

"They're tired!" Hugh shouted back. "They only just got to sleep after saving you the last time!" But he could see that there was no other way—Emma's arms were pinned, Bronwyn was busy protecting both her trunk and Olive from a trio of angry train conductors, and there were more adults on the way—so Hugh began pounding his chest as if trying to dislodge a piece of stuck food. A moment later he let out a reverberating belch, and ten or so bees flew out of his mouth. They did a few circles overhead, then got their bearings and began stinging every adult in sight.

The men holding Emma dropped her and fled. The one holding me got stung right on the tip of his nose, and he hollered and flapped his arms as if possessed by demons. Soon all the adults were running, trying to defend themselves from tiny, stinging attackers with spastic dance moves, to the delight of all the children still on the platform, who laughed and cheered and threw their arms in the air in imitation of their ridiculous elders.

With everyone thus distracted, we picked ourselves up, bolted for the turnstiles, and ran out into a bustling London afternoon.

* * *

We became lost in the chaos of the streets. It felt like we'd been plunged into a jar of stirred liquid, racing with particles: gentlemen, ladies, laborers, soldiers, street kids, and beggars all rushing purposefully in every direction, weaving around tiny, sputtering cars and cart vendors crying their wares and buskers blowing horns and buses blowing horns and shuddering to stops to spill more people onto the teeming sidewalks. Containing all this was a canyon of column-fronted buildings that stretched to vanishing down a street half in shadow, the afternoon sun low and muted, reduced by the smokes of London to a murky glow, a lantern winking through fog.

Dizzy from it, I half closed my eyes and let Emma pull me along while with my free hand I reached into my pocket to touch the cold glass of my phone. I found this strangely calming. My phone was a useless relic of the future but an object which retained some power nevertheless—that of a long, thin filament connecting this baffling world to the sane and recognizable one I'd once belonged to; a thing that said to me as I touched it, *You are here and this is real and you are not dreaming and you are still you,* and somehow that made everything around me vibrate a little less quickly.

Enoch had spent his formative years in London and claimed to still know its streets, so he led. We stuck mostly to alleys and back lanes, which made the city seem at first like a maze of gray walls and gutter pipes, its grandness revealed in glimpses as we dashed across wide boulevards and back to the safety of shadows. We made a game of it, laughing, racing one another between alleys. Horace pretended to trip over a curb, then bounced up nimbly and bowed like a dancer, tipping his hat. We laughed like mad, strangely giddy, half in disbelief that we'd made it this far—across the water, through the woods, past snarling hollows and death squads of wights, all the way to London.

We put a good long way between us and the train station and then stopped in an alley by some trash cans to catch our breath. Bronwyn set down her trunk and lifted Miss Peregrine out, and she wobbled drunkenly across the cobblestones. Horace and Millard broke out laughing.

"What's so funny?" said Bronwyn. "It ain't Miss P's fault she's dizzy."

Horace swept his arms out grandly. "Welcome to beautiful London!" he said. "It's ever so much grander than you described it, Enoch. And oh, did you describe it! For seventy-five years: London, London, London! The greatest city on Earth!"

Millard picked up a trash-can lid. "London! The finest refuse available anywhere!"

Horace doffed his hat. "London! Where even the rats wear top hats!"

"Oh, I didn't go on about it *that* much," Enoch said.

"You did!" said Olive. "'Well, that's not how they do things in *London*,' you'd say. Or, 'In London, the food is *much* finer!'"

"Obviously, we're not on a grand tour of the city right now!" Enoch said defensively. "Would you rather walk through alleys or be spotted by wights?"

Horace ignored him. "London: where every day's a holiday . . . for the trash man!"

He broke down laughing, and his laughter was infectious. Soon nearly all of us were giggling—even Enoch. "I suppose I did glamorize it a *bit*," he admitted.

"I don't see what's so amusing about London," Olive said with a frown. "It's dirty and smelly and full of cruel, nasty people who make children cry and I hate it!" She scrunched her face into a scowl and added, "And I'm becoming *quite peckish*!"—which made us all laugh harder.

"Those people in the station *were* nasty," said Millard. "But they got what they deserved! I'll never forget that man's face when Bronwyn stuffed him into the phone box."

"Or that horrible woman when she got stung in the bum by a bee!" said Enoch. "I'd pay money to see that again."

I glanced at Hugh, expecting him to chime in, but his back was to us, his shoulders trembling.

"Hugh?" I said. "You all right?"

He shied away. "No one gives a whit," he said. "Don't bother checking on old Hugh, he's just here to save everyone's hindquarters with no word of thanks from anybody!"

Shamed, we offered him our thanks and apologies.

"Sorry, Hugh."

"Thanks again, Hugh."

"You're our man in a pinch, Hugh."

He turned to face us. "They were my friends, you know."

"We still are!" said Olive.

"Not *you*—my bees! They can only sting once, and then it's lights out, the big hive in the sky. And now I've only Henry left, and he can't fly 'cause he's missing a wing." He put out his hand and slowly opened the fingers, and there in his palm was Henry, waving his only wing at us.

"C'mon, mate," Hugh whispered to it. "Time to go home." He stuck out his tongue, set the bee upon it, and closed his mouth.

Enoch patted him on the shoulder. "I'd bring them back to life for you, but I'm not sure it would work on creatures so small."

"Thanks anyway," Hugh said, and then he cleared his throat and wiped his cheeks roughly, as if annoyed at his tears for exposing him.

"We'll find you more just as soon as we get Miss P fixed up," said Bronwyn.

"Speaking of which," Enoch said to Emma, "did you manage to get through to any ymbrynes on that phone?"

"Not a one," Emma replied, then sat down on an overturned trash can, her shoulders slumping. "I was really hoping we might catch a bit of good luck for once. But no."

"Then it seems the dog was correct," said Horace. "The great loops of London have fallen to our enemies." He bowed his head solemnly. "The worst has come to pass. All our ymbrynes have been kidnapped."

We all bowed our heads, our giddy mood gone.

"In that case," said Enoch, "Millard, you'd better tell us all you know about the punishment loops. If that's where the ymbrynes are, we're going to have to stage a rescue."

"No," said Millard. "No, no, no."

"What do you mean, *no*?" said Emma.

Millard made a strangled noise in his throat and started breathing weirdly. "I mean . . . we can't . . ."

He couldn't seem to get the words out.

"What's wrong with him?" said Bronwyn. "Mill, what's the matter?"

"You'd better explain right now what you mean by 'no,'" Emma said threateningly.

"Because we'll *die*, that's why!" Millard said, his voice breaking.

"But back at the menagerie you made it sound so easy!" I said. "Like we could just waltz into a punishment loop . . ."

Millard was hyperventilating, hysterical—and it scared me. Bronwyn found a crumpled paper bag and told him to breathe into it. When he'd recovered a bit, he answered.

"Getting *into* one is easy enough," he said, speaking slowly, working to control his breaths. "Getting out again is trickier. Getting out *alive*, I should say. Punishment loops are everything the dog said and worse. Rivers of fire . . . bloodthirsty Vikings . . . pestilence so thick you can't breathe . . . and mixed into all that, like some devilish bouillabaisse, bird knows how many wights and hollowgast!"

"Well, that's fantastic!" said Horace, tossing up his hands. "You might've told us earlier, you know—like back at the menagerie, when we were planning all this!"

"Would it have made any difference, Horace?" He took a few more breaths from the bag. "If I'd made it sound more frightening, would you have chosen to simply let Miss Peregrine's humanity expire?"

"Of course not," said Horace. "But you should've told us the truth."

Millard let the bag drop. His strength was returning, and his conviction with it. "I admit I somewhat downplayed the punishment loops' dangers. But I never thought we'd actually have to go into them! Despite all that irritating dog's doomsaying about the state of London, I was certain we'd find at least *one* unraided loop here, its ymbryne still present and accounted for. And for all we know, we may still! How can we be sure they've all been kidnapped? Have we seen their raided loops with our own eyes? What if the ymbrynes' phones were simply . . . disconnected?"

"*All* of them?" Enoch scoffed.

Even Olive, eternally optimistic Olive, shook her head at that.

"Then what do you suggest, Millard?" said Emma. "That we tour London's loops and hope to find someone still at home? And what would you say the odds are that the corrupted, *who are looking for us*, would leave all those loops unguarded?"

"I think we'd have a better chance of surviving the night if we spent it playing Russian roulette," said Enoch.

"All I mean," Millard said, "is that we have no *proof* . . ."

"What more proof do you want?" said Emma. "Pools of blood? A pile of plucked ymbryne feathers? Miss Avocet told us the corrupted assault began here weeks ago. Miss Wren clearly believed that all of London's ymbrynes had been kidnapped—do you know better than Miss Wren, an ymbryne herself? And now we're here, and none of the loops are answering their telephones. So please, tell me why going loop to loop would be anything other than a suicidally dangerous waste of time."

"Wait a minute—that's it!" Millard exclaimed. "What about Miss Wren?"

"What about her?" said Emma.

"Don't you remember what the dog told us? Miss Wren came to London a few days ago, when she heard that her sister ymbrynes had been kidnapped."

"So?"

"What if she's still here?"

"Then she's probably been captured by now!" said Enoch.

"And if she hasn't?" Millard's voice was bright with hope. "She could help Miss Peregrine—and then we wouldn't have to go anywhere *near* the punishment loops!"

"And how would you suggest we find her?" Enoch said shrilly. "Shout her name from the rooftops? This isn't Cairnholm; it's a city of millions!"

"Her pigeons," said Millard.

"Come again?"

"It was Miss Wren's peculiar pigeons who told her where the ymbrynes had been taken. If they knew where all the other ymbrynes went, then they should know where Miss Wren is, too. They belong to her, after all."

"Hah!" said Enoch. "The only thing commoner here than plain-looking middle-aged ladies are flocks of pigeons. And you want to search all of London for *one flock* in particular?"

"It does seem a bit mad," Emma said. "Sorry, Mill, I just don't see how that could work."

"Then it's a lucky thing for you I spent our train ride studying rather than making idle gossip. Someone hand me the *Tales*!"

Bronwyn fished the book from her trunk and gave it to him. Millard dove right in, flipping pages. "There are many answers to be found within," he said, "if you only know what to look for." He stopped at a certain page and stabbed the top with his finger. "Aha!" he said, turning the book to show us what he'd found.

The title of the story was "The Pigeons of St. Paul's."

"I'll be blessed," said Bronwyn. "Could those be the same pigeons we're talking about?"

"If they're written about in the *Tales*, they're almost certainly peculiar pigeons," said Millard, "and how many flocks of peculiar pigeons could there possibly be?"

Olive clapped her hands and cried, "Millard, you're brilliant!"

"Thank you, yes, I was aware."

"Wait, I'm lost," I said. "What's St. Paul's?"

"Even *I* know that," said Olive. "The cathedral!" And she went to the end of the alley and pointed up at a giant domed roof rising in the distance.

"It's the largest and most magnificent cathedral in London," said Millard, "and if my hunch is correct, it's also the nesting place of Miss Wren's pigeons."

"Let's hope they're at home," said Emma. "And that they've got some good news for us. We've had quite a drought of it lately."

*   *   *

As we navigated a labyrinth of narrow streets toward the cathedral, a brooding quiet settled over us. For long stretches no one spoke, leaving only the tap of our shoes on pavement and the sounds of the city: airplanes, the ever-present hum of traffic, sirens that warbled and pitch-shifted around us.

The farther we got from the train station, the more evidence we saw of the bombs that had been raining down on London. Building fronts pocked by shrapnel. Shattered windows. Streets that glinted with frosts of powdered glass. The sky was speckled with puffy silver blimps tethered to the ground by long webs of cable. "Barrage balloons," Emma said when she saw me craning my neck toward one. "The German bombers get caught up in their cables at night and crash."

Then we came upon a scene of destruction so bizarre that I had to stop and gape at it—not out of some morbid voyeurism, but because it was impossible for my brain to process without further study. A bomb crater yawned across the whole width of the street like a monstrous mouth with broken pavement for teeth. At one edge, the blast had sheared away the front wall of a building but left what was inside mostly intact. It looked like a doll's house, its interior rooms all exposed to the street: the dining room with its table still set for a meal; family pictures knocked crooked in a hallway but still hanging; a roll of toilet paper unspooled and caught in the breeze, waving in the air like a long, white flag.

"Did they forget to finish building it?" Olive asked.

"No, dummy," said Enoch. "It got hit by a bomb."

For a moment Olive looked as if she might cry, but then her face went hard and she shook her fist at the sky and yelled, "Nasty Hitler! Stop this horrible war and go right away altogether!"

Bronwyn patted her arm. "Shhh. He can't hear you, love."

"It isn't fair," Olive said. "I'm tired of airplanes and bombs and war!"

"We all are," said Enoch. "Even me."

Then I heard Horace scream and I spun around to see him pointing at something in the road. I ran to see what it was, and then I did see and I stopped, frozen, my brain shouting *Run away!* but my legs refusing to listen.

It was a pyramid of heads. They were blackened and caved,

mouths agape, eyes boiled shut, melted and pooled together in the gutter like some hydra-headed horror. Then Emma came to see and gasped and turned away; Bronwyn came and started moaning; Hugh gagged and clapped his hands over his eyes; and then finally Enoch, who seemed not in the least disturbed, calmly nudged one of the heads with his shoe and pointed out that they were only mannequins made of wax, having spilled from the display window of a bombed wig shop. We all felt a little ridiculous but somehow no less horrified, because even though the heads weren't real, they represented something that was, hidden beneath the rubble around us.

"Let's go," Emma said. "This place is nothing but a graveyard."

We walked on. I tried to keep my eyes to the ground, but there was no shutting out all the ghastly things we passed. A scarred ruin belching smoke, the only fireman dispatched to extinguish it slouched in defeat, blistered and weary, his hose run dry. Yet there he stood watching anyway, as if, lacking water, his job now was to bear witness.

A baby in a stroller, left alone in the street, bawling.

Bronwyn slowed, overcome. "Can't we help them somehow?"

"It wouldn't make any difference," said Millard. "These people belong to the past, and the past can't be changed."

Bronwyn nodded sadly. She'd known it was true but had needed to hear it said. We were barely here, ineffectual as ghosts.

A cloud of ash billowed, blotting out fireman and child. We went on, choking in an eddy of windborne wreck dust, powdered concrete blanching our clothes, our faces bone white.

*   *   *

We hurried past the ruined blocks as quickly as we could, then marveled as the streets returned to life around us. Just a short walk from Hell, people were going about their business, striding down sidewalks, living in buildings that still had electricity and windows and walls. Then we rounded a corner and the cathedral's dome revealed itself, proud and imposing despite patches of fire-blackened stone and a few crumbling arches. Like the spirit of the city itself, it would take more than a few bombs to topple St. Paul's.

Our hunt began in a square close to the cathedral, where old men on benches were feeding pigeons. At first it was mayhem: we bounded in, grabbing wildly as the pigeons took off. The old men grumbled, and we withdrew to wait for their return. They did, eventually, pigeons not being the smartest animals on the planet, at which point we all took turns wading casually into the flock and trying to catch them by surprise, reaching down to snatch at them. I thought Olive, who was small and quick, or Hugh, with his peculiar connection to another sort of winged creature, might have some luck, but both were humiliated. Millard didn't fare any better, and they couldn't even *see* him. By the time my turn came, the pigeons must've been sick of us bothering them, because the moment I strolled into the square they all burst into flight and took one big, simultaneous cluster-bomb crap, which sent me flailing toward a water fountain to wash my whole head.

In the end, it was Horace who caught one. He sat down next to the old men, dropping seeds until the birds circled him. Then, leaning slowly forward, he stretched out his arm and, calm as could be, snagged one by its feet.

"Got you!" he cried.

The bird flapped and tried to get away, but Horace held on tight.

He brought it to us. "How can we tell if it's peculiar?" he said, flipping the bird over to inspect its bottom, as if expecting to find a label there.

"Show it to Miss Peregrine," Emma said. "She'll know."

So we opened Bronwyn's trunk, shoved the pigeon inside with Miss Peregrine, and slammed down the lid. The pigeon screeched like it was being torn apart.

I winced and shouted, "Go easy, Miss P!"

When Bronwyn opened the trunk again, a poof of pigeon feathers fluttered into the air, but the pigeon itself was nowhere to be seen.

"Oh, no—she's ate it!" cried Bronwyn.

"No she hasn't," said Emma. "Look beneath her!"

Miss Peregrine lifted up and stepped aside, and there underneath her was the pigeon, alive but dazed.

"Well?" said Enoch. "Is it or isn't it one of Miss Wren's?"

Miss Peregrine nudged the bird with her beak and it flew away. Then she leapt out of the trunk, hobbled into the square, and with one loud squawk scattered the rest of the pigeons. Her message was clear: not only was Horace's pigeon not peculiar, *none* of them were. We'd have to keep looking.

Miss Peregrine hopped toward the cathedral and flapped her wing impatiently. We caught up to her on the cathedral steps. The building loomed above us, soaring bell towers framing its giant dome. An army of soot-stained angels glared down at us from marble reliefs.

"How are we ever going to search this whole place?" I wondered aloud.

"One room at a time," Emma said.

A strange noise stopped us at the door. It sounded like a faraway car alarm, the note pitching up and down in long, slow arcs. But there were no car alarms in 1940, of course. It was an air-raid siren.

Horace cringed. "The Germans are coming!" he cried. "Death

from the skies!"

"We don't know *what* it means," Emma said. "Could be a false alarm, or a test."

But the streets and the square were emptying fast; the old men were folding up their newspapers and vacating their benches.

"*They* don't seem to think it's a test," Horace said.

"Since when are we afraid of a few bombs?" Enoch said. "Quit talking like a Nancy Normal!"

"Need I remind you," said Millard, "these are not the sort of bombs we're accustomed to. Unlike the ones that fall on Cairnholm, we don't know where they're going to land!"

"All the more reason to get what we came for, and quickly!" Emma said, and she led us inside.

*   *   *

The cathedral's interior was massive—it seemed, impossibly, even larger than the outside—and though damaged, a few hardy believers knelt here and there in silent prayer. The altar was buried under a midden of debris. Where a bomb had pierced the roof, sunlight fell down in broad beams. A lone soldier sat on a fallen pillar, gazing at the sky through the broken ceiling.

We wandered, necks craned, bits of concrete and broken tile crunching beneath our feet.

"I don't see anything," Horace complained. "There are enough hiding places here for ten thousand pigeons!"

"Don't look," Hugh said. *"Listen."*

We stopped, straining to hear the telltale coo of pigeons. But there was only the ceaseless whine of air-raid sirens, and below that a series of dull cracks like rolling thunder. I told myself to stay calm, but my heart thrummed like a drum machine.

Bombs were falling.

"We need to go," I said, panic choking me. "There has to be a shelter nearby. Somewhere safe we can hide."

"But we're so close!" said Bronwyn. "We can't quit now!"

There was another crack, closer this time, and the others started to get nervous, too.

"Maybe Jacob's right," said Horace. "Let's find somewhere safe to hide until the bombing's through. We can search more when it's over."

"Nowhere is truly safe," said Enoch. "Those bombs can penetrate even a deep shelter."

"They can't penetrate a loop," Emma said. "And if there's a tale about this cathedral, there's probably a loop entrance here, too."

"Perhaps," said Millard, "perhaps, perhaps. Hand me the book and I shall investigate."

Bronwyn opened her trunk and handed Millard the book.

"Let me see now," he said, turning its pages until he reached "The Pigeons of St. Paul's."

Bombs are falling and we're reading stories, I thought. *I have entered the realm of the insane.*

"Listen closely!" Millard said. "If there's a loop entrance nearby, this tale may tell us how to find it. It's a short one, luckily."

A bomb fell outside. The floor shook and plaster rained from the ceiling. I clenched my teeth and tried to focus on my breathing.

Unfazed, Millard cleared his throat. "The Pigeons of St. Paul's!" he began, reading in a big, booming voice.

"We know the title already!" said Enoch.

"Read faster, please!" said Bronwyn.

"If you don't stop interrupting me, we'll be here all night," said Millard, and then he continued.

"Once upon a peculiar time, long before there were towers or steeples or any tall buildings at all in the city of London, there was a flock of pigeons who got it into their minds that they wanted a nice, high place to roost, above the bustle and fracas of human society. They knew just how to build it, too, because pigeons are builders by nature, and much more intelligent than we give them credit for being. But the people of ancient London weren't interested in constructing tall things, so one night the pigeons snuck into the bedroom of the most industrious human they could find and whispered into his ear the plans for a magnificent tower.

"In the morning, the man awoke in great excitement. He had dreamed—or so he thought—of a magnificent church with a great, reaching spire that would rise from the city's tallest hill. A few years later, at enormous cost to the humans, it was built. It was a very towering sort of tower and had all manner of nooks and crannies inside it where the pigeons could roost, and they were very satisfied with themselves.

"Then one day Vikings sacked the city and burned the tower to the ground, so the pigeons had to find another architect, whisper in his ear, and wait patiently for a new church tower to be built—this one even grander and taller than the first. And it was built, and it was very grand and very tall. And then it burned, too.

"Things went on in this fashion for hundreds of years, the towers burning and the pigeons whispering plans for still grander and taller towers to successive generations of nocturnally inspired architects. Though these architects never realized the debt they owed the birds, they still regarded them with tenderness, and allowed them to hang about wherever they liked, in the naves and belfries, like the mascots and guardians of the place they truly were."

"This is *not helpful*," Enoch said. "Get to the loop entrance part!"

"I am getting to what I am *getting to*!" Millard snapped. "Eventually, after many church towers had come and gone, the pigeons' plans became so ambitious that it took an exceedingly long time to find a human intelligent enough to carry them out. When they finally did, the man resisted, believing the hill to be cursed, so many churches having burned there in the past. Though he tried to put the idea out of his mind, the pigeons kept returning, night after night, to whisper it in his ear. Still, the man would not act. So they came to him during the day, which they had never done before, and told him in their strange laughing language that he was the only human capable of constructing their tower, and he simply had to do it. But he refused and chased them from his house, shouting, 'Shoo, begone with ye, filthy creatures!'

"The pigeons, insulted and vengeful, hounded the man until he was nearly mad—following him wherever he went, picking at his clothes, pulling his hair, fouling his food with their hind-feathers, tapping on his windows at night so he couldn't sleep—until one day he fell to his knees and cried, 'O pigeons! I will build whatever you ask, so long as you watch over it and preserve it from the fire!'

"The pigeons puzzled over this. Consulting among themselves, they decided that they might've been better guardians of past towers if they hadn't come to enjoy building them so much, and vowed to do everything they could to protect them in the future. So the man built it, a soaring cathedral with two towers and a dome. It was so grand, and both the man and the pigeons were so pleased with what they'd made that they became great friends; the man never went anywhere for the rest of his life without a pigeon close at hand to advise him. Even after he died at a ripe and happy old age, the birds still went to visit him, now and again, in the land below. And to this very day, you'll find the cathedral they built standing on the tallest hill in London, the pigeons watching over it."

Millard closed the book. "The end."

Emma made an exasperated noise. "Yes, but watching over it *from where?*"

"That could not have been less helpful to our present situation," said Enoch, "were it a story about cats on the moon."

"I can't make heads or tails of it," said Bronwyn. "Can anyone?"

I nearly could—felt close to something in that line about "the land below"—but all I could think was, *The pigeons are in Hell?*

Then another bomb fell, shaking the whole building, and from high overhead came a sudden flutter of wingbeats. We looked up to see three frightened pigeons shoot out of some hiding place in the rafters. Miss Peregrine squawked with excitement—as if to say, *That's them!*—and Bronwyn scooped her up and we all went racing after the birds. They flew down the length of the nave, turned sharply, and disappeared through a doorway.

We reached the doorway a few seconds later. To my relief, it didn't lead outside, where we'd never have a hope of catching them, but to a stairwell, down a set of spiral steps.

"Hah!" Enoch said, clapping his pudgy hands. "They've gone and done it now—trapped themselves in the basement!"

We sprinted down the stairs. At the bottom was a large, dimly lit room walled and floored with stone. It was cold and damp and almost completely dark, the electricity having been knocked out, so Emma sparked a flame in her hand and shone it around, until the nature of the space became apparent. Beneath our feet, stretching from wall to wall, were marble slabs chiseled with writing. The one below me read:

BISHOP ELDRIDGE THORNBRUSH, DYED ANNO 1721

"This is no basement," Emma said. "It's a crypt."

A little chill came over me, and I stepped closer to the light and warmth of Emma's flame.

"You mean, there are people buried in the floor?" said Olive, her voice quavering.

"What of it?" said Enoch. "Let's catch a damned pigeon before one of those bombs buries *us* in the floor."

Emma turned in a circle, throwing light on the walls. "They've got to be down here somewhere. There's no way out but that staircase."

Then we heard a wing flap. I tensed. Emma brightened her flame and aimed it toward the sound. Her flickering light fell on a flat-topped tomb that rose a few feet from the floor. Between the tomb and the wall was a gap we couldn't see behind from where we stood; a perfect hiding spot for a bird.

Emma raised a finger to her lips and motioned for us to follow. We crept across the room. Nearing the tomb, we spread out, surrounding it on three sides.

Ready? Emma mouthed.

The others nodded. I gave a thumbs-up. Emma tiptoed forward to peek behind the tomb—and then her face fell. "Nothing!" she said, kicking the floor in frustration.

"I don't understand!" said Enoch. "They were *right here*!"

We all came forward to look. Then Millard said, "Emma! Shine your light on top of the tomb, please!"

She did, and Millard read the tomb's inscription aloud:

HERE LIETH SIR CHRISTOPHER WREN
BUILDER OF THIS CATHEDRAL

"Wren!" Emma exclaimed. "What an odd coincidence!"

"I hardly think it's a coincidence," said Millard. "He must be related to *Miss* Wren. Perhaps he's her father!"

"That's very interesting," said Enoch, "but how does that help us find her, or her pigeons?"

"That is what I am attempting to puzzle out." Millard hummed to himself and paced a little and recited a line from the tale: "the birds still went to visit him, now and again, in the land below."

Then I thought I heard a pigeon coo. "Shh!" I said, and made everyone listen. It came again a few seconds later, from the rear corner of the tomb. I circled around it and knelt down, and that's when I noticed a small hole in the floor at the tomb's base, no bigger than a fist—just large enough for a bird to wriggle through.

"Over here!" I said.

"Well, I'll be stuffed!" said Emma, holding her flame up to the hole. "Perhaps that's 'the land below'?"

"But the hole is so small," said Olive. "How are we supposed to get the birds out of there?"

"We could wait for them to leave," said Horace, and then a bomb fell so close by that my eyes blurred and my teeth rattled.

"No need for that!" said Millard. "Bronwyn, would you please open Sir Wren's tomb?"

"No!" cried Olive. "I don't want to see his rotten old bones!"

"Don't worry, love," Bronwyn said, "Millard knows what he's doing." She planted her hands on the edge of the tomb lid and began to push, and it slid open with a slow, grating rumble.

The smell that came up wasn't what I'd expected—not of death, but mold and old dirt. We gathered around to look inside.

"Well, I'll be stuffed," Emma said.

CHAPTER NINE

*W*here a coffin should've been, there was a ladder, leading down into darkness. We peered into the open tomb.

"There's no *way* I'm climbing down there!" Horace said. But then a trio of bombs shook the building, raining chips of concrete on our heads, and suddenly Horace was pushing past me, grasping for the ladder. "Excuse me, out of my way, best-dressed go first!"

Emma caught him by the sleeve. "I have the light, so *I'll* go first. Then Jacob will follow, in case there are . . . *things* down there."

I flashed a weak smile, my knees going wobbly at the thought.

Enoch said, "You mean things *other than* rats and cholera and whatever sorts of mad trolls live beneath crypts?"

"It doesn't matter *what's* down there," Millard said grimly. "We'll have to face it, and that's that."

"Fine," said Enoch. "But Miss Wren had better be down there, too, because rat bites don't heal quickly."

"Hollowgast bites even less so," said Emma, and then she swung her foot onto the ladder.

"Be careful," I said. "I'll be right above you."

She saluted me with her flaming hand. "Once more into the breach," she said, and began to climb down.

Then it was my turn.

"Do you ever find yourself climbing into an open grave during a bombing raid," I said, "and just wish you'd stayed in bed?"

Enoch kicked my shoe. "Quit stalling."

I grabbed the lip of the tomb and put my foot on the ladder.

Thought briefly of all the pleasant, boring things I might've been doing with my summer, had my life gone differently. Tennis camp. Sailing lessons. Stocking shelves. And then, through some Herculean effort of will, I made myself climb.

The ladder descended into a tunnel. The tunnel dead-ended to one side, and in the other direction disappeared into blackness. The air was cold and suffused with a strange odor, like clothes left to rot in a flooded basement. The rough stone walls beaded and dripped with moisture of mysterious origin.

As Emma and I waited for everyone to climb down, the cold crept into me, degree by degree. The others felt it, too. When Bronwyn reached the bottom, she opened her trunk and handed out the peculiar sheep's wool sweaters we'd been given in the menagerie. I slipped one over my head. It fit me like a sack, the sleeves falling past my fingers and the bottom sagging halfway to my knees, but at least it was warm.

Bronwyn's trunk was empty now and she left it behind. Miss Peregrine rode inside her coat, where she'd practically made a nest for herself. Millard insisted on carrying the *Tales* in his arms, heavy and bulky as it was, because he might need to refer to it at any moment, he said. I think it had become his security blanket, though, and he thought of it as a book of spells which only he knew how to read.

We were an odd bunch.

I shuffled forward to feel for hollows in the dark. This time, I got a new kind of twinge in my gut, ever so faint, as if a hollow had been here and gone, and I was sensing its residue. I didn't mention it, though; there was no reason to alarm everyone unnecessarily.

We walked. The sound of our feet slapping the wet bricks echoed endlessly up and down the passage. There'd be no sneaking up on whatever was waiting for us.

Every so often, from up ahead, we'd hear a flap of wings or a pigeon's warble, and we'd pick up our pace a little. I got the uneasy feeling we were being led toward some nasty surprise. Embedded in the walls were stone slabs like the ones we'd seen in the crypt, but older, the writing mostly worn away. Then we passed a coffin, graveless, on the floor—then a whole stack of them, leaned against a wall like discarded moving boxes.

"What *is* this place?" Hugh whispered.

"Graveyard overflow," said Enoch. "When they need to make room for new customers, they dig up the old ones and stick them down here."

"What a terrible loop entrance," I said. "Imagine walking through here every time you needed in or out!"

"It's not so different from our cairn tunnel," Millard said. "Unpleasant loop entrances serve a purpose—normals tend to avoid them, so we peculiars have them all to ourselves."

So rational. So wise. All I could think was, *There are dead people everywhere and they're all rotted and bony and dead and, oh God . . .*

"Uh-oh," Emma said, and she stopped suddenly, causing me to run into her and everyone else to pile up behind me.

She held her flame to one side, revealing a curved door in the wall. It hung open slightly, but only darkness showed through the crack.

We listened. For a long moment there was no sound but our breath and the distant drip of water. Then we heard a noise, but not the kind we were expecting—not a wing-flap or the scratch of a bird's feet—but something human.

Very softly, someone was crying.

"Hello?" called Emma. "Who's in there?"

"Please don't hurt me," came an echoing voice.

Or was it a pair of voices?

Emma brightened her flame. Bronwyn crept forward and nudged the door with her foot. It swung open to expose a small chamber filled with bones. Femurs, shinbones, skulls—the dismembered fossils of many hundreds of people, heaped up in no apparent order.

I stumbled backward, dizzy with shock.

"Hello?" Emma said. "Who said that? Show yourself!"

At first I couldn't see anything in there but bones, but then I heard a sniffle and followed the sound to the top of the pile, where two pairs of eyes blinked at us from the murky shadows at the rear of the chamber.

"There's no one here," said a small voice.

"Go away," came a second voice. "We're dead."

"No you're not," said Enoch, "and I would know!"

"Come out of there," Emma said gently. "We're not going to hurt you."

Both voices said at once: "Promise?"

"We promise," said Emma.

The bones began to shift. A skull dislodged from the pile and clattered to the floor, where it rolled to a stop at my feet and stared up at me.

Hello, future, I thought.

Then two young boys crawled into the light, on hands and knees atop the bone pile. Their skin was deathly pale and they peeped at us with black-circled eyes that wheeled dizzyingly in their sockets.

"I'm Emma, this is Jacob, and these are our friends," Emma said. "We're peculiar and we're not going to hurt you."

The boys crouched like frightened animals, saying nothing, eyes spinning, seeming to look everywhere and nowhere.

"What's wrong with them?" Olive whispered.

Bronwyn hushed her. "Don't be rude."

"Can you tell me your names?" Emma said, her voice coaxing and gentle.

"I am Joel and Peter," the larger boy said.

"Which are you?" Emma said. "Joel or Peter?"

"I am Peter and Joel," said the smaller boy.

"We don't have time for games," said Enoch. "Are there any birds in there with you? Have you seen any fly past?"

"The pigeons like to hide," said the larger.

"In the attic," said the smaller.

"What attic?" said Emma. "Where?"

"In our house," they said together, and raising their arms they pointed down the dark passage. They seemed to speak cooperatively, and if a sentence was more than a few words long, one would start and the other finish, with no detectable pause between. I also noticed that whenever one was speaking and the other wasn't, the quiet one would mouth the other's words in perfect synchronicity—as if they shared one mind.

"Could you please show us the way to your house?" asked Emma. "Take us to your attic?"

Joel-and-Peter shook their heads and shrank back into the dark.

"What's the matter?" Bronwyn said. "Why don't you want to go?"

"Death and blood!" cried one boy.

"Blood and screaming!" cried the other.

"Screaming and blood and shadows that bite!" they cried together.

"Cheerio!" said Horace, turning on his heels. "I'll see you all back in the crypt. Hope I don't get squashed by a bomb!"

Emma caught Horace by his sleeve. "Oh, no you don't! You're the only one of us who's managed to catch any of those blasted pigeons."

"Didn't you hear them?" Horace said. "That loop is full of shadows that bite—which could only mean one thing. Hollows!"

"It *was* full of them," I said. "But that might have been days ago."

"When was the last time you were inside your house?" Emma asked the boys.

Their loop had been raided, they explained in their strange and broken way, but they'd managed to escape into the catacombs and hide among the bones. How long ago that was, they couldn't say. Two days? Three? They'd lost all track of time down here in the dark.

"Oh, you poor dears!" said Bronwyn. "What terrors you must've endured!"

"You can't stay here forever," said Emma. "You'll age forward if you don't reach another loop soon. We can help you—but first we have to catch a pigeon."

The boys gazed into one another's spinning eyes and seemed to speak without uttering a word. They said in unison, "Follow us."

They slid down from their bone pile and started down the passage. We followed. I couldn't take my eyes off them; they were fascinatingly odd. They kept their arms linked at all times, and every few steps, they made loud clicking sounds with their tongues.

"What are they doing?" I whispered.

"I believe that's how they see," said Millard. "It's the same way bats see in the dark. The sounds they make reflect off things and then back to them, which forms a picture in their minds."

"We are echolocators," Joel-and-Peter said.

They were also, apparently, very sharp of hearing.

The passage forked, then forked again. At one point I felt a sudden pressure in my ears and had to wiggle them to release it. That's when I knew we'd left 1940 and entered a loop. Finally we came to a dead-end wall with vertical steps cut into it. Joel-and-Peter stood at the base of the wall and pointed to a pinpoint of daylight overhead.

"Our house—" said the elder.

"Is up there," said the younger.

And with that, they retreated into the shadows.

The steps were slimed with moss and difficult to climb, and I had to go slowly or risk falling. They ascended the wall to meet a circular, person-sized door in the ceiling, through which shone a single gleam of light. I wedged my fingers into the crack and pushed sideways, and the doors slid open like a camera shutter, revealing a tubular conduit of bricks that rose twenty or thirty feet to a circle of sky. I was at the false bottom of a fake well.

I pulled myself into the well and climbed. Halfway up I had to stop and rest, pushing my back against the opposite side of the shaft. When the burn in my biceps subsided, I climbed the rest of the way, scrambling over the lip of the well to land in some grass.

I was in the courtyard of a shabby-looking house. The sky was an infected shade of yellow, but there was no smoke in it and no sound of engines. We were in some older time, before the war—before cars, even. There was a chill in the air, and errant flakes of snow drifted down and melted on the ground.

Emma came up the well next, then Horace. Emma had decided that only the three of us should explore the house. We didn't know what we would find up here, and if we needed to leave in a hurry, it was better to have a small group that could move fast. None who stayed below argued; Joel-and-Peter's warning of blood and shadows had scared them. Only Horace was unhappy, and kept muttering to himself that he wished he'd never caught that pigeon in the square.

Bronwyn waved to us from below and then pulled closed the circular door at the bottom of the well. The top side was painted to look like the surface of water—dark, dirty water you'd never want to drop a drinking bucket into. Very clever.

The three of us huddled together and looked around. The courtyard and the house were suffering from serious neglect. The grass around the well was tamped down, but everywhere else it grew up in weedy thickets that reached higher than some of the ground-floor windows. A doghouse sat rotting and half collapsed in one corner, and near it a toppled laundry line was gradually being swallowed by brush.

We stood and waited, listening for pigeons. From beyond the house's walls, I could hear the tap of horses' hooves on pavement. No, this definitely wasn't London circa 1940.

Then, in one of the upper-floor windows, I saw a curtain shift. "Up there!" I hissed, pointing at it.

I didn't know if a bird or a person had done it, but it was worth checking out. I started toward a door that led into the house, beckoning the others after me—then tripped over something. It was a body lying on the ground, covered head to ankle with a black tarp. A pair of worn shoes poked from one end, pointing at the sky. Tucked into one cracked sole was a white card, on which had been written in neat script:

Mr. A. F. Crumbley
Lately of the Outer Provinces
Aged forward rather than be taken alive
Kindly requests his remains be deposited in the Thames

"Unlucky bastard," Horace whispered. "He came here from the country, probably after his own loop was raided—only to have the one he'd escaped to raided, as well."

"But why would they leave poor Mr. Crumbley out in the open this way?" whispered Emma.

"Because they had to leave in a hurry," I said.

Emma bent down and reached for the edge of Mr. Crumbley's tarp. I didn't want to look but couldn't help myself, and I half turned away but peeked back through split fingers. I had expected a withered corpse, but Mr. Crumbley looked perfectly intact and surprisingly young, perhaps only forty or fifty years old, his black hair graying just around the temples. His eyes were closed and peaceful, as if he might've just been sleeping. Could he really have aged forward, like the leathery apple I took from Miss Peregrine's loop?

"Hullo, are you dead or asleep?" Emma said. She nudged the man's ear with her boot, and the side of his head caved and crumbled to dust.

Emma gasped and let the tarp fall back. Crumbley had become a desiccated cast of himself, so fragile that a strong wind could blow him apart.

We left poor, crumbling Mr. Crumbley behind and went to the door. I grasped the knob and turned it. The door opened and we stepped through it into a laundry room. There were fresh-looking clothes in a hamper, a washboard hung neatly above a sink. This place had not been abandoned long.

The Feeling was stronger here, but was still only residue. We opened another door and came into a sitting room. My chest tightened. Here was clear evidence of a fight: furniture scattered and overturned, pictures knocked off the mantel, stripes of wallpaper shredded to ribbons.

Then Horace muttered, "Oh, *no*," and I followed his gaze upward, to a dark stain discoloring a roughly circular patch of ceiling. Something awful had happened upstairs.

Emma squeezed her eyes closed. "Just listen," she said. "Listen for the birds and don't think about anything else."

We closed our eyes and listened. A minute passed. Then, finally, the fluttering coo of a pigeon. I opened my eyes to see where it had come from.

The staircase.

We mounted the stairs gently, trying not to creak them under our feet. I could feel my heartbeat in my throat, in my temple. I could handle old, brittle corpses. I wasn't sure if I could take a murder scene.

The second-floor hallway was littered with debris. A door, torn from its hinges, lay splintered. Through the broken doorway was a fallen tower of trunks and dressers; a failed blockade.

In the next room, the white carpet was soaked with blood—the stain that had leaked through the floor to the ceiling below. But whomever it had leaked from was long gone.

The last door in the hall showed no signs of forced entry. I pushed it open warily. My eyes scanned the room: there was a wardrobe, a dresser topped with carefully arranged figurines, lace curtains fluttering in a window. The carpet was clean. Everything undisturbed.

Then my eyes went to the bed, and what was in it, and I stumbled back against the doorjamb. Nestled under clean white covers were two men, seemingly asleep—and between them, two skeletons.

"Aged forward," said Horace, his hands trembling at his throat. "Two of them considerably more than the others."

The men who looked asleep were as dead as Mr. Crumbley downstairs, Horace said, and if we touched them, they would disintegrate in just the same way.

"They gave up," Emma whispered. "They got tired of running and they gave up." She looked at them with a mix of pity and disgust.

She thought they were weak and cowardly—that they'd taken the easy way out. I couldn't help wondering, though, if these peculiars simply knew more than we did about what the wights did with their captives. Maybe we would choose death, too, if we knew.

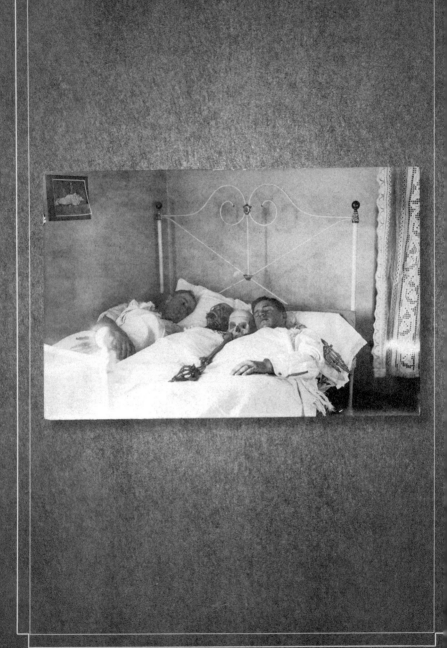

We drifted into the hall. I felt dizzy and sick, and I wanted out of this house—but we couldn't leave yet. There was one last staircase to climb.

At the top, we found a smoke-damaged landing. I imagined peculiars who'd withstood the initial attack on this house gathering here for a last stand. Maybe they'd tried to fight the corrupted with fire—or maybe the corrupted had tried to smoke them out. Either way, it looked like the house had come close to burning down.

Ducking through a low doorway, we entered a narrow, slope-walled attic. Everything here was burned black. Flames had made gaping holes in the roof.

Emma prodded Horace. "It's here somewhere," she said quietly. "Work your magic, bird-catcher."

Horace tiptoed into the middle of the room and sing-songed, "Heeeeere, pigeon, pigeon, pigeon . . ."

Then, from behind us, we heard a wingbeat and a strangled chirp. We turned to see not a pigeon but a girl in a black dress, half hidden in the shadows.

"Is this what you're after?" the girl said, raising one arm into a shaft of sunlight. The pigeon squirmed in her hand, struggling to free itself.

"Yes!" Emma said. "Thank heaven you caught it!" She moved toward the girl with her hands out to take the pigeon, but the girl shouted, "Stop right there!" and snapped her fingers. A charred throw rug flew out from beneath Emma and took her feet with it, sending her crashing to the floor.

I rushed to Emma. "Are you okay?"

"On your knees!" the girl barked at me. "Put your hands on your head!"

"I'm fine," Emma said. "Do as she says. She's telekinetic and clearly unstable."

I knelt down by Emma and laced my fingers behind my head.

Emma did the same. Horace, trembling and silent, sat heavily and placed his palms on the floor.

"We don't mean you any harm," Emma said. "We're only after the pigeon."

"Oh, I know perfectly well what you're after," the girl said with a sneer. "Your kind never gives up, do you?"

"Our *kind*?" I said.

"Lay down your weapons and slide them over!" barked the girl.

"We don't have any," Emma said calmly, trying her best not to upset the girl any further.

"This will go easier for you if you don't assume I'm stupid!" the girl shouted. "You're weak and have no powers of your own, so you rely on guns and things. Now lay them on the floor!"

Emma turned her head and whispered, "She thinks we're wights!"

I almost laughed out loud. "We aren't wights. We're *peculiar*!"

"You aren't the first blank-eyes to come here pigeon-hunting," she said, "nor the first to try impersonating peculiar children. And you wouldn't be the first I've killed, neither! Now put your weapons on the floor before I snap this pigeon's neck—and then yours!"

"But we aren't wights!" I insisted. "Look at our pupils if you don't believe us!"

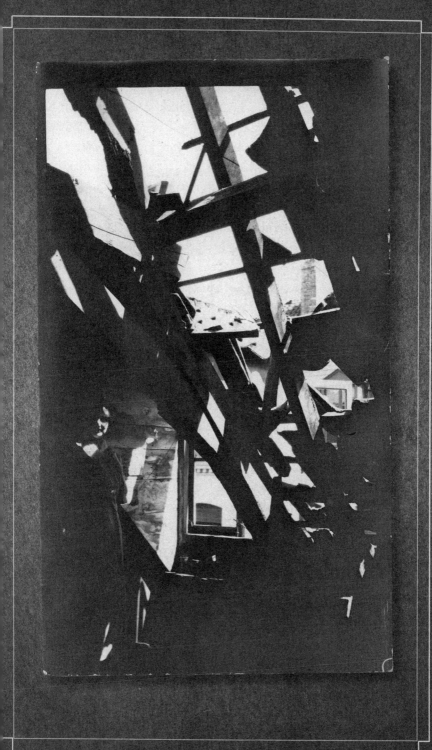

"Your eyes don't mean *nothing*!" the girl said. "False lenses are the oldest trick in the book—and trust me, I know 'em all."

The girl took a step toward us, into the light. Hate smoldered in her eyes. She was tomboyish, except for the dress, with short hair and a muscular jaw. She had the glassy look of someone who hadn't slept in days; who was running now on instinct and adrenaline. Someone in that condition wouldn't be kind to us, nor patient.

"We *are* peculiar, I swear!" Emma said. "Watch—I'll show you!" She lifted one hand from her head and was about to make a flame when a sudden intuition made me grab her wrist.

"If there are hollows close by, they'll sense it," I said. "I think they can feel us kind of like I feel them—but it's much easier for them when we use our powers. It's like setting off an alarm."

"But you're using *your* power," she said, irritated. "And she's using hers!"

"Mine is passive," I said. "I can't turn it off, so it doesn't leave much of a trail. As for her—maybe they already know she's here. Maybe it's not her they want."

"How convenient!" the girl said to me. "And that's supposed to be your power? Sensing shadow creatures?"

"He can see them, too," said Emma. "And kill them."

"You need to invent better lies," the girl said. "No one with half a brain would buy that."

Just as we were talking about it, a new Feeling blossomed painfully inside me. I was no longer sensing the left-behind residue of a hollow, but the active presence of one.

"There's one nearby," I said to Emma. "We need to get out of here."

"Not without the bird," she muttered.

The girl started across the room toward us. "Time to get on with it," she said. "I've given you more than enough chances to prove yourselves. Anyway, I'm beginning to *enjoy* killing you things. After what you did to my friends, I just can't seem to get enough of it!"

She stopped a few feet from us and raised her free hand—about to bring what was left of the roof down on our heads, maybe. If we were going to make a move, it had to be now.

I sprang from my crouched position, threw my arms in front of me, and collided with the girl, knocking her to the floor. She cried out in angry surprise. I rammed my fist into the palm of her free hand so she couldn't snap her fingers again. She let the bird go, and Emma grabbed it.

Then Emma and I were up, rushing toward the open door. Horace was still on the floor in a daze. "Get up and run!" Emma shouted at him.

I was pulling Horace up by his arms when the door slammed in my face and a burned dresser lifted out of the corner and flew across the room. The edge of it connected with my head and I went sprawling, taking Emma down with me.

The girl was in a rage, screaming. I was certain we had only seconds to live. Then Horace stood up and shouted at the top of his lungs:

"*Melina Manon!*"

The girl froze. "What did you say?"

"Your name is Melina Manon," he said. "You were born in Luxembourg in 1899. You came to live with Miss Thrush when you were sixteen years old, and have been here ever since."

Horace had caught her off guard. She frowned, then made an arcing motion with her hand. The dresser that had nearly knocked me unconscious sailed through the air and then stopped, hovering, directly above Horace. If she let it drop, it would crush him. "You've done your homework," said the girl, "but any wight could know my name and birthplace. Unfortunately for you, I no longer find your deceptions interesting."

And yet, she didn't quite seem ready to kill him.

"Your father was a bank clerk," Horace said, speaking quickly. "Your mother was very beautiful but smelled strongly of onions, a lifelong condition she could do nothing to cure."

The dresser wobbled above Horace. The girl stared at him, her brows knit together, hand in the air.

"When you were seven, you badly wanted an Arabian horse," Horace continued. "Your parents couldn't afford such an extravagant animal, so they bought a donkey instead. You named him Habib, which means *beloved*. And loved him you did."

The girl's mouth fell open.

Horace went on.

"You were thirteen when you realized you could manipulate objects using only your mind. You started with small things, paper clips and coins, then larger and larger ones. But you could never pick up Habib with your mind, because your ability did not extend to living creatures. When your family moved houses, you thought it had gone away entirely, because you couldn't move anything at all anymore. But it was simply that you hadn't gotten to know the new house yet. Once you became familiar with it, mapped it in your mind, you could move objects within its walls."

"How could you possibly know all this?" Melina said, gaping at him.

"Because I dreamed about you," said Horace. "That's what *I* can do."

"My God," said the girl, "you *are* peculiar."

And the dresser drifted gently to the floor.

✳   ✳   ✳

I wobbled to my feet, head throbbing where the dresser had hit me.

"You're bleeding!" Emma said, jumping up to inspect my cut.

"I'm fine, I'm fine," I said, dodging her. The Feeling was shifting inside me, and being touched while it was happening made it harder to interpret; interrupted its development somehow.

"Sorry about your head," Melina Manon said. "I thought I was the only peculiar left!"

"There's a whole gang of us down your well, in the catacomb tunnel," Emma said.

"Really?" Melina's face lit up. "Then there's still hope!"

"There was," said Horace. "But it just flew out the hole in your roof."

"What—you mean Winnifred?" Melina put two fingers in her mouth and whistled. A moment later, the pigeon appeared, flying down through the hole to land on her shoulder.

"Marvelous!" said Horace, clapping his hands. "How'd you do that?"

"Winnie's my chum," Melina said. "Tame as a house cat."

I wiped some blood from my forehead with the back of my hand, then chose to ignore the pain. There wasn't time to be hurt. I said to the girl, "You mentioned that wights have been here, chasing pigeons."

Melina nodded. "Them and their shadow beasts came three nights ago. Surrounded the place, took Miss Thrush and half our wards here, then set fire to the house. I hid on the roof. Since then, wights have come back every day, in little groups, hunting for Winnifred and her friends."

"And you killed them?" Emma asked.

Melina looked down. "That's what I said, ain't it?"

She was too proud to admit she'd lied. It didn't matter.

"Then we're not the only ones hunting for Miss Wren," Emma said.

"That means she's still free," I said.

"Maybe," said Emma. "Maybe."

"We think the pigeon can help us," I said. "We need to find Miss Wren, and we think the bird knows how."

"I never heard of any Miss Wren," said Melina. "I just feed Winnie when she comes into our courtyard. We're friends, she and I. Ain't we, Winnie?"

The bird chirped happily on her shoulder.

Emma moved close to Melina and addressed the pigeon. "Do you know Miss Wren?" she said, enunciating loudly. "Can you help us find her? *Miss Wren?*"

The pigeon leapt off Melina's shoulder and flapped across the room to the door. She warbled and fluttered her wings, then flew back.

This way, it seemed to say.

That was proof enough for me. "We need to take the bird with us," I said.

"Not without me," said Melina. "If Winnie knows how to find this ymbryne, then I'm coming, too."

"Not a good idea," said Horace. "We're on a dangerous mission, you see—"

Emma cut him off. "Give us the bird. We'll come back for you, I promise."

A sudden jolt of pain made me gasp and double over.

Emma rushed to my side. "Jacob! Are you all right?"

I couldn't speak. Instead I hobbled to the window, forced myself upright, and projected my Feeling out toward the cathedral dome, visible over the rooftops just a few blocks away—then down at the street, where horse-drawn wagons rattled past.

Yes, there. I could feel them approaching from a side street, not far away.

Them. Not one hollow, but two.

"We have to go," I said. "*Now.*"

"Please," Horace begged the girl. "We *must* have the pigeon!"

Melina snapped her fingers, and the dresser that had nearly killed me raised up off the floor again. "I can't allow that," she said, narrowing her eyes and flicking them toward the dresser just to make sure we understood one another. "But take me along and you get Winnie in the bargain. Otherwise . . ."

The dresser pirouetted on one wooden leg, then tipped and crashed onto its side.

"Fine then," Emma said through her teeth. "But if you slow us down, we take the bird and leave you behind."

Melina grinned, and with a flick of her hand the door banged open.

"Whatever you say."

*   *   *

We flew down the stairs so fast that our feet hardly seemed to touch the ground. In twenty seconds we were back in the courtyard, leaping over dead Mr. Crumbley, diving down the dry well. I went first, kicking in the mirrored door at the bottom rather than wasting time sliding it open. It broke from its hinges and fell in pieces. "Look out below!" I called, then lost my grip on the wet stone steps and fell flailing and tumbling into the dark.

A pair of strong arms caught me—Bronwyn's—and set my feet on the floor. I thanked her, my heart pounding.

"What happened up there?" asked Bronwyn. "Did you catch the pigeon?"

"We got it," I said as Emma and Horace reached the bottom, and a cheer went up among our friends. "That's Melina," I said, pointing up at her, and that was all the time for introductions we had. Melina was still at the top of the steps, fooling with something. "Come on!" I shouted. "What are you doing?"

"Buying us time!" she shouted back, and then she pulled shut and locked a wooden lid that capped the well, closing out the last rays of light. As she climbed down in darkness, I explained about the hollows that were chasing us. In my panicked state, this came out as *"GO NOW RUN HOLLOWS NOW,"* which was effective if not terribly articulate, and threw everyone into hysterics.

"How can we run if we can't see?!" Enoch shouted. "Light a flame, Emma!"

She'd been holding off because of my warning back in the attic.

Now seemed like a good time to reinforce that, so I grabbed her arm and said, "Don't! They'll be able to pinpoint us too easily!" Our best hope, I thought, was to lose them in this forking maze of tunnels.

"But we can't just run blindly in the dark!" said Emma.

"Of course," said the younger echolocator.

"We can," said the older.

Melina stumbled toward their voices. "Boys! You're alive! It's me—it's Melina!"

Joel-and-Peter said:

"We thought you were—"

"Dead every last—"

"One of you."

"Everyone link hands!" Melina said. "Let the boys lead the way!"

So I took Melina's hand in the dark and Emma took mine, then she felt for Bronwyn's, and so on until we'd formed a human chain with the blind brothers in the lead. Then Emma gave the word and the boys took off at an easy run, plunging us into the black.

We forked left. Splashed through puddles of standing water. Then from the tunnel behind us came an echoing crash that could only have meant one thing: the hollows had smashed through the well door.

"They're in!" I shouted.

I could almost feel them narrowing their bodies, wriggling down into the shaft. Once they made it to level ground and could run, they'd overtake us in no time. We'd only passed one split in the tunnels—not enough to lose them. Not nearly enough.

Which is why what Millard said next struck me as patently insane: "Stop! Everyone stop!"

The blind boys listened to him. We piled up behind them, tripping and skidding to a halt.

"What the hell is wrong with you?!" I shouted. *Run!*

"So sorry," Millard said, "but this just occurred to me—one of us will have to pass through the loop exit before the echolocators or the girl do, or they will cross into the present and we into 1940, and we'll be separated. For them to travel to 1940 with us, one of *us* has to go first and open the way."

"You didn't come from the present?" Melina said, confused.

"From 1940, like he said," Emma replied. "It's raining bombs out there, though. You might want to stay behind."

"Nice try," said Melina, "you ain't getting rid of me that easy. It's got to be worse in the present—wights everywhere! That's why I never left Miss Thrush's loop."

Emma stepped forward and pulled me with her. "Fine! We'll go first!"

I stuck out my free arm, feeling blindly in the dark. "But I can't see a thing!"

The elder echolocator said, "It's just twenty paces ahead there, you—"

"Can't miss it," said the younger.

So we plodded ahead, waving our hands in front of us. I kicked something with my foot and stumbled. My left shoulder scraped the wall.

"Keep it straight!" Emma said, pulling me to the right.

My stomach lurched. I could feel it: the hollows had made it down the well shaft. Now, even if they couldn't sense us, there was a fifty-fifty chance they'd choose the right spur of the tunnel and find us anyway.

The time for sneaking around was over. We had to run.

"Screw it," I said. "Emma, give me a light!"

"Gladly!" She let my hand go and made a flame so large I felt the hair on the right side of my head singe.

I saw the transition point right away. It was just ahead of us, marked by a vertical line painted on the tunnel wall. We took off running for it in a mob.

The moment we passed it, I felt a pressure in my ears. We were back in 1940.

We bolted through the catacombs, Emma's fire casting manic shadows across the walls, the blind boys clicking loudly with their tongues and shouting out "Left!" or "Right!" when we came to splits in the tunnel.

We passed the stack of coffins, the landslide of bones. Finally we returned to the dead end and the ladder to the crypt. I shoved Horace up ahead of me, then Enoch, and then Olive took off her shoes and floated up.

"We're taking too long!" I shouted.

Down the passage I could feel them coming. Could hear their tongues pounding the stone floor, propelling them forward. Could picture their jaws beginning to drip black goo in anticipation of a kill.

Then I saw them. A blur of dark motion in the distance.

I screamed, "*Go!*" and leapt onto the ladder, the last one to climb it. When I was near the top, Bronwyn reached down her arm and yanked me up the last few rungs, and then I was in the crypt with everyone else.

Groaning loudly, Bronwyn picked up the stone slab that topped Christopher Wren's tomb and dropped it back in place. Not two seconds later, something slammed violently against the underside of it, making the heavy slab leap. It wouldn't hold the hollows for long—not two of them.

They were so close. Alarms blared inside me, my stomach aching like I'd drunk acid. We dashed up the spiral staircase and into the nave. The cathedral was dark now, the only illumination a weird orange glow eking through the stained-glass windows. I thought for a moment it was the last strains of sunset, but then, as we dashed toward the exit, I caught a glimpse of the sky through the broken roof.

Night had fallen. The bombs were falling still, thudding like an irregular heartbeat.

We ran outside.

CHAPTER TEN

*F*rom where we stood, arrested in awe on the cathedral steps, it looked as if the whole city had caught fire. The sky was a panorama of orange flame bright enough to read by. The square where we'd chased pigeons was a smoking hole in the cobblestones. The sirens droned on, a soprano counterpoint to the bombs' relentless bass, their pitch so eerily human it sounded like every soul in London had taken to their rooftops to cry out collective despair. Then awe gave way to fear and the urgency of self-preservation, and we rushed down the debris-strewn steps into the street—past the ruined square, around a double-decker bus that looked like it had been crushed in the fist of an angry giant—running I knew not where, nor cared, so long as it was away from the Feeling that grew stronger and sicker inside me with each passing moment.

I looked back at the telekinetic girl, pulling the blind brothers along by their hands while they clicked with their tongues. I thought of telling her to let the pigeon go so we could follow it—but what use would it be to find Miss Wren now, while hollows were chasing us? We'd reach her only to be slaughtered at her doorstep, and we'd put her life in danger, too. No, we had to lose the hollows first. Or better yet, kill them.

A man in a metal hat stuck his head out of a doorway and shouted, "You are advised to take cover!" then ducked back inside.

Sure, I thought, *but where?* Maybe we could hide in the debris and the chaos around us, and with so much noise and distraction everywhere, the hollows would pass us by. But we were still too close to them, our trail too fresh. I warned my friends not to use their abilities, no matter what, and Emma and I led them zigzagging through the streets, hoping this would make us harder to track.

Still, I could feel them coming. They were out in the open now, out of the cathedral, lurching after us, invisible to all but me. I wondered if even I would be able to see them here, in the dark: shadow creatures in a shadow city.

We ran until my lungs burned. Until Olive couldn't keep up anymore and Bronwyn had to scoop her into her arms. Down long blocks of blacked-out windows staring like lidless eyes. Past a bombed library snowing ash and burning papers. Through a bombed cemetery, long-forgotten Londoners unearthed and flung into trees, grinning in rotted formal wear. A curlicued swing set in a cratered playground. The horrors piled up, incomprehensible, the bombers now and then dropping flares to light it all with the pure, shining white of a thousand camera flashes. As if to say: *Look. Look what we made.*

Nightmares come to life, all of it. Like the hollows themselves. *Don't look don't look don't look . . .*

I envied the blind brothers, navigating a mercifully detail-free topography; the world in wireframe. I wondered, briefly, what their dreams looked like—or if they dreamt at all.

Emma jogged alongside me, her wavy, powder-coated hair flowing behind her. "Everyone's knackered," she said. "We can't keep going like this!"

She was right. Even the fittest of us were flagging now, and soon the hollows would catch up to us and we'd have to face them in the middle of the street. And that would be a bloodbath. We had to find cover.

I steered us toward a row of houses. Because bomber pilots were more likely to target a cheerfully lit house than another smudge in the dark, every house was blacked out—every porch light dark, every window opaque. An empty house would be safest for us, but blacked out like this, there was no way to tell which houses were occupied and which weren't. We'd have to pick one at random.

I stopped us in the road.

"What are you doing?" Emma said, puffing to catch her breath. "Are you mad?"

"Maybe," I said, and then I grabbed Horace, swept my hand toward the row of houses, and said, "Choose."

"What?" he said. "Why me?"

"Because I trust your random guesses more than my own."

"But I never dreamed about this!" he protested.

"Maybe you did and don't remember," I said. "*Choose.*"

Realizing there was no way out of it, he swallowed hard, closed his eyes for a second, then turned and pointed to a house behind us. "That one."

"Why that one?" I asked.

"Because you made me choose!" Horace said angrily.

That would have to do.

*　　*　　*

The front door was locked. No problem: Bronwyn wrenched off the knob and tossed it into the street, and the door creaked open on its own. We filed into a dark hallway lined with family photos, the faces impossible to make out. Bronwyn closed the door and blocked it with a table she found in the hall.

"Who's there?" came a voice from further inside the house.

Damn. We weren't alone. "You were supposed to pick an *empty* house," I said to Horace.

"I'm going to hit you very hard," Horace muttered.

There was no time to switch houses. We'd have to introduce ourselves to whoever was here and hope they were friendly.

"*Who is there!*" the voice demanded.

"We aren't thieves or Germans or anything like that!" Emma said. "Just here to take cover!"

No response.

"Stay here," Emma told the others, and then she pulled me after her down the hall. "We're coming to say hello!" she called out, loud and friendly. "Don't shoot us, please!"

We walked to the end of the hall and rounded a corner, and there, standing in a doorway, was a girl. She held a wicked-down lantern in one hand and a letter opener in the other, and her hard, black eyes flicked nervously between Emma and me. "There's nothing of value here!" she said. "This house has been looted already."

"I told you, we're not thieves!" Emma said, offended.

"And I told you to leave. If you don't, I'll scream and . . . and my father will come running with his . . . guns and things!"

The girl looked at once childish and prematurely adult. She had her hair in a short bob and wore a little girl's dress with big white buttons trailing down the front, but something in her stony expression made her seem older, world-weary at twelve or thirteen.

"Please don't scream," I said, thinking not about her probably fictitious father but about what other things might come running.

Then a small voice piped up behind her, through the doorway she'd been conspicuously blocking. "Who's there, Sam?"

The girl's face pinched in frustration. "Only some children," she said. "I asked you to keep quiet, Esme."

"Are they nice? I want to meet them!"

"They were just leaving."

"There are lots of us and two of you," Emma said matter-of-factly. "We're staying here for a bit, and that's that. You're not going to scream, either, and we're not going to steal anything."

The girl's eyes flashed with anger, then dulled. She knew she'd lost. "All right," she said, "but try anything and I'll scream *and* bury this in your belly." She brandished the letter opener weakly, then lowered it to her waist.

"Fair enough," I said.

"Sam?" said the little voice. "What's happening now?"

The girl—Sam—stepped reluctantly aside, revealing a bathroom that danced with the flickering light of candles. There was a sink and a toilet and a bathtub, and in the bathtub a little girl of perhaps five. She peeped curiously at us over the rim. "This is my sister, Esme," Sam said.

"Hullo!" said Esme, waggling a rubber duck at us. "Bombs can't get you when you're in the bath, did you know that?"

"I didn't," Emma replied.

"It's her safe place," Sam whispered. "We spend every raid in here."

"Wouldn't you be safer in a shelter?" I said.

"Those are awful places," Sam said.

The others had tired of waiting and began coming down the hall. Bronwyn leaned through the doorway and waved hello.

"Come in!" Esme said, delighted.

"You're too trusting," Sam scolded her. "One day you're going to meet a bad person and then you'll be sorry."

"They aren't bad," said Esme.

"You can't tell just by *looking*."

Then Hugh and Horace pressed their faces through the doorway, curious to see whom we'd met, and Olive scooted between their legs and sat in the middle of the floor, and pretty soon all of us were squeezed into the bathroom together, even Melina and the blind brothers, who stood creepily facing the corner. Seeing so many people, Sam's legs shook and she sat down heavily on the toilet, overwhelmed—but her sister was thrilled, asking everyone's name as they came in.

"Where are your parents?" Bronwyn asked.

"Father's shooting bad people in the war," Esme said proudly. She mimed holding a rifle and shouted, *"Bang!"*

Emma looked at Sam. "You said your father was upstairs," she said flatly.

"You broke into our house," Sam replied.

"True."

"And your mother?" said Bronwyn. "Where is she?"

"A long time dead," Sam said with no apparent feeling. "So when Father went to war they tried shipping us off to family elsewhere—and because Father's sister in Devon is terribly mean and would only take one of us, they tried shipping Esme and me off to different places. But we jumped off the train and came back."

"We won't be split up," Esme declared. "We're *sisters*."

"And you're afraid if you go to a shelter they'll find you?" Emma said. "Send you away?"

Sam nodded. "I won't let that happen."

"It's safe in the tub," said Esme. "Maybe you should get in, too. That way we'd all be safe."

Bronwyn touched her hand to her heart. "Thank you, love, but we'd never fit!"

While the others talked, I turned my focus inward, trying to sense the hollows. They weren't running anymore. The Feeling had stabilized, which meant they weren't getting closer or farther away, but were probably sniffing around nearby. I took this as a good sign; if they knew where we were, they'd be coming straight for us. Our trail had gone cold. All we had to do was keep our heads down for a while, and then we could follow the pigeon to Miss Wren.

We huddled on the bathroom floor listening to bombs fall in other parts of the city. Emma found some rubbing alcohol in the medicine cabinet and insisted on cleaning and bandaging the cut on my head. Then Sam began to hum some tune I knew but couldn't quite name, and Esme played with her duck in the tub, and ever so slowly, the Feeling began to diminish. For a scant few minutes, that twinkling bathroom became a world unto itself; a cocoon far away from trouble and war.

But the war outside refused to be ignored for long. Anti-aircraft guns rattled. Shrapnel skittered like claws across the roof. The bombs drew closer until their reports were followed by lower, more ominous sounds—the dull thud of walls collapsing. Olive hugged herself. Horace put his fingers in his ears. The blind boys moaned and rocked on their feet. Miss Peregrine wriggled deep into the folds of Bronwyn's coat and the pigeon trembled in Melina's lap.

"What sort of madness have you led us into?" Melina said.

"I warned you," Emma replied.

The water in Esme's tub rippled with each blast. The little girl clutched her rubber duck and began to cry. Her sobs filled the little room. Sam hummed louder, pausing to whisper, "You're safe, Esme, you're safe in here," between melody lines, but Esme only cried harder. Horace took his fingers out of his ears and tried to distract Esme by making shadow animals on the wall—a crocodile snapping its jaws, a bird flying—but she hardly noticed. Then, the last person I'd expect to care about making a little girl feel better scooted over to the tub.

"Look here," Enoch said, "I have a little man who'd like to ride on your duck, and he'd just about fit, too." From his pocket he took a clay homunculus figure, three inches tall, the last of those he'd made on Cairnholm. Esme's sobs abated as she watched him bend the clay man's legs and sit him on the edge of the tub. Then, with a press of Enoch's thumb against the clay man's tiny chest, he came to life. Esme's face glowed with delight as the clay man sprang to his feet and strolled along the lip of the tub.

"Go on," said Enoch. "Show her what you can do."

The clay man jumped up and clicked his heels, then took an exaggerated bow. Esme laughed and clapped her hands, and when a bomb fell close by a moment later, causing the clay man to lose his balance and fall into the tub, she only laughed harder.

A sudden chill rolled up the back of my neck and prickled my scalp, and then the Feeling came over me so swiftly and sharply that I groaned and doubled over where I sat. The others saw me and knew instantly what it meant.

They were coming. They were coming very quickly.

Of course they were: Enoch had used his power, and I hadn't even thought to stop him. We might as well have sent up a signal flare.

I staggered to my feet, the pain attacking me in debilitating waves. I tried to shout—*Go, run! Run out the back!*—but couldn't force the words. Emma put her hands on my shoulders. "Collect yourself, love, we need you!"

Then something was beating at the front door, each impact echoing through the house. "They're here!" I finally managed to say, but the sound of the door shaking on its hinges had said it for me.

Everyone scrambled to their feet and squeezed into the hall in a panicked knot. Only Sam and Esme stayed put, baffled and cowering. Emma and I had to pry Bronwyn away from the tub. "We can't just *leave* them!" she cried as we dragged her toward the door.

"Yes, we can!" said Emma. "They'll be all right—they aren't

the ones the hollows are after!"

I knew that was true, but I also knew the hollows would tear apart anything in their path, including a couple of normal girls.

Bronwyn struck the wall in anger, leaving a fist-shaped hole. "I'm sorry," she said to the girls, then let Emma push her into the hall.

I hobbled after them, my stomach writhing. "Lock this door and don't open it for anyone!" I shouted, then looked back to catch a last glimpse of Sam's face, framed in the closing door, her eyes big and scared.

I heard a window smash in the front hall. Some suicidal curiosity made me peek around the corner. Squirming through the black-out curtains was a mass of tentacles.

Then Emma took my arm and yanked me away—down another hall—into a kitchen—out the back door—into an ash-dusted garden—down an alley where the others were running in a loose group. Then someone said "Look, look!" and, still running, I swiveled to see a great white bird fluttering high above the street. Enoch said, "Mine—it's a mine!" and what had seemed like gossamer wings resolved suddenly and clearly into a parachute, the fat silver body hanging below it packed with explosives; an angel of death floating serenely toward earth.

The hollows burst outside. I could see them distantly, loping through the garden, tongues waving in the air.

The mine landed by the house with a gentle *clink*.

"*Get down!*" I screamed.

We never had a chance to run for cover. I'd only just hit the ground when there was a blinding flash and a sound like the earth ripping open and a shock wave of searing hot wind that knocked the air from my lungs. Then a black hail of debris whipped hard against my back and I hugged my knees to my chest, making myself as compact as I could.

After that, there was only wind and sirens and a ringing in my ears. I gasped for air and choked on the swirling dust. Pulling the collar of my sweater up over my nose and mouth to filter it, I slowly caught my breath.

I counted my limbs: two arms, two legs.

Good.

I sat up slowly and looked around. I couldn't see much through the dust, but I heard my friends calling out for one another. There was Horace's voice, and Bronwyn's. Hugh's. Millard's.

Where was Emma?

I shouted her name. Tried to get up and fell back again. My legs were intact but shaking; they wouldn't take my weight.

I shouted again. *"Emma!"*

"I'm here!"

My head snapped toward her voice. She materialized through the smoke.

"Jacob! Oh, God. Thank God."

Both of us were shaking. I put my arms around her, running my hands over her body to make sure she was all there.

"Are you all right?" I said.

"Yes. Are you?"

My ears hurt and my lungs ached and my back stung where I'd been pelted by debris, but the pain in my stomach was gone. The moment the blast went off, it was as if someone had flipped a switch inside me, and just like that, the Feeling had vanished.

The hollows had been vaporized.

"I'm okay," I said. "I'm okay."

Aside from scrapes and cuts, so were the rest of us. We staggered together in a cluster and compared injuries. All were minor. "It's some kind of miracle," Emma said, shaking her head in disbelief.

It seemed even more so when we realized that everywhere around us were nails and bits of concrete and knifelike splinters of wood, many of them driven inches into the ground by the blast.

Enoch wobbled to a car parked nearby, its windows smashed,

its frame so pocked with shrapnel that it looked like it had been sprayed by a machine gun. "We should be dead," he marveled, poking his finger into one of the holes. "Why aren't *we* full of holes?"

Hugh said, "Your shirt, mate," then went to Enoch and plucked a crumpled nail from the back of his grit-encrusted sweater.

"And yours," said Enoch, pulling a jagged spike of metal from Hugh's.

Then we all checked our sweaters. Embedded in each were long shards of glass and pieces of metal that should have passed right through our bodies—but hadn't. Our itchy, ill-fitting, peculiar sweaters weren't fireproof or waterproof, as the emu-raffe had guessed. They were *bulletproof*. And they had saved our lives.

"I never dreamed I'd owe my life to such an appalling article of clothing," said Horace, testing the sweater's wool between his fingers. "I wonder if I could make a tuxedo jacket out of it instead."

Then Melina appeared, pigeon on her shoulder, blind brothers at her side. With their sonarlike senses, the brothers had discovered a low wall of reinforced concrete—it had *sounded* hard—and pulled Melina behind it just as the bomb exploded. That left only the two normal girls unaccounted for. But as the dust settled and their house came into view—or what was left of it—any hope of finding them alive seemed to fade. The upper floor had collapsed, pancaking down onto the lower. What remained was a skeletal wreck of exposed beams and smoking rubble.

Bronwyn took off running toward it anyway, shouting the sisters' names. Numbly, I watched her go.

"We could've helped them and we didn't," Emma said miserably. "We left them to die."

"It wouldn't have made the least bit of difference," Millard said. "Their deaths had been written into history. Even if we'd saved their lives today, something else would've taken them tomorrow. Another bomb. A bus crash. They were of the past, and the past always mends itself, no matter how we interfere."

"Which is why you can't go back and kill baby Hitler to stop the war from happening," said Enoch. "History heals itself. Isn't that interesting?"

"No," Emma snapped, "and you're a heartless bastard for talking about killing babies at a time like this. Or ever."

"Baby *Hitler*," said Enoch. "And talking loop theory is better than going into pointless hysterics." He was looking at Bronwyn, who was climbing the rubble, digging in the wreckage, flinging debris this way and that.

She turned and waved her arms at us. "Over here!" she cried.

Enoch shook his head. "Someone please retrieve her. We've got an ymbryne to find."

"Over here!" Bronwyn shouted, louder this time. "I can hear one of them!"

Emma looked at me. "Wait. What did she say?"

And then we were all running to meet her.

*   *   *

We found the little girl beneath a slab of broken ceiling. It had fallen across the bathtub, which was wrecked but had not entirely collapsed. Cowering inside was Esme—wet, filthy, and traumatized—but alive. The tub had protected her, just like her sister promised it would.

Bronwyn lifted the slab enough for Emma to reach in and pull Esme out. She clung to Emma, trembling and weeping. "Where's my sister?" she said. "Where's Sam?"

"Hush, baby, hush," Emma said, rocking her back and forth. "We're going to get you to a hospital. Sam will be along later." That was a lie, of course, and I could see Emma's heart breaking as she told it. That we had survived and the little girl had also were two miracles in one night. To expect a third seemed greedy.

But then a third miracle did happen, or something like one: her sister answered.

"I'm here, Esme!" came a voice from above.

"*Sam!*" the little girl shouted, and we all looked up.

Sam was dangling from a wooden beam in the rafters. The beam was broken and hung down at a forty-five-degree angle. Sam was near the low end, but still too high for any of us to reach.

"Let go!" Emma said. "We'll catch you!"

"I can't!"

Then I looked more closely and saw why she couldn't, and I nearly fainted.

Sam's arms and legs were dangling free. She wasn't hanging *onto* the beam, but *from* it. She'd been impaled through the center of her body. And yet her eyes were open, and she was blinking alertly in our direction.

"I appear to be stuck," she said calmly.

I was sure Sam would die at any moment. She was in shock, so she felt no pain, but pretty soon the adrenaline pumping through her system would dissipate, and she'd fade, and be gone.

"Someone get my sister down!" Esme cried.

Bronwyn went after her. She climbed a crumbling staircase to the ruined ceiling, then reached out to grab onto the beam. She pulled and pulled, and with her great strength was able to angle the beam downward until the broken end was nearly touching the rubble below. This allowed Enoch and Hugh to reach Sam's dangling legs and, very gently, slide her forward until she came free with a soft *ploop!* and landed on her feet.

Sam regarded the hole in her chest dully. It was nearly six inches in diameter and perfectly round, like the beam she'd been impaled on, and yet it didn't seem to concern her much.

Esme broke away from Emma and ran to her sister. "Sam!" she cried, throwing her arms around the injured girl's waist. "Thank Heaven you're all right!"

"I don't think she is!" Olive said. "I don't think she is at all!"

But Sam worried only for Esme, not for herself. Once she'd hugged the stuffing out of her, Sam knelt down and held the little girl at arm's length, scanning for cuts and bruises. "Tell me where it hurts," she said.

"My ears are ringy. I scraped my knees. And I got some dirt in my eye . . ."

Then Esme began to tremble and cry, the shock of what had happened overcoming her again. Sam hugged her close, saying, "There, there . . ."

It made no sense that Sam's body was functioning in any capacity. Stranger still, her wound wasn't even bleeding, and there was no gore or little bits of entrails hanging out of it, like I knew to expect from horror movies. Instead, Sam looked like a paper doll that had been attacked with a giant hole-punch.

Though everyone was dying for an explanation, we had elected to give the girls a moment to themselves, and stared in amazement from a respectful distance.

Enoch, however, paid them no such courtesy. "Excuse me," he said, crowding into their personal space, "but could you please explain how it is that you're alive?"

"It's nothing serious," Sam said. "Although my dress may not survive."

"Nothing serious?!" said Enoch. "I can see clear through you!"

"It does smart a little," she admitted, "but it'll fill in in a day or so. Things like this always do."

Enoch laughed dementedly. "*Things like this?*"

"In the name of all that's peculiar," Millard said quietly. "You know what this means, don't you?"

"She's one of us," I said.

*　　*　　*

We had questions. Lots of questions. As Esme's tears began to
fade, we worked up the courage to ask them.

Did Sam realize she was peculiar?

She knew she was different, she said, but had never heard the
term *peculiar*.

Had she ever lived in a loop?

She had not ("A what?"), which meant she was just as old as
she appeared to be. Twelve, she said.

Had no ymbryne ever come to find her?

"Someone came once," she answered. "There were others like
me, but to join them I would've had to leave Esme behind."

"Esme can't . . . *do* anything?" I asked.

"I can count backward from one hundred in a duck voice,"
Esme volunteered through her sniffles, and then began to demonstrate, quacking: "One hundred, ninety-nine, ninety-eight . . ."

Before she could get any further, Esme was interrupted by a
siren, this one high-pitched and moving fast in our direction. An ambulance careened into the alley and raced toward us, its headlights
blacked out so that only pinpricks of light shone through. It skidded
to a stop nearby, cut its siren, and a driver leapt out.

"Is anyone hurt?" the driver said, rushing over to us. He wore
a rumpled gray uniform and a dented metal hat, and though he was
full of energy, his face looked haggard, like he hadn't slept in days.

His eyes met the hole in Sam's chest, and he stopped dead in his
tracks. "Cor blimey!"

Sam got to her feet. "It's nothing, really!" she said. "I'm fine!"
And to demonstrate how fine she was, she passed her fist in and out
of the hole a few times and did a jumping jack.

The medic fainted.

"Hm," said Hugh, nudging the fallen man with his foot.

"You'd think these chaps would be made of tougher stuff."

"Since he's clearly unfit for service, I say we borrow his ambulance," Enoch said. "There's no knowing where in the city that pigeon's leading us. If it's far, it could take us all night to reach Miss Wren on foot."

Horace, who'd been sitting on a chunk of wall, sprang to his feet. "That's a fine idea!" he said.

"It's a *reprehensible* idea!" Bronwyn said. "You can't steal an ambulance—injured persons need it!"

"*We're* injured persons," Horace whined. "*We* need it!"

"It's hardly the same thing!"

"Saint Bronwyn!" Enoch said sarcastically. "Are you so concerned with the well-being of normals that you'd risk Miss Peregrine's life to protect a few of theirs? A thousand of them aren't worth one of her! Or one of us, for that matter!"

Bronwyn gasped. "What a thing to say in front of . . ."

Sam stalked toward Enoch with a humorless look on her face. "Look here, boy," she said, "if you imply that my sister's life is worthless again, I will clobber you."

"Calm down, I wasn't referring to your sister. I only meant that . . ."

"I know exactly what you meant. And I'll clobber you if you say it again."

"I'm sorry if I've offended your delicate sensibilities," Enoch said, his voice rising in exasperation, "but you've never had an ymbryne and you've never lived in a loop, and so you couldn't possibly understand that this—right now—is not *real*, strictly speaking. It's the *past*. The life of every normal in this city has already been lived. Their fates are predetermined, no matter how many ambulances we steal! So it doesn't bloody *matter*, you see."

Looking a bit baffled, Sam said nothing, but continued to give Enoch the evil eye.

"Even so," said Bronwyn. "It's not right to make people suffer unnecessarily. We *can't* take the ambulance!"

"That's all well and good, but think of Miss Peregrine!" said Millard. "She can't have more than a day left."

Our group seemed evenly divided between stealing the ambulance or going on foot, so we put it to a vote. I myself was against taking it, but mostly because the roads were so pocked with bomb holes that I didn't know how we'd drive the thing.

Emma took the vote. "Who's for taking the ambulance?" she said.

A few hands shot up.

"And against?"

Suddenly there was a loud pop from the direction of the ambulance, and we all turned to see Miss Peregrine standing by as one of its rear tires hissed air. Miss Peregrine had voted with her beak—by stabbing it into the ambulance's tire. Now *no one* could use it—not us, not injured persons—and there was no point in arguing or delaying any further.

"Well, that simplifies things," said Millard. "We go on foot."

"Miss Peregrine!" Bronwyn cried. "How could you?"

Ignoring Bronwyn's indignation, Miss Peregrine hopped over to Melina, looked up at the pigeon on her shoulder, and screeched. The message was clear: *Let's go already!*

What could we do? Time was wasting.

"Come with us," Emma said to Sam. "If there's any justice in the world, we'll be somewhere safe before the night is through."

"I told you, I won't leave my sister behind," Sam replied. "You're going to one of those places she can't enter, aren't you?"

"I—I don't know," Emma stammered. "It's possible . . ."

"I don't care either way," Sam said coldly. "After what I just saw, I wouldn't so much as cross the road with you."

Emma drew back, going a bit pale. In a small voice she asked, "Why?"

"If even outcasts and downtrodden folk like yourselves can't muster a bit of compassion for others," she said, "then there's no hope for this world." And she turned away and carried Esme toward the ambulance.

Emma reacted as if she'd been slapped, her cheeks going red. She ran after Sam. "We don't all think the way Enoch does! And as for our ymbryne, I'm sure she didn't mean to do what she did!"

Sam spun to face her. "That was no accident! I'm glad my sister's not like all of you. Wish to God I wasn't."

She turned away again, and this time Emma didn't follow. With wounded eyes she watched Sam go, then slouched after the others. Somehow the olive branch she'd extended had turned into a snake and bitten her.

Bronwyn peeled off her sweater and set it down on the rubble. "Next time bombs start falling, have your sister wear this," she called to Sam. "It'll keep her safer than any bathtub."

Sam said nothing; didn't even look. She was bending over the ambulance driver, who was sitting up now and mumbling, "I had the queerest dream . . ."

"That was a stupid thing to do," Enoch said to Bronwyn. "Now *you* don't have a sweater."

"Shut your fat gob," Bronwyn replied. "If you'd ever done a nice thing for another person, you might understand."

"I *did* do something nice for another person," Enoch said, "and it nearly got us eaten by hollows!"

We mumbled goodbyes that went unreturned and slipped quietly into the shadows. Melina took the pigeon from her shoulder and tossed it skyward. It flew a short distance before a string she'd tied around its foot snapped taut and it hovered, caught in the air, like a dog straining at its lead. "Miss Wren's this way," Melina said, nodding in the direction the bird was pulling, and we followed the girl and her pigeon friend down the alley.

I was about to assume hollow-watch, my now-customary position near the head of the group, when something made me glance back at the sisters. I turned in time to see Sam lift Esme into the ambulance, then bend forward to plant a kiss on each of her scraped knees. I wondered what would happen to them. Later, Millard would tell me that the fact that none of them had ever heard of Sam—and someone with such a unique peculiarity would've been well known—meant she probably had not survived the war.

The whole episode had really gotten to Emma. I don't know why it was so important for her to prove to a stranger that we were good-hearted, when we knew ourselves to be—but the suggestion that we were anything less than angels walking the earth, that our natures were more complexly shaded, seemed to bother her. "They don't understand," she kept saying.

Then again, I thought, *maybe they do.*

CHAPTER ELEVEN

*S*o it had come to this: everything depended on a pigeon. Whether we would end the night in the womblike safety of an ymbryne's care or half chewed in the churning black of a hollow's guts; whether Miss Peregrine would be saved or we'd wander lost through this hellscape until her clock ran out; whether I would live to see my home or my parents again—it all depended on one scrawny, peculiar pigeon.

I walked at the front of the group, feeling for hollows, but it was really the pigeon who led us, tugging on its leash like a bloodhound after a scent. We turned left when the bird flew left, and right when it jerked right, obedient as sheep even when it meant fumbling down streets cratered with ankle-breaking bomb holes or bristling with the bones of dismembered buildings, their jagged iron spear tips lurking dimly in the wavering fire glow, angled at our throats.

Coming down from the terrifying events of that evening, I'd reached a new low of exhaustion. My head tingled strangely. My feet dragged. The rumble of bombs had quieted and the sirens had finally wound down, and I wondered if all that apocalyptic noise had been keeping me awake. Now the smoky air was alive with subtler sounds: water gushing from broken mains, the whine of a trapped dog, hoarse voices moaning for help. Occasionally fellow travelers would materialize out of the dark, wraithlike figures escaped from some lower world, eyes shining with fear and suspicion, clutching random things in their arms—radios, looted silver, a gilt box, a funerary urn. Dead bearing the dead.

We came to a T in the road and stopped, the pigeon deliberating between left and right. The girl murmured encouragements: "Come on, Winnie. There's a good pigeon. Show us the way."

Enoch leaned in and whispered, "If you don't find Miss Wren, I will personally roast you on a spit."

The bird leapt into the air, urging left.

Melina glowered at Enoch. "You're an ass," she said.

"I get results," he replied.

Eventually we arrived at an underground station. The pigeon led us through its arched entry into a ticket lobby, and I was about to say *We're taking the subway—smart bird*, when I realized the lobby was deserted and the ticket booth shuttered. Though it didn't look like trains would be visiting this station anytime soon, we forged ahead regardless, through an unchained gate, along a hallway lined with peeling notices and chipped white tiles, to a deep staircase where we spiraled down and down into the city's humming, electric-lit belly.

At each landing, we had to step around sleeping people wrapped in blankets: lone sleepers at first, then groups lying like scattered matchsticks, and then, as we reached bottom, an unbroken human tide that swept across the underground platform—hundreds of people squeezed between a wall and the tracks, curled on the floor, sprawled on benches, sunk into folding chairs. Those who weren't sleeping rocked babies in their arms, read paperbacks, played cards, prayed. They weren't waiting for a train; no trains were coming. They were refugees from the bombs, and this was their shelter.

I tried sensing for hollows, but there were too many faces, too many shadows. Luck, if we had any left, would have to sustain us for a while.

Now what?

We needed directions from the pigeon, but it seemed briefly confused—like me, it was probably overwhelmed by the crowd—so we stood and waited, the breaths and snores and mumbles of the sleepers murmuring weirdly around us.

After a minute the pigeon stiffened and flew toward the tracks, then reached the end of its leash and bounced back into Melina's hand like a yo-yo.

We tiptoed around the bodies to the edge of the platform, then hopped down into the pit where the tracks ran. They disappeared into tunnels on either end of the station. I had a sinking feeling that our future lay somewhere inside one of these dark, gaping mouths.

"Oh, I hope we don't have to go mucking about in *there*," said Olive.

"Of course we do," Enoch said. "It isn't a proper holiday until we've plumbed every available sewer."

The pigeon bopped rightward. We started down the tracks.

I hopscotched around an oily puddle and a legion of rats scurried away from my feet, sending Olive into Bronwyn's arms with a shriek. The tunnel yawned before us, black and menacing. It occurred to me that this would be a very bad place to meet a hollowgast. Here there'd be no walls to climb, no houses to shelter in, no tomb lids to close behind us. It was long and straight and lit only by a few red bulbs, glinting feebly at scattered intervals.

I walked faster.

The darkness closed around us.

*   *   *

When I was a kid, I used to play hide-and-seek with my dad. I was always the hider and he the seeker. I was really good at it, primarily because I, unlike most kids of four or five, had the then-peculiar ability to be extremely quiet for long periods of time, and also because I suffered from absolutely no trace of anything resembling claustrophobia: I could wedge myself into the smallest rear-closet crawl space and stay there for twenty or thirty minutes, not making a sound, having the time of my life.

Which is why you'd think I wouldn't have a problem with the

whole dark, enclosed spaces thing. Or why, at the very least, you'd think a tunnel meant to contain trains and tracks and nothing else would be easier for me to handle than one that was essentially an open cemetery, with all manner of Halloweenish things spilling out along it. And yet, the farther into this tunnel we walked, the more I was overcome by clammy, creeping dread—a feeling entirely apart from the one I sensed hollows with; this was simply a *bad feeling*. And so I hurried us through as fast as the slowest of us could go, prodding Melina until she barked at me to back off, a steady drip of adrenaline keeping my deep exhaustion at bay.

After a long walk and several Y-shaped tunnel splits, the pigeon led us to a disused section of track where the ties had warped and rotted and pools of stagnant water spanned the floor. The pressure of trains passing in far-off tunnels pushed the air around like breaths in some great creature's gullet.

Then, way down ahead of us, a pinpoint of light winked into being, small but growing fast. Emma shouted, "Train!" and we split apart and pressed our backs to the walls. I covered my ears, expecting the deafening roar of a train engine at close range, but it never came—all I could hear was a small, high-pitched whine, which I was fairly certain was coming from inside my own head. Just as the light was filling the tunnel, its white glow surrounding us, I felt a sudden pressure in my ears and the light disappeared.

We stumbled away from the walls in a daze. Now the tracks and ties under our feet were new, as if they'd just been laid. The tunnel smelled somewhat less intensely of urine. The bulbs along it had gotten brighter, and instead of giving a steady light, they flickered—because they weren't electric bulbs at all, but gaslamps.

"What just happened?" I said.

"We crossed into a loop," said Emma. "But what was that light? I've never seen anything like that."

"Every loop entrance has its quirks," said Millard.

"Anyone know when we are?" I asked.

"I'd guess the latter half of the nineteenth century," said Millard. "Prior to 1863 there wasn't an underground system in London at all."

Then, from behind us, another light appeared—this one accompanied by a gust of hot wind and a thunderous roar. *"Train!"* Emma shouted again, and this time it really was. We threw ourselves against the walls as it shot past in a cyclone of noise and light and belching smoke. It looked less like a modern subway train than a miniature locomotive. It even had a caboose, where a man with a big black beard and a guttering lantern in his hand gaped at us in surprise as the train strafed away around the next bend.

Hugh's cap had blown off his head and been crushed. He went to pick it up, found it shredded, and threw it down again angrily. "I don't care for this loop," he said. "We've been here all of ten seconds and already it's trying to kill us. Let's do what we have to and get gone."

"I couldn't agree more," said Enoch.

The pigeon guided us on down the track. After ten minutes or so, it stopped, pulling toward what looked like a blank wall. We couldn't understand why, until I looked up and noticed a partially camouflaged door where the wall met the ceiling, twenty feet overhead. Because there seemed no other way to reach it, Olive took off her shoes and floated up to get a closer look. "There's a lock on it," she said. "A combination lock."

There was also a pigeon-sized hole rusted through the door's bottom corner, but that was no help to us—we needed the combination.

"Any idea what it could be?" Emma asked, putting the question out to everyone.

She was met with shrugs and blank looks.

"None," said Millard.

"We'll have to guess," she said.

"Perhaps it's my birthday," said Enoch. "Try three–twelve–

ninety-two."

"Why would anyone know your birthday?" said Hugh.

Enoch frowned. "Just try it."

Olive spun the dial back and forth, then tried the lock. "Sorry, Enoch."

"What about our loop day?" Horace suggested. "Nine–three–forty."

That didn't work, either.

"It's not going to be something easy to guess, like a date," said Millard. "That would defeat the purpose of having a lock."

Olive began to try random combinations. We stood by watching, growing more anxious with each failed attempt. Meanwhile, Miss Peregrine slipped quietly from Bronwyn's coat and hopped over to the pigeon, who was waddling around at the end of its lead, pecking at the ground. When it saw Miss Peregrine, it tried to hop away, but the headmistress followed, making a low, vaguely threatening warble in her throat.

The pigeon flapped its wings and flew up to Melina's shoulder, out of Miss Peregrine's reach. Miss Peregrine stood by Melina's feet, squawking at it. This seemed to make the pigeon extremely nervous.

"Miss P, what are you up to?" said Emma.

"I think she wants something from your bird," I said to Melina.

"If the pigeon knows the way," said Millard, "perhaps it knows the combination, too."

Miss Peregrine turned toward him and squawked, then looked back at the pigeon and squawked louder. The pigeon tried to hide behind Melina's neck.

"Perhaps the pigeon knows the combination but doesn't know how to tell us," said Bronwyn, "but it could tell Miss Peregrine, because both of them speak bird language, and then Miss Peregrine could tell us."

"Make your pigeon talk to our bird," said Enoch.

"Your bird's twice Winnie's size and sharp on three ends," Melina said, backing away a step. "She's scared and I don't blame her."

"There's nothing to be scared of," said Emma. "Miss P would never hurt another bird. It's against the ymbryne code."

Melina's eyes widened, then narrowed. "That bird is an *ymbryne?*"

"She's our headmistress!" said Bronwyn. "Alma LeFay Peregrine."

"Full of surprises, ain't you?" Melina said, then laughed in a way that wasn't exactly friendly. "If you've got an ymbryne right there, what d'you need to find another one for?"

"It's a long story," said Millard. "Suffice to say, our ymbryne needs help that only another ymbryne can give."

"Just put the blasted pigeon on the ground so Miss P can talk to it!" said Enoch.

Finally, reluctantly, Melina agreed. "Come on, Winnie, there's a good girl." She lifted the pigeon from her shoulder and placed it gently at her feet, then pinned its leash under her shoe so it couldn't fly away.

Everyone circled around to watch as Miss Peregrine advanced on the pigeon. It tried to run but was caught short by the leash. Miss Peregrine got right in its face, warbling and clucking. It was like watching an interrogation. The pigeon tucked its head under its wing and began to tremble.

Then Miss Peregrine pecked it on the head.

"Hey!" said Melina. "Stop that!"

The pigeon kept its head tucked and didn't respond, so Miss Peregrine pecked it again, harder.

"That's enough!" Melina said, and lifting her shoe from the leash, she reached down for the pigeon. Before she could get her fingers around it, though, Miss Peregrine severed the leash with a quick slash of her talons, clamped down with her beak on one of the pigeon's twiggy legs, and bounded away, the pigeon screeching and flailing.

Melina freaked out. "Come back here!" she shouted, furious, about to run after the birds when Bronwyn caught her by the arms.

"Wait!" said Bronwyn. "I'm sure Miss P knows what she's doing . . ."

Miss Peregrine stopped a little way down the track, well out of anyone's reach. The pigeon struggled in her beak, and Melina struggled against Bronwyn, both in vain. Miss Peregrine seemed to be waiting for the pigeon to tire out and give up, but then she got impatient and began swinging the pigeon around in the air by its leg.

"Please, Miss P!" Olive shouted. "You'll kill it!"

I was close to rushing over and breaking it up myself, but the birds were a blur of talons and beaks, and no one could get close enough to separate them. We yelled and begged Miss Peregrine to stop.

Finally, she did. The pigeon dropped from her mouth and wobbled on its feet, too stunned to flee. Miss Peregrine warbled at it the way she had earlier, and this time the pigeon chirped in response. Then Miss Peregrine tapped the ground with her beak three times, then ten times, then five.

Three–ten–five. Olive tried the combination. The lock popped open, the door swung inward, and a rope ladder unrolled down the wall to meet the floor.

Miss Peregrine's interrogation had worked. She'd done what she needed to do to help us all, and given that, we might've overlooked her behavior—if not for what happened next. She took the dazed pigeon by its leg again and, seemingly out of spite, flung it hard against the wall.

We reacted with a great collective gasp of horror. I was shocked beyond speaking.

Melina broke away from Bronwyn and ran to pick up the pigeon. It hung limply from her hand, its neck broken.

"Oh my bird, she's killed it!" cried Bronwyn.

"All we went through to catch that thing," said Hugh, "and now look."

"I'm going to stomp your ymbryne's head!" Melina shrieked, crazed with rage.

Bronwyn caught her arms again. "No, you're not! Stop it!"

"Your ymbryne's a savage! If that's how she conducts herself, we're better off with the wights!"

"You take that back!" shouted Hugh.

"I won't!" Melina said.

More harsh words were exchanged. A fistfight was narrowly avoided. Bronwyn held Melina, and Emma and I held Hugh, until the fight went out of them, if not the bitterness.

No one could quite believe what Miss Peregrine had done.

"What's the big fuss?" said Enoch. "It was just a stupid pigeon."

"No, it wasn't," said Emma, scolding Miss Peregrine directly. "That bird was a personal friend of Miss Wren's. It was hundreds of years old. It was written about in the *Tales*. And now it's dead."

"Murdered," said Melina, and she spat on the ground. "That's what it's called when you kill something for no reason."

Miss Peregrine nibbled casually at a mite under her wing, as if she hadn't heard any of this.

"Something wicked's gotten into her," said Olive. "This isn't like Miss Peregrine at all."

"She's changing," said Hugh. "Becoming more animal."

"I hope there's still something human left in her to rescue," Millard said darkly.

So did we all.

We climbed out of the tunnel, each of us lost in our own anxious thoughts.

*　　*　　*

Beyond the door was a passage that led to a flight of steps that led to another passage and another door, which opened onto a room filled with daylight and packed to the rafters with clothes: racks and closets and wardrobes stuffed with them. There were also two wooden privacy screens to change behind, some freestanding mirrors, and a worktable laid out with sewing machines and bolts of raw fabric. It was half boutique, half workshop—and a paradise to Horace, who practically cartwheeled inside, crying, "I'm in Heaven!"

Melina lurked sullenly at the rear, not speaking to anyone.

"What is this place?" I asked.

"It's a disguising room," Millard answered, "designed to help visiting peculiars blend in with this loop's normals." He pointed out a framed illustration demonstrating how clothes of the period were worn.

"When in Rome!" said Horace, bounding toward a rack of clothes.

Emma asked everyone to change. In addition to helping us blend in, new clothes might also throw off any wights who'd been tracking us. "But keep your sweaters on underneath, in case more trouble finds us."

Bronwyn and Olive took some plain-looking dresses behind a screen. I traded my ash-coated, sweat-stained pants and jacket for a mismatched but relatively clean suit. Instantly uncomfortable, I wondered how, for so many centuries, people wore such stiff, formal clothes all the time.

Millard put on a sharp-looking outfit and sat down in front of a mirror. "How do I look?" he said.

"Like an invisible boy wearing clothes," replied Horace.

Millard sighed, lingered in front of the mirror a bit longer, then stripped and disappeared again.

Horace's initial excitement had already waned. "The selection here is atrocious," he complained. "If the clothes aren't moth-eaten, they're patched with clashing fabric! I am *so* weary of looking like a street urchin."

"Street urchins blend," Emma said from behind her changing screen. "Little gents in top hats do not." She emerged wearing shiny red flats and a short-sleeved blue dress that fell just below the knee. "What do you think?" she said, twirling to make the dress billow.

She looked like Dorothy from *The Wizard of Oz*, only cuter. I didn't know how to tell her this in front of everybody, though, so instead I gave her an awkward grin and a thumbs-up.

She laughed. "Like it? Well, that's too bad," she said with a coy smile. "I'd stick out like a sore thumb." Then a pained expression crossed her face, as if she felt guilty for laughing—for having had even a moment of fun, given all that had happened to us and everything yet to be resolved—and she ducked behind the screen again.

I felt it, too: the dread, the weight of the horrors we'd seen, which replayed themselves in an endless, lurid loop in my mind. But you can't feel bad *every second*, I wanted to tell her. Laughing doesn't make bad things worse any more than crying makes them better. It doesn't mean you don't care, or that you've forgotten. It just means you're human. But I didn't know how to say this, either.

When she came out again, she had on a sacklike blouse with ripped sleeves and a broomstick skirt that brushed the top of her feet. (Much more urchin like.) She'd kept the red shoes, though. Emma could never resist a touch of glitter, however small.

"And this?" said Horace, waving a poofy orange wig he'd found. "How's this going to help anyone 'blend in with the normals'?"

"Because it seems we're going to a carnival," said Hugh, looking up at a poster on the wall that advertised one.

"Just a moment!" Horace said, joining Hugh beneath the poster. "I've heard of this place! It's an old tourist loop."

"What's a tourist loop?" I asked.

"Used to be you could find them all across peculiardom," Millard explained, "placed strategically at times and locations of historical import. They made up a sort of Grand Tour that was once considered an essential part of any well-bred peculiar's education. This was many years ago, of course, when it was still relatively safe to travel abroad. I didn't realize there were any left."

Then he got quiet, lost in memories of a better time.

When we'd all finished changing, we left our twentieth-century clothes in a heap and followed Emma through another door, out into an alleyway stacked with trash and empty crates. I recognized the sounds of a carnival in the distance: the arrhythmic wheeze of pipe organs, the dull roar of a crowd. Even through my nerves and exhaustion, I felt a jangle of excitement. Once, this was something peculiars had come from far and wide to see. My parents had never even taken me to Disney World.

Emma gave the usual instructions: "Stay together. Watch Jacob and me for signals. Don't talk to anyone, and look no one in the eye."

"How will we know where to go?" asked Olive.

"We'll have to think like ymbrynes," Emma said. "If you were Miss Wren, where would you be hiding?"

"Anywhere but London?" said Enoch.

"If only someone hadn't *murdered the pigeon*," Bronwyn said, staring bitterly at Miss Peregrine.

The headmistress stood on the cobblestones looking up at us, but no one wanted to touch her. We had to keep her out of sight, though, so Horace went back into the disguising room and fetched a denim sack. Miss Peregrine wasn't enthusiastic about this arrangement, but when it became clear that no one was going to pick her up—least of all Bronwyn, who seemed entirely disgusted with her—she climbed inside and let Horace knot the top closed with a strip of leather.

We followed the drunken sound of the carnival through a snarl of cramped lanes, where from wooden carts vendors hawked vegetables and dusty sacks of grain and freshly killed rabbits; where children and thin cats skulked and prowled with hungry eyes, and women with proud, dirty faces squatted in the gutter peeling potatoes, building little mountains with the tossed-away skins. Though we tried very hard to slink by unnoticed, every one of them seemed to turn and stare as we passed: the vendors, the children, the women, the cats, the dead, milk-eyed rabbits swinging by their legs.

Even in my new, period-appropriate clothes, I felt transparently out of place. Blending in was as much about performance as about costume, I realized, and my friends and I carried ourselves with none of the slump-shouldered, shifty-eyed attitude that these people did. In the future, if I wanted to disguise myself as effectively as the wights, I'd have to sharpen my acting skills.

The carnival grew louder as we went, and the smells stronger— overcooked meats, roasting nuts, horse manure, human manure, and the smoke from coal fires all mixing together into something so sickly sweet that it thickened the very air. Finally, we reached a wide square where the carnival was in full, rollicking swing, packed with masses of people and brightly colored tents and more activity than my eyes could take in at once. The whole scene was an assault on my senses. There were acrobats and ropedancers and knife-throwers and fire-eaters and street performers of every type. A quack doctor pitched patent medicines from the back of a wagon: "A rare cordial to fortify the innards against infective parasites, unwholesome damps, and malignant effluvia!" Competing for attention on an adjacent stage was a loudmouthed showman in coattails and a large, prehistoric-looking creature whose gray skin hung from its frame in cascading wrinkles. It took me ten full seconds, as we threaded the crowd past the stage, to recognize it as a bear. It had been shaved and tied to a chair and made to wear a woman's dress, and as its eyes bulged in its head, the showman grinned and pretended to serve it tea, shouting, "Ladies and gentlemen! Presenting the most beautiful lady in all of Wales!"—which earned him a big laugh from the crowd. I half hoped it would break its chains and eat him, right there in front of everyone.

To combat the dizzying effect of all this dreamlike madness, I reached into my pocket to palm the smooth glass of my phone, eyes closed for a moment, and whispered to myself, "I am a time traveler. This is real. I, Jacob Portman, am traveling in time."

This was astonishing enough. More astonishing, perhaps, was the fact that time travel hadn't broken my brain; that by some miracle, I had not yet devolved into a gibbering crazy person ranting on a street corner. The human psyche was much more flexible than I'd imagined, capable of expanding to contain all sorts of contradictions and seeming impossibilities. Lucky for me.

"Olive!" Bronwyn shouted. "Get away from there!" I looked up to see her yank Olive away from a clown who had bent down to talk to her. "I've told you time and again, *never* talk to normals!"

Our group was large enough that keeping it together could be a challenge, especially in a place like this, full of distractions tailor-made to fascinate children. Bronwyn acted as den mother, rounding us up every time one of us strayed to get a closer look at a stall of brightly colored pinwheels or steaming boiled candy. Olive was the most easily distractible, and often seemed to forget that we were in serious danger. It was only possible to keep so many kids in line because they were not actually kids—because there was some older nature inside them, warring against and balancing their childish impulses. With actual children, I'm sure it would've been hopeless.

For a while we wandered aimlessly, looking for anyone who resembled Miss Wren, or anywhere it seemed peculiars were likely to hide. But *everything* here seemed peculiar—this entire loop, with all its chaotic strangeness, was perfect camouflage for peculiars. And yet, even here, people noticed us, their heads turning subtly as we passed. I started to get paranoid. How many of the people around us were spies for the wights—or wights themselves? I was especially wary of the clown, the one Bronwyn had pulled Olive away from. He kept turning up. We must've passed him five times in as many minutes: loitering at the mouth of an alley, staring down from a window, watching us from a tented photo booth, his mussed hair and horrific makeup clashing bizarrely with a backdrop painting of bucolic countryside. He seemed to be everywhere at once.

"It's not good being out in the open like this," I said to Emma. "We can't just circle around forever. People are noticing us. *Clowns.*"

"Clowns?" she said. "Anyway, I agree with you—but it's difficult to know where to start in all this madness."

"We should start at what is always the most peculiar part of *any* carnival," said Enoch, butting between us. "The sideshow." He pointed at a tall, gaudy facade at the edge of the square. "Sideshows and peculiars go together like milk and cookies. Or hollows and wights."

"Usually they do," said Emma, "but the wights know that as well. I'm sure Miss Wren hasn't kept her freedom this long by hiding in such obvious places."

"Have you got a better idea?" said Enoch.

We didn't, and so we shifted direction toward the sideshow. I looked back for the leering clown, but he had melted into the crowd.

At the sideshow, a scruffy carnival barker was shouting through a megaphone, promising glimpses of "the most shocking errors of nature allowed on view by law" for a trivial fee. It was called the Congress of Human Oddities.

"Sounds like dinner parties I've attended," said Horace.

"Some of these 'oddities' might be peculiar," said Millard, "in which case they might know something about Miss Wren. I say it's worth the price of admission."

"We don't have the price of admission," said Horace, pulling a single, lint-flecked coin from his pocket.

"Since when have we ever paid to get into a sideshow?" said Enoch.

We followed Enoch around to the back of the sideshow, where its wall-like facade gave way to a big, flimsy tent. We were scouting for openings to slip through when a flap pulled back and a well-dressed man and woman burst out, the man holding the lady, the lady fanning herself.

"Move aside!" the man barked. "This woman needs air!"

A sign above the flap read: PERFORMERS ONLY.

We slipped inside and were immediately stopped. A plain-looking boy sat on a tufted stool near the entrance, apparently in some official capacity. "You performers?" he said. "Can't come in 'less you're performers."

Feigning offense, Emma said, "Of *course* we're performers," and to demonstrate, she made a tiny flame on the tip of her finger and stubbed it out in her eye.

The boy shrugged, unimpressed. "Go on, then."

We shuffled past him, blinking, our eyes adjusting slowly to the dark. The sideshow was a low-ceilinged maze of canvas—a single, dramatically torchlit aisle that took sharp turns every twenty or thirty feet, so that around each corner we were confronted by a new "abomination of nature." A trickle of spectators, some laughing, others pale and shaking, stumbled past us in the opposite direction.

The first few freaks were standard-issue sideshow fare, and not especially peculiar: an "illustrated" man covered in tattoos; a bearded lady stroking her long chin-whiskers and cackling; a human pincushion who pierced his face with needles and drove nails into his nostrils with a hammer. While I thought this was pretty impressive, my friends, some of whom had traveled Europe in a sideshow with Miss Peregrine, could hardly stifle their yawns.

Under a banner that read THE AMAZING MATCHSTICK MEN, a gentleman with hundreds of matchbooks glued to his suit body-slammed a man similarly clothed in matchsticks, causing flames to erupt across the matchstick man's chest as he flailed in fake terror.

"Amateurs," Emma muttered as she pulled us on to the next attraction.

The oddities got progressively odder. There was a girl in a long, fringed dress who wore a giant python around her body, which wriggled and danced at her command. Emma allowed that this was at least marginally peculiar, since the ability to enchant snakes was something only *syndrigasti* could do. But when Emma mentioned Miss Wren to the girl, she gave us a hard stare and her snake hissed and showed its fangs, and we moved on.

"This is a waste of time," said Enoch. "Miss Peregrine's clock is running out and we're touring a carnival! Why not get some sweets and make a day of it?"

There was only one more freak to see, though, so we continued on. The final stage was empty but for a plain backdrop, a small table with flowers on it, and an easel-propped sign that read: THE WORLD-FAMOUS FOLDING MAN.

A stagehand walked onto the stage lugging a suitcase. He set the case down and left.

A crowd gathered. The suitcase sat there, center stage. People began to shout, "On with the show!" and "Bring out the freak!"

The suitcase jiggled. Then it began to shake, wobbling back and forth until it toppled onto its side. The crowd pressed toward the stage, fixated on the case.

Its latches popped, and very slowly, the case began to open. A pair of white eyes peeped out at the crowd, and then the case opened a little more to reveal a face—that of an adult man, with a neatly trimmed mustache and little round glasses, who had somehow folded himself into a suitcase no larger than my torso.

The crowd burst into applause, which increased as the freak proceeded to unfold himself, limb by limb, and step out of the impossibly small case. He was very tall and as skinny as a beanpole—so alarmingly thin, in fact, that it looked as if his bones were about to break through his skin. He was a human exclamation point, but carried himself with such dignity that I couldn't laugh at him. He studied the hooting crowd dourly before taking a deep bow.

He then took a minute to demonstrate how his limbs could bend in all sorts of exotic ways—his knee twisting so that the top of his foot touched his hip, then his hips folding so that the knee touched his chest—and after more applause and more bows, the show was over.

We lingered as the crowd filtered away. The folding man was leaving the stage when Emma said to him, "You're peculiar, aren't you?"

The man stopped. He turned slowly to look at her with an air of imperious annoyance. "Excuse me?" he said in a thick Russian accent.

"Sorry to corner you this way, but we need to find Miss Wren," Emma said. "We know she's here someplace."

"Peh!" said the man, dismissing her with a noise halfway between laughing and hawking spit.

"It's an emergency!" Bronwyn pleaded.

The folding man crossed his arms in a bony X and said, "I dunno anything what you say," then walked off the stage.

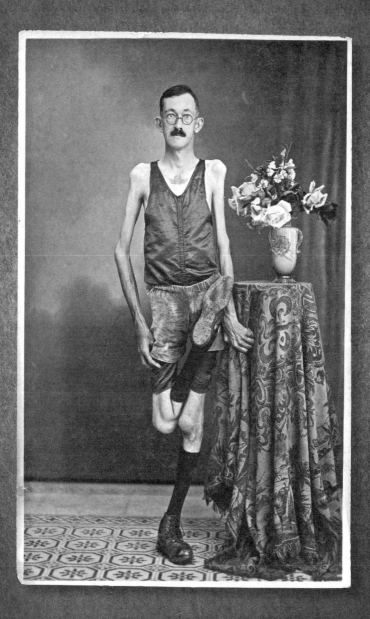

"Now what?" asked Bronwyn.

"We keep looking," said Emma.

"And if we don't find Miss Wren?" said Enoch.

"We *keep looking*," Emma said through her teeth. "Everyone understand?"

Everyone understood perfectly well. We were out of options. If this didn't work—if Miss Wren wasn't here or we couldn't find her soon—then all our efforts would have been for nothing, and Miss Peregrine would be lost just the same as if we'd never come to London at all.

We walked out of the sideshow the way we'd come, dejected, past the now-empty stages, past the plain-looking boy, out of the tent and into the daylight. We were standing outside the exit, unsure what to do next, when the plain-looking boy leaned out through the flap. "Wotsa trouble?" he said. "Show weren't to your liking?"

"It was . . . fine," I said, waving him off.

"Not peculiar enough for you?" he asked.

That got our attention. "What'd you say?" said Emma.

"Wakeling and Rookery," he said, pointing past us toward the far side of the square. "That's where the *real* show is." And then he winked at us and ducked back inside the tent.

"That was mysterious," said Hugh.

"Did he say *peculiar*?" said Bronwyn.

"What's Wakeling and Rookery?" I said.

"A place," said Horace. "Someplace in this loop, maybe."

"Could be the intersection of two streets," said Emma, and she pulled back the tent flap to ask the boy if this was what he meant—but he was already gone.

So we set off through the crowd, toward the far end of the square where he'd pointed, our one last, thin hope pinned to a couple of oddly named streets we weren't even sure existed.

* * *

There was a point, a few blocks beyond the square, where the noise of the crowd faded and was replaced by an industrial clank and clamor, and the rich funk of roasting meat and animal waste was replaced by a stench far worse and unnameable. Crossing a walled river of Stygian sludge, we entered a district of factories and workhouses, of smokestacks belching black stuff into the sky, and this is where we found Wakeling Street. We walked one way down Wakeling looking for Rookery until it dead-ended at a large open sewer which Enoch said was the River Fleet, then turned and came back the other way. When we'd passed the point along Wakeling where we'd started, the street began to curve and twist, the factories and workhouses shrinking down into squat offices and unassuming buildings with blank faces and no signs, like a neighborhood purpose-built to be anonymous.

The bad feeling I'd been nursing got worse. What if we'd been set up—sent to this deserted part of the city to be ambushed out of view?

The street twisted and straightened again, and then I crashed into Emma, who'd been walking in front of me but had come to a sudden stop.

"What's the matter?" I said.

In lieu of an answer, she just pointed. Up ahead, at a T-shaped intersection, there was a crowd. Though it had been sticky-hot back at the carnival, many of them were bundled in coats and scarves. They were assembled around a particular building, and stood gazing up at it in dumbfounded wonder—just as we were, now. The building itself was nothing special—four stories, the top three just rows of narrow, rounded windows, like an old office building. It was, in fact, nearly identical to all the buildings around it, with one exception: it was totally encased in ice. Ice coated its windows and doors. Icicles hung like fangs from every sill and ledge. Snow spilled from its doorways, collecting in giant heaps on the sidewalk. It looked like a blizzard had struck the building—from the *inside*.

I peered at a snow-blasted street sign: R—KERY STRE—.

"I know this place," said Melina. "It's the peculiar archives, where all our official records are kept."

"How do you know that?" said Emma.

"Miss Thrush was grooming me to be second assistant to the ombudswoman there. The examination's very difficult. I've been studying for twenty-one years."

"Is it supposed to be covered in ice like that?" asked Bronwyn.

"Not that I'm aware," said Melina.

"It's also where the Council of Ymbrynes convene for the annual Nitpicking of the Bylaws," said Millard.

"The Council of Ymbrynes meets *here*?" said Horace. "It's awfully humble. I expected a castle or somesuch."

"It's not meant to stand out," said Melina. "You aren't supposed to notice it at all."

"They're doing a poor job of keeping it hidden, then," said Enoch.

"As I said, it's not usually covered in ice."

"What do you think happened here?" I asked.

"Nothing good," said Millard. "Nothing good at all."

There was no question we'd have to get closer and explore, but that didn't mean we had to rush in like fools. We hung back and watched from a distance. People came and went. Someone tried the door but it was frozen shut. The crowd thinned a bit.

"Tick, tick, tick," said Enoch. "We're wasting time."

We cut through what was left of the crowd and stepped onto the icy sidewalk. The building emanated cold, and we shivered and jammed our hands into our pockets against it. Bronwyn used her strength to pull open the door, and it came straight off, hinges flying—but the hallway it let onto was completely obstructed by ice. It stretched from wall to wall, floor to ceiling, and into the building in a blue and cloudy blur. The same was true of the windows: I wiped the frost from one pane and then another, and through both I could see only ice. It was as if a glacier was being born somewhere in the heart of the place, and its frozen tongues were squeezing out wherever there was an opening.

We tried every way we could think of to get inside. We rounded the building looking for a door or window that wasn't blocked, but every potential entrance was filled with ice. We picked up stones and loose bricks and tried hacking at the ice, but it was almost supernaturally hard—even Bronwyn could dig no more than a few inches into it. Millard scanned the *Tales* for any mention of the building, but there was nothing, no secrets to be found.

Finally, we decided to take a calculated risk. We formed a semicircle around Emma to block her from view, and she heated her hands and placed them against the ice wall that filled the hallway. After a minute they began to sink into the ice, meltwater trickling down to puddle around our feet. But the progress was painfully slow, and after five minutes she'd only gotten up to her elbows.

"At this rate, it'll take the rest of the week just to get down the hall," she said, pulling her arms from the ice.

"Do you think Miss Wren could really be inside?" said Bronwyn.

"She *has* to be," Emma said firmly.

"I find this contagion of optimism positively flabbergasting," said Enoch. "If Miss Wren is in there, then she's frozen solid."

Emma erupted at him. "Doom and gloom! Ruin and ruination! I think you'd be happy if the world came to an end tomorrow, just so you could say *I told you so*!"

Enoch blinked at her, surprised, then said very calmly, "You may choose to live in a world of fantasy if you like, my dear, but I am a realist."

"If you *ever* offered more than simple criticism," Emma said, "if you *ever* gave a single useful suggestion during a crisis, rather than just shrugging your shoulders at the prospect of failure and death, I might be able to tolerate your unrelenting black moods! But as it stands—"

"We've tried everything!" Enoch interjected. "What could I possibly suggest?"

"There's *one* thing we haven't tried," Olive said, piping up from the edge of our group.

"And what's that?" asked Emma.

Olive decided to show rather than tell us. Leaving the sidewalk, she went into the crowd, turned to face the building, and called at the top of her lungs, *"Hello, Miss Wren! If you're in there, please come out! We need your—"*

Before she could finish, Bronwyn had tackled her, and the rest of Olive's sentence was delivered into the big girl's armpit. "Are you *insane*?" Bronwyn said, bringing Olive back to us under her arm. "You're going to get us all found out!"

She set Olive on the sidewalk and was about to chastise her further when tears began streaming down the little girl's face. "What does it matter if we're found out?" Olive said. "If we can't find Miss Wren and we can't save Miss Peregrine, what does it matter if the whole wight army descends on us right now?"

A lady stepped out of the crowd and approached us. She was older, back bent with age, her face partly obscured by the hood of a cloak. "Is she all right?" the lady asked.

"She's fine, thank you," Emma said dismissively.

"I'm *not*!" said Olive. "*Nothing* is right! All we ever wanted was to live in peace on our island, and then bad things came and hurt our headmistress. Now all we want to do is help her—and we can't even do *that*!"

Olive hung her head and began to weep pitifully.

"Well then," said the woman, "it's an awfully good thing you came to see me."

Olive looked up, sniffled, and said, "Why is that?"

And then the woman vanished.

Just like that.

She disappeared right out of her clothes, and her cloak, suddenly empty, collapsed onto the pavement with an airy *whump*. We were all too stunned to speak—until a small bird came hopping out from beneath the folds of the cloak.

I froze, not sure if I should try to catch it.

"Does anyone know what sort of bird that is?" asked Horace.

"I believe that's a wren," said Millard.

The bird flapped its wings, leapt into the air, and flew away, disappearing around the side of the building.

"Don't lose her!" Emma shouted, and we all took off running after it, slipping and sliding on the ice, rounding the corner into the snow-choked alley that ran between the glaciated building and the one next to it.

The bird was gone.

"Drat!" Emma said. "Where'd she go?"

Then a series of odd sounds came up from the ground beneath our feet: metallic clanks, voices, and a noise like water flushing. We kicked the snow away to find a pair of wooden doors set into the bricks, like the entrance to a coal cellar.

The doors were unlatched. We pulled them open. Inside were steps that led down into the dark, covered in quick-melting ice, the

meltwater draining loudly into an unseen gutter.

Emma crouched and called into the darkness. "Hello? Is anyone there?"

"If you're coming," returned a distant voice, "come quickly!"

Emma stood up, surprised. Then shouted: "Who are you?"

We waited for an answer. None came.

"What are we waiting for?" said Olive. "It's Miss Wren!"

"We don't know that," said Millard. "We don't know *what* happened here."

"Well, I'm going to find out," Olive said, and before anyone could stop her she'd gone to the cellar doors and leapt through them, floating gently to the bottom. "I'm still alive!" her voice taunted us from the dark.

And so we were shamed into following her, and climbed down the steps to find a passage tunneled through thick ice. Freezing water dripped from the ceiling and ran down the walls in a steady stream. And it wasn't completely dark, after all—gauzy light glowed from around a turn in the passage ahead.

We heard footsteps approaching. A shadow climbed the wall in front of us. Then a cloaked figure appeared at the turn in the passage, silhouetted in the light.

"Hello, children," the figure said. "I am Balenciaga Wren, and I'm so pleased you're here."

CHAPTER TWELVE

I am Balenciaga Wren.

*H*earing those words was like uncorking a bottle under pressure. First came the initial release—gasps, giddy laughter—and then an outpouring of joy: Emma and I jumped and hugged each other; Horace fell to his knees and tossed up his arms in a wordless *hallelujah!* Olive was so excited that she lifted into the air even with her weighted shoes on, stuttering, "We-we-we—we thought we might never—never see another ymbryne ever-ever again!"

This, finally, was Miss Wren. Days ago she'd been nothing more to us than the obscure ymbryne of a little-known loop, but since then she'd achieved mythic stature: she was, as far as we knew, the last free and whole-bodied ymbryne, a living symbol of hope, something we'd all been starving for. And here she was, right in front of us, so human and frail. I recognized her from Addison's photo, only now there was no trace of black left in her silver hair. Deep-set worry lines stacked her brow and held her mouth in parentheses, and her shoulders were hunched as if she were not merely old, but straining under some monumental burden; the weight of all our desperate hope piling down on her.

The ymbryne pulled back the hood of her cloak and said, "I am very glad to meet you, too, dears, but you must come inside at once; it isn't safe out here."

She turned and hobbled away into the passage. We fell into line, waddling behind her through the tunneled ice like a train of ducklings after their mother, feet shuffling and arms held out in awkward balance poses to keep from slipping. Such was the power of an ymbryne over peculiar children: the very presence of one—even one we'd only just met—had an immediate pacifying effect on us.

The floor ramped upward, leading us past silent furnaces bearded with frost, into a large room clogged floor to ceiling and wall to wall with ice except for the tunnel we were in, which had been carved straight through the middle. The ice was thick but clear, and in some places I could see twenty or thirty feet into it with only a slight waver of distortion. The room appeared to be a reception area, with rows of straight-backed chairs facing a massive desk and some filing cabinets, all trapped inside tons of ice. Blue-filtered daylight shone from a row of unreachable windows, beyond which was the street, a smear of indistinct gray.

A hundred hollows could spend a week hacking at that ice and not reach us. If not for the tunnel entrance, this place would make a perfect fortress. Either that or a perfect prison.

On the walls hung dozens of clocks, their stilled hands pointed every which way. (To keep track of the time in different loops, maybe?) Above them, directional signs pointed the way to certain offices:

← UNDERSECRETARY OF TEMPORAL AFFAIRS

← CONSERVATOR OF GRAPHICAL RECORDS

NONSPECIFIC MATTERS OF URGENCY →

DEPT. OF OBFUSCATION AND DEFERMENT →

Through the door to the Temporal Affairs office, I saw a man trapped in the ice. He was frozen in a stooped posture, as if he'd been trying to dislodge his feet as ice overtook the rest of him. He'd been there a long time. I shuddered and looked away.

The tunnel came to an end at a fancy, balustraded staircase that was free of ice but awash in loose papers. A girl stood on one of the lower steps, and she watched our halting, slip-sliding approach without enthusiasm. She had long hair that was parted severely down the middle and fell all the way to her hips, small, round glasses she was constantly adjusting, and thin lips that looked like they'd never once curled into a smile.

"Althea!" Miss Wren said sharply. "You mustn't wander off like that while the passage is open—anything at all might wander in here!"

"Yes, mistress," the girl said, then cocked her head slightly. "Who are they, mistress?"

"These are Miss Peregrine's wards. The ones I was telling you about."

"Have they brought any food with them? Or medicine? Or anything useful at all?" The girl spoke with excruciating slowness, her voice as wooden as her expression.

"No more questions until you've closed up," Miss Wren said. "Quick now!"

"Yes, mistress," the girl said, and with no apparent sense of urgency she ambled away down the tunnel, dragging her hands along the walls as she went.

"Apologies for that," said Miss Wren. "Althea doesn't mean to be obstinate; she's just naturally mulish. But she keeps the wolves at bay, and we badly need her. We'll wait here until she returns."

Miss Wren sat on the bottom step, and as she lowered herself I could almost hear her old bones creaking. I didn't know what she meant by *keeps the wolves at bay*, but there were too many other questions to be asked, so that one would have to wait.

"Miss Wren, how did you know who we are?" asked Emma. "We never said."

"It's an ymbryne's business to know," she replied. "I have watchers in the trees from here to the Irish Sea. And besides, you're famous! There's only one ymbryne whose wards were able to slip the corrupted's grasp complete and entire, and that's Miss Peregrine. But I've no idea how you made it this far without being captured—or how in peculiardom you found me!"

"A boy at the carnival directed us here," said Enoch. He raised a hand level with his chin. "About yea big? Wearing a silly hat?"

"One of our lookouts," said Miss Wren, nodding. "But how did you find *him*?"

"We caught one of your spy pigeons," Emma said proudly, "and she led us to this loop." (She left out the part about Miss Peregrine having killed it.)

"My pigeons!" Miss Wren exclaimed. "But how did you know about them? Much less *catch* one?"

Then Millard stepped forward. He had borrowed Horace's disguising-room overcoat to keep from freezing, and though Miss Wren didn't seem surprised to see a coat hovering in the air, she was astonished when the invisible boy wearing it said, "I deduced your birds' location from the *Tales of the Peculiar*, but we first heard of them in your mountaintop menagerie, from a pretentious dog."

"But *no one* knows the location of my menagerie!"

Miss Wren was now almost too astonished to speak, and since every answer we gave her only sparked more questions, we laid out our whole story for her, as quickly as we could, stretching all the way back to our escape from the island in those tiny, open boats.

"We nearly drowned!" said Olive.

"And got shot, and bombed, and eaten by hollows," said Bronwyn.

"And run over by an underground train," said Enoch.

"And squashed by a dresser," said Horace, scowling at the tele-kinetic girl.

"We've traveled a long way across dangerous country," Emma said, "all to find someone who could help Miss Peregrine. We were quite hoping that person would be you, Miss Wren."

"Counting on it, really," said Millard.

It took Miss Wren a few moments to find her voice, and when she did, it was gravelly with emotion. "You brave, wonderful children. You're miracles, every one of you, and any ymbryne would be lucky to call you her wards." She dabbed at a tear with the sleeve of her cloak. "I was so sorry to hear about what happened to your Miss Peregrine. I didn't know her well, as I'm a retiring sort of person, but I promise you this: we'll get her back. She and all our sisters!"

Get her back?

That's when I realized Miss Peregrine was still hidden in the sack that Horace was carrying. Miss Wren hadn't seen her yet!

Horace said, "Why, she's right here!" and he put the sack down and untied it.

A moment later, Miss Peregrine came tottering out, dizzy after spending so long in the dark.

"By the Elderfolk!" Miss Wren exclaimed. "But . . . I heard she'd been taken by the wights!"

"She *was* taken," Emma said, "and then we took her back!"

Miss Wren was so excited that she leapt up without her cane, and I had to steady her elbow to keep her from toppling over. "Alma, is that really you?" Miss Wren said breathlessly, and when she had her balance again she rushed over to scoop up Miss Peregrine. "Hullo,

Alma? Is that you in there?"

"It's her!" Emma said. "That's Miss Peregrine!"

Miss Wren held the bird at arm's length, turning her this way and that while Miss Peregrine squirmed. "Hum, hum, hum," Miss Wren said under her breath, her eyes narrowing and lips drawing tight. "Something's not right with your headmistress."

"She got hurt," said Olive. "Hurt on the inside."

"She can't turn human anymore," said Emma.

Miss Wren nodded grimly, as if she'd already figured this out. "How long's it been?"

"Three days," said Emma. "Ever since we stole her back from the wights."

I said, "Your dog told us that if Miss Peregrine didn't change back soon, she'd never be able to."

"Yes," Miss Wren said. "Addison was quite right about that."

"He also said that the sort of help she needed was something only another ymbryne could give her," said Emma.

"That's right, too."

"She's changed," said Bronwyn. "She isn't herself anymore. We need the old Miss P back!"

"We can't let this happen to her!" said Horace.

"So?" said Olive. "Can you turn her human now, please?"

We had surrounded Miss Wren and were pressing in on her, our desperation palpable.

Miss Wren put up her hands in a plea for quiet. "I wish it were that simple," she said, "or so immediate. When an ymbryne remains a bird for too long, she becomes rigid, like a cold muscle. If you try and bend her back to shape too quickly, she'll snap. She's got to be massaged into her true form, delicately; worked and worked like clay. If I work with her through the night, I might have it done by morning."

"If she has that long," said Emma.

"Pray that she does," said Miss Wren.

The long-haired girl returned, walking slowly toward us, dragging her hands along the tunnel walls. Everywhere they touched, layer upon layer of new ice formed. The tunnel behind her had already narrowed to just a few feet wide; soon it would be closed completely, and we'd be sealed in.

Miss Wren waved the girl over. "Althea! Run upstairs ahead of us and have the nurse prepare an examination room. I shall need all my medicinal remedies!"

"When you say remedies, do you mean your solutions, your infusions, or your suspensions?"

"All of them!" Miss Wren shouted. "And quickly—this is an emergency!"

Then I saw the girl notice Miss Peregrine, and her eyes widened a bit—the most I'd seen her react to anything—and she started up the stairs.

This time, she was running.

*　　*　　*

I held Miss Wren's arm, steadying her as we climbed the stairs. The building had four stories, and we were heading for the top. Aside from the stairwell, that was the only part of the building still accessible; the other floors were all frozen shut, walls of ice clogging their rooms and hallways. We were, in effect, climbing through the hollowed center of a gigantic ice cube.

I glanced into some of the frozen rooms as we hurried past them. Bulging tongues of ice had broken doors off their hinges, and through their splintered jambs I could see evidence of a raid: kicked-over furniture, drawers torn open, snows of paper on the floor. A machine gun leaned against a desk, its owner frozen in flight. A peculiar slumped in a corner beneath a slash of bullet holes. Like the victims of Pompeii, arrested in ice rather than ash.

It was hard to believe one girl could have been responsible for all this. Apart from ymbrynes, Althea had to be one of the most powerful peculiars I'd ever met. I looked up in time to see her disappear around the landing above us, that endless mane of hair trailing behind her like a blurred afterimage.

I snapped an icicle off the wall. "She really did all this?" I said, turning it in my hand.

"She did indeed," said Miss Wren, puffing beside me. "She is— or was, I should say—apprenticed to the minister of obfuscation and deferment, and was here performing her duties on the day the corrupted raided the building. At the time she knew little of her power other than that her hands radiated unnatural cold. To hear Althea tell it, her ability was the sort of thing that came in useful during hot summer days, but which she'd never thought of as a defense weapon until two hollows began devouring the minister before her very eyes. In mortal fear, she called upon a well of power previously unknown to her, froze the room—and the hollows—and then the entire building, all in the space of a few minutes."

"Minutes!" Emma said. "I don't believe it."

"I rather wish I'd been here to witness it," said Miss Wren, "though if I had, I likely would've been kidnapped along with the other ymbrynes who were present at the time—Miss Nightjar, Miss Finch, and Miss Crow."

"Her ice didn't stop the wights?" I asked.

"It stopped many of them," said Miss Wren. "Several are still with us, I imagine, frozen in the building's recesses. But despite their losses, the wights ultimately got what they came for. Before the entire building froze, they managed to secrete the ymbrynes out through the roof." Miss Wren shook her head bitterly. "I swear on my life, one day I'll personally escort all those that hurt my sisters to Hell."

"All that power she has didn't do any good at all, then," said Enoch.

"Althea wasn't able to save the ymbrynes," Miss Wren said, "but she made this place, and that's blessing enough. Without it we'd have no refuge anywhere. I've been using it as our base of operations for the past few days, bringing back survivors from raided loops as I come across them. This is our fortress, the only safe place for peculiars in all of London."

"And what of *your* efforts, madam?" said Millard. "The dog said you came here to help your sisters. Have you had any luck?"

"No," she said quietly. "My efforts have not been successful."

"Maybe Jacob can help you, Miss Wren," Olive said. "He's very special."

Miss Wren looked sideways at me. "Is that so? And what is your talent, young man?"

"I can see hollows," I said, a little embarrassed. "And sense them."

"And *kill* them, sometimes," added Bronwyn. "If we hadn't found you, Miss Wren, Jacob was going to help us slip past the hollows that guard the punishment loops, so that we could rescue one of the ymbrynes being held there. In fact, maybe he could help *you* . . ."

"That's kind of you," said Miss Wren, "but my sisters are not being held in the punishment loops, or anywhere near London, I'm sure."

"They aren't?" I said.

"No, and they never were. That business about the punishment loops was a ruse concocted to ensnare those ymbrynes whom the corrupted weren't able to capture in their raids. Namely, myself. And it nearly worked. Like a fool, I flew right into their trap—the punishment loops are prisons, after all! I'm lucky to have escaped with only a few scars to show for it."

"Then where were the kidnapped ymbrynes taken?" asked Emma.

"I wouldn't tell you even if I knew, because it's none of your concern," Miss Wren said. "It isn't the duty of peculiar children to worry for the welfare of ymbrynes—it's ours to worry for yours."

"But, Miss Wren, that's hardly fair," Millard began, but she cut him short with a curt "I won't hear anything else about it!" and that was that.

I was shocked by this sudden dismissal, especially considering that if we *hadn't* worried about Miss Peregrine's welfare—and risked our lives to bring her here!—she would've been condemned to spend the rest of her days trapped in the body of a bird. So it did seem like our duty to worry, since the ymbrynes had clearly not done a good enough job worrying to keep their loops from being raided. I didn't like being talked down to that way, and judging from Emma's knitted brow, she didn't, either—but to have said so would've been unthinkably rude, so we finished our climb in awkward silence.

We came to the top of the stairs. Only a few of the doorways on this level were iced over. Miss Wren took Miss Peregrine from Horace and said, "Come on, Alma, let's see what can be done for you."

Althea appeared in an open door, her face flushed, chest heaving. "Your room's all ready, mistress. Everything you asked for."

"Good, good," said Miss Wren.

"If we can do anything to help you," Bronwyn said, "anything at all . . ."

"All I need is time and quiet," Miss Wren replied. "I'll save your ymbryne, young ones. On my life I will." And she turned and took Miss Peregrine into the room with Althea.

Not knowing what else to do with ourselves, we drifted after her and congregated around the door, which had been left open a crack. We took turns peeking inside. In a cozy room dimly lit by oil lamps, Miss Wren sat in a rocking chair holding Miss Peregrine in her lap. Althea stood mixing vials of liquid at a lab table. Every so often she'd lift a vial and swirl it, then walk to Miss Peregrine and pass it under her beak—much the way smelling salts are waved under the nose of someone who's fainted. All the while, Miss Wren rocked in the chair and stroked Miss Peregrine's feathers, singing her a soft, lilting lullaby:

"*Eft kaa vangan soorken, eft ka vangan soorken, malaaya . . .*"

"That's the tongue of the old peculiars," Millard whispered. "Come home, come home . . . remember your true self . . . something like that."

Miss Wren heard him and looked up, then waved us away. Althea crossed the room and shut the door.

"Well, then," said Enoch. "I can see we're not wanted here."

After three days of the headmistress depending on us for everything, we had suddenly become extraneous. Though we were grateful to Miss Wren, she'd made us all feel a bit like children who'd been ordered to bed.

"Miss Wren knows her business," came a Russian-accented voice from behind us. "Best leave her to it."

We turned to see the stick-thin folding man from the carnival, standing with his bony arms crossed.

"You!" said Emma.

"We meet again," the folding man said, his voice deep as an ocean trench. "My name is Sergei Andropov, and I am captain of peculiar resistance army. Come, I will show you around."

*   *   *

"I *knew* he was peculiar!" Olive said.

"No, you didn't," said Enoch. "You only *thought* he was."

"I knew you were peculiar the second I saw you," said the folding man. "How you weren't captured long time ago?"

"Because we're *wily*," said Hugh.

"He means lucky," I said.

"But mostly just hungry," said Enoch. "Got any food around here? I could eat an emu-raffe."

At the mere mention of food, my stomach growled like a wild animal. None of us had eaten since our train ride to London, which seemed eons ago.

"Of course," said the folding man. "This way."

We followed him down the hall.

"So tell me about this peculiar army of yours," Emma said.

"We will crush the wights and take back what's ours. Punish

them for kidnapping our ymbrynes." He opened a door off the hallway and led us through a wrecked office where people lay sleeping on the floor and under desks. As we stepped around them, I recognized a few of their faces from the carnival: the plain-looking boy, the frizzy-haired snake-charmer girl.

"They're all peculiar?" I asked.

The folding man nodded. "Rescued from other loops," he said, holding a door open for us.

"And you?" said Millard. "Where did you come from?"

The folding man led us into a vestibule where we could talk without disturbing the sleepers, a room dominated by two large wooden doors emblazoned with dozens of bird insignias. "I come from land of frozen desert beyond Icy Waste," he said. "Hundred years ago, when hollows first born, they strike my home first. Everything destroy. All in village killed. Old woman. Baby. All." He made a chopping motion in the air with his hand. "I hide in butter churn, breathe through reed of straw, while own brother killed in same house. After, I come to London to escape the hollows. But they come, too."

"That's awful," said Bronwyn. "I'm so sorry for you."

"One day we take revenge," he said, his face darkening.

"You mentioned that," said Enoch. "How many are in your army, then?"

"Right now six," he said, gesturing to the room we'd just left.

"Six people?!" said Emma. "You mean . . . *them*?"

I didn't know whether to laugh or cry.

"With you, makes seventeen. We growing quick."

"Whoa, whoa, whoa," I said. "We didn't come here to join any army."

He gave me a look that could freeze Hell, then turned and threw open the double doors.

We followed him into a large room dominated by a massive oval table, its wood polished to a mirror shine. "This is Ymbryne Council meeting place," the folding man said.

All around us were portraits of famous old peculiars, not framed but drawn directly onto the walls in oil and charcoal and grease pencil. The one closest to me was a face with wide, staring eyes and an open mouth, inside of which was a real, functioning water fountain. Around its mouth was a motto written in Dutch, which Millard, standing next to me, translated: "From the mouths of our elders comes a fountain of wisdom."

Nearby was another, this one in Latin. "*Ardet nec consomitur*," Melina said. "Burned but not destroyed."

"How fitting," said Enoch.

"I can't believe I'm really here," said Melina. "I've studied this place and dreamed about it for so many years."

"It's just a room," said Enoch.

"Maybe to you. To me, it's the heart of the whole peculiar world."

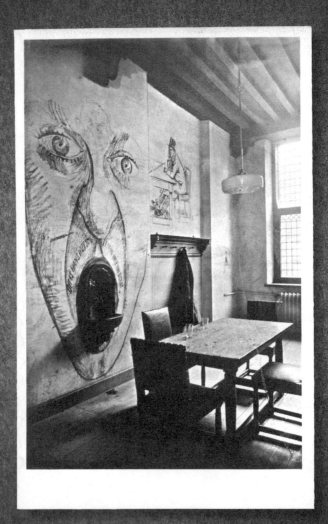

"A heart that's been ripped out," said someone new, and I looked to see a clown striding toward us—the same one who'd been stalking us at the carnival. "Miss Jackdaw was standing right where you are when she was taken. We found a whole pile of her feathers on the floor." His accent was American. He stopped a few feet from us and stood, chewing, one hand on his hip. "This them?" he asked the folding man, pointing at us with a turkey leg. "We need *soldiers*, not little kids."

"I'm a hundred and twelve!" said Melina.

"Yeah, yeah, I've heard it all before," said the clown. "I could tell you people were peculiar from across the fairgrounds, by the way. You're the most obviously peculiar bunch of peculiars I've ever laid eyes on."

"I told them same thing," said the folding man.

"How they made it all the way here from Wales without being captured is beyond me," said the clown. "In fact, it's suspicious. Sure one of you ain't a wight?"

"How dare you!" said Emma.

"We *were* captured," Hugh said proudly, "but the wights who took us didn't live to tell about it."

"Uh-huh, and I'm the king of Bolivia," the clown said.

"*It's true!*" Hugh thundered, going red in the face.

The clown tossed up his hands. "Okay, okay, calm down, kid! I'm sure Wren wouldn't have let you in if you weren't legitimate. Come on, let's be friends, have a turkey leg."

He didn't have to offer twice. We were too hungry to stay offended for long.

The clown showed us to a table stacked with food—the same boiled nuts and roasted meats that had tempted us at the carnival. We crowded around the table and stuffed our faces shamelessly. The folding man ate five cherries and a small hunk of bread and then announced he'd never been so full in his life. Bronwyn paced along the wall, chewing her fingers, too consumed by worry to eat.

When we were done, and the table was a battlefield of gnawed bones and grease stains, the clown leaned back in his chair and said, "So, peculiar children, what's your story? Why'd you come here all the way from Wales?"

Emma wiped her mouth and said, "To help our ymbryne."

"And when she's helped?" the clown asked. "What then?"

I'd been busy sopping up turkey gravy with the last of the bread, but now I looked up. The question was so straightforward, so simply put—so obvious—that I couldn't believe none of us had asked it before.

"Don't talk like that," said Horace. "You'll jinx us."

"Wren's a miracle worker," the clown said. "There's nothing to worry about."

"I hope you're right," said Emma.

"Of course I am. So what's your plan? You'll stay and help us fight, obviously, but where will you sleep? Not with me, my room's a single. Exceptions rarely made." He looked at Emma and raised an eyebrow. "Note I said *rarely.*"

All of a sudden everyone was looking off at the paintings on the walls or adjusting their collars—except for Emma, whose face was turning a certain shade of green. Maybe we were naturally pessimistic, and our chances of success had seemed so tiny that we'd never bothered to wonder what we'd do if we actually fixed Miss Peregrine—or maybe the crises of the past few days had been so constant and pressing that we'd never had a chance to wonder. Either way, the clown's question had caught us off guard.

What if we really pulled this off? What would we do if Miss Peregrine walked into the room, right now, restored to her old self?

It was Millard who finally gave an answer. "I suppose we would head west again, back where we come from. Miss Peregrine could make another loop for us. One where we'd never be found."

"That's it?" the clown said. "You'll *hide*? What about all the other ymbrynes—the ones who weren't so lucky? What about *mine*?"

"It isn't our job to save the whole world," Horace said.

"We're not *trying* to save the whole world. Just all of peculiar-dom."

"Well, that's not our job, either." Horace sounded weak and defensive, ashamed to have been cornered into saying this.

The clown leaned forward in his chair and glared at us. "Then whose job is it?"

"There's got to be someone else," said Enoch. "People who are better equipped, who've trained for this sort of thing . . ."

"The first thing the corrupted did three weeks ago was attack the Peculiar Home Guard. In less than a day, they were scattered to the four winds. With them gone, and now our ymbrynes, who does the defense of peculiardom fall to, eh? People like you and me, that's who." The clown threw down his turkey leg. "You cowards disgust me. I just lost my appetite."

"They are tired, had long journey," said the folding man. "Give them break."

The clown waved his finger in the air like a schoolmarm. "Uh-uh. Nobody rides for free. I don't care if you're here for an hour or a month, as long as you're here, you've got to be willing to fight. Now, you're a scrawny-looking bunch, but you're peculiar, so I know you've all got hidden talents. Show me what you can do!"

He got up and moved toward Enoch, one arm extended like he was going to search Enoch's pockets for his peculiar ability. "You there," he said. "Do your thing!"

"I'll need a dead person in order to demonstrate," Enoch said. "That could be you, if you so much as lay one finger on me."

The clown rerouted himself toward Emma. "Then how about you, sweetheart," he said, and Emma held a particular finger up and made a flame dance atop it like a birthday candle. The clown laughed and said, "Sense of humor! I like that," and moved on to the blind brothers.

"They're connected in the head," said Melina, putting herself between the clown and the brothers. "They can see with their ears, and always know what the other's thinking."

The clown clapped his hands. "Finally, something useful! They'll be our lookouts—put one in the carnival and keep the other here. If anything goes wrong out there, we'll know right away!"

He pushed past Melina. The brothers shied away from him.

"You can't separate them!" said Melina. "Joel-and-Peter don't like being apart."

"And I don't like being hunted by invisible corpse beasts," said the clown, and he began to pry the older brother from the younger. The boys locked arms and moaned loudly, their tongues clicking and eyes rolling wildly in their heads. I was about to intervene when the brothers came apart and let out a doubled scream so loud and piercing I feared my head would break. The dishes on the table shattered, everyone ducked and clapped their hands over their ears, and I thought I could hear, from the frozen floors below, cracks spidering through the ice.

As the echo faded, Joel-and-Peter clutched each other on the floor, shaking.

"See what you did!" Melina shouted at the clown.

"Good *God*, that's impressive!" the clown said.

With one hand Bronwyn picked the clown up by his neck. "If you continue to harass us," she said calmly, "I'll put your head through the wall."

"Sorry . . . about . . . that," the clown wheezed through his closing windpipe. "Put . . . me . . . down?"

"Go on, Wyn," said Olive. "He said he's sorry."

Reluctantly, Bronwyn set him down. The clown coughed and straightened his costume. "Looks like I misjudged you," he said. "You'll make fine additions to our army."

"I told you, we're not joining your stupid army," I said.

"What's the point of fighting, anyway?" Emma said. "You don't even know where the ymbrynes are."

The folding man unfolded from his chair to tower above us. "Point is," he said, "if corrupted get rest of ymbrynes, they become unstoppable."

"It seems like they're pretty unstoppable already," I said.

"If you think that's unstoppable, you ain't seen nothin' yet," said the clown. "And if you think that while your ymbryne is free they'll ever stop hunting you, you're stupider than you look."

Horace stood up and cleared his throat. "You've just laid out the worst-case scenario," he said. "Of late, I've heard a great many worst-case scenarios presented. But I haven't heard a single argument laid for the *best*-case scenario."

"Oh, this should be rich," said the clown. "Go ahead, fancy boy, let's hear it."

Horace took a deep breath, working up his courage. "The wights wanted the ymbrynes, and now they have them—or most of them, anyway. Say, for the sake of argument, that's all the wights need, and now they can follow through with their devilish plans. And they do: they become superwights, or demigods, or whatever it is they're after. And then they have no more use for ymbrynes, and no more use for peculiar children, and no more use for time loops, so they go away to be demigods elsewhere and leave us alone. And then things not only go back to normal, they're *better* than they were before, because no longer is anyone attempting to eat us or kidnap our ymbrynes. And then maybe, once in a great while, we could take a vacation abroad, like we used to, and see the world a bit, and put our toes in the sand somewhere that isn't cold and gray three hundred days of the year. In which case, what's the use in staying here and fighting? We'd be throwing ourselves onto their swords when everything might turn out just rosy without our intervention."

For a moment no one said anything. Then the clown began to laugh. He laughed and laughed, his cackles bouncing off the walls, until finally he fell out of his chair.

Then Enoch said, "I simply have no words. Wait—no—I do!

Horace, that is the most stunningly naive and cowardly bit of wishful thinking that I've ever heard."

"But it is *possible*," Horace insisted.

"Yes. It's also possible that the moon is made of cheese. It's just not bloody likely."

"I can end argument right now," said the folding man. "You want to know what wights will do with us once free to do anything? Come—I show you."

"Strong stomachs only," said the clown, glancing at Olive.

"If *they* can handle it, I can, too," she said.

"Fair warning," the clown shrugged. "Follow us."

"I wouldn't follow you off a sinking ship," said Melina, who was just getting the shaking blind brothers to their feet again.

"Stay, then," said the clown. "Anyone who'd rather not go down with the ship, follow us."

*   *   *

The injured lay in mismatched beds in a makeshift hospital room, watched over by a nurse with a bulging glass eye. There were three patients, if you could call them that—a man and two women. The man lay on his side, half catatonic, whispering and drooling. One of the women stared blankly at the ceiling, while the other writhed under her sheets, moaning softly, in the grip of some nightmare. Some of the children watched from outside the door, keeping their distance in case whatever these people suffered from was contagious.

"How are they today?" the folding man asked the nurse.

"Getting worse," she replied, buzzing from bed to bed. "I keep them sedated all the time now. Otherwise they just bawl."

They had no obvious wounds. There were no bloody bandages, no limbs wrapped in casts, no bowls brimming with reddish liquid. The room looked more like overflow from a psychiatric ward than a hospital.

"What's the matter with them?" I asked. "They were hurt in the raid?"

"No, brought here by Miss Wren," answered the nurse. "She found them abandoned inside a hospital, which the wights had converted into some sort of medical laboratory. These pitiful creatures were used as guinea pigs in their unspeakable experiments. What you see is the result."

"We found their old records," the clown said. "They were kidnapped years ago by the wights. Long assumed dead."

The nurse took a clipboard from the wall by the whispering man's bed. "This fellow, Benteret, he's supposed to be fluent in a hundred languages, but now he'll only say one word—over and over again."

I crept closer, watching his lips. *Call, call, call*, he was mouthing. *Call, call, call.*

Gibberish. His mind was gone.

"That one there," the nurse said, pointing her clipboard at the moaning girl. "Her chart says she can fly, but I've never seen her so much as lift an inch out of that bed. As for the other one, she's meant to be invisible. But she's plain as day."

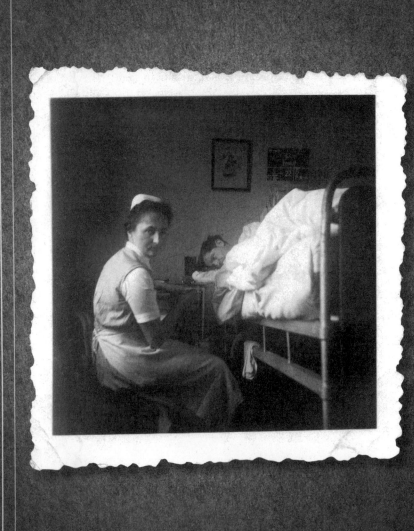

"Were they tortured?" Emma asked.

"Obviously—they were tortured out of their minds!" said the clown. "Tortured until they forgot how to be peculiar!"

"You could torture me all day long," said Millard. "I'd never forget how to be invisible."

"Show them the scars," said the clown to the nurse.

The nurse crossed to the motionless woman and pulled back her sheets. There were thin red scars across her stomach, along the side of her neck, and beneath her chin, each about the length of a cigarette.

"I'd hardly call this evidence of torture," said Millard.

"Then what *would* you call it?" the nurse said angrily.

Ignoring her question, Millard said, "Are there more scars, or is this all she has?"

"Not by a long shot," said the nurse, and she whisked the sheets off to expose the woman's legs, pointing out scars on the back of the woman's knee, her inner thigh, and the bottom of her foot.

Millard bent to examine the foot. "That's odd placement, wouldn't you say?"

"What are you getting at, Mill?" said Emma.

"Hush," said Enoch. "Let him play Sherlock if he wants. I'm rather enjoying this."

"Why don't we cut *him* in ten places?" said the clown. "Then we'll see if he thinks it's torture!"

Millard crossed the room to the whispering man's bed. "May I examine him?"

"I'm sure he won't object," said the nurse.

Millard lifted the man's sheets from his legs. On the bottom of one of his bare feet was a scar identical to the motionless woman's.

The nurse gestured toward the writhing woman. "She's got one too, if that's what you're looking for."

"Enough of this," said the folding man. "If that is not torture, then what?"

"Exploration," said Millard. "These incisions are precise and surgical. Not meant to inflict pain—probably done under anesthetic, even. The wights were *looking* for something."

"And what was that?" Emma asked, though she seemed to dread the answer.

"There's an old saying about a peculiar's foot," said Millard. "Do any of you remember it?"

Horace recited it. "A peculiar's sole is the door to his soul," he said. "It's just something they tell kids, though, to get them to wear shoes when they play outside."

"Maybe it is and maybe it's not," said Millard.

"Don't be ridiculous! You think they were looking for—"

"Their souls. And they found them."

The clown laughed out loud. "What a pile of baloney. Just because they lost their abilities, you think their second souls were removed?"

"Partly. We know the wights have been interested in the second soul for years now."

Then I remembered the conversation Millard and I had had on the train, and I said, "But you told me yourself that the peculiar soul is what allows us to enter loops. So if these people don't have their souls, how are they *here*?"

"Well, they're not *really* here, are they?" said Millard. "By which I mean, their *minds* are certainly elsewhere."

"Now you're grasping at straws," said Emma. "I think you've taken this far enough, Millard."

"Bear with me for just a moment longer," Millard said. He was pacing now, getting excited. "I don't suppose you heard about the time a normal actually *did* enter a loop?"

"No, because everyone knows that's impossible," said Enoch.

"It *nearly* is," said Millard. "It isn't easy and it isn't pretty, but it has been done—once. An illegal experiment conducted by Miss Peregrine's own brother, I believe, in the years before he went mad and formed the splinter group that would become the wights."

"Then why haven't I ever heard about this?" said Enoch.

"Because it was extremely controversial and the results were immediately covered up, so no one would attempt to replicate them. In any event, it turns out that you *can* bring a normal into a loop, but they have to be *forced* through, and only someone with an ymbryne's power can do it. But because normals do not have a second soul, they cannot handle a time loop's inherent paradoxes, and their brains turn to mush. They become drooling, catatonic vegetables from the moment they enter. Not unlike these poor people before us."

There was a moment of quiet while Millard's words registered. Then Emma's hands went to her mouth and she said quietly, "Oh, hell. He's right."

"Well, then," said the clown. "In that case, things are even worse than we thought."

I felt the air go out of the room.

"I'm not sure I follow," said Horace.

"He said the monsters stole their souls!" Olive shouted, and then she ran crying to Bronwyn and buried her face in her coat.

"These peculiars didn't *lose* their abilities," said Millard. "They were stolen from them—extracted, along with their souls, which were then fed to hollowgast. This allowed the hollows to evolve sufficiently to enter loops, a development which enabled their recent assault on peculiardom—and netted the wights even more kidnapped peculiars whose souls they could extract, with which they evolved still more hollows, and so on, in a vicious cycle."

"Then it isn't just the ymbrynes they want," said Emma. "It's us, too—and our souls."

Hugh stood at the foot of the whispering man's bed, his last bee buzzing angrily around him. "All the peculiar children they kidnapped over the years . . . *this* is what they were doing to them? I figured they just became hollowgast food. But this . . . this is *leagues* more evil."

"Who's to say they don't mean to extract the ymbrynes' souls, too?" said Enoch.

That sent a special chill through us. The clown turned to Horace and said, "How's your best-case scenario looking now, fella?"

"Don't tease me," Horace replied. "I bite."

"Everyone out!" ordered the nurse. "Souls or no souls, these people are ill. This is no place to bicker."

We filed sullenly into the hall.

"All right, you've given us the horror show," Emma said to the clown and the folding man, "and we are duly horrified. Now tell us what you want."

"Simple," said the folding man. "We want you to stay and fight with us."

"We just figured we'd show you how much it's in your own best interest to do so," said the clown. He clapped Millard on the back. "But your friend here did a better job of that than we ever could've."

"Stay here and fight for what?" Enoch said. "The ymbrynes aren't even in London—Miss Wren said as much."

"Forget London! London's finished!" the clown said. "The battle's over here. We lost. As soon as Wren has saved every last peculiar she can from these ruined loops, we'll posse up and travel—to other lands, other loops. There must be more survivors out there, peculiars like us, with the fight still burning in them."

"We will build army," said the folding man. "*Real* one."

"As for finding out where the ymbrynes are," said the clown, "no problem. We'll catch a wight and torture it out of him. Make him show us on the Map of Days."

"You have a Map of Days?" said Millard.

"We have two. The peculiar archives is downstairs, you know."

"That is good news indeed," Millard said, his voice charged with excitement.

"Catching a wight is easier said than done," said Emma. "And they lie, of course. Lying is what they do best."

"Then we'll catch two and compare their lies," the clown said. "They come sniffing around here pretty often, so next time we see one—bam! We'll grab him."

"There's no need to wait," said Enoch. "Didn't Miss Wren say there are wights in this very building?"

"Sure," said the clown, "but they're frozen. Dead as door-nails."

"That doesn't mean they can't be interrogated," Enoch said, a grin spreading across his face.

The clown turned to the folding man. "I'm really starting to like these weirdos."

"Then you are with us?" said the folding man. "You stay and fight?"

"I didn't say that," said Emma. "Give us a minute to talk this over."

"What is there to talk over?" said the clown.

"Of course, take all time you need," said the folding man, and he pulled the clown down the hall with him. "Come, I will make coffee."

"All *right*," the clown said reluctantly.

We formed a huddle, just as we had so many times since our troubles began, only this time rather than shouting over one another, we spoke in orderly turns. The gravity of all this had put us in a solemn state of mind.

"I think we should fight," said Hugh. "Now that we know what the wights are doing to us, I couldn't live with myself if we just went back to the way things were, and tried to pretend none of this was happening. To fight is the only honorable thing."

"There's honor in survival, too," said Millard. "Our kind survived the twentieth century by hiding, not fighting—so perhaps all we need is a better way to hide."

Then Bronwyn turned to Emma and said, "I want to know

what *you* think."

"Yeah, I want to know what Emma thinks," said Olive.

"Me too," said Enoch, which took me by surprise.

Emma drew a long breath, then said, "I feel terrible for the other ymbrynes. It's a crime what's happened to them, and the future of our kind may depend on their rescue. But when all is said and done, my allegiance doesn't belong to those other ymbrynes, or to other peculiar children. It belongs to the woman to whom I owe my life—Miss Peregrine, and Miss Peregrine alone." She paused and nodded—as if testing and confirming the soundness of her own words—then continued. "And when, bird willing, she becomes herself again, I'll do whatever she needs me to do. If she says fight, I'll fight. If she wants to hide us away in a loop somewhere, I'll go along with that, too. Either way, my creed has never changed: Miss Peregrine knows best."

The others considered this. Finally Millard said, "Very wisely put, Miss Bloom."

"Miss Peregrine knows best!" cheered Olive.

"Miss Peregrine knows best!" echoed Hugh.

"I don't care what Miss Peregrine says," said Horace. "I'll fight."

Enoch choked back a laugh. "You?"

"Everyone thinks I'm a coward. This is my chance to prove them wrong."

"Don't throw your life away because of a few jokes made at your expense," said Hugh. "Who gives a whit what anyone else thinks?"

"It isn't just that," said Horace. "Remember the vision I had back on Cairnholm? I caught a glimpse of where the ymbrynes are being kept. I couldn't show you on a map, but I'm sure of this—I'll know it when I see it." He tapped his forehead with his index finger. "What I've got up here might just save those chaps a heap of trouble. And save those other ymbrynes, too."

"If some fight and some stay behind," said Bronwyn, "I'll protect whoever stays. Protecting's always been my vocation."

And then Hugh turned to me and said, "What about you, Jacob?" and my mouth went instantly dry.

"Yeah," said Enoch. "What *about* you?"

"Well," I said, "I . . ."

"Let's take a walk," Emma said, hooking her arm around mine. "You and I need to have a chat."

*　　*　　*

We walked slowly down the stairs, saying nothing to each other until we'd reached the bottom and the curved wall of ice where Althea had frozen shut the exit tunnel. We sat together and looked into the ice for a long while, at the forms trapped there, blurred and distorted in the darkening light, suspended like ancient eggs in blue amber. We sat, and I could tell from the silence collecting between us that this was going to be a hard conversation—one neither of us wanted to start.

Finally Emma said, "Well?"

I said, "I'm like the others—I want to know what *you* think."

She laughed in the way people do when something's not funny but awkward, and said, "I'm not entirely sure you do."

She was right, but I prodded her to speak anyway. "Come on."

Emma laid a hand on my knee, then retracted it. She fidgeted. My chest tightened.

"I think it's time you went home," she said finally.

I blinked. It took a moment to convince myself she'd really said it. "I don't understand," I mumbled.

"You said yourself you were sent here for a reason," she said quickly, staring into her lap, "and that was to help Miss Peregrine. Now it seems she may be saved. If you owed her any debts, they're paid. You helped us more than you'll ever realize. And now it's time for you to go home." Her words came all in a rush, like they were a painful thing she'd been carrying a long time, and it was a relief to finally be rid of them.

"This *is* my home," I said.

"No, it isn't," she insisted, looking at me now. "Peculiardom is dying, Jacob. It's a lost dream. And even if somehow, by some miracle, we were to take up arms against the corrupted and prevail, we'd be left with a shadow of what we once had; a shattered mess. You *have* a home—one that isn't ruined—and parents who are alive, and who love you, in some measure."

"I told you. I don't want those things. I chose *this*."

"You made a promise, and you've kept it. And now that's over, and it's time for you to go home."

"Quit saying that!" I shouted. "Why are you pushing me away?"

"Because you have a real home and a real family, and if you think any of us would've chosen *this* world over those things—wouldn't have given up our loops and longevity and peculiar powers long ago for even a *taste* of what you have—then you really are living in a fantasy world. It makes me absolutely ill to think you might throw that all away—and for what?"

"For *you*, you idiot! I love you!"

I couldn't believe I'd said it. Neither could Emma—her mouth had fallen open. "No," she said, shaking her head like she could erase my words. "No, that's not going to help anything."

"But it's *true*!" I said. "Why do you think I stayed instead of going home? It wasn't because of my grandfather or some stupid sense of duty—not *really*—or because I hated my parents or didn't appreciate my home and all the nice things we had. I stayed because of you!"

She didn't say anything for a moment, just nodded and then looked away and ran her hands through her hair, revealing a streak of white concrete dust I hadn't noticed before, which made her look suddenly older. "It's my own fault," she said finally. "I should never have kissed you. Perhaps I made you believe something that wasn't true."

That stung me, and I recoiled instinctively, as if to protect myself. "Don't say that to me if you don't mean it," I said. "I may not have a lot of dating experience, but don't treat me like some pathetic loser who's powerless in the face of a pretty girl. You didn't *make* me stay. I stayed because I wanted to—and because what I feel for you is as real as anything I've ever felt." I let that hang in the air between us for a moment, feeling the truth of it. "You feel it too," I said. "I know you do."

"I'm sorry," she said. "I'm sorry, that was cruel, and I shouldn't have said it." Her eyes watered a little and she wiped at them with her hand. She had tried to make herself like stone, but now the facade was falling away. "You're right," she said. "I care about you very much. That's why I can't watch you throw your life away for nothing."

"I *wouldn't* be!"

"Dammit, Jacob, yes you would!" She was so incensed that she inadvertently lit a fire in her hand—which, luckily, she'd since removed from my knee. She clapped her hands together, snuffed the flame, and then stood up. Pointing into the ice, she said, "See that potted plant on the desk in there?"

I saw. Nodded.

"It's green now, preserved by the ice. But inside it's dead. And the moment that ice melts, it'll turn brown and wither into mush." She locked eyes with me. "I'm like that plant."

"You aren't," I said. "You're . . . perfect."

Her face tightened into a expression of forced patience, as if she were explaining something to a thick-headed child. She sat down again, took my hand, and raised it to her smooth cheek. "This?" she said. "Is a lie. It's not really me. If you could see me for what I really am, you wouldn't want me anymore."

"I don't *care* about that stuff—"

"I'm an old woman!" she said. "You think we're alike, but we aren't. This person you say you love? She's really a hag, an old crone hiding in a body of a girl. You're a young man—a *boy*—a baby compared to me. You could never understand what it's like, being this close to death all the time. And you shouldn't. I never want you to. You've still got your whole life to look forward to, Jacob. I've already spent mine. And one day—soon, perhaps—I will die and return to dust."

She said it with such cold finality that I knew she believed it. It hurt her to say these things, just as it hurt me to hear them, but I understood why she was doing it. She was, in her way, trying to save me.

It stung anyway—partly because I knew she was right. If Miss Peregrine recovered, then I would have done what I'd set out to do: solved the mystery of my grandfather; settled my family's debts to Miss Peregrine; lived the extraordinary life I'd always dreamed of— or part of one, anyway. At which point my only remaining obligation was to my parents. As for Emma, I didn't care at all that she was older than me, or different from me, but she'd made up her mind that I should and it seemed there was no convincing her otherwise.

"Maybe when this is all over," she said, "I'll send you a letter, and you'll send one back. And maybe one day you can come see me again."

A letter. I thought of the dusty box of them I'd found in her room, written by my grandfather. Was that all I'd be to her? An old man across the ocean? A memory? And I realized that I was about to follow in my grandfather's footsteps in a way I'd never thought possible. In so many ways, I was living his life. And probably, one day, my guard would relax too much, I'd get old and slow and distracted, and I would die his death. And Emma would continue on without me, without either of us, and one day maybe someone would find *my* letters in her closet, in a box beside my grandfather's, and wonder who we were to her.

"What if you need me?" I said. "What if the hollows come back?"

Tears shimmered in her eyes. "We'll manage somehow," she said. "Look, I can't talk about this anymore. I honestly don't think my heart can take it. Shall we go upstairs and tell the others your decision?"

I clenched my jaw, suddenly irritated by how hard she was pushing me. "I haven't decided anything," I said. "*You* have."

"Jacob, I just told you—"

"Right, you *told* me. But *I* haven't made up my mind yet."

She crossed her arms. "Then I can wait."

"No," I said, and stood up. "I need to be by myself for a while."

And I went up the stairs without her.

CHAPTER THIRTEEN

I moved quietly through the halls. I stood outside the ymbryne meeting room for a while, listening to muffled voices through the door, but I didn't go in. I peeked into the nurse's room and saw her dozing on a stool between the single-souled peculiars. I cracked the door to Miss Wren's room and saw her rocking Miss Peregrine in her lap, gently kneading her fingers into the bird's feathers. I said nothing to anyone.

Wandering through empty halls and ransacked offices, I tried to imagine what home would feel like, if after all this I chose to go back. What I would tell my parents. I'd tell them nothing, most likely. They'd never believe me, anyway. I would say I'd gotten mad, written a letter to my father filled with crazy stories, then caught a boat to the mainland and run away. They'd call it a stress reaction. Chalk it up to some invented disorder and adjust my meds accordingly. Blame Dr. Golan for suggesting I go to Wales. Dr. Golan, whom of course they'd never hear from again. He'd skipped town, they'd say, because he was a fraud, a quack whom we never should've trusted. And I'd go back to being Jacob the poor, traumatized, mentally disturbed rich kid.

It sounded like a prison sentence. And yet, if my best reason for staying in peculiardom didn't want me anymore, I wouldn't debase myself by clinging to her. I had my pride.

How long could I stand Florida, now that I'd had a taste of this peculiar life? I was not nearly as ordinary as I used to be—or if it was true that I'd never been ordinary, now I knew it. I had changed. And that, at least, gave me some hope: that even under ordinary circumstances, I still might find a way to live an extraordinary life.

Yes, it was best to go. It really was best. If this world was dying and there was nothing to be done for it, then what was left for me here? To run and hide until there was no safe place left to go, no loop to sustain my friends' artificial youth. To watch them die. To hold Emma as she crumbled and broke apart in my arms.

That would kill me faster than any hollow could.

So yes, I would go. Salvage what was left of my old life. Goodbye, peculiars. Goodbye, peculiardom.

It was for the best.

I wandered until I came to a place where the rooms were only half frozen, and the ice had risen halfway to the ceiling like water in a sinking ship and then stopped, leaving the tops of desks and the heads of lamps sticking out like faltering swimmers. Beyond the iced windows the sun was sinking. Shadows bloomed across the walls and multiplied in the stairwells, and as the light died it got bluer, painting everything around me a deep-sea cobalt.

It occurred to me that this was probably my last night in peculiardom. My last night with the best friends I'd ever had. My last night with Emma.

Why was I spending it alone? Because I was sad, and Emma had hurt my pride, and I needed to sulk.

Enough of this.

Just as I turned to leave the room, though, I felt it: that old familiar twinge in my gut.

A hollow.

I stopped, waiting for another hit of pain. I needed more information. The intensity of the pain corresponded to the nearness of the hollow and the frequency of the hits with its strength. When two strong hollows had been chasing us, the Feeling had been one long, unbroken spasm, but now it was a long time before I felt another—nearly a minute—and when it came, it was so faint I wasn't even sure I'd felt it.

I crept slowly out of the room and down the hall. As I passed the next doorway, I felt a third twinge: a little stronger now, but still only a whisper.

I tried to open the door carefully and quietly, but it was frozen shut. I had to yank on it, then rattle the door, then kick it, until finally it flew open to reveal a doorway and a room filled with ice that rose to mid-chest height. I approached the ice cautiously and peered across it, and even in the weak light, I saw the hollow right away. It was crouched on the floor, encased in ice up to its ink-black eyeballs. Only the top half of its head was exposed above the ice; the rest of it, the dangerous parts, its open jaws and all its teeth and tongues, were all caught below the surface.

The thing was just barely alive, its heart slowed almost to nothing, beating maybe once per minute. With each feeble pulse I felt a corresponding stitch of pain.

I stood at the mouth of the room and stared at it, fascinated and repulsed. It was unconscious, immobilized, totally vulnerable. It would've been easy to climb onto the ice and drive the point of an icicle into the hollow's skull—and if anyone else had known it was here, I'm sure they would've done just that. But something stopped me. It was no threat to anyone now, this creature. Every hollow I'd come into contact with had left a mark on me. I saw their decaying faces in my dreams. Soon I'd be going home, where I'd no longer be Jacob the hollow-slayer. I didn't want to take this one with me, too. It wasn't my business anymore.

I backed out of the room and closed the door.

*   *   *

When I returned to the meeting hall, it was nearly dark outside and the room was black as night. Because Miss Wren wouldn't allow the gaslamps to be lit for fear they'd be seen from the street, everyone had gathered around a few candles at the big oval table, some in chairs and others perched cross-legged on the table itself, talking in low voices and peering down at something.

At the creak of the heavy doors, everyone turned to look at me. "Miss Wren?" Bronwyn said hopefully, straightening in her chair and squinting.

"It's only Jacob," said another shadowy form.

After a chorus of disappointed sighs, Bronwyn said, "Oh, hullo Jacob," and returned her attention to the table.

As I walked toward them, I locked eyes with Emma. Holding her gaze, I saw something raw and unguarded there—a fear, I imagined, that I had in fact decided to do what she'd urged me to. Then her eyes dulled and she looked down again.

I'd been half hoping Emma had taken pity on me and told the others I was leaving already. But of course she hadn't—I hadn't told *her* yet. She seemed to know, though, just from reading my face as I crossed the room.

It was clear the others had no idea. They were so accustomed to my presence, they'd forgotten it was even under consideration. I steeled myself and asked for everyone's attention.

"Wait a moment," said a heavily accented voice, and in the candlelight I saw the snake girl and her python looking at me. "This boy here was just spewing a lot of rubbish about the place I hail from." She turned to the only chair at the table which was empty and said, "My people call it *Simhaladvipa*—dwelling place of lions."

From the chair Millard replied, "I'm sorry, but it says right here in plain calligraphy: *The Land of Serendip*. The peculiar cartographers who made this were not in the business of making things up!"

Then I got a little closer and saw what it was they were arguing over. It was a Map of Days, though a much larger edition than the one we'd lost at sea. This one stretched practically across the table, and was as thick as a brick stood on end. "I know my own home, and it's called *Simhaladvipa*!" the snake girl insisted, and her python uncoiled from her neck and shot across the table to bang its nose against the Map, indicating a teardrop-shaped island off India's coast. On this map, however, India was called *Malabar*, and the island, which I knew to be Sri Lanka, was overlaid with slinky script that read *Land of Serendip*.

"It's pointless to argue," said Millard. "Some places have as many names as they have occupants to name them. Now please ask your serpent to back away, lest he crinkle the pages."

The snake girl harrumphed and muttered something, and the python slunk away to coil around her neck again. All the while, I couldn't stop staring at the book. The one we'd lost was impressive enough, though I'd seen it opened only once, at night, by the skittish orange firelight of the burning home for peculiar children. This one was of another scale entirely. Not only was it orders of magnitude larger, but it was so ornate that it made the other look like so much leather-bound toilet paper. Colorful maps spilled across its pages, which were made from something stronger than paper, calfskin maybe, and edged with gold. Lush illustrations and legends and blocks of explanatory text stuffed the margins.

Millard noticed me admiring it and said, "Isn't it stunning? Excepting perhaps the *Codex Peculiaris*, this edition of the Map is the finest book in all peculiardom. It took a team of cartographers, artists, and bookmakers a lifetime to create, and it's said that Perplexus Anomalous himself drew some of the maps. I've wanted to see it in person ever since I was a boy. Oh, I am *so* pleased!"

"It's really something," I said, and it was.

"Millard was just showing us some of his favorite parts," said Olive. "I like the pictures best!"

"To take their minds off things," Millard explained, "and make the waiting easier. Here, Jacob, come and help me turn the pages."

Rather than ruin Millard's moment with my sad announcement, I decided it could wait a little while. I wasn't going anywhere until morning, at least, and I wanted to enjoy a few more minutes with my friends unburdened by weightier things. I sidled up next to

Millard and slipped my fingers under the page, which was so large that it took both my hands and his to turn.

We pored over the Map. I was absorbed by it—especially the far-flung and lesser-known parts. Naturally, Europe and its many loops were well-defined, but farther afield things got sketchier. Vast swaths of Africa were simply blank. *Terra incognita.* The same was true of Siberia, although the Map of Days had its own name for Russia's Far East: *The Great Far-Reaching Solitude.*

"Are there loops in these places?" asked Olive, pointing to a void that stretched across much of China. "Are there peculiars there, like us?"

"Certainly there are," Millard said. "Peculiarness is determined by genes, not geography. But large portions of the peculiar world have simply not been explored."

"Why not?"

"I suppose we were too busy surviving."

It occurred to me that the business of surviving precluded a great many things, exploring and falling in love not least among them.

We turned more pages, hunting for blank spots. There were many, and all had fanciful names. *The Mournful Kingdom of Sand. The Land Made in Anger. A High Place Full of Stars.* I mouthed the words silently to myself, appreciating their roundness.

At the margins lurked fearsome places the Map called *Wastes.* The far north of Scandinavia was *The Icy Waste.* The middle of Borneo: *The Stifling Waste.* Much of the Arabian peninsula: *The Pitiless Waste.* The southern tip of Patagonia: *The Cheerless Waste.* Certain places weren't represented at all. New Zealand. Hawaii. Florida, which was just an ingrown nub at America's foot, barely there.

Looking at the Map of Days, even the places that sounded most forbidding evoked in me a strange longing. It reminded me of long-ago afternoons spent with my grandfather studying historic maps in *National Geographic*—maps drawn long before the days of airplanes and satellites, when high-resolution cameras couldn't see into the world's every nook and cranny. When the shape of now-familiar coastlines was guesswork. When the depths and dimensions of icy seas and forbidding jungles were cobbled together from rumors and legends and the wild-eyed ramblings of expeditioners who'd lost half their party exploring them.

While Millard rambled on about the history of the Map, I traced with my finger a vast and trackless desert in Asia. *Where the Winged Creature Ends Not Its Flight.* Here was a whole world yet to be discovered, and I had only just cracked its surface. The thought filled me with regret—but also a shameful kind of relief. I would see my home again, after all, and my parents. And maybe it was childish, this old urge to explore for exploring's sake. There was romance in the unknown, but once a place had been discovered and cataloged and mapped, it was diminished, just another dusty fact in a book, sapped of mystery. So maybe it was better to leave a few spots on the map blank. To let the world keep a little of its magic, rather than forcing it to divulge every last secret.

Maybe it was better, now and then, to wonder.

And then I told them. There was no point in waiting any longer. I just blurted it out: "I'm leaving," I said. "When this is all over, I'm going back home."

There was a moment of shocked silence. Emma met my eyes, finally, and I could see tears standing in them.

Then Bronwyn got up from the table and threw her arms around me. "Brother," she said. "We'll miss you."

"I'll miss you, too," I said. "More than I can say."

"But *why?*" said Olive, floating up to my eye level. "Was I too irritating?"

I put my hand on her head and pushed her back down to the floor. "No, no, it's got nothing to do with you," I said. "You were great, Olive."

Emma stepped forward. "Jacob came here to help us," she said. "But he has to go back to his old life, while it's still there waiting for him."

The children seemed to understand. There was no anger. Most of them seemed genuinely happy for me.

Miss Wren popped her head into the room to give us a quick update—everything was going marvelously, she said. Miss Peregrine was well on her way to recovery. She'd be ready by morning. And then Miss Wren was gone again.

"Thank the gods," said Horace.

"Thank the birds," said Hugh.

"Thank the gods *and* the birds," said Bronwyn. "All the birds in all the trees in all the forests."

"Thank Jacob, too," said Millard. "We never would've made it this far without him."

"We never even would've made it off the *island*," said Bronwyn. "You've done so much for us, Jacob."

They all came and hugged me, each of them, one by one. Then they drifted away and only Emma was left, and she hugged me last—a long, bittersweet embrace that felt too much like goodbye.

"Asking you to leave was the hardest thing I've ever had to do," she said. "I'm glad you came around. I don't think I'd have had the strength to ask again."

"I hate this," I said. "I wish there were a world where we could be together in peace."

"I know," she said. "I know, I know."

"I wish . . . ," I started to say.

"Stop," she said.

I said it anyway. "I wish you could come home with me."

She looked away. "You know what would happen to me if I did."

"I know."

Emma disliked long goodbyes. I could feel her steeling herself, trying to pull her pain inside. "So," she said, businesslike. "Logistics. When Miss Peregrine turns human, she'll lead you back through the carnival, into the underground, and when you pass through the changeover, you'll be back in the present. Think you can manage from there?"

"I think so," I said. "I'll call my parents. Or go to a police station, or something. I'm sure there's a poster of my face in every precinct in Britain by now, knowing my dad." I laughed a little, because if I hadn't, I might've started crying.

"Okay, then," she said.

"Okay, then," I said.

We looked at each other, not quite ready to let go, not sure what else to do. My instinct was to kiss her, but I stopped myself. That wasn't allowed anymore.

"You go," she said. "If you never hear from us again, well, one day you'll be able to tell our story. You can tell your kids about us. Or your grandkids. And we won't entirely be forgotten."

I knew then that, from now on, every word that passed between us would hurt, would be wrapped up with and marked by the pain of this moment, and that I needed to pull away now or it would never stop. So I nodded sadly, hugged her one more time, and retreated to a corner to sleep, because I was very, very tired.

After awhile, the others dragged mattresses and blankets into the room and made a nest around me, and we packed together for warmth against the encroaching chill. But as the others began to bed down, I found myself unable to sleep, despite my exhaustion, and I got up and paced the room for a while, watching the children from a distance.

I'd felt so many things since our journey began—joy, fear, hope, horror—but until now, I'd never once felt alone. Bronwyn had called me brother, but that didn't sound right anymore. I was a second cousin to them at best. Emma was right: I could never understand. They were so old, had seen so much. And I was from another world. Now it was time to go back.

* * *

Eventually, I fell asleep to the sound of ice groaning and cracking in the floors beneath us and the attic above. The building was alive with it.

That night, strange and urgent dreams.

I am home again, doing all the things I used to do. Tearing into a fast-food hamburger—big, brown, and greasy. Riding shotgun in Ricky's Crown Vic, bad radio blaring. At the grocery store with my parents, sliding down long, too-bright aisles, and Emma is there, cooling her hands in the ice at the fish counter, meltwater running everywhere. She doesn't recognize me.

Then I'm at the arcade where I had my twelfth birthday party, firing a plastic gun. Bodies bursting, blood-filled balloons.

Jacob where are you

Then school. Teacher's writing on the board, but the letters don't make sense. Then everyone's on their feet, hurrying outside. Something's wrong. A loud noise rising and falling. Everyone standing still, heads craned to the sky.

Air raid.

Jacob Jacob where are you

Hand on my shoulder. It's an old man. A man without eyes. Come to steal mine. Not a man—a thing—a monster.

Running now. Chasing my old dog. Years ago she'd broken away from me, run off with her leash still attached and got it wrapped around a branch while trying to tree a squirrel. Strangled herself. We spent two weeks wandering the neighborhood calling her name. Found her after three. Old Snuffles.

The siren deafening now. I run and a car pulls alongside and picks me up. My parents are inside, in formal wear. They won't look at me. The doors lock. We're driving and it's stifling hot outside, but the heater is on and the windows are up, and the radio is loud but tuned to the garble between stations.

Mom where are we going

She doesn't answer.

Dad why are we stopping here

Then we're out, walking, and I can breathe again. Pretty green place. Smell of fresh-cut grass. People in black, gathered around a hole in the ground.

A coffin open on a dais. I peer inside. It's empty but for an oily stain slowly spreading across the bottom. Blacking the white satin. *Quick, close the lid!* Black tar bubbles out from the cracks and grooves and drips down into the grass and sinks into the earth.

Jacob where are you say something

The headstone reads: ABRAHAM EZRA PORTMAN. And I'm tumbling into his open grave, darkness spinning up to swallow me, and I keep falling and it's bottomless, and then I'm somewhere underground, alone and wandering through a thousand interconnecting tunnels, and I'm wandering and it's cold, so cold I'm afraid my skin will freeze and my bones will splinter, and everywhere there are yellow eyes watching me from the dark.

I follow his voice. *Yakob, come here. Don't be afraid.*

The tunnel angles upward and there's light at the end, and standing at its mouth, calmly reading a book, is a young man. And he looks just like me, or almost like me, and maybe he is me, I think, but then he speaks, and it's my grandfather's voice. *I have something to show you.*

For a moment I jolted awake in the dark and knew I was dreaming, but I didn't know where I was, only that I was not in bed anymore, not in the meeting hall with the others. I'd gone elsewhere and the room I was in was all black, with ice beneath me, my stomach writhing . . .

Jacob come here where are you

A voice from outside, down the hall—a real voice, not something from a dream.

And then I'm in the dream again, just outside the ropes of a boxing ring, and on the canvas, in the haze and lights, my grandfather faces off against a hollowgast.

They circle each other. My grandfather is young and nimble on his feet, stripped to the waist, a knife in one hand. The hollow is bent and twisted, its tongues waving in the air, open jaws dripping black on the mat. It whips out a tongue and my grandfather dodges it.

Don't fight the pain, that's the key, my grandfather says. *It's telling you something. Welcome it, let it speak to you. The pain says: Hello, I am not other than you; I am of the hollow, but I am you also.*

The hollow whips at him again. My grandfather anticipates it, makes room in advance of the strike. Then the hollow strikes a third time, and my grandfather lashes out with his knife and the tip of the hollow's black tongue falls to the mat, severed and jolting.

They are stupid creatures. Highly suggestible. Speak to them, Yakob. And my grandfather begins to speak, but not in English, nor Polish, nor any language I've heard outside my dreams. It's like some guttural outgassing, the sounds made with something other than a throat or a mouth.

And the creature stops moving, merely swaying where it stands, seemingly hypnotized. Still speaking his frightening gibberish, my grandfather lowers his knife and creeps toward it. The closer he gets, the more docile the creature becomes, finally sinking down to the mat, on its knees. I think it's about to close its eyes and go to sleep when suddenly the hollow breaks free of whatever spell my grandfather has cast over it, and it lashes out with all its tongues and impales my grandfather. As he falls, I leap over the ropes and run toward him, and the hollow slips away. My grandfather is on his back on the mat and I am kneeling by his side, my hand on his face, and he is whispering something to me, blood bubbling on his lips, so I bend closer to hear him. *You are more than me, Yakob,* he says. *You are more than I ever was.*

I can feel his heart slow. Hear it, somehow, until whole seconds elapse between beats. Then tens of seconds. And then . . .

Jacob where are you

I jolted awake again. Now there was light in the room. It was morning, just the blue beginning of it. I was kneeling on the ice in the half-filled room, and my hand wasn't on my grandfather's face but resting atop the trapped hollow's skull, its slow, reptilian brain. Its eyes were open and looking at me, and I was looking right back. *I see you.*

"Jacob! What are you doing? I've been looking for you every-where!"

It was Emma, frantic, out in the hall. "What are you doing?" she said again. She couldn't see the hollow. Didn't know it was there.

I took my hand away from its head, slid back from it. "I don't know," I said. "I think I was sleepwalking."

"It doesn't matter," she said. "Come quick—Miss Peregrine's about to change!"

*   *   *

Crowded into the little room were all the children and all the freaks from the sideshow, pale and nervous, pressed against the walls and crouched on the floor in a wide berth around the two ymbrynes, like gamblers in a backroom cockfight. Emma and I slipped in among them and huddled in a corner, eyes glued to the unfolding spectacle. The room was a mess: the rocking chair where Miss Wren had sat all night with Miss Peregrine was toppled on its side, the table of vials and beakers pushed roughly against the wall. Althea stood on top of it clutching a net on a pole, ready to wield it.

In the middle of the floor were Miss Wren and Miss Peregrine. Miss Wren was on her knees, and she had Miss Peregrine pinned to the floorboards, her hands in thick falconing gloves, sweating and chanting in Old Peculiar, while Miss Peregrine squawked and flailed with her talons. But no matter how hard Miss Peregrine thrashed, Miss Wren wouldn't let go.

At some point in the night, Miss Wren's gentle massage had turned into something resembling an interspecies pro-wrestling match crossed with an exorcism. The bird half of Miss Peregrine had so thoroughly dominated her nature that it was refusing to be driven away without a fight. Both ymbrynes had sustained minor injuries: Miss Peregrine's feathers were everywhere, and Miss Wren had a long, bloody scratch running down one side of her face. It was a disturbing sight, and many of the children looked on with openmouthed shock. Wild-eyed and savage, the bird Miss Wren was grinding into the floor was one we hardly recognized. It seemed incredible that a fully restored Miss Peregrine of old might result from this violent display, but Althea kept smiling at us and giving us encouraging nods as if to say, *Almost there, just a little more floor-grinding!*

For such a frail old lady, Miss Wren was giving Miss Peregrine a pretty good clobbering. But then the bird jabbed at Miss Wren with her beak and Miss Wren's grasp slipped, and with a big flap of her wings Miss Peregrine nearly escaped from her hands. The children reacted with shouts and gasps. But Miss Wren was quick, and she leapt up and managed to catch Miss Peregrine by her hind leg and thump her down against the floorboards again, which made the children gasp even louder. We weren't used to seeing our ymbryne treated like this, and Bronwyn actually had to stop Hugh from rushing into the fight to protect her.

Both ymbrynes seemed profoundly exhausted now, but Miss Peregrine more so; I could see her strength failing. Her human nature seemed to be winning out over her bird nature.

"Come on, Miss Wren!" Bronwyn cried.

"You can do it, Miss Wren!" called Horace. "Bring her back to us!"

"Please!" said Althea. "We require absolute silence."

After a long time, Miss Peregrine quit struggling and lay on the ground with her wings splayed, gasping for air, feathered chest heaving. Miss Wren took her hands off the bird and sat back on her haunches.

"It's about to happen," she said, "and when it does, I don't want any of you to rush over here grabbing at her. Your ymbryne will likely be very confused, and I want the first face she sees and voice she hears to be mine. I'll need to explain to her what's happened." And then she clasped her hands to her chest and murmured, "Come back to us, Alma. Come on, sister. Come back to us."

Althea stepped down from the table and picked up a sheet, which she unfolded and held up in front of Miss Peregrine to shield her from view. When ymbrynes turned from birds into humans, they were naked; this would give her some privacy.

We waited in breathless suspense while a succession of strange noises came from behind the sheet: an expulsion of air, a sound like someone clapping their hands once, sharply—and then Miss Wren jumped up and took a shaky step backward.

She looked frightened—her mouth was open, and so was Althea's. And then Miss Wren said, "No, this can't be," and Althea stumbled, faint, letting the sheet drop. And there on the floor we saw a human form, but not a woman's.

He was naked, curled into a ball, his back to us. He began to stir, and uncurl, and finally to stand.

"Is that Miss Peregrine?" said Olive. "She came out funny."

Clearly, it was not. The person before us bore no resemblance whatsoever to Miss Peregrine. He was a stunted little man with knobby knees and a balding head and a nose like a used pencil eraser, and he was stark naked and slimed head to toe with sticky, translucent gel. While Miss Wren gaped at him and grasped for something to steady herself against, in shock and anger the others all began to shout, "Who are you? Who are you? What have you done with Miss Peregrine!"

Slowly, slowly, the man raised his hands to his face and rubbed his eyes. Then, for the first time, he opened them.

The pupils were blank and white.

I heard someone scream.

Then, very calmly, the man said, "My name is Caul. And you are all my prisoners now."

*   *   *

"Prisoners!" said the folding man with a laugh. "What he mean, we are prisoners?"

Emma shouted at Miss Wren. "Where's Miss Peregrine? Who's this man, and what have you done with Miss Peregrine?"

Miss Wren seemed to have lost the ability to speak.

As our confusion turned to shock and anger, we barraged the little man with questions. He endured them with a slightly bored expression, standing at the center of the room with his hands folded demurely over his privates.

"If you'd actually permit me to speak, I'll explain everything," he said.

"Where is Miss Peregrine?!" Emma shouted again, trembling with rage.

"Don't worry," Caul said, "she's safely in our custody. We kidnapped her days ago, on your island."

"Then the bird we rescued from the submarine," I said, "that was . . ."

"That was me," Caul said.

"Impossible!" said Miss Wren, finally finding her voice. "Wights can't turn into birds!"

"That is true, as a general rule. But Alma is my sister, you see, and though I wasn't fortunate enough to inherit any of her talents for manipulating time, I do share her most useless trait—the ability to turn into a vicious little bird of prey. I did a rather excellent job impersonating her, don't you think?" And he took a little bow. "Now, may I trouble you for some pants? You have me at a disadvantage."

His request was ignored. Meanwhile, my head was spinning. I remembered Miss Peregrine once mentioning that she'd had two brothers—I'd seen their photo, actually, when they were all in the care of Miss Avocet together. Then I flashed back to the days we'd spent with the bird we had believed was Miss Peregrine; all we'd gone though, everything we'd seen. The caged Miss Peregrine that Golan had thrown into the ocean—that had been the real one, while the one we "rescued" had been her brother. The cruel things Miss Peregrine had done recently made more sense now—that hadn't been Miss Peregrine at all—but I was still left with a million questions.

"All that time," I said. "Why did you stay a bird? Just to watch us?"

"While my lengthy observations of your childish bickering were incontrovertibly fascinating, I was quite hoping you could help me with a piece of unfinished business. When you killed my men in the countryside, I was impressed. You proved yourselves to be quite resourceful. Naturally, my men could've swept in and taken you at any point after that, but I thought it better to let you twist in the wind awhile and see if your ingenuity might not lead us to the one ymbryne who's consistently managed to evade us." With that, he turned to Miss Wren and grinned broadly. "Hello, Balenciaga. So good to see you again."

Miss Wren moaned and fanned herself with her hand.

"You idiots, you cretins, you morons!" the clown shouted. "You led them right to us!"

"And as a nice bonus," said Caul, "we paid a visit to your menagerie, as well! My men came by not long after we left; the stuffed heads of that emu-raffe and boxer dog will look *magnificent* above my mantelpiece."

"You monster!" Miss Wren screeched, and she fell back against the table, legs failing her.

"Oh, my bird!" exclaimed Bronwyn, her eyes wide. "Fiona and Claire!"

"You'll see them again soon," Caul said. "I've got them in safekeeping."

It all began to make a terrible kind of sense. Caul knew he'd be welcomed into Miss Wren's menagerie disguised as Miss Peregrine, and when she wasn't at home to be kidnapped, he'd nudged us after her, toward London. In so many ways, we'd been manipulated from the very beginning—from the moment we chose to leave the island and I chose to go along. Even the tale he'd chosen for Bronwyn to read that first night in the forest, about the stone giant, had been a manipulation. He wanted us to find Miss Wren's loop, and think that it was we who'd cracked its secret.

Those of us who weren't reeling in horror frothed with anger. Several people were shouting that Caul should be killed, and were busily hunting for sharp objects to do the job with, while the few who'd kept their heads were trying to hold them back. All the while, Caul stood calmly, waiting for the furor to die down.

"If I may?" he said. "I wouldn't entertain any ideas about killing me. You *could*, of course; no one can stop you. But it will go much easier for you if I am unharmed when my men arrive." He pretended to check a nonexistent watch on his wrist. "Ah, yes," he said, "they should be here now—yes, just about now—surrounding the building, covering every conceivable point of exit, including the roof. And might I add, there are fifty-six of them and they are armed positively to the teeth. *Beyond* the teeth. Have you ever seen what a mini-gun can do to a child-sized human body?" He looked directly at Olive and said, "It would turn you to cat's meat, darling."

"You're bluffing!" said Enoch. "There's no one out there!"

"I assure you, there is. They've been watching me closely since we left your depressing little island, and I gave my signal to them the moment Balenciaga revealed herself to us. That was over twelve hours ago—more than ample time to muster a fighting force."

"Allow me to verify this," said Miss Wren, and she left to go to the ymbryne meeting room, where the windows were obstructed from ice mostly from the outside, and a few had small telescope tunnels melted through them with mirror attachments that let us look down at the street below.

While we waited for her to return, the clown and the snake girl debated the best ways to torture Caul.

"I say we pull out his toenails first," said the clown. "Then stick hot pokers in his eyes."

"Where I come from," the snake girl said, "the punishment for treason is being covered in honey, bound to an open boat, and floated out into a stagnant pond. The flies eat you alive."

Caul stood cricking his neck from side to side and stretching his arms boredly. "Apologies," he said. "Remaining a bird for so long tends to cramp the muscles."

"You think we're kidding?" said the clown.

"I think you're amateurs," said Caul. "If you found a few young bamboo shoots, I could show you something really wicked. As delightful as that would be, though, I do recommend you melt this ice, because it'll save us all a world of trouble. I say this for your sake, out of genuine concern for your well-being."

"Yeah, right," said Emma. "Where was your concern when you were stealing those peculiars' souls?"

"Ah, yes. Our three pioneers. Their sacrifice was necessary—all for the sake of progress, my dears. What we're trying to do is advance the peculiar species, you see."

"What a joke," she said. "You're nothing but power-hungry sadists!"

"I know you're all quite sheltered and uneducated," said Caul, "but did your ymbrynes not teach you about our people's history? We peculiars used to be like gods roaming the earth! Giants—kings—the world's rightful rulers! But over the centuries and millennia, we've suffered a terrible decline. We mixed with normals to such an extent that the purity of our peculiar blood has been diluted almost to nothing. And now look at us, how degraded we've become! We hide in these temporal backwaters, afraid of the very people we should be ruling, arrested in a state of perpetual childhood by this confederacy of busybodies—these *women*! Don't you see how they've reduced us? Are you not ashamed? Do you have any idea of the power that's rightfully ours? Don't you feel the blood of *giants* in your veins?" He was losing his cool now, going red in the face. "We aren't trying to eradicate peculiardom—we're trying to *save* it!"

"Is that right?" said the clown, and then walked over to Caul and spat right in his face. "Well, you've got a twisted way of going at it."

Caul wiped the spit away with the back of his hand. "I knew it would be pointless to reason with you. The ymbrynes have been feeding you lies and propaganda for a hundred years. Better, I think, to take your souls and start again fresh."

Miss Wren returned. "He speaks the truth," she said. "There must be fifty soldiers out there. All of them armed."

"Oh, oh, oh," moaned Bronwyn, "what are we to *do*?"

"Give up," said Caul. "Go quietly."

"It doesn't matter how many of them there are," Althea said. "They'll never be able to get through all my ice."

The ice! I'd nearly forgotten. We were inside a fortress of ice!

"That's right!" Caul said brightly. "She's absolutely right, they can't get in. So there's a quick and painless way to do this, where you melt the ice voluntarily right now, or there's the long, stubborn, slow, boring, sad way, which is called a siege, where for weeks and months my men stand guard outside while we stay in here, quietly starving to death. Maybe you'll give up when you're desperate and hungry enough. Or maybe you'll start cannibalizing one another. Either way, if my men have to wait that long, they'll torture every last one of you to death when they get in, which inevitably they will. And if we *must* go the slow, boring, sad route, then please, for the sake of the children, bring me some trousers."

"Althea, fetch the man some damned trousers!" said Miss Wren. "But do *not*, under any circumstances, melt this ice!"

"Yes, ma'am," replied Althea, and she went out.

"Now," said Miss Wren, turning to Caul. "Here's what we'll do. You tell your men to allow us safe passage out of here, or we'll kill you. If we have to do it, I assure you we will, and we'll dump your stinking corpse out a hole in the ice a piece at a time. While I'm sure your men won't like that much, we'll have a very long time to devise our next move."

Caul shrugged and said, "Oh, all right."

"Really?" Miss Wren said.

"I thought I could scare you," he said, "but you're right, I'd rather not be killed. So take me to one of these holes in the ice and I'll do as you've asked and shout down to my men."

Althea came back in with some pants and threw them at Caul, and he put them on. Miss Wren appointed Bronwyn, the clown, and the folding man to be Caul's guards, arming them with broken icicles. With their points aimed at his back, we proceeded into the hall. But as we were bottlenecking through the small, dark office that led to the ymbryne meeting room, everything went wrong. Someone tripped over a mattress and went down, and then I heard a scuffle break out in the dark. Emma lit a flame just in time to see Caul dragging Althea away from us by the hair. She kicked and flailed while Caul held a sharpened icicle to her throat and shouted, "Stay back or I drive this through her jugular!"

We followed Caul at a careful distance. He dragged Althea thrashing and kicking into the meeting hall, and then up onto the oval table, where he put her in a choke hold, the icicle held an inch from her eye, and shouted, "*These are my demands!*"

Before he could get any further, though, Althea slapped the icicle from his hand. It flew and landed point-down in the pages of the Map of Days. While his mouth was still forming an O of surprise, Althea's hand latched onto the front of Caul's pants, and the O broadened into a grimace of shock.

"*Now!*" Emma bellowed, and then she and I and Bronwyn rushed toward them through the wooden doors. But as we ran, the distance across that big room seemed to yawn, and in seconds the fight between Althea and Caul had taken another turn: Caul let go of Althea and fell to the table, his arms stretched and grasping for the icicle. Althea fell with him but did not let go—now had both hands wrapped around his thigh—and a coating of ice was spreading quickly across Caul's lower half, paralyzing him from the waist down and freezing Althea's hands to his leg. He got one finger around the icicle, and then his whole hand, and groaning with effort and pain, he wrenched it free from the Map and twisted his upper body until he had the point of it poised above Althea's back. He screamed at her to stop and let him go and melt the ice or he'd plunge it into her.

We were just yards from them now, but Bronwyn caught Emma and me and held us back.

Caul screamed, "Stop! Stop this!" as his face contorted in pain, the ice racing up his chest and over his shoulders. In a few seconds, his arms and hands would be encased, too.

Althea didn't stop.

And then Caul did it—he stabbed the icicle into her back. She tensed in shock, then groaned. Miss Wren ran toward them, screaming Althea's name while the ice that had spread across most of Caul's body began, very quickly, to recede. By the time Miss Wren reached them, he was nearly free of it. But then the ice everywhere was melting, too—fading and retracting just as quickly as Althea's life was—the ice in the attic dripping and raining down through the ceiling just as Althea's own blood ran down her body. She was in Miss Wren's arms now, slack, going.

Bronwyn was on the table, Caul's throat in one hand, his weapon crushed to snow in her other. We could hear the ice in floors below us melting, too, and then it was gone from the windows. We rushed to look out, and could see water flooding from lower windows into the street, where soldiers in gray urban camo were clinging to lampposts and fire hydrants to keep from being washed away by the icy waves.

Then we heard their boots stomping on the stairs below and coming down from the roof above, and moments later they burst in with their guns, shouting. Some of the men wore night-vision headsets and all of them bristled with weapons—compact machine guns, laser-sighted pistols, combat knives. It took three of them to pry Bronwyn away from Caul, who wheezed through his half-crushed windpipe, "Take them away, and don't be gentle!"

Miss Wren was shouting, begging us to comply—"Do as they say or they'll hurt you!"—but she wouldn't let go of Althea's body, so they made an example of her; they tore Althea away and kicked Miss Wren to the ground, and one of the soldiers fired his machine pistol into the ceiling just to scare us. When I saw Emma about to make a fireball with her hands, I grabbed her by the arm and begged her not to—"Don't, please don't, they'll kill you!"—and then a rifle butt slammed into my chest and I fell gasping to the floor. One of the soldiers noosed my hands together behind me.

I heard them counting us, Caul listing our names, making sure even Millard was accounted for—because of course by now, having spent the last three days with us, he knew all of us, knew everything about us.

I was pulled to my feet and we were all pushed out through the doors into the hallway. Stumbling along next to me was Emma, blood in her hair, and I whispered, "Please, just do what they say," and though she didn't acknowledge it, I knew she'd heard me. The look on her face was all rage and fear and shock—and I think pity, too, for all I'd just had snatched away from me.

In the stairwell, the floors and stairs below were a white-water river, a vortex of cascading waves. Up was the only way out. We were shoved up the stairs, through a door and into strong daylight, onto the roof. Everyone wet, frozen, frightened into silence.

All but Emma. "Where are you taking us?" she demanded.

Caul came right to her and grinned in her face while a soldier held her cuffed hands behind her. "A very special place," Caul said, "where not a drop of your peculiar souls will go to waste."

She flinched, and he laughed and turned away, stretching his arms above his head and yawning. From his shoulder blades jutted a weird pair of knobby protrusions, like the stems of aborted wings: the only outward clue that this twisted man bore any relation to an ymbryne.

Voices shouted from the top of another building. More soldiers. They were laying down a collapsible bridge between rooftops.

"What about the dead girl?" one of the soldiers asked.

"Such a pity, such a waste," Caul said, clucking his tongue. "I should have liked to dine on her soul. It's got no taste on its own, the peculiar soul," he said, addressing us. "Its natural consistency is a bit gelatinous and pasty, really, but whipped together with a soupçon of remoulade and spread upon white meat, it's quite palatable."

Then he laughed, very loudly, for a long time.

As they led us away, one by one, over the wide collapsible bridge, I felt a familiar twinge in my gut—faint but strengthening, slow but quickening—the hollowgast, unfrozen now, coming slowly back to life.

*　　*　　*

Ten soldiers marched us out of the loop at gunpoint, past the carnival tents and sideshows and gaping carnival-goers, down the rats' warren of alleys with their stalls and vendors and ragamuffin kids staring after us, into the disguising room, past the piles of cast-off clothes we'd left behind, and down into the underground. The soldiers prodded us along, barking at us to keep quiet (though no one had said a word in minutes), to keep our heads down and stay in line or be pistol-whipped.

Caul was no longer with us—he had stayed behind with the larger contingent of soldiers to "mop up," which I think meant scouring the loop for hiders and stragglers. The last time we saw him, he was pulling on a pair of modern boots and an army jacket and told us he was absolutely sick of our faces but would see us "on the other side," whatever that meant.

We passed through the changeover, and forward in time again—but not to a version of the tunnels I recognized. The tracks and ties were all metal now, and the lights in the tunnels were different, not red incandescents but flickering fluorescent tubes that glowed a sickly green. Then we came out of the tunnel and onto the platform, and I understood why: we were no longer in the nineteenth century, nor even the twentieth. The crowd of sheltering refugees was gone now; the station nearly deserted. The circular staircase we'd come down was gone, too, replaced by an escalator. A scrolling LED screen hung above the platform: TIME TO NEXT TRAIN: 2 MINUTES. On the wall was a poster for a movie I'd seen earlier in the summer, just before my grandfather died.

We'd left 1940 behind. I was back in the present.

A few of the kids took note of this with looks of surprise and fear, as if afraid they would age forward in a matter of minutes, but for most of them I think the shock of our sudden captivity was not about to be trumped by an unexpected trip to the present; they were worried about having their souls extracted, not about developing gray hair and liver spots.

The soldiers corralled us in the middle of the platform to wait for the train. Hard shoes clicked toward us. I risked a look over my shoulder and saw a policeman coming. Behind him, stepping off the escalator, were three more.

"Hey!" Enoch shouted. "Policeman, over here!"

A soldier punched Enoch in the gut, and he doubled over.

"Everything good here?" said the closest policeman.

"They've taken us prisoner!" said Bronwyn. "They aren't really soldiers, they're—"

And then she got a punch to the gut, too, though it didn't seem to hurt her. What stopped her from saying more was the policeman himself, who took off his mirrored sunglasses to reveal stark white eyes. Bronwyn shrank back.

"A bit of advice," the policeman said. "No help is coming to you. We are everywhere. Accept that, and this will all be easier."

Normals were starting to fill the station. The soldiers pressed in on us from all sides, keeping their weapons hidden.

A train hissed into the station, filled with people. Its electric doors whooshed open and a glut of passengers spilled out. The soldiers began pushing us toward the nearest car, the policemen going ahead to scatter what few passengers remained inside. "Find another car!" they barked. "Get out!" The passengers grumbled but complied. But there were more people behind us on the platform, trying to push into the car, and a few of the soldiers who'd been ringing us had to break away to stop them. And then there was just enough confusion—the doors trying to close but the police holding them open until a warning alarm began to sound; the soldiers shoving us forward so hard that Enoch tripped, sending other children tripping over him in a chain reaction—that the folding man, whose wrists were so skinny he'd been able to slip his cuffs, decided to make a break for it, and ran.

A shot rang out, then a second, and the folding man tumbled and splayed onto the ground. The crowd swarmed away in a panic, people screaming and scrambling to escape the gunshots, and what had been merely confusion deteriorated into total chaos.

Then they were shoving us and kicking us onto the train. Beside me, Emma was resisting, making the soldier who was pushing her get close. Then I saw her cuffed hands flare orange, and she reached behind her and grabbed him. The soldier crumpled to the ground, shrieking, a hand-shaped hole melted through his camo. Then the soldier who was pushing *me* raised the butt of his gun and was about to bring it down on Emma's neck when some instinct triggered in me and I drove my shoulder into his back.

He stumbled.

Emma melted through her metal cuffs, which fell away from her hands in a deformed mass of red-hot metal. My soldier turned his gun on me now, howling with rage, but before he could fire, Emma came at him from behind and clapped her hands around his face, her fingers so hot they melted through his cheeks like warm butter. He dropped the gun and collapsed, screaming.

All this happened very quickly, in a matter of seconds.

Then two more soldiers were coming at us. Nearly everyone else was on the train now—all but Bronwyn and the blind brothers, who had never been cuffed and were merely standing by with arms linked. Seeing that we were about to be shot to death, Bronwyn did something I could never have imagined her doing under any other circumstances: she slapped the older brother hard across the face, then took the younger one and wrenched him roughly away from the older.

The moment their connection was severed, they let out a scream so powerful it generated its own wind. It tore through the station like a tornado of pure energy—blowing Emma and me backwards, shattering the soldiers' glasses, eclipsing most of the frequencies my ears could detect so that all I heard was a squeaking, high-pitched *Eeeeeeeeee . . .*

I saw all the windows of the train break and the LED screens shiver to knife shards and the glass light tubes along the roof explode, so that we were plunged for a moment into pure blackness, then the hysterical red flashing of emergency lights.

I had fallen onto my back, the wind knocked out of me, my ears ringing. Something was pulling me backwards by the collar, away from the train, and I couldn't quite remember how to work my arms and legs well enough to resist. Beneath the ringing in my ears I could make out frantic voices shouting, *"Go, just go!"*

I felt something cold and wet against the back of my neck, and was dragged into a phone booth. Emma was there, too, folded into a ball in the corner, semiconscious.

"Pull your legs up," I heard a familiar voice say, and from around back of me came trotting a short, furry thing with a pushed-in snout and a jowly mouth.

The dog. Addison.

I pulled my legs into the booth, my wits returning enough to move but not speak.

The last thing I saw, in the hellish red flashing, was Miss Wren being shoved into the train car and the doors snapping closed, and all my friends inside with her, cowering at gunpoint, framed by the shattered windows of the train, surrounded by men with white eyes.

Then the train roared away into the darkness, and was gone.

* * *

I startled awake to a tongue licking my face.

The dog.

The door of the phone booth had been pulled closed, and the three of us were crammed inside on the floor.

"You passed out," said the dog.

"They're gone," I said.

"Yes, but we can't stay here. They'll come back for you. We have to go."

"I don't think I can stand up just yet."

The dog had a cut on his nose, and a hunk of one ear was missing. Whatever he'd done to get here, he'd been through hell, too.

I felt a tickle against my leg, but was too tired to look and see what it was. My head was heavy as a boulder.

"Don't go to sleep again," said the dog, and then he turned to Emma and began to lick her face.

The tickle again. This time I shifted my weight and reached for it.

It was my phone. My phone was vibrating. I couldn't believe it. I dug it out of my pocket. The battery was nearly dead, the signal almost nonexistent. The screen read: DAD (177 MISSED CALLS).

If I hadn't been so groggy, I probably wouldn't have answered. At any moment a man with a gun might arrive to finish us off. Not a good time for a conversation with my father. But I wasn't thinking straight, and anytime my phone rang, my old Pavlovian impulse was to pick it up.

I pressed ANSWER. "Hello?"

A choked cry on the other end. Then: "Jacob? Is that you?"

"It's me."

I must've sounded awful. My voice a faint rasp.

"Oh, my God, oh, my God," my father said. He hadn't expected me to answer, maybe had given me up for dead already and was calling now out of some reflexive grief instinct that he couldn't switch off. "I don't—where did you—what happened—where *are* you, son?"

"I'm okay," I said. "I'm alive. In London."

I don't know why I told him that last part. I guess I felt like I owed him some truth.

Then it sounded like he aimed his head away from the receiver to shout to someone else, "It's Jacob! He's in London!" Then back to me: "We thought you were *dead*."

"I know. I mean, I'm not surprised. I'm sorry about leaving the way I did. I hope I didn't scare you too much."

"You scared us to *death*, Jacob." My father sighed, a long, shivering sound that was relief and disbelief and exasperation all at once. "Your mother and I are in London, too. After the police couldn't find you on the island . . . anyway, it doesn't matter, just tell us where you are and we'll come get you!"

Emma began to stir. Her eyes opened and she looked at me, bleary, like she was somewhere deep inside herself and peering out at me through miles of brain and body. Addison said, "Good, very good, now stay with us," and began licking her hand instead.

I said into the phone, "I can't come, Dad. I can't drag you into this."

"Oh, God, I knew it. You're on drugs, aren't you? Look, whoever you've gotten mixed up with, we can help. We don't have to bring the police into it. We just want you back."

Then everything went dark for a second in my head, and when I came to again, I felt such a gut-punch of pain in my belly that I dropped the phone.

Addison jerked his head up to look at me. "What is it?"

That's when I saw a long, black tongue pressing against the outside of the booth's glass. It was quickly joined by a second, then a third.

The hollow. The unfrozen hollowgast. It had followed us.

The dog couldn't see it, but he could read the look on my face easily enough. "It's one of them, isn't it?"

I mouthed, *Yes*, and Addison shrank into a corner.

"Jacob?" My dad's tinny voice from the phone. "Jacob, are you there?"

The tongues began to wrap around the booth, encircling us. I didn't know what to do, only that I had to do *something*, so I shifted my feet under me, planted my hands on the walls, and struggled to my feet.

Then I was face to face with it. Tongues fanned from its gaping, bladed mouth. Its eyes were black and weeping more black and they stared into mine, inches away through the glass. The hollow let out a low, guttural snarl that turned my insides to jelly, and I half wished the beast would just kill me and be done with it so all this pain and terror could end.

The dog barked in Emma's face. "Wake up! We need you, girl! Make your fire!"

But Emma could neither speak nor stand, and we were alone in the underground station but for two women in raincoats who were backing away, holding their noses against the hollow's fetid stench.

And then the booth, the whole booth with all of us in it, swayed one way and then the other, and I heard whatever bolts anchored it to the floor groan and snap. Slowly, the hollow lifted us off the ground—six inches, then a foot, then two—only to slam us back down again, shattering the booth windows, raining glass on us.

Then there was nothing at all between the hollow and me. Not an inch, not a pane of glass. Its tongues wriggled into the booth, snaking around my arm, my waist, then around my neck, squeezing tighter and tighter until I couldn't breathe.

That's when I knew I was dead. And because I was dead, and there was nothing I could do, I stopped fighting. I relaxed every muscle, closed my eyes, and gave in to the hurt bursting inside my belly like fireworks.

Then a strange thing happened: the hurt stopped hurting. The pain shifted and became something else. I entered into it, and it enveloped me, and beneath its roiling surface I discovered something quiet and gentle.

A whisper.

I opened my eyes again. The hollow seemed frozen now, staring at me. I stared back, unafraid. My vision was spotting black from lack of oxygen, but I felt no pain.

The hollow's grip on my neck relaxed. I took my first breath in minutes, calm and deep. And then the whisper I'd found inside me traveled up from my belly and out of my throat and past my lips, making a noise that didn't sound like language, but whose meaning I knew innately.

Back.

Off.

The hollow retracted its tongues. Drew them all back into its bulging mouth and shut its jaws. Bowed its head slightly—a gesture, almost, of submission.

And then it sat down.

Emma and Addison looked up at me from the floor, surprised by the sudden calm. "What just happened?" said the dog.

"There's nothing to be afraid of," I said.

"Is it gone?"

"No, but it won't hurt us now."

He didn't ask how I knew this; just nodded, assured by the tone of my voice.

I opened the booth door and helped Emma to her feet. "Can

you walk?" I asked her. She put an arm around my waist, leaned her weight against mine, and together we took a step. "I'm not leaving you," I said. "Whether you like it or not."

Into my ear she whispered, "I love you, Jacob."

"I love you, too," I whispered back.

I stooped to pick up the phone. "Dad?"

"What was that noise? Who are you with?"

"I'm here. I'm okay."

"No, you're not. Just stay where you are."

"Dad, I have to go. I'm sorry."

"Wait. Don't hang up," he said. "You're confused, Jake."

"No. I'm like Grandpa. I have what Grandpa had."

A pause on the other end. Then: "Please come home."

I took a breath. There was too much to say and no time to say it. This would have to do:

"I hope I'll be able to come home, someday. But there are things I need to do first. I just want you to know I love you and Mom, and I'm not doing any of this to hurt you."

"We love you, too, Jake, and if it's drugs, or whatever it is, we don't care. We'll get you right again. Like I said, you're confused."

"No, Dad. I'm peculiar."

Then I hung up the phone, and speaking a language I didn't know I knew, I ordered the hollow to stand.

Obedient as a shadow, it did.

About the Photography

Like those in the first book, *Miss Peregrine's Home for Peculiar Children*, all the pictures in *Hollow City* are authentic, vintage, found photographs, and with the exception of a handful that have undergone digital postprocessing, they are unaltered. They were painstakingly collected over several years: discovered at flea markets, vintage paper shows, and, more often than not, in the archives of photo collectors much more accomplished than I, who were kind enough to part with some of their most peculiar treasures to help create this book.

The following photos were graciously lent for use by their owners:

PAGE	TITLE	FROM THE COLLECTION OF
8	Jacob in silhouette	Roselyn Leibowitz
8	Emma Bloom	Muriel Moutet
9	Enoch O'Connor	David Bass
10	Claire Densmore	Davis Bass
10	Fiona	John Van Noate
11	Miss Avocet	Erin Waters
212	Girl boarding train	John Van Noate
226	Crying baby	John Van Noate
246	Peculiar brothers	John Van Noate
283	Sam	John Van Noate
300	Millard in the mirror	John Van Noate
309	The lookout	John Van Noate

Acknowledgments

In the acknowledgments of *Miss Peregrine's Home for Peculiar Children*, I thanked my editor, Jason Rekulak, for his "seemingly endless" patience. Now, after a second book that took twice as long to write, I'm afraid I need to thank him for his truly legendary, nay, saintly, patience; verily, he hath the patience of Job! I hope it was worth the wait, and I'll be forever grateful to him for helping me find my way.

Thanks to the team at Quirk Books—Brett, David, Nicole, Moneka, Katherine, Doogie, Eric, John, Mary Ellen, and Blair—for being at once the sanest and most creative people in publishing. Thanks, too, to everyone at Random House Publisher Services, and to my publishers abroad for somehow managing to gracefully translate my oddball, made-up words into other languages (and for occasionally hosting a tall, pale, and slightly confused American author in your country; sorry for the mess I made of your guest room).

Thanks to my agent, Jodi Reamer, for reading many drafts of this book, for always giving notes that made the book better, and for (almost) always using her first-degree black belt for good, not evil.

A hearty thank-you to my photo collector friends, who helped enormously in the creation of this book. Robert E. Jackson, Peter J. Cohen, Steve Bannos, Michael Fairley, Stacy Waldman, John Van Noate, David Bass, Yefim Tovbis, and Fabien Breuvart—I couldn't have done it without you.

Thanks to the teachers who challenged and encouraged me over the years: Donald Rogan, Perry Lentz, P. F. Kluge, Jonathan Tazewell, Kim McMullen, Linda Janoff, Philip Eisner, Wendy MacLeod, Doe Mayer, Jed Dannenbaum, Nina Foch, Lewis Hyde, and John Kinsella, among many others.

Thanks most of all to Tahereh, who has brightened my life in uncountable ways. I love you, *azizam*.

A Conversation
with Ransom Riggs

R ansom Riggs grew up in Florida and studied at Kenyon
College and the University of Southern California's School
of Cinema. His first novel, *Miss Peregrine's Home for
Peculiar Children*, was a #1 *New York Times* best seller. He recently
sat down with Quirk Books publisher Jason Rekulak to discuss writing the sequel, *Hollow City*.

When describing how you wrote *Miss Peregrine's Home for Peculiar Children*, you once explained that "the photos came first," and then you shaped the story around the imagery. Was the process different this time around?

Very much so! When I was starting the first book, the slate was blank. I had a pile of strange photographs and some strange ideas, but nothing was set in stone yet. So, a great photograph could lead the way, sparking whole plotlines and inspiring major characters. With *Hollow City*, so much of the story was already in motion that the photos had to play a subtler role. Rather than writing a scene around a photograph, I would go looking for the perfect photograph to fit a scene I knew had to be in the book.

That's interesting. Were there any instances where you had multiple "perfect" photographs but had to choose the most perfect one?

One of the challenges of searching for a photo to fit a scene I'd already written was that there was often no perfect photo. I'd have one in my mind, but it didn't exist—I would have had to stage it like a movie and shoot it myself, which would've been extraordinarily expensive! Usually what happens is, I'll find a photo that's in the neighborhood of the perfect photo, but it's a few houses to the left and the garage is painted the wrong color and the hedges are all wrong. But it's as close as I'm going to get.

So, with that almost-perfect photo in mind, I go back and rewrite the scene a bit to match what I found, tweaking details to align with the specific image. Luckily, where the scene ends up is usually more interesting than where it started, all thanks to the challenge of finding the right picture.

However, there were a few instances where several different photos would've worked for a scene—at least, before I rewrote it to fit one image in particular. An example is the photo of the wights' zeppelins flying over the beach (shown on page 34). Early twentieth-century photos of zeppelins and hot-air balloons are fairly common. I just really happened to like the one I chose, which I thought had a nice foreboding quality. But I could've gone with something like this instead:

Of course, it has French writing on the front of it, and explaining that would've presented a challenge.

Another example: when Addison describes the various indignities suffered by peculiar animals over the years, he shows a photo of a dog pulling a boy in a cart.

Unfortunately, pictures of animals being humiliated by humans are easy to find. I considered but ultimately decided against using this insane photo of a baby riding an eagle, which I'm really happy to have an excuse to share with you here, because it's a picture of a baby riding an eagle.

What was the most challenging aspect of writing *Hollow City*?

The plotting. The ending of *Miss Peregrine* was so open, almost anything could've happened to those kids in their little boats. They were embarking into a world of time loops and infinite possibility, and my temptation as a writer is always to explore everything, every nook and cranny of the world I'm creating, but that's never possible (or advisable). Winnowing those endless possibilities is the hardest part of my job, because it feels like I'm saying no to all these story threads that could be great. But there's only so much time, only so many pages, only so much story I can tell in one book. More's the pity!

You wrote *Miss Peregrine's Home for Peculiar Children* in relative anonymity. Did the blockbuster success of that book—two million copies sold, dozens of translations, a huge movie deal—have an impact on your writing process?

I'd like to think it didn't. I'm probably my own harshest critic, so the judgments of others don't faze me much. I suppose it might be different if I had to, say, read the book aloud in front of an audience of two million people. That would be crazy intimidating. But I still write alone in a quiet room, like I always have, where I can at least pretend that no one's going to read the thing I'm typing besides my wife and my mom.

One of the pleasures of *Hollow City* is that we get to spend more time with the individual peculiars. Do you have a favorite among the children? Are any of the characters especially fun to write?

Each character reflects a slightly exaggerated aspect of my own personality, I think, so whom I enjoy writing about depends on how I'm feeling at the time. Enoch is me when I'm grumpy and petulant. I sometimes have a tendency to deliver mini lectures on obscure subjects people may or may not have any interest in, and I channel that when writing Millard. Emma is always a joy to write because she says exactly what she means, sometimes too forcefully for her own good, which can be cathartic. I aspire to be as noble and loyal as Bronwyn. So, it depends. I love finding new characters along the way, too, like Addison, and seeing where the story takes them.

I was completely floored by Caul's arrival in the finale of _Hollow City_. Were you planning this twist all along? Or did he surprise you, too?

I wish I could say I knew all along, but the idea of having the bird who the kids thought was Miss Peregrine be her evil brother instead came to me about halfway through the writing of the book. When it occurred to me, I clapped my hands and cackled so loud it scared the cat out of the room.

Do you have a favorite photograph in the book?

It's hard to choose a favorite, but I'm partial to the woman in the horned chair smoking a pipe.

The photographs in _Hollow City_ depict so many strange and fantastic visions: a house atop a stack of railroad ties, a man snared in a fishing net. Are you ever tempted to research any of their "real" origins?

Yes, and I often do, though I rarely uncover any substantive information. That's a relief, ultimately, because I like having the freedom to make up stories about my photos, and I think knowing the "real" stories—as curious as I am—might take away some of the fun and fantasy.

It's clear that some of these photographers used early forms of trick

photography. I'm thinking particularly of the emu-raffe on page 89 and the invisible boy on page 300. Do you know how these effects were achieved?

I have no idea about the invisible boy. My only guess is that it was some sort of double-exposure applied only to the bottom of the frame, where his feet would be—one photo of him in the chair married to one without him, but just the feet. Then again, maybe he just didn't have any feet! It's Occam's razor: sometimes the simplest answer is the most likely. As for the emu-raffe, my assumption is that it's a really bizarre piece of taxidermy, not a photo manipulation.

Last but not least: We know you're putting the finishing touches on the next book, and we can't wait to see what happens. How about a sneak preview?

Book three picks up right where *Hollow City* left off. Jacob, Emma, and Addison follow their kidnapped friends' quickly vanishing trail to Devils' Acre, the most dangerous loop in peculiardom. It's home to the worst of the worst: peculiar criminals, exiles, addicts, and, at its festering heart, the wights' lair. With the help of a mysterious defector and his ingenious loop-making machine, our peculiar heroes will finally make their stand against the wights. Should they fail, it's not only their lives that hang in the balance, but the future of all peculiars. In other words, fans can expect lots of action, loads of atmosphere, and plenty more peculiar photos:

SUCH AS THIS BLOATED WATER-MONSTER . . .

. . . MYSTERIOUS LADIES AT CEMETERY GATES . . .

. . . MASKED WEIRDOS AND COWBOYS . . .

. . . AND THIS YOUNG MAN, WHO'S BEEN WAITING
FOR YOU. WAITING A LONG, LONG TIME.

COMING IN SEPTEMBER 2015

THE THIRD NOVEL OF

MISS PEREGRINE'S
PECULIAR CHILDREN

TURN THE PAGE FOR
AN EXCLUSIVE SNEAK PREVIEW!

*T*he monster stood not a tongue's length away, eyes fixed on our throats, shriveled brain crowded with fantasies of murder. Its hunger for us charged the air. Hollows are born lusting after the souls of peculiars, and here we were arrayed before it like a buffet: bite-sized Addison bravely standing his ground at my feet; Emma moored against me for support, still too dazed from the impact we'd taken to make more than a match flame; our backs laddered against the wrecked phone booth. Beyond our grim circle, the underground station looked like the aftermath of a nightclub bombing. Steam from burst pipes shrieked forth in ghostly curtains. Splintered monitors swung broken-necked from the ceiling. A sea of shattered glass spread all the way to the tracks, flashing in the hysterical strobe of red emergency lights like an acre-wide disco ball. We were boxed in, a wall hard to one side and glass shin-deep on the other, two strides from a creature whose only natural instinct was to disassemble us—and yet it made no move to close the gap. It seemed rooted to the floor, swaying on its heels like a drunk or a sleepwalker, death's head drooping, its tongues a nest of snakes I'd charmed to sleep.

Me. I'd done that. Jacob Portman, boy nothing from Nowhere, Florida. It was not currently murdering us—this horror made of gathered dark and nightmares harvested from sleeping children—because I had asked it not to. Told it, in no uncertain terms, to unwrap its tongue from around my neck. *Back off*, I'd said. *Stand*, I'd said—in a language I did not know I knew, made of sounds I hadn't realized a human mouth could make—

and, miraculously, it had, its eyes challenging me while its body obeyed. Somehow I had tamed the nightmare, cast a spell over it, interrupted the impulse to kill during its microsecond journey from monstrous mind to monstrous limbs. But sleeping things wake and spells wear off, especially those cast by accident, and beneath a surface that betrayed all the urgency of an old man waiting for a bus, I could feel the hollow boiling.

Addison nudged my calf with his nose. "More wights will be coming. Will the beast let us pass?"

"Talk to it again," Emma said, her voice woozy and vague. "Tell it to sod off."

I searched for the words, but they'd gotten shy. "I don't know how."

"You did a minute ago," Addison said. "It sounded like there was a demon inside you."

A minute ago, before I'd known I could do it, the words had been right there on my tongue, just waiting to be spoken. Now that I wanted them back, it was like trying to catch fish with my bare hands; every time I touched one, it slipped out of my grasp.

Go away! I shouted.

The words came in English. The hollow didn't move. I stiffened my back, glared into its inkpot eyes, and tried again.

Get out of here! Leave us alone!

English again. The hollow tilted its head like a curious dog, but was otherwise a statue.

"Is he gone?" Addison asked.

"Still there. I don't know what's wrong."

I felt silly and deflated. Had my gift vanished so quickly?

"Never mind," Emma said. "Hollows aren't meant to be reasoned with, anyway." She stuck out a hand and tried to light a flame, but it fizzled. The effort seemed to sap her. I tightened my grip around her waist lest she topple over.

"Save your strength, matchstick," said Addison. "I'm sure

we'll need it."

"I'll fight it with cold hands if I have to," said Emma. "All that matters is we find the others before it's too late."

The others. I could see them still, their afterimage fading by the tracks: weeping in terror, kicked onto a train at gunpoint, gone. Gone with the ymbryne we'd nearly killed ourselves to find, hurtling now through London's guts toward a fate worse than death. *It's already too late*, I thought. It was too late the moment Caul's soldiers stormed our frozen hideout. It was too late the night we mistook Miss Peregrine's wicked brother for the ymbryne herself. Now it was past midnight; the clock had stopped, caught fire, melted like a surrealist painting. But I swore to myself that we'd find our friends and find our ymbryne anyway, no matter the cost, even if there were only bodies to recover—even if it meant adding our own to the pile. I was all in.

So, then: somewhere in the flashing dark was an escape to the street. A door, a staircase, an escalator, way against the far wall. But how to reach them?

Get the hell out of our way! I shouted, giving it one last try.

English, naturally. The hollow grunted like a cow but didn't move. It was no use. The words were gone, a remote control lost between couch cushions.

"Plan B," I said. "It won't listen to me, so we go around it, hope it stays put."

"Go around it where?" said Emma.

To give it a wide berth, we'd have to wade through heaps of glass—but it would slice Emma's bare calves and tear Addison's paws to ribbons. I thought through a few bad alternatives: I could carry the dog, but that still left Emma. I could find a swordlike shard of glass and stab the thing through its eyes—a technique that had served me well in the past—but if I didn't manage to kill it with the first strike, it would surely snap awake and kill us, instead. The only other way around it was through a small, glass-free gap between the hollow and the wall. But it was so narrow—a foot, maybe a foot and a half wide—a tight squeeze even if we flattened our backs to the wall. I worried that getting so close to the hollow, or worse, touching it by accident, would break the fragile trance that seemed to be holding it in check. Short of growing wings and flying over its head, though, it seemed like our only option.

"Can you walk a little?" I asked Emma. "Or at least hobble?"

She locked her knees and loosened her grip on my waist, testing her weight.

"I can limp."

"Then here's what we're going to do. Slide past it, backs to the wall, through that gap there. It's not a lot of space, but if we're careful . . ."

Addison saw what I meant and shrank back into the phone booth. "Do you think we should get so close to it?"

"Probably not."

"What if it wakes up while we're—?"

"It won't," I said, faking confidence. "Just don't make any sudden moves. And whatever you do, don't touch it."

"No sudden moves, skip the hug," said Emma. "Got it."

At another time, her sarcasm might've annoyed me, but now it was comforting. Despite everything we'd gone through, Emma was still herself—funny, biting; hard and soft.

I chose a nice long shard of glass from the floor and slid it into my pocket, just in case. Shuffling two steps to the wall, we pressed ourselves against the cold tiles.

"You're our eyes now," Addison said. "Bird preserve us."

We inched toward the hollow. Its eyes moved as we did, locked on me. A few creeping sidesteps later, we were enveloped by a pocket of hollow-stink so foul that it made my eyes water. Addison coughed and Emma cupped a hand over her nose.

"Just a little farther," I said, my voice reedy with forced calm. I took the shard from my pocket, gripped it point out, and took another step, and another.

We were close enough now that I could've touched it with an outstretched arm. I heard its heart knocking inside its ribs, the beat quickening with each step we took. It was getting worked up, straining against me, fighting with every neuron to wrest my clumsy hands from its controls. *Don't move*, I said, mouthing the words in English. *You're mine. I control you. Don't move.*

I sucked in my chest, lined up and laddered each vertebra against the wall—I imagined myself as two-dimensional—and crab-walked into the tight gap between the wall and the hollow.

Don't move, don't move.

Slide, shuffle, slide. I held my breath while the hollow's quickened, wet and wheezing, a vile black mist blooming from its nostrils. The urge to devour us must've been excruciating. So was my urge to run, but I ignored it; that would be acting like prey, not master.

Don't move. Do not move.

Another few steps, a few more feet, and we'd be past it. Its shoulder a hairsbreadth from my chest.

Don't—

—and then it did. In one swift motion, the hollow swiveled its head and pivoted on its heels to face me.

I went rigid. "Don't move," I said, this time aloud, to the others. Addison buried his face between his paws and Emma froze, her arm squeezing mine like a vise. I steeled myself for what was to come—its tongues, its teeth, the end.

Get back, get back, get back.

English, English, English.

Seconds passed in which, astonishingly, we weren't killed. But for the rising and falling of its chest, the creature had seemingly turned once again to stone.

Experimentally, moving by micrometers, I slid farther along the wall. The hollow followed my movements with slight turns of its head—locked onto me like a heat-seeking missile, a compass needle, its body in perfect sympathy with mine—but it didn't follow, didn't open its jaws. If whatever spell I'd cast had been broken, we'd already be dead.

The hollow was only watching me. Awaiting instructions that I didn't know how to give.

"False alarm," I said, and Emma breathed an audible sigh of relief.

We slid out of the gap, peeled ourselves from the wall, and hurried away as fast as Emma could limp. When we'd put a little distance between us and the hollow, I looked back. It had turned all the way around to face me.

Stay, I muttered in English. *Good dog.*

*   *   *

We passed through a veil of steam, and the escalator came into view, frozen into stairs, its power cut. Around it glowed a halo of weak daylight, tantalizing envoy from the world above. World of the living, world of now. A world where I had parents. They were here, both of them, in London, breathing this air. A stroll away.

Oh, hi there!

Unthinkable. Still more unthinkable: not five minutes ago, I'd told my father everything. The super–Cliff's Notes version, anyway: *I'm like Grandpa Portman was. I'm peculiar.* They wouldn't understand, but at least now they knew. It would make my absence feel like less of a betrayal. I could still hear my father's voice, begging me to come home. *Don't do this to us* is what he meant, and it stung. As we limped toward the light, I had to fight a sudden urge to shake off Emma's arm and run for it—to escape this suffocating dark, to find my parents and beg forgiveness, and then to crawl into their posh hotel bed and sleep.

That was most unthinkable of all, and a flush of hot shame came over me for even flirting with the idea. Because I could never. I loved Emma, and I'd told her so, and I wouldn't leave her behind for anything. And not because I was noble or brave or chivalrous. I'm not any of those things. I was afraid it would rip me in half.

And the others, the others. Our poor, doomed friends. We had to go after them—but how? A train hadn't come through the station since the one that spirited them away, and after the blast and gunshots that had rocked the place, I was sure there'd be no more trains coming. That left us two options, each terrible: go after them on foot through the tunnels and hope we didn't meet any more hollows, or climb the escalator and face whatever was waiting for us up there—most likely a wight mop-up crew—then regroup, reassess.

I knew which option I preferred. I'd had enough of the dark, and more than enough of hollows.

"Let's go up," I said, urging Emma toward the stalled escalator. "We'll find somewhere safe to plan our next move while you get your strength back."

"Absolutely not!" she said. "We can't just abandon the others, never mind how I feel."

"We aren't. But we need to be realistic. We're hurt, defenseless, and the others are probably miles away by now, out of the underground and halfway to somewhere else. How would we even find them?"

"The same way I found you," said Addison. "With my nose. Peculiar folk have an aroma all their own, you see—one which only dogs of my persuasion can sniff out—and you happen to be one powerfully odoriferous bunch. Fear enhances it, I think, and skipping baths . . ."

"Then we go after them!" Emma said.

She pulled me toward the tracks with a surprising burst of strength. I resisted, tug-of-warring our linked arms. "No, no—there's no *way* the trains are still running, and if we go in there on *foot*—"

"I don't care if it's dangerous. I won't leave them."

"It isn't just dangerous; it's pointless. They're already gone, Emma."

She took back her arm and started hobbling toward the tracks. Stumbled, caught herself. *Say something*, I mouthed to Addison, and he circled around to block her.

"I'm afraid he's right. If we follow on foot, our friends' scent trail will dissipate long before we're able to find them. Even my profound abilities have limits."

Emma gazed into the tunnel, then back at me, her expression tortured. I held out my hand. "Please, let's go. It doesn't mean we're giving up."

"All right," she said heavily. "All right."

But just as we were starting toward the escalator, someone called out from the dark, back along the tracks.

"Over here!"

The voice was weak but familiar, the accent Russian.

"Sergei!" cried Emma.

It was the folding man. Peering into the dark, I could just make out his crumpled form by the tracks, one arm raised. He had been shot during the melee, and I assumed he'd been shoved onto the train with the others—but there he lay, waving to us.

"You know him?" Addison said suspiciously.

"He was one of Miss Wren's peculiar refugees," I said, my ears pricking at the wail of distant sirens echoing down to us from the surface. Trouble was coming—maybe trouble disguised as help—and I worried that our best chance at a clean exit was slipping away.

Addison scuttled toward the folding man, dodging the deepest reefs of glass. Emma let me take her arm again and we shuffled after. The folding man was lying on his side, covered in glass and streaked with blood. He'd been shot somewhere vital. His little wire-framed spectacles were cracked and he was adjusting them, trying to get a good look at me. "Is miracle, is miracle," he rasped, his voice thin as twice-strained tea. "I heard you speak with monster's tongue. Is miracle."

"It's not," I said, kneeling beside him. "It's gone, I've already lost it."

"If gift is inside you, is forever."

Footsteps and voices echoed from the escalator passage. I started clearing away glass so that I could get my hands under Sergei and pick him up. "We're taking you with us," I said.

"Leave me," he croaked. "I'll be gone soon enough. . . ." He grabbed my hand and pressed a small square of paper into it. A photograph. "Find them," he said. "Make army."

Since we met him, he'd talked nonstop about raising an army of peculiars. He wanted to go loop to loop recruiting able-bodied survivors of the raids and purges. It had sounded far-fetched then; now it seemed insane.

"There's no army," I said. "Everything's changed."

I tried to slip my hands beneath him, but he rolled away.

"No," he insisted. "They are underground, in the ancient home. Navel of worlds. *Gurehmeh.*"

I glanced at the photo he'd given me long enough to see a clutch of men standing in a strange, brightly lit cavern, then I stuffed it into my coat. "We'll talk about it later," I said, and this time he didn't resist when I tried to lift him. He was ladder long but light as a feather, and I held him in my arms like a big baby, his skinny legs dangling over my elbow while his head lolled against my shoulder.

Two figures banged down the last few escalator steps and then stood at the bottom, rim-lit by pale daylight and peering into the new dark. Emma pointed at the floor, and we sank quietly to our knees, hoping they'd miss us—hoping they were just civilians come to catch a train. But then I heard the squelch of a walkie-talkie, and they each fired up a flashlight, the beams making their bright reflective jackets pop.

They might've been emergency responders, or wights disguised as such. I wasn't sure until, in synchrony, they peeled off wraparound sunglasses.

Of course.

Our options had just narrowed by half. Now there were only the tracks, the tunnels. We could never outrun them, damaged as we were, but escape was still possible if they didn't see us—and they hadn't yet, amid the chaos of the ruined station. Their flashlight beams dueled across the floor. Emma and I backed toward the tracks. If we could just slip into the tunnels unnoticed . . . but Addison, damn him, wasn't moving.

"Come *on*," I hissed.

"They are ambulance drivers, and this man needs help," he said too loudly, and right away the flashlight beams bounced up from the floor and whipped toward us.

"Stay where you are!" one of the men boomed, unholstering a gun while the other fumbled for his walkie-talkie.

Then, two unexpected things happened in quick succession. The first was that, just as I was about to drop the folding man onto the tracks and dive after him with Emma, a thunderous horn blew from inside the tunnel and a single brilliant headlight flashed into view. The rush of stale wind I'd been too distracted to register belonged to a train. The second thing, announced by a painful twinge in my gut, was that the hollow had come unstuck and was loping in our direction. The instant after I felt it, I saw it, too, plowing at us through a billow of steam, black lips peeled wide, tongues thrashing the air.

We were trapped. If we ran for the stairs, we'd be shot and mauled. If we jumped onto the tracks, we'd be crushed by the train. And we couldn't escape *onto* the train because it would be ten seconds at least before it stopped and twelve before its doors opened and ten more before they shut again, and by then we'd be dead three ways. And so I did as I often do when I'm out of ideas: I looked to Emma. I could read in the desperation on her face that she understood fully the hopelessness of our situation and in the stony set of her jaw that she meant to act anyway. I remembered only as she began to stagger forward, palms out, that she couldn't see the hollow, and I tried to tell her, reach for her, stop her, but I couldn't get the words out and couldn't grab her without dropping the folding man, and then Addison was alongside her, too, barking at the wight while Emma tried uselessly to make a flame—spark, spark, nothing, like a lighter low on juice.

The wight broke out laughing, pulled back the hammer of his gun, and aimed it at her. The hollowgast ran at me, howling in counterpoint to the squeal of train brakes behind me. That's when I knew the end had come, and there was nothing I could do to stop it. At that moment, something inside me relaxed, and as it did, the pain I felt whenever a hollow was near faded, too. That pain was like a high-pitched whine, and as it hushed, I discovered hidden beneath it another sound, a murmur at the edge of consciousness.

A word.

I dove for it. Wrapped both arms around it. Wound up and shouted it with all the force of a major league pitcher. *Him,* I said, in a language not my own. It was only one syllable but held volumes of meaning, and the moment it rattled from my throat, the result was instant. The hollow stopped running at me—stopped dead, skidding on its feet—then turned sharply to one side and lashed out a tongue that whipped across the platform and wrapped three times around the wight's leg. Knocked off balance, he fired a shot that caromed off the ceiling, and then he was flipped upside down and hauled thrashing and screaming into the air.

It took my friends a moment to realize what had happened. While they stood gaping and the other wight shouted into his walkie-talkie, I heard the train doors whoosh open behind me.

Here was our moment.

"COME ON!" I shouted, and they did, Emma stumble-running and Addison tangling her feet and me trying to wedge the gangly and blood-slick folding man through the narrow doors until we all crashed together across the threshold into the train car.

More gunshots rang out, the wight firing blindly at the hollow.

The doors closed halfway, then popped back open. "Clear the doors, please," came a cheerful recorded announcement.

"His feet!" Emma said, pointing at the shoes at the end of the folding man's long legs, the toes of which were poking through the doors. I scrambled to kick his feet clear, and in the interminable seconds before the doors closed again, the dangling wight fired more wild shots until the hollow grew tired of him and flung him against the wall, where he slid to the floor in an unmoving heap.

The other wight scurried for the exit. *Him, too,* I tried to say, but it was too little too late. The doors were closing anyway, and with an awkward jolt, the train began to move.

I looked around, grateful the car we'd tumbled into was empty. What would regular people make of us?

"Are you okay?" I asked Emma. She was sitting up, breathing hard, studying me intensely.

"Thanks to you," she said. "Did you really make the hollow do all that?"

"I think so," I said, not quite believing it myself.

"That's amazing," she said quietly. I couldn't tell if she was frightened or impressed, or both.

"We owe you our lives," said Addison, nuzzling his head sweetly against my arm. "You're a very special boy."

The folding man laughed, and I looked down to see him

grinning at me through a mask of pain. "You see?" he said. "I told you. Is miracle." And then he relaxed into a spreading pool of blood on the floor.

"He doesn't have long," Addison said, moving to lick his face.

"I might have enough heat to cauterize the wound," said Emma, and she scooted toward him and began rubbing her hands together.

Addison nosed the folding man's shirt near his abdomen. "Here. He's hurt here." Emma put her hands on either side of the spot, and at the sickly sizzle of flesh I stood up, feeling faint.

I looked out the window. We were still pulling out of the station, slowed perhaps by debris on the tracks. The emergency lights' SOS flicker picked details from the dark at random. The body of a dead wight, half buried in glass. The crumpled phone booth, scene of my breakthrough. The hollow—I registered its form with a little shock—trotting along the platform alongside us, a few cars back, casual as a jogger.

Stop. Stay away, I spat at the window, in English. My head wasn't clear, the hurt and the whine getting in the way again.

We picked up speed and passed into the tunnel. I pressed my face to the glass, angling backward for another glimpse. It was dark, dark—and then, in a millisecond burst of light like a camera flash, I saw the hollow as a momentary still image. Flying, its feet lifting from the platform, tongues lassoing the rail of the last car.

Miracle. Curse. I hadn't quite worked out the difference.